M 3 A

LAND
OF THE
HEADLESS

Also by Adam Roberts from Gollancz:

Salt
Stone
On
The Snow
Polystom
Gradisil

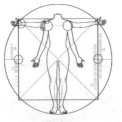

LAND
OF THE
HEADLESS

A Simple Story

ADAM
ROBERTS

GOLLANCZ

LONDON

The right of Adam Roberts to be identified as the author
of this work has been asserted by him in accordance with
the Copyright, Designs and Patents Act 1988.

First published in Great Britain in 2007
by Gollancz
An imprint of the Orion Publishing Group
Orion House, 5 Upper St Martin's Lane,
London WC2H 9EA

A CIP catalogue record for this book
is available from the British Library

ISBN 978 0 57507 588 7 (cased)
ISBN 978 0 57507 799 7 (trade paperback)

1 3 5 7 9 10 8 6 4 2

Typeset by Input Data Services Ltd, Frome

Printed and bound at Mackays of Chatham plc, Chatham, Kent

The Orion Publishing Group's policy is to use papers that
are natural, renewable and recyclable products and
made from wood grown in sustainable forests. The logging
and manufacturing processes are expected to conform to
the environmental regulations of the country of origin.

www.orionbooks.co.uk

PART ONE

What Happened on the Way to Cainon

One

On Tuesday a genetic materials test confirmed my guilt (but of course this confirmation was only a formality) and on Wednesday I was beheaded. My crime was adultery.

There is a traditional belief, which many still share, that adultery is the least of the three offences which our penal code punishes by decapitation. For it consists of injuring another's life, whereas *murder* is a crime that fully deprives another of their life; and *blasphemy* is a crime against the divine principle, which is clearly a wholly other affair. But I do not say this in self-exculpation. The punishment is the same whichever of the three you commit. Holy law sanctions no legalistic evasions or hairsplittings. How could it be holy if it did?

On the Wednesday morning the maior, Bil Charis, came to see me in my cell. He was there to oversee the fitting of the ordinator. Two security employees lay me naked on my front and strapped me down. The strap was not necessary, as I assured them, but they applied it nevertheless. 'It is,' said Bil, as the surgeons started about their surgical work, 'the usual procedure.'

'And let us not,' I replied bitterly, 'ever depart from the *usual*. Let us never *reform*, or *improve*, the ancient barbarities.'

'Boh, Jon Cavala,' Bil replied. 'For you cannot deny that these beheadings have indeed been thoroughly reformed and improved since the old days!'

I said nothing.

The surgeons touched the base of my spine with an analgesic proboscis. They spliced swiftly and precisely into my spine, affixing the primary and secondary node and embedding the ordinator. The analgesic meant that I felt none of this, except for the butterfly pressure of the machines moving over my back. I could hear only the whizz and click of their tools. I could see nothing but the portion of grey bench immediately in front of my eyes. This, by a chain of association, brought into my mind the thought of my impending blindness, and my

3

dissatisfactions found voice. I will admit that I spoke peevishly.

'You will shortly be blinding me,' I pointed out to Bil. 'Taking my sight, and my hearing and taste and smell, as well as my head. The latter necessarily includes all the former.'

'By no means,' returned Bil, in an easy voice. 'There are many forms of prosthetic sight on the market, even for somebody with funds as limited as, perhaps, are yours. Only last month Medicom released a new design: fashioned as a webbed cloak worn around the shoulders and granting one hundred and eighty degrees of vision behind the wearer. Or you may choose to wear the cloak on your front and enable forward vision.'

'By repute,' I complained, 'the visual input from this new device is grainy and has a limited range of colours.'

'Then choose another,' said Bil. 'Your ordinator has multiple compatibilities. Cameras on stalks, pods for the wrist or palm, bio-devices, all can be connected to your new brain.'

'Any such device I must furnish for myself, at my own expense,' I said.

'Naturally. The same is true of your future clothes, food, housing. You do not expect the State to provide you with such things freely? Such charity would be demeaning.'

'I do not *expect*,' I said, becoming heated, 'the State to decapitate me for a so-called crime that—' But Bil stopped me.

'Come come, no sermonising here,' he said. 'It is fruitless to harangue me. Besides, the surgeons have completed their work.'

And so they had.

I was taken to a separate room for the download, which was accomplished in a matter of minutes: mapping all cortices and lobes of my brain and copying all their patterns and potential synaptic arrangements electronically into the ordinator at the base of my spine. Then I was dressed in loose pants, but no other clothing. The surgical analgesia was beginning to wear off by this time, and I was conscious of a vague ache on my back where the incisions had been made. And I was aware of the weight of the wallet-sized metal ordinator under my skin, at the base of my back, just above the top of my buttocks. I have heard stories that condemned men and women experience oddly doubled and near-hallucinogenic sensations whilst possessing both head and ordinator. I cannot confirm these stories. I felt no doubleness of consciousness. I felt nothing but anxiety at my approaching execution.

After that everything happened quickly. I was hurried up a dozen steps and through a door onto the outside platform. It was a hot afternoon. The air smelt strongly of a city summer. The sunlight was sharp on my face, like a zest. Florettes of white cloud were arranged with a perfect aesthetic harmony across a blue sky, and there were neither too many nor too few of these clouds. It was a beautiful arrangement. The colour of this sky, a delicate and exquisite blue, was the last I saw with my fleshly eyes.

Beyond the yellow walls of the execution yard I could see the city of Doué baking in the sun, and very beautiful it seemed to me there, at that time, before my beheading. How often I had walked around it and never noticed anything about it! Alleys of lime trees flanked the straight roads: scores of silver trunks nearly phosphorescent in the sunlight, each topped with a foam of tiny leaves. Pavements of tessellated brick deserted in the afternoon heat. A muddle of tiled roofs, most of them the colour of carrots or pumpkin and all of them textured like pineapple skin. In every direction white walls, and in every wall white-shuttered windows, giving the city a blank face, perfectly uninterested in me or my execution. To my right the river ran cyan with dyes from the fabric factory. Behind the river stood the metal stalks of the telecommunications park. The moon was very skinny in the afternoon sky, a curve of scalpel silver against the blue. Above it the tiny hieroglyph of an airliner moved slowly, hurdling the moon in slow motion.

That sky-blue! That colour!

I said, 'The weather is hot.' This was merely stating the obvious, of course, and a poor bid for last words; but witnesses at executions will confirm that only very rarely do the condemned utter profundities. You should not expect wisdom from people in such a position. Their minds, after all, will tend to be elsewhere.

I walked forward, and sweat started dotting my skin.

There were no more than five people lolling in the execution yard. A century ago, of course, the public executions drew swarms of eager spectators. Our modern, high-tech tastes are less bloody, I suppose. Or perhaps the spectacle is less entertaining nowadays, since the human headsman has been replaced by the flawless mechanics of the Clapper.

The herald read my crime, declaring me, in the whole world's hearing, an adulterer and a rapist. My panic at the impending event took a sudden, hyperbolic swerve upwards. I was blinking, and I was sweating in the heat. I felt as if I were choking on my hump-pumping heart, as if the heart were somehow lodged in my gullet and grown four times its normal size. Its throb was restricting my breathing and clogging my whole chest with palpitating grossness. I could not command my own legs. I was told to walk forward, but I could not do so. I was shoved.

The herald muttered in my ear – these were the last words my fleshly ear would ever hear – 'Drop your shoulders, lad.' He spoke kindly, I believe. It is of course better if the cut does not pass through the shoulders as well as the neck. But it was hard for me to comply: every muscle in my frame had tensed taut as hardwood. This was something beyond my conscious control.

I heard the hum of the Clapper behind me, floating up and positioning itself. I almost called out, but I did not, and then the blade spun and bit, and my world went instantly dark and silent.

I did not feel any pain.

This is what I felt: I was conscious of a sudden forceful pressure, as if I had been punched firmly on the back of my neck. The loss of sight and sound was as if a capacious lead helmet had landed on my head with abrupt force. I'm sure I staggered. My ordinator was routing my auton-omics now. It registered that I had leaned from the vertical, and I put my right foot to steady myself, and then shimmied my left foot to stop myself toppling that way. Then I felt the Clapper clamp itself onto the stump of my neck, and only with that sensation did I become aware that my shoulders, my chest and back were wet, slick with my own blood. At that realisation I felt a giddiness, doubtless more a matter of intellectual shock than physical distress. I suppose I lost no more than a pint of blood before the Clapper sealed the wound. But the understanding that what had happened to me had actually happened to me was– I don't know. I was going to write *disorienting*, but that does not capture it at all.

It is difficult to convey the sensation.

I felt the stomatic value being slid into the severed opening of my throat, its biprong separating oesophagus and trachea. But I did not feel the machine knit artery to artery, or feel it polyseal the plastic cap to my skin. Or, it would be more accurate to say, I could not determine which of the many pricking, pressing, crimping, penetrating, wrenching and tickling sensations of which I was aware related to these processes.

Then, as is common in decapitation autobiographies, I must report a hiatus. This, I understand, is known as the aporia. With no visual or aural inputs, only a close darkness, the sensory deprivation plays games with one's apprehension of the passage of time. I have no memory of Bil Charis standing beside me on the platform, or of him saying, 'As Maior of Doué I declare you punished for your crime. Go now and live a good life.' He must have said this, because the law requires it, but I had no way of hearing the words, deaf to the world, blind to world, the world tasteless and odourless to me now.

Two

My family had disowned me, and no friend of mine from my former life cared to offer me aid in this extremity. I had been, in former life, a successful man: a poet, a musician, to some degree even a scholar. But that life had been struck as clean away from me as my head.

It fell to a philanthropic group named the Friends of the Headless to lead me, blind and deaf, from the platform and away through the city. These people perform such duties out of charity and religious piety. I cared nothing for this. All I cared for was the sense of heat on my torso, and my awareness of those places on my skin where my blood had become sticky and dry. I could feel, because the sensors inside my ordinator told me, that I was moving, that my legs were working. But I was sealed away from the cosmos in darkness. Eventually the walking stopped, and my guides encouraged me to sit, to lie down. I slept, fitfully at first, then coma-like. It had been a stressful day.

The next day, or the one afterwards, I am not sure, I heard a voice. It came as a direct input into my ordinator, through its port at the base of my spine – a synthetic voice asking if I wished the senses of sight and hearing returned to my consciousness. Some decapitees, I have heard, opt for complete deprivation as their decreed punishment. Not the majority, of course, but perhaps those few who are more devoutly religious. I replied that I wanted both, but that I had very little money left from my funds, after paying prison fees and legal subventions. I had just enough for three mid-range prostheses; after which I would depend wholly upon the charity of others, or upon such work as I could obtain in my newly denuded physical condition.

But, meagre though my funds were, the thought of remaining in the silent dark was intolerable to me. So, and even though it cost me almost everything I had, I asked for epaulette eyes, for ears, and a torso-mounted microphone, on my front between my nipples; and for these I authorised payment. I spoke with the somewhat uninflected voice broadcast out of the ordinator itself. It is possible to buy software that gives the headless person's voice more heft and resonance, but I could not afford this. It is sometimes said that it is not the ordinator's voice itself that offends decapitees' sensibilities, but rather than fact that, after a lifetime of having one's ears located close to one's own mouth, it is a disconcertingly alienating thing to hear one's own voice coming from a completely different part of the body. It sounds, even as one formulates and speaks one's own words, as if somebody else is speaking. A schizophrenic circumstance.

My ears were fitted, and wired in to my ordinator. This was a simple matter. My eyes were inserted into my shoulders and connected to my new brain. These devices gave me a rabbit-like vision, two wide arcs from opposite sides of my neck stump. The effect was to distort objects in my visual field according to an elongated oval pattern, making things thinner and longer and slightly curved as they moved in front or behind me. I could not see things that were behind me, for my ordinator could not process two contradictory fields of view simultaneously. Even as it was, with forward-only vision, objects acquired a double aspect when they moved, for although my ordinator could integrate the two visual fields as long as things were still, any movement confused the programming and single objects split into two, overlapping shadows, like projections on a screen, until they were still again. This took getting-used-to. In addition to this limitation, the eyes had a much-reduced colour range: I saw many blues, some greens, a single hue of red, a single shade of yellow. Many things that I would have recognised immediately with my old eyes were puzzles to my new eyes. It was a while before I became accustomed to all this.

I spent a dizzy day. Merely getting off my pallet bed caused my senses to spill, and often I was compelled to sit down again. I experimented with walking around my room. A volunteer from the Friends had agreed to help me move towards rehabilitation-in-the-world, and her name was Siuzan Delage. 'This will soon be second nature for you,' she assured me.

'It is hard to believe so,' I replied.

'I have come,' she told me, 'to accompany you to church. Assuming you want company.' And by this I knew that it was Sunday.

I went to church with Siuzan Delage, and prayed for the first time since my punishment, thoughts clattering and rattling about my new metal brain. I joined in the singing of antiphonal hymns. The congregation was more or less evenly divided between headless individuals such as myself, scraping the air with their metal voices, and the headed zealots and enthusiasts of the Friends organisation.

8

Afterwards Siuzan Delage walked back with me to my room, her hand on my elbow to stop me from walking into one or other of the double-visioned shimmying obstacles I came across. Wall. Door. Chair. Person. 'So many of the headless,' I said. 'The church was crowded with them. Have so many people been decapitated recently?'

'Only a small number,' said Siuzan. 'Most of those in church today are headless volunteers who work now for the Friends, helping us rehabilitate people such as yourself.'

'I suppose,' I said, 'that there are few enough employment opportunities for such folk. Perhaps volunteer work for your philanthropic organisation is the best they can manage.' My thoughts were sour and sarcastic, but the words emerged as blandly synthetic as all my other statements.

'It is more likely,' she replied blithely, 'that they work from a sense of remorse, of duty, and a belief in the importance of making the mercy of the All'God prevail, even to murderers, heretics and adulterers.'

We were back at my room. I sat upon my cot, surprisingly exhausted by the short walk. 'From your words,' I said, 'you are a zealot.'

I saw her nod, her features blurring between two vertically bouncing faces momentarily, before recomposing into a single item. She was a beautiful young woman, with straight, plump nose and lips and fat-lidded wide-set eyes of pronounced clarity and blueness, although perhaps the vivid shine of blue was a function more of my visual software than her eyes. Her dark hair was webbed into plaits and tied behind her head. Her skin seemed sunshine-white to my new eyes, and was blemishless and smooth. She wore modest but expensive clothes: a mauve droho with white stripes, and expensive-looking meadhres. She was smiling at me.

'Indeed,' she said. 'I have been a zealot for seven years.' She could not have been more than twenty years old. 'I confess I cannot understand how one can worship the Divine and not do so with zeal. A frank, heretical denial of the All'God seems more logical to me, in a way, than any half-hearted adherence to the church.'

'Some people are by nature half-hearted in their lives,' I said. 'It is the minority who are enthusiasts.'

'And which are you?'

I considered. 'It may offend you,' I said, 'and indeed may approach heresy, but I suppose that I have lost much of my confidence in the church. Until this affliction,' and I put my hands up to wave in the air over my neck stump, 'I thought little of the headless. Of course, I saw them from time to time, working at their menial jobs, or shuffling along

9

the streets, but I was too caught up in my own business and my own thoughts to pay them much attention. But now that I have become what I did not used to notice, I am shaken by the extremity of the condition.'

'Many amongst the newly headless speak as you speak,' she said. She was still smiling. 'It can take time for a person to overcome the injury to their pride.'

'I speak of the general, not of my particular. I ask, *is* this the way to organise our society? This code, this penal code; it is from a medieval past, from a time when life was brutal. But life is no longer brutal. We are a space-faring, technologically advanced civilisation. We have a sophisticated and liberal culture. No other inhabited world still abides by so barbaric a practice.'

'But every world,' she said, 'must have a legal code, and must punish wrongdoing. All worlds have punishments, and some are more barbaric than ours. What of Oudart, for instance, where murder and treason are punishable by death?'

'Our own code calls for death!' I said. 'For centuries our criminals were decapitated and buried in criminal graves.'

'But no longer,' she said, still calm. 'Because we understand the central points of our scriptures to be *compassion* and *mercy*, and so we are merciful and compassionate. Because the All'God has enabled us to develop new technologies, so it is that we can mitigate the necessity of death.'

'It remains a monstrously antiquated creed,' I insisted, 'for a modern society.'

'On the contrary. It is precisely modernity that enables you to speak to me, even though your head has been struck from your body.'

'For crimes that other worlds view as pastimes! As hobbies!'

For the first time her expression cooled. 'Murder and blasphemy cannot be described as hobbies!'

'I was not beheaded for either.'

'Nor,' she said, 'are there civilised worlds where rape is a pastime.'

This deflated me, and took the conviction from my statements. My torso sagged a little on the bed. 'But,' I continued in a quieter voice, 'I speak of the principles behind the punishment. Anybody committing adultery faces the same punishment that I have faced, regardless of the benignity of the offence, adultery being defined as any illicit sexual activity whatsoever. Two teenagers committing fornication, an unhappy wife seeking solace with a lover, a man—'

But she stopped me, holding up her hand like a traffic policeman. 'The All'God's law is the All'God's law,' she said sternly. Then, in a kinder tone, 'The divine We is who we are. Our religion is the spinal cord of our civilisation. Without the All'God all its richness would crumble.'

'It seems to me,' I said, after a silence, 'that the worship of God evolves over time, as cultures evolve. Is it heresy to say so?'

'Many scholars,' said Siuzan, 'and many theologians have argued the point. It can hardly be called heresy to discuss it. The All'God is duality, and relishes discussion.'

'Yet a man was beheaded last year for insisting the practice of decapitation be discontinued!' I said. 'It is heresy to oppose the beheadings, and heresy results in beheading. Is it surprising that the practice has never been reformed?'

'The All'God's law,' she said again, 'is the All'God's law.'

'A circular statement,' I said.

This animated her. 'Is our world not harmonious, ordered, beautiful? Is ours not a complex and satisfying culture in which to live, to grow, to love and be loved, to study, to work, to grow old and die? Are our cities not free of crime, almost wholly so, and the people well mannered, polite, engaged, selfless and pure? Would you truly prefer a world like Rivy, where the populace carry guns and dozens die in street brawls every day? Would you prefer to live on Hoffmanwelt, where suicide outnumbers all other manners of death, and half the population live bleakly secular and alcoholic lives?'

'These,' I said shortly, 'are merely rhetorical questions.'

'Religion gives shape and meaning to our existences,' she said. 'Empirically this cannot be denied. The people of our world benefit from that. We are happy with a profound happiness. Would you jeopardise this, for the right to fornicate and kill at your pleasure?'

'Though we speak to one another, you and I, perhaps,' I said, 'are having different conversations.'

Three

I stayed in the House of the Friends of the Headless for two weeks, and during that time the two of us had many similar discussions, Siuzan Delage and I. To begin with I assumed that all newly beheaded individuals received such devoted attention from the zealots of this organisation. But it dawned on me that Siuzan Delage held a special place for me in her heart. She wanted, perhaps, to return me to the path of the Divine. The conversion mania is common to many zealots.

'I know the work you used to do,' she told me. 'The poetry you composed before your execution. It is beautiful.'

'Thank you,' I said, surprised.

'Your music, your lyricism.'

'Yes.'

'It is spiritual,' she said.

'Thank you again,' I said. 'I tried to celebrate the spiritual within the ordinary.'

'Precisely,' she said with energy, as if I had pressed a button that released all her agitation, 'precisely! The church is not for Sundays and high days, but for every day! God is not the *decoration* of our lives, God *is* our lives!'

'I am not sure,' I said tentatively, 'that this is what my poetry expresses – not exactly this.'

It seemed to depress her that I said so, and she became surly. After a while she brightened. 'But who can say? Music can be interpreted in many ways, after all. Not even the artist can encompass every resonance of his or her art.'

'Musical poetry can be interpreted many ways,' I conceded. 'More so than conventional narratives, more so than the visuals. And yet music is not open to every interpretation. Happy music is happy, after all. Sad music is sad.' I had no need to add that my poetry had been sad. But my poetry was all behind me now, struck away with my old life.

'These are only the broadest criteria of interpretation,' she said. 'Within that, we may find a spectrum of meanings.'

'Is the same not true,' I hazarded, 'of Scripture also?'

It upset her, I believe, that I returned to this topic. 'Scripture is precise where it needs to be precise,' she said stiffly, 'and general when it needs to be general. The All'God lays down specific rules we must follow, but also general principles we must interpret for ourselves in our actions – the principle of mercy, for instance, which is core to the Divine being.'

I replied that I had had little sense of that mercy.

This annoyed Siuzan further. 'That you have not perceived All'God's mercy tells me much about you, and little about Him,' she snapped.

At mealtimes I fed little parcels of vegetable or meat pulp into the valve at my neck stump, and swallowed them down into my stomach. This food of course lacked any flavour or quality. Whatever drink I poured into the same valve slid down into my stomach the same way, tastelessly, distinguished only by subtle variations in viscosity and texture of flow. There was one exception, namely wine, which of course entails certain aftereffects which other drinks would not. But in general no savour remained to the business of eating and drinking. I took no pleasure in it any more. When my stomach creased with hunger, I fed myself. That was all.

I became acquainted with the other recent headless. A dozen had been received into the house from execution over the month, ten men and two women. I spoke to most of them, and two of them left the house in my company, joining me on my travels, and I shall say something more about this pair.

I sat in the courtyard, in the white heat of the summer sun, trying to read a book, or more exactly experimenting with different positions of holding the text so that my eyes could absorb it. The best way, I discovered, was to cover one eye, and position the book beside the other shoulder.

Two headless came out of the refectory into the courtyard and sat on the hot marble of the bench. They were wearing white meadhres and yellow shifts: one, like me, had epaulette eyes; and his shift was cut open about the shoulders to facilitate their vision. The other had stalk eyes placed on his neck stump, like antennae; a more expensive prosthesis.

We introduced ourselves. 'My name is Jon Cavala,' said I.

'Mine,' said the stalk-eye, 'is Mark Pol Treherne.'

'Gymnaste Peri,' said the second.

'You are the Cavala,' said Mark Pol, 'famous for his poetry? I know your poetry. I have heard some of your music.' His voice emerged from some device in his neck stump rather than from his ordinator, and it had a more melodious timbre than mine, although it was nevertheless unmistakably synthetic. Such a device must have been expensive.

'I am flattered,' I replied.

'I enjoy music,' said Mark Pol. 'Why were you beheaded?'

'You are direct,' I said, 'in your questions. I was beheaded for adultery.'

'Aha! Adultery, is it? But that covers several crimes, that word. What form of adultery?'

I angled my shoulders away from him a little, to express my discomfort. 'Rape,' I said shortly.

'It is always rape, isn't it?' he said. 'In our so-exacting legal definition. Adultery always means rape, doesn't it?'

'Not so,' I contradicted. 'Last year in this very city, in Doué, a young couple were both beheaded for adulterous fornication. There was no rape in that instance. This was a mutually consensual sexual relationship.'

'I remember the case,' said Mark Pol. 'Although I insist it was an exceptional affair, and that "adultery" almost always does mean rape. But they were a fine couple, were they not? A handsome couple they were, both of them very good-looking. Neither of them older than twenty-four. But she was married to somebody else, as I recall. She shouldn't have married the other man if she wanted the first fellow, I would say.'

'They could not,' said Gymnaste, 'live without each other.' He paused. 'So they said.'

'Indeed,' said the more garrulous Mark Pol. 'And so they faced execution together. Is it romantic? I don't know. I heard that her husband has put her aside. He will divorce her, it seems, although the legal process takes seven years. So, in six years they will be together, a headless couple, enjoying legally sanctioned sexual congress in wedlock. Headless parents giving birth to headed children! How droll that thought is!'

'There is no reason,' I said, my thoughts on my own possible future, 'that one of the headless might not marry and have children.'

'Indeed not,' said Mark Pol. 'But would a beautiful woman marry one of our sort? Perhaps beauty is only on the surface, as the saying says, but who could fall in love with somebody in our poor, truncated condition? Yourself, *Sieur* Cavala, you are – I see it – a muscular individual. You have a good body, a strong torso, two strong arms, well-proportioned legs. You have exercised assiduously.'

'I have,' I said. 'And fortune has given me a robust constitution.'

'Yours was a pretty face, I suppose?' Mark Pol asked, seemingly offhand.

'It is no vanity,' I said, 'to admit that I was handsome.'

14

'And now that handsome visage is rotting in a ditch! So the world turns.' He laughed his ersatz laugh, a tinnily mechanical noise, very grating to hear.

'And why,' I asked, encouraged by his boldness, 'were *you* executed?'

'For murder,' he said, turning his torso flat to face mine, so that his stalk eyes were looking directly at me.

'Indeed?' I said, uncertain how to respond.

'Yes,' he said. 'Yes, murder. They say that blasphemy is the worst of the three crimes, don't they? A crime against the All'God rather than man, which makes it worse. I can't believe so. Surely murder is the worse, for heresy is just words, where murder is deeds, and deeds against flesh. Ask Gymnaste here – he lost his head for heresy. Didn't you, Gymnaste?'

'So I did,' said Gymnaste, after a pause.

'And a milder mannered individual you'll not find amongst all the headless,' declared Mark Pol Treherne loudly. 'And yet I am *far* from mild mannered. I am quarrelsome and prone to anger.'

'You killed a man?' I asked.

'I did.'

'Under what circumstances?'

'Oh,' he said, giving his hands alternately a rub and a squeeze, 'you'd like to know, would you? The violence and the death intrigue you, do they? Well, I have no objection to telling you. I was drinking in a bar here in Doué, and I became involved in a discussion with the person sitting next to me–a man I had never before met. Our discussion became more animated, until it would be accurate to describe it as an argument. The heat increased under the pressure applied to it by our two per-sonalities, and before long we were fighting. I struck him with one of the long-necked bottles of wine for which the region of Brignol, far to the east of here, is so famous. The bottle was full, and accordingly heavy. It broke his skull, and he died inside an ambulance on the road to hospital. There.' He held his hands before himself, showing the palms. 'My whole story. I blamed what I had drunk. I said the wine had killed him and not I. But the court thought differently. They thought, fan-tastically, that the blame was mine.'

'An engrossing story,' I said.

'Doué is full of such stories,' he replied. 'And now my victim is in one of Doué's many graveyards, and my own head is rotting like yours on a rubbish heap, and the world turns again.'

We three sat together, and the heat and the faint pressure of the sunlight squeezed our skins. I had an itch at my neck stump, which was a frequent occurrence, although it was not always possible to reach the itching area with my fingernails. I scratched as well as I could at the place near the broad cap of the stump-fitting.

'Where,' said Gymnaste shortly, 'will you go, *Sieur* Cavala?'

'I am no *sieur*,' I said. 'My name is Jon. And I will travel into the countryside, hoping to find work on a farm or factory.'

'I have thought a great deal about this very question,' said Mark Pol, stretching himself on the bench. 'The family of my victim are resident in Doué, and it would be uncomfortable to encounter them on the street. Unlikely, I suppose, in a city so large, but certainly possible. Perhaps it would be best to travel to the country. But at the same time, there is much to be said for city life, particularly from a headless perspective. After all, there are many hundred headless individuals in the city. Citizens are used to seeing them coming and going about their business. This is not so in the country, where villages may not see one of the headless from year's end to year's end. In such places one runs the risk of ridicule, of persecution, fingers pointed and doors slammed in one's – face, I was going to say. Neck, I suppose I should say instead.'

'There is Montmorillon,' said Gymnaste slowly. 'They call it the Land of the Headless.'

'Yes,' said Mark Pol impatiently. 'I have heard of this place. But is it truly a Land of the Headless? Or is it merely a province where many of the headless have gone, such that they form a higher proportion of the general population? There they go to work the mines, isn't it so? Perhaps you would be happy in the mines, Gymnaste: in those low-ceilinged tunnels, with light-amplifiers fitted to your epaulettes, servicing the mining machines and lugging cargo. Perhaps that would suit you. But it would not suit me. Even though I no longer have a face upon which to feel the sunlight, I would prefer to live above ground. Are you of the same mind, Jon?'

'I have no strong feelings on the subject of working subterraneously,' I said. 'It is merely my whim to travel to the country. My' – and I hesitated, but it was necessary that I become used to the locution – 'my *victim* also lives in Doué, and I do not wish to encounter her. It would distress her, and discommode me. Better to leave the city altogether, and continue life in a new environment.'

'I see,' said Mark Pol. 'I see.'

But this was the direct opposite of the truth. In truth my victim no longer lived in Doué, for she had moved to her family's estate in Cainon. Her family name was Benet. My only wish (and I had nothing else with which to give purpose to my life) was to see her again. And so I planned to travel to Cainon. I had been revolving possibilities in my mind ever since coming to the House of Friends: perhaps to travel incognito, to apply to the Estate of Benets as a labourer under a false identity. Without my head I was virtually unrecognisable as the person I had once been. It could be that the Estate of Benets hired headless workers for menial chores; such was a common charity amongst the more devout families. Then, working on the estate, I might contrive a chance to see Bernardise. For this was the name of the woman for whose sake I had been decapitated. But, naturally, I could tell nobody this, since if it became clear that I was travelling specifically to see Bernardise I would be prevented, by law. A headless man can be imprisoned, as can any other person. A headless man can suffer any penalty under the law except decapitation– and the law says that should he commit a second crime for which that is the punishment there is only the final execution, and burial in a criminal's grave.

I did not tell Siuzan Delage that this was my plan; and nor did I tell these two other headless men. 'I have experience of working on farms,' I told them, 'from my youth. The work agrees with me. Besides, one of the headless can hardly pick and choose which work he wants to do. I will be lucky to earn the merest labourer's wage.'

'True,' said Mark Pol. 'Too true.'

'How will you travel?' asked the taciturn Gymnaste.

'My friend means to ask,' interrupted Mark Pol, 'how much money you possess. He means to ask, will you fly? Or take the overland? Or will you, perhaps, walk?' He laughed again his artificial laugh. 'Of course, you must know where you are going before you can buy a ticket.'

'I have no particular plans,' I said disingenuously. 'Besides, my funds are very limited. I spent most of my monies on the law, and what little was left paid for my prostheses. I have, perhaps, fifteen totales, and some odd divizos.' I thought about the overland fare to Cainon, a hundred or more miles distant: it would be at least ten totales. I did not like the thought of arriving at Cainon with only five totales in my account.

'I will walk,' I said expansively.

'I shall accompany you,' said Mark Pol. 'If you have no objections?'

'None,' I said.

'Will you come too,' Mark Pol asked Gymnaste, as if on the spur of the moment. 'Or do you have other plans?'

Gymnaste was silent for a while, and then said: 'I will walk.'

Four

Our walk to Cainon lasted four days and three nights. My account of it need not detain the reader any longer than twenty pages of this text; but I must tell you about it because so much of what followed was shaped by it. From this walk so much else, both evil and good, flowed. These few days have proved to be the dominant event of my life.

That Siuzan declared her intention to accompany us upon this walk did not, perhaps, surprise me as much as it ought to have done. She talked of her desire to go to Cainon and explore the possibilities of mission work in that city. The walk, she said, would be a pilgrimage. We were all pilgrims.

We were, but in ways neither she nor I could anticipate. I fear I flattered myself that Siuzan accompanied us because of some indefinable magnetism of mine. Headless as I was, infatuated as I was becoming, I could not see clearly, alas. But then again: why might not a woman love a man, though he lacks a head? Why does any woman fall in love with any man? Not for the outsides, or insides, of their heads, surely. For their *hearts*, surely.

We set out early one day, walking through the streets of Doué before most of the population were awake. Eager to be out of the city and away from the judgemental eyes of so many citizens, we agreed to take a central bus to the northern outskirts of the city. This cost us seventy divizos each, and Mark Pol grumbled at the expense, even so little an outgoing as this. 'I see no reason why we should not have walked proudly through the city,' he said, 'holding our—' And he stopped, with an electronic snickering sound. 'I was going to say,' he added, '*holding our heads high*, but that is not the best expression, perhaps.'

'Can you not afford seventy divizos?' Siuzan Defarge asked him, earnestly. It may have been that she was thinking of gifting him some money. Here I intervened crossly.

'Do not pity him his lack of money,' I said. 'He spent more on his prostheses than either of us – the very best in visual and auditory augmentation. Nothing but the best was good enough for—'

Mark Pol laughed. 'Are you envious?' he demanded.

'—good enough for the luxurious Mark Pol—'

'Envious?' he repeated. 'Are you envious, *Sieur* Cavala?'

'There is nothing you have that merits envy; nor do I covet anything you have ever possessed,' I returned, rather stiffly. I cannot say where my dislike of this man came from, except to note that it was there from the very first time I met him.

'The bus is stopping,' said Gymnaste, standing up.

'I will say only this,' said Siuzan in a severe voice. 'If you, Mark Pol, and you, Jon, intend to bicker and fight throughout the whole of this trek, it will become quickly tedious for myself and Gymnaste. Most tedious, indeed.'

I felt the sting of this rebuke keenly, for the last thing I wished was to offend Siuzan; and so I resolved at that very moment to leave Mark Pol be – neither to provoke him, nor to allow him to provoke me. But I did not remain true to this resolution. The more time I spent in the company of the chittering, preening, headless Mark Pol the more furious I became, and this fury frequently spilled out.

We began to walk, and the sun low to our right pulled tremendously long shadows from the putty-stuff of our bodies and draped them over the objects to our left. Yet even these early morning shadows, longer than serpents, made clear the headlessness of our bodies, shadow-arms trailing from flared shadow-shoulders. The valves in our neck stumps clicked quietly as each of us breathed in, and breathed out. This regular percussion from the three of us, synchronising into a single beat and then falling away from it again into intricate syncopation, aligning and de-aligning, this was the constant accompaniment of our trek.

We walked for twenty minutes and came into an outlying industrial zone of Doué. Here we saw some other headless, making their way into a large factory building for their morning shift. It was not clear what the factory produced, or even (to be truthful) if it was a factory at all. Perhaps it was a prison, or an office, or a warehouse, I do not know. There are only a small number of industries prepared to employ the headless, and those that do pay poorly for what is often dangerous work, preferring cheap headless to expensive robotic devices.

My visual software was still strange to my senses, such that the scene acquired a more vivid and surreal aspect than otherwise it would. I might, in former days, have passed such a place without a second glance; but now I lingered staring at the irregular line of headless, all dressed in purple or scarlet overalls, all making their way across a tarmac field littered with boxes and randomly parked trolleys, beneath the peach-pink and treacle-yellow sky of a summer dawn. Their lack of heads gave them a caricature look, as if they were so despondent at their lowly jobs that they were hanging their heads far below their shoulder-blades. They made a sulky-looking, lumpish crew.

Because of the nature of this workforce we found a café in which to break our fast that did not forbid the headless from entering, or make them eat in the alley down the side, or lecture them on their duty of atonement, or any of the things most eateries did in the city. Inside, indeed, Siuzan Delage was the only patron with a head; and since the menu was mostly tasteless sludge, the cheapest of foods, palatable only to those without tongues to taste it, she did not eat.

'I have been thinking,' said Mark Pol, breaking the silence (because he could never bear to remain silent for long), 'about my longer-term future.'

None of us replied.

'Have you not, my fellow decapitatees, given thought to the matter? This countryside walk up to Cainon is all very good, but we have many years of life left to us. And the employment opportunities for the headless are rare. Surely observing the workforce in this dour place brings these thoughts into your minds as well?' Even when created by a neutral electronic device, through a speaker, rather than out of his flesh, there was some unmistakable and unpleasant tone in his voice: a smugness, a selfishness. I recalled my new resolution to leave him be and though I shuddered privately I said nothing.

'I am glad to hear you planning for the long term,' said Siuzan.

'Your gladness gladdens me, *chère* lady,' said Mark Pol, in winsome imitation of the hero from courtly love. This infuriated me; for it sounded too close to flirtation, and the thought of this grotesque truncated murderer setting his sights so high as the pure lady Siuzan, even in jest, was too revolting. Yet still I strove not to antagonise the fellow, and limited myself to speaking in general terms.

'We have no future,' I growled. 'It is fruitless to speculate. We must endure, and be grateful for any charity offered us.'

'My dear melancholic poet,' said Mark Pol. 'But I disagree! There are many options.'

'Name one.'

'We might,' said Mark Pol, 'join the army.'

This had not occurred to me. 'The military?'

'Providing only that their prostheses are of a good enough quality,' said Mark Pol, 'the headless make excellent soldiery. They are far less vulnerable than headed troops, the head being (of course) the most fragile portion of any body in combat. You present a less dangerous profile to the enemy if you are headless, and yet you can fight as well as any man.' He put out the palms of his hands. 'Some headless join the army for no better reason than that they are thereby guaranteed the better prostheses, and a regular supply of endocrine pharmocopies.'

'I have no experience as a fighter,' I said.

Mark Pol put his palms out again, a gesture that seemed to substitute for a smile in his body language. 'That matters not in the least,' he said. 'For would they not train us? Of course they would.'

'But it would be repugnant to me to become, in effect, a professional killer—' I said. I stopped myself, remembering that Mark Pol had been beheaded for murder. But rather than being offended by my remark, he misinterpreted it.

'I, too, would not like to put myself in danger. I confess, it is the idea of a consistent and uninterrupted endocrine supply that mostly attracts me. It is no easy matter to guarantee a proper supply of endocrine chemicals, or so I understand. This is what other headless have told me. The pouches of pharmocopy are expensive, though vital, and many headless work long hours and spend most of their money only to obtain them. Nor can we simply do without them, or we will sicken and die. But in the army, the highest quality of synthetic endocrine materials are on guaranteed supply.'

'Perhaps,' I hazarded, 'this might be thought a trivial reason for enlisting?'

'Indeed,' he said. We fell silent. Gymnaste was spooning pap into the valve at the top of his neck. This action made a series of clicking and scraping noises.

After a while, irrepressible, Mark Pol began speaking again. 'I believe that, on the world of Sung, the soldiers have their heads removed and stored prior to battle. Imagine that! The heads are cut away, but carefully, surgically, and kept chilled. After the battle the heads are reattached, specific nano-pharmakos reattaching the nervous pathways, as good as new in two days. Soldiers are thereby assured that their heads will suffer no injury in the battle.'

'This is idle speculation,' I said. 'A mere fantasy.'

'Perhaps,' agreed Mark Pol, 'you are correct. Or did I only see such scenes in a drama? Perhaps I have confused fiction and real life.' He laughed.

'Time isn't loitering,' said Siuzan, 'and neither should we. Gentlemen, shall we go?'

We stepped out and walked away, making towards the north. The city fell behind us, shrinking from tall buildings into single-storey, from close-packed to more sparsely arranged. The ground between was parched by the summer, a scrub upon which strands of grass grew brittle as crystal, all very yellow and tan, all very pale and dry.

This whole time Mark Pol chattered on. He commented upon the landscape, and the nature of the road. He goaded me with references to the barrenness of my poetry, and his preference for music over poetry ('Why must there be any words set to music at all?'). He laughed. He commented that I was sweating more than the others, and that I was unused to physical hardship. I swallowed my anger and did not reply.

Instead I focused upon a separate irritation of my walk. For I had no *staff*. It cannot be denied that, for any lengthy walk or trek, a staff – a wand of wood reaching from the ground up to the walker's shoulder – makes the process very much smoother and easier. I do not know why this might be, but I do know (having enjoyed several walking holidays in the Apollo foothills to the east of the Mild Sea before my disgrace) that it is so. And now, as I trekked to Cainon, I regretted my not obtaining a similar staff, at first ruefully, and then more bitterly. My feet began aching very soon after beginning the walk. I felt the friction of my pedestrian action in my heels, along the sides of my feet, in my knees and hips.

Why had I not thought of giving myself a staff?

At mid-morning we crossed the wide road-bridge over the River Goidel, which is the main river of Doué, flowing from the north-west into the city and out again into the Mild Sea. North of this landmark there were no buildings; only the outback landscape patched here and there by grass. It was a baked land. The sun was high enough now to drop a palpable heat upon us. It marked a brimming white circle in my field of vision; and its light, perhaps owing to some glitch in the software, registered almost as a pulsing throb, such as is produced by a badly tuned neon bulb. The river eeled away towards the eastern horizon, a very striking dark blue against the yellow.

On the far side of the bridge we crossed a wide star of tarmac, a surface marked with the monotonous runes of truck tyre rubber. This was the junction of several roads, one to the city in the west, another east, following the river for a while before turning off to other cities (to Hainly, to Crowne) and another. A smartpole sat inert in the centre of this junction waiting for traffic to direct. Our footsteps did not disturb it.

Dust trickled over the road like fluid gauze, moved by an intermittent ground breeze. My trachea felt dry as I breathed, and the click of my throat valve was increasingly noisy.

'You are not used to such exercise,' Mark Pol said again, 'despite your well-developed physique. Gym-built muscles, perhaps?'

I restrained the urge to reply in anger, and I held my peace.

The roads went straight east and straight west and straight north, and a smaller road curled away to the north-east. It was the north road we took, walking in silence for a while.

We saw no trucks at all for another half hour, by which time the river was beyond the horizon behind us and there was nothing but yellow scrub in all directions. Then one of those enormous robot-driven lorries announced its presence with a distant grinding noise, a groan which swelled to a shout and swelled and bore down upon us. It passed us with a roar to shame the largest lion, and a swaying sidewind rocked us on our heels in the aftermath. Then it was receding, shrinking in size and diminuendoing its noise.

Then it was gone.

After this noise, the silence returned with a greater intensity.

'Planes have taken most of the trade from those trucks, as I was reading in a newsbook only last month,' said Mark Pol conversationally. Chatter, chatter, chatter: could he never be quiet? But I restrained myself. 'They were more common ten years ago, but those new elemag engines have brought the cost of jet flight down considerably.'

As if anybody cared!

We did not see another truck for another hour. After that two passed us in the space of ten minutes. Then nothing for several hours.

We walked through the heat of the day. My body slipped into a steady rhythm. The heat was uncomfortable but bearable. I pondered the sort of staff I would buy if I had the money: with a knob for the palm of the hand, as tall as from the ground to my breast, made of white wood.

Mark Pol fell into step beside me. 'Siuzan Delage is a beautiful woman,' he observed, as if to the air. Siuzan herself was perhaps thirty feet away from us.

'Do not talk about her,' I retorted. 'And certainly do not talk about her *in that way*.'

'Oho,' he said, amused. 'I have touched a tender spot, have I? And why not? We may all dream. You, *Sieur* Cavala – you have as much right to love as any, I think? As much right to fantasise about taking a woman in your arms ...'

'Be quiet!'

'Have I offended you?' he asked, in mock surprise. 'Was it because I referred to you as *Sieur* Cavala? I apologise; I had forgotten your dislike of the honorific.'

'You speak to vex me,' I said. 'Leave me alone – go back.'

'Not at all. Speak to vex you? No, no. Why should it vex you that I call Siuzan Delage a beautiful young woman? Is she not beautiful? Don't *I* have as much right to admire her as you?'

'Stop!'

'You can't be jealous, Jon Cavala, surely,' he joked. 'Although I have been wondering whether she has some special taste or fetish for headless men – for why else would she agree to accompany us on this tedious walk? I *have* been wondering. And *if* she has a taste for headless men then why might her favour not fall on me, as like as you?'

I quickened my pace, his words (*if she has a taste for headless men*) burning in my mind. I walked on in a fury, and indeed got far ahead of the other three, before stopping at the side to wait for them to catch up. I repeated to myself, silently, over and over, *be calm*.

Mountains serrated the line of the northern horizon, rising up very slowly as we approached them. My vision recognition software represented them to me as a dark blue that was nearly purple, blistered and capped at the top with pure white. The flat land leading up to them registered as a sharp and artificial-looking yellow. These were not the real colours, but were instead a function of the crudeness of my vision software. I could not tell you what colours the landscape truly possessed. But it made a very striking visual composition.

Above the mountains the sky looked white. A wide lenticular raincloud, with a white border and a heart the colour of plain chocolate, dominated that empty space over the peaks. But the air was dry. That raincloud would never relinquish its yield. It would slide (and indeed I watched it slide) away over the horizon to the east unpunctured and whole. Dust was blowing over the road before us, as fine and yellow as pollen. The unnatural straightness of the tarmac had the effect of foreshortening it, such that it appeared to be only a few tapering metres long.

One foot stepped in front of another, over and over.

Once again I regretted the lack of a staff to aid my walking. I chided myself silently. Why had I not taken the foresight to provide myself with a simple staff of wood? How could I have been so remiss?

'Perhaps you could explain again to me,' said Mark Pol to Siuzan, 'why you are prepared to walk this long and gritty path with us. I only mean,' he added, angling his torso towards her a little, 'that a woman such as yourself – so blameless, so wealthy, so beautiful! – could easily take passage in a jet. Surely you could afford it. And we could, if you wished, still rendezvous with you at Cainon.'

'Is my company irksome to you, *Sieur* Mark?' said Siuzan, smiling.

'Not in the slightest,' Mark Pol replied gaily. 'Not in the least irksome, *Chère* Siuzan.' I did not like the way he used the honorific; it smacked, I thought, of too great an assumption of intimacy, of too much levity, and I thought the way Mark Pol drew out the second 'e' of the word almost lascivious. But Siuzan did not seem offended.

'I view this,' said Siuzan, 'after the manner of a pilgrimage. I pay duty to the All'God by walking with you. It is my honour.'

'But precisely, it is your *honour*,' said Mark Pol, 'which is my chief concern. It is your *honour* that is uppermost in my mind.' It is difficult to decipher nuance with an artificial voice, even of the more sophisticated sort that Mark Pol was using. But nevertheless I felt I detected a lewd double-meaning here, as if he were saying that he himself wished to take her virginity, and thereby her honour. I bridled. 'Mark Pol, restrain yourself,' I barked.

'But what prompts your outrage, *Sieur* Cavala?' he replied, as if surprised. 'I spoke sincerely. Or did you think I had some pornographic intention behind my innocent words?'

'Do not apply the honorific to me,' I replied, my electric voice gruff. 'For I do not deserve it.'

'Then plain Cavala it shall be,' Mark Pol said straightaway, with a chuckle in his voice. 'But I must press the point. Why do you rebuke me for my perfectly genuine expression of interest in the lady's honour?'

This was approaching impertinence. 'I say: leave this conversation wholly behind you, Mark Pol.'

There was no mistaking the gloating tone that was in Mark Pol's artificial voice. 'No, Cavala, no,' he said. 'This cannot be. You have impugned *my* honour, and although perhaps, like you, I do not deserve to be addressed as "Sieur", nevertheless I cannot let *that* pass. Even a headless may want to preserve such tatters of honour as remain to him. You impute to me lewd and base motivations...'

'Please,' said Siuzan. 'No quarrelling. No fighting.'

'*Chère* Siuzan,' Mark Pol said. 'A moment, by your gracious consent. Allow me merely to impress upon Cavala, here, the gravity of what he has said. Lewd motivation? Some base *sexual* motivation to my—?'

'Mark Pol!' I cried, almost in an agony.

'—to my words? This is insupportable. This was not in my mind *at all*. It is not *I*, after all, who was beheaded for sexual crimes. It was not *I* who forced my sexual attentions on a woman – that is something *I* would never do.'

I could feel the flush on my chest. For once I was grateful that I no longer possessed a face, for that would have been as dark as wine with my embarrassment. But, of course, I had permitted Mark Pol to force me into this situation. It served me poorly to over-react to his goading. I could do nothing but concede.

'Very well,' I said. 'You have won the victory here, Mark Pol.'

But he chose not to be pacified. 'Victory? This is not what I was thinking, not in the least. No, no, I am not in conflict with you, my fellow headless.'

'Whatever you will,' I said. 'Take it any way you choose. I give way. The ground is yours.'

He carried on protesting that this was not his intention, but I quickened my stride and walked ahead of the group. My emotions were cast into a profound turmoil by this little exchange and by the fact that Mark Pol had so easily fooled me in front of Siuzan Delage. I was angry as much with myself as with him. This forge of shame inside me flamed hot.

A little later, perhaps a quarter of an hour, Siuzan hurried up to walk beside me. Because my legs were longer than hers, and I was striding fiercely in my miserable anger, she had to insert little running trots into her own step to keep up. 'Do not be concerned by Mark Pol, I beg of you,' she said.

'He is a mocker,' I said.

'I can hardly be unaware of *that*! It is his nature.'

'His intentions towards you,' I growled, 'are dishonourable.'

'I am indeed appreciative, Jon Cavala, of your attempt to protect me from his roguery. But you need not be so worried. I have worked for years now amongst the newly headless. Do you think I am unfamiliar with inappropriate words and actions? The truth is that, especially amongst the *newly* decapitated, there is much anger and resentment, and on occasion this becomes directed at me. I have listened to obscenity and sexual suggestion much more upsetting than anything Mark Pol has said a dozen times a day. Besides, he is not capable of true obscenity. He is a clown. He may joke with me, and attempt to provoke me, but he would never assault me.'

This, naturally, stung me, and further stirred up my furious shame and anger; although I believe Siuzan spoke carelessly, for the moment forgetting the reason I had been beheaded.

'You should be more careful of him,' I told her. But, in truth, I meant: *you should be more careful of me.* For, from the time I had first known her and day by day since then, I was finding it harder and harder to look upon her without instantly sinking into the imaginative rehearsal of erotic possibility. I pushed my stride out longer, walking so fast now as to be almost running, and I left her behind.

Can a man escape himself? Not merely by quickening his stride, alas.

We came to a bridge over a railway line. The steel rails were inset into a trench, ten metres below us, and we paused on the bridge to drink from our water bottles. The sun had swung through the sky. I could feel it on the backs of my shoulders. The covering of my neck stump was made of a plastic darker than skin-tone, and this had heated during my walk.

Gymnaste came and stood beside me. 'If you'll forgive me, Jon Cavala,' he said gently. 'You should not allow Mark Pol to make you angry. When he speaks, I beg of you: consider his words as nothing more than the whining of a mosquito.'

I was silent for a while, staring at the view with my artificial eyes. But Gymnaste's words were kindly meant, so I said: 'Thank you. I know, of course, that what you say is right.'

'He cannot help himself, perhaps,' Gymnaste said. 'He *must* infuriate and madden those around him. It is a habit with him. Perhaps he feels he would expire were people not to direct their attention upon him.'

As we stood there a train passed under the bridge: a lengthy robot-driven goods train of perhaps a hundred metal cars. We all watched it approach, drawing closer and louder, until it rolled directly beneath us and conversation was swallowed by the whoop of steel on steel, the grinding, swaying chunter of the carriages. And then we turned about, and watched it recede again, the noise diminishing until once again we were left with pure silence, the sort that is so clear it rings bell-like inside you.

We walked on, and within two hours we reached the outskirts of a small town. A sign announced its name: Lacon. 'We must find a place to stay for the night,' said Siuzan Delage, and immediately she added, 'Here,' pointing to a one-storey wooden hostel set a little way back from the side of the road.

'At the very first place we come to?' I asked.

'Do not forget our condition, for that declares our crimes to the world,' said Mark Pol. 'We will be lucky if they will give us a roof over our— over our heads I was going to say.' He laughed. 'But a roof at any rate, even though we have no heads that need housing. A place where we can curl up together.' His torso was angled towards Siuzan when he said this last.

27

It occurred to me at that moment that I hated Mark Pol enough to want to kill him.

We walked up a short gravel path between two wide flower beds and up three steps onto a wooden terrace. Tables were arranged for diners, although none was occupied. 'Stay here,' said Siuzan. 'I shall explain the circumstance to the owner.'

She went inside.

The three of us stood, headless and awkward, in silence. The late afternoon sunlight was bright upon the little terrace. The wooden lattice roof above us was wholly grown over with vines. Bunch after bunch of grapes hung down like dozens of irregular toy chandeliers. Between the grape clusters moth-shaped leaves plucked and stirred in the breeze.

'Beautiful roses,' said Mark Pol, gesturing with his right hand at the flower bed through which we had just walked. Of course he was unable simply to stand there in silence, as Gymnaste and I were doing. 'My visual recognition software is of a higher quality than yours, *Sieurs* Cavala and Gymnaste, so I am able to appreciate the extraordinary delicacy and loveliness of the coloration. But perhaps even you can see how well-grown these flowers are, even though your prostheses are considerably inferior to mine.'

I looked at the roses. I looked at the little eye-shaped leaves on the stems, the luxuriant upholstery of their petals clustering around their buds. 'They are pretty,' I said.

Mark Pol angled his torso towards me to bring his stalk eyes more directly to bear upon me. He was intending, I am sure, to say something galling to me; but in this event he was interrupted by the hostel owner coming through the main door and onto the porch. 'No,' this fellow was saying. 'I say it again, *chère* lady. You are welcome to any room you choose, but these lopped fellows cannot stay under my roof.'

'I ask you to think again,' said Siuzan. 'I beg you, in piety and mercy.'

'This is a respectable house,' said the owner. 'Lacon is a respectable town. No hotel will accommodate them. If they intend staying they should make their way, perhaps, to the church barracks behind the ammonia sink.' He was pointing, but none of us followed the line of his arm with our eyes.

'Please put your preconceptions aside,' said Siuzan.

'*Chère* lady, your business is your business. But I am surprised to see you walking the high road in the company of three such …' He trailed off, looking at us with disgust.

'I assure you,' Mark Pol, said, with almost a giggle in his voice, 'that you, *sieur* landlord, should not include me with these other two in your disdain.'

'I know these men,' said Siuzan in a placatory tone. 'They have repented of their crimes. I trust them more readily than I would men I know with heads.'

The landlord was a small-framed, corpulent man with spiky black hair and a turf-like beard over his chin and neck. His dark eyes flicked from Siuzan to the three of us. 'Your business is your business,' he repeated.

'And will you not give them shelter?' Siuzan pressed.

'*Chère* lady,' he said. 'They can, if they like, sleep in the yard at the back. That is more than many hostels would do, I assure you. If they are newly headless, as I see they are, then I'd recommend they reconcile themselves to their new circumstances – they will not be welcome in most respectable towns. They had better get used to sleeping outdoors and tucking themselves out of the sight and way of decent people.'

'The yard at the back then,' said Siuzan. 'Thank you.'

'Shall I prepare a room for you inside, *chère* lady?'

'I shall stay in the yard at the back,' said Siuzan. 'With them.'

The hostel owner swallowed this information. He started speaking, and stopped in surprise. Then he said: 'Your business is yours,' one final time, before going inside again.'

That evening Siuzan joined us as we sat in the backyard of the café. Mark Pol began chittering and chattering again. His favoured topic was himself, and he liked to ponder aloud, making plans for his life. 'We could leave the world altogether.'

'That,' I pointed out, 'would require us to obtain passage on a spaceship.'

'Of course. But on other worlds the stigma of being headless might well be lessened. Or perhaps there would be no stigma at all. Perhaps we would be interesting curios, or objects of pity.'

'This seems unlikely to me.'

'How many worlds practise so severe a punishment? None but ours.'

'I shall say prayers for all of us,' said Siuzan, 'after I have washed.'

She went into the hostel and returned a few minutes later with a bowl of water, which she placed on the floor. Then she pulled off her coat and crouched down to wash her hands and face. We all watched her, without moving. As she bent forward over the bowl, her shirt rode up a little way– no more than a hand's width – at the base of her spine. Several of the knuckles of her spine were visible, and the taut skin stretched over them.

My breathing was very shallow. My male organ had become aroused.

This disgusted me, of course. I disgusted myself. But I could not remove my gaze from her back. I stared as a starving man stares at fresh food. I was furious with myself, simultaneously revolted and angry and yet excited, and though I rebuked myself internally yet I could not stop looking. I was visited with an urge to reach over and touch her, an urge so powerful it almost made me gasp. I held myself rigid. Only by doing so could I restrain my shameful desire.

She sat back on her heels, and her shirt dropped to conceal her flesh again. She looked around, fresh-faced and beaming. 'Shall I lead the prayers?' she asked.

We prayed, but all the time that I grated out those words in my electronic voice, my thoughts were very far from pure. I was thinking of the glimpse of Siuzan's skin. Eventually I fell asleep, but in the night a revolting thing happened, almost too revolting to repeat in this narrative except that I have promised myself to be wholly truthful and spare none of the degradations that I have brought on myself. What happened was this: there was emission of fluid from my male organ, and I awoke to discover this seminal phlegm cold and crusted to my belly and thigh. I apologise for reporting this, but I have vowed that this account be as truthful as possible and omit nothing, though it shames me, all of it, shames me.

That morning we walked through Lacon, along the main street. We passed shops and factories, and eventually came into the northern suburbs. Within the hour we were in the scrublands again.

There was one more notable thing I remember from this town. In a farm on the outskirts of it I saw a headless horse. It stood like an unfinished statue in a straw-yellow field under the massive blue bar of the sky and the perfect circle of the sun. Why would its master have decapitated it? It was impossible to say. As we came closer we could see the pommel-like protuberance of its ordinator, just to the front of that place where a saddle would be placed were the horse ever to be ridden. Its neck resembled a fat tentacle stretching out at nothing. I could not see whether it had been fitted with any sensory devices. What sort of consciousness had been downloaded into that metal block on its back? Perhaps its master had loved the horse and had responded to some fatal sickness or head injury in this manner. Perhaps it had been an act of kindness. Or perhaps merely an experiment – the first human ordinators had been tested on animals after all, although that had been a century before. Surely nobody needed repeat the experiment. But perhaps this was a new design of ordinator being developed. Perhaps – and I could not help thinking this – perhaps the horse had killed somebody, or pressed its amorous desires upon some neighbour's mare, and a religiously over-literal farmer had punished him in this manner. Such an explanation seemed bizarre, but it was at least possible. The horse did not move as we walked by its field. Further along the road I looked back, and it was still there, motionless.

We walked all day, pausing only to drink water as we needed it, and stopping once to eat. Siuzan had bought a pack of breads and vat-meats, and we ate this. '*Chère* Siuzan,' Mark Pol chattered. 'There is no need to be so generous! Pap will suffice us. We cannot taste the malt in this bread, the savour in these meats.'

'But there are also your stomachs to consider,' she said cheerily. 'Is it good to place in them nothing but pap? Surely variety, and good food, will keep you stronger.'

She said a short prayer, and passed round a little wine. This we did not refuse.

'We cannot taste your wine, my lady,' said Mark Pol. 'I regret.'

'And yet wine is a holy drink, whether you can taste it or not. I beg you: think of the All'God when you drink, of his blood and spirit.'

I angled my torso forward, and tried to think of this. But instead my thoughts were distracted by the shapes made by Siuzan's face; the smoothness of her skin; the curves and planes of her cheeks. Her brow. Her nose and lips. The dance of her features when she laughed, har-monious and delightful.

That night we slept in the desert, with nothing but foilweave blankets to keep us warm. Siuzan wrapped a stone in her coat to make a pillow. 'We have no need for such ingenuity!' declared Mark Pol. 'Not us. Lacking a head has advantages as well as disadvantages, I think. No need of pillows! No expensive hats! No costly sunglasses!'

'Be quiet,' I hissed. 'Go to sleep. Or if you do not, then at least let *us* go to sleep.'

'I shall be silent as the night sky,' he promised. But even when he was himself asleep he muttered and chattered to himself, scraps and orts of words, symptoms of a restless soul.

I woke, pinched by cold, in the nothing hours. My blanket had slid from my legs and they were cramping in the frost, but even after replacing the covering and feeling the flesh warm, I could not sleep. I lay looking at the stars, at their broadcast scatter of bleaching dots, distinct and isolated, or flowing into one another where the galaxy's arm reaches round in its spectral embrace of us. My vision software gave the stars a precision that was quite unlike my former vision, as if each focus of light were defined and picked out exactly. This made the larger spread of dark purple almost prickly with brightness. For long minutes my thoughts were wholly occupied by the immensity of this dappled blackness. I fancied myself looking into the pupil of the eye of the Creator. I imagined my sight falling through impossible depths, almost to the point where I quite forgot myself, hovering on the edge of that place where there is no self at all.

Siuzan Delage called out. She was still asleep, and the word she uttered was simply the fin of some great fish breaking the water's surface only for a moment before sinking to the depths of her unconscious once more. But the sound of her voice sent a smack and a recoil through my nerves. The universe fled away, to an impossible infinite distance. The only thing of which I was aware was her: her proximity. Her flesh. I desired her with a completeness for which the very word *desire* seems inadequate. I lay and I trembled like a fever victim. My male organ was hard as metal, as planed and carved wood, and was striving to become even harder.

This is the basic question of our lives. Why must the spiritual be tethered to the gross with this rope? Is it a second and brute consciousness that fights with the wisdom of the head? It has rightly been said that the male organ is a serpent, a rat nosing out of a bed of hair. How much better the judges of Doué had severed that part of my body and left me with my head! I urged it down, I tried to focus my will on subduing it. That my lust was provoked by so pure and perfect a woman seemed to me doubly shameful, and almost impossible hideousness of my own soul.

She had given me no cause for my repulsive reaction. She had neither flirted with me, nor acted in any way inappropriate. And yet the urge was almost overwhelming in me to touch her – hold her, to cover her with my body.

I wrestled against this urge with all my force. Even though I lay motionless I struggled more fiercely than any athlete. Eventually, after an indeterminate length of time, I fell asleep again. I was worn out by my motionless struggle.

That sky, so darkly purple! Those stars, each so distinctly defined by its dimensionless intensity of light, and yet spread with such profusion over the sky they might have been grains of bright pollen!

I often think of that night.

When I awoke it was bright sky above me, although the chill had not yet left the ground. The others were up, and the headless body of Mark Pol Treherne was shaking me. The motion of his arm made his shoulder-mounted stalk eyes wobble slightly. 'Up!' he said. 'Up *sieur* poet, for the day-sky has his head on again – you can see it resting its chin on the eastern horizon. Though I fear the day-sky has committed some crime, for the horizon is a blade that will sever it, mark my words, and set that head rolling into the bowl of day.'

I was too tired even to tell him to hold his tongue at all this foolishness.

We walked all day, and even Mark Pol's incessant chatter dried in the migraine heat. Siuzan Delage seemed distracted, and stopped often to sip from her water bottle, or to replenish her sunblock. Of course we, lacking heads and otherwise clothed, needed none of this.

We stopped for lunch, and were refreshed with food and water, but the conversation between us was not refreshed. Mark Pol tried a few hopeless sallies, but soon gave up. After a brief rest we set off again, walking in a line.

The unrelenting boredom of it, the lack of sensory stimulation, played tricks with the sense of time. It was tedious, and uncomfortable, almost to the point of ascetic meditation. After a while the motion of the sun though the sky became discernible, a relentless pressure of movement as the source of heat and light pivoted about the world. Eventually the horizon swallowed this bolus up and it was dark again. Gymnaste hastened over to me and laid a hand on my upper arm, and the spell was broken – for I would have trudged on mindlessly into the night if not stopped. I ate in silence, drank in silence, wrapped myself about and fell asleep almost at once. Rarely in my life have I been so tired.

I did not wake that night.

I had an insight, as I gathered myself in that morning, of the way lengthily prolonged and monotonous action – walking, working – redefines a person. If the wilderness had stretched on for weeks, I would have fallen without thought or regret into that blank routine. I would have walked, and stopped to eat; I would have walked on, and stopped to sleep. And with the new dawn I would have done it again. This might have gone on indefinitely.

But we did not have weeks of walking ahead of us. 'We should reach Cainon today,' croaked Siuzan Delage, in a voice unused to speaking. Her face looked almost sorrowful, as if over-weary. I even wondered if she was sorry that her trek was soon to end. Perhaps, I reasoned, she had achieved some spiritual state in the labour of it, something like physical prayer.

We kicked a shallow bowl out of the dust of the ground, and turned our backs (Mark Pol covered his eye stalks with his hands) whilst Siuzan Delage voided her bladder, only turning back when the sound of scuffing made it clear that she had filled in this makeshift latrine. She then walked on ahead as we performed similar functions, and we afterwards jogged to catch her up. Her manner towards us seemed to have changed. There was a hauteur in it, some disinclination to be part of our company.

As in the previous day we fell into a silent rhythm. The mountains ahead were imperceptibly taller. The whole range seemed to float on a scintillating mist of mirage, which made them more like angular clouds of white and tan and purple. They did not look real.

Five

We come to the most painful portion of my narrative. It is here that the need for an absolute truthfulness becomes most pressing, although the events I must relate are of a sort naturally revolting to civilised sensibilities. But I shall not flinch. I ask you to be similarly braced.

We approached Cainon. The first symptom of the city was industrial: a series of circular concrete mushrooms, large as ocean liners, marking the heads of groundsinks. It took us more than an hour to walk past these giant objects, looking over at them frequently, for after the days of monotonous landscape it was in some way marvellous to see anything new. Beyond them were several power substations, each with its roof-set loom of electrical cable. Finally we moved into a manufacturing zone, where such factories as could be staffed with robots were located, humming, and nobody went to or came from them. Enough moisture dripped from these places into the parched earth, by design or accident, that banks of blue and black thistles grew, crowding into heaps and piles and burst mattresses of shards, spikes, thorns.

Finally we were close enough to the city to see human habitation. On one wide building, perhaps a barracks, a large flag flowed constantly towards the west, its zigzag design impatient with the undulations of the cloth. It made an unmistakable clapping noise against its pole.

'Like a tablecloth being shaken to lose its crumbs,' said Mark Pol. 'How I love to see a flag in a stiff breeze! How it cheers the heart inside me! I feel the urge to salute.' Reaching the town, evidently, had lifted his spirits.

Siuzan flinched at his words, or perhaps merely at the sound of his voice after the long silence. She seemed cowed, almost fearful, but of what I did not know.

Beyond this building we came to a suburb of the city proper. The central towers and domes were visible straight ahead. Now we were walking on pavement, and the road itself was busy with cars, driverless and driven. We were passing open restaurants, serving late lunches to the accompaniment of northern music, the trickling of a melody over a constant and erratic mesh of drumbeats. It is a style that has always sounded to me like somebody playing a flute beside a malfunctioning machine. People were coming and going. Some people looked blankly at us, or scowled with distrust and dislike. Others pointedly avoided looking at us at all.

This day I had my first taste of one of the various hormonal imbalances that tend to afflict the headless. With enough money it is possible to keep the necessary pharmocopies always to hand, and to dose oneself with whichever of the cranially-produced hormones are required. We had all of us purchased purses of the proper range of pharmocopies in Doué, yet in foolishness I had purchased too much of one sort and not enough of another. The loss of the head involves the loss of both the pineal and the pituitary glands. From the former the body receives its melatonin, which amongst other things regulates circadian rhythms. The latter produces many hormones. The headless also lose the hypothalamus. Without replacement pharmocopies, we would suffer a variety of debilitating and ultimately fatal illnesses, including Insipid Diabetes, a form of the disease which is, despite its name, far from insipid – for it entails fatigue; hypersensitivity to cold; weight gain; dry skin and a shrivelling of the sex organs which results in infertility. It is, fortunately for the many headless on our world, a simple matter to replace the missing hormones by swallowing a purse of medication.

I had done this before beginning the walk, but now I was beginning to feel unsteady. I felt the need to urinate frequently, and I was thirsty and sensitive to cold. 'I fear,' I said, 'that my pharmocopy pouch has malfunctioned. I feel increasingly unwell.'

'What do you suggest we do?' asked Mark Pol. 'Are you asking for our sympathy? You should have ensured you swallowed an appropriate dose before beginning this trek.'

'I must purchase a replacement,' I said. 'Let us find a chemist.'

'Can't it wait?'

'It is imperative,' I snapped.

'But can you *spare* the money?' said Mark Pol, in a more insinuating tone of voice.

'It is a necessity and not a luxury,' I replied angrily.

'Come along,' said Siuzan, peacemaker as ever. 'We shall find a chemist.' And yet she spoke in a voice that was weary, and she avoided looking at us.

We walked the streets until we found a large chemist's shop. The others waited outside whilst I stepped up to the door, shivering slightly. Inside

36

was a long room with many shelves, and a bar at the back behind which stood the chemist. But as I walked towards him he demonstrated the symptoms of dismay. 'No, no,' he said. 'We do not serve your sort – go away.'

'I beg your pardon,' I said, 'but I am in great need of ...'

'Go away!'

'Please ... I am ill, and I need medication for ...'

'We do not serve your sort!' His voice was raised. I flinched, but I was propelled onward by physical necessity. 'If you do not stock it,' I said, 'then it should be a simple matter to concoct the ...'

He lifted a small datablock. 'Shall I contact the police? Will you leave? We serve only the headed.'

I left the shop.

Outside the others were impatient with me. 'Let us get on,' said Mark Pol.

'I was unable to purchase any pharmocopy.'

'Did they not stock it?'

'They refused to serve me.'

'On what grounds?' asked Gymnaste.

'On grounds of distrust and dislike of the headless,' I said. 'He refused any trade with our sort.'

'Then we are no better than we were before!' exclaimed Mark Pol in an exasperated voice. 'After this goose-chase search for a chemist's and all that time wasted!'

'I cannot go on without pharmocopy,' I said urgently.

'Then perhaps we should leave you here,' snapped Mark Pol.

'No!' I cried. 'Do not abandon me!'

'But none of *us*,' Mark Pol sneered, with exaggerated relish for my predicament, 'will be able to purchase your pharmocopies from *that shop*.'

I looked at Siuzan. She did not return my gaze. She seemed, indeed, to be staring at the floor. Perhaps she was worn out. Or (the thought occurred to me again) in a state of fear for some reason.

'I shall go in,' she said shortly, gazing over the road at the chemist's shop.

'Thank you,' I said earnestly. 'Please, let me give you my money.'

But she did not take my money, and would not be persuaded to do so. As she crossed the road, with the three of us hunched followers dancing attendance, I tried to tell her that she must take money, or at the least that she must let me know the cost of the pharmocopy after she had purchased it and I would reimburse her, but she said nothing.

She stepped quickly up the ramp and passed through the whispery sliding doors. Mark Pol, Gymnaste and I loitered for a while outside. Through the glass we could see piled and filled rectangles of the shelving. The crown of Siuzan's head was just about visible over the top of a shop display. She was talking to the serving man. This conversation went on for a long time.

A policeman approached, and told us to move away from the doorway of the shop. We complied at once, of course; and sat, the three of us, on a bench on the other side of the road. We sat in silence whilst awaiting Siuzan's return.

She did not come out of the chemist's shop.

After twenty minutes or so we were becoming increasingly agitated, although it was Mark Pol who was the most agitated of all. 'What's the delay?' he cried. 'Why does she loiter in this shop? What can be taking her so long? There! There!' He was pointing at the shop's main entrance, through which the policeman was now stepping. 'People come and go! Where is she? I'm going in to see if she is all right.'

'I would not advise that,' I said. 'The owner of the establishment will, I assure you, be very unwelcoming.'

'Nonsense. I will go and fetch her from the store, nothing else. What can be taking her so long?'

He jumped to his feet and trotted through the slow-moving traffic. Gymnaste and I watched as he made his way to the door, and the two panes (from the angle at which we saw them, both mirrored with the reflection of our side of the street) slid aside to reveal the policeman standing in the threshold. We could not hear what words passed between them, but it was clear that Mark Pol had been forbidden from going inside.

He trotted back to us in a state of fury. 'Extraordinary!' he said. 'I was given no explanation – I was merely repulsed!'

'Did you see Siuzan?' I asked. 'Did you see what she was doing?'

'I did not. I was burlied away from the door. This treatment is extra-ordinary and outrageous!'

There was nothing to do but settle down to wait. The traffic passed and repassed on the street. Of course my prostheses could detect no smell; but I was hypnotised by the distinct quality of the light, a pollen-like yellow smoke, or dust, that moved languidly in the air, sometimes clearing to bring this building, or that person, into a slightly sharper focus. This dust brought odour to my memory if not to my actual senses: memories of spices and petrol, of lemon and sugar and grit. I cannot of course say whether the actual dust, thrown into the air of Cainon by its traffic, smelt of any of these things.

Late afternoon passed and the light thickened into evening. People came and went, none giving us more than a brief and disapproving glance. A caterpillar, long as my forefinger and bristling with hairs thick as eyelashes, crawled over my lap. I did not remove it. I seemed to have entered some manner of fugue state, unwilling, or unable, to move so much as a finger. There was, I recall, a great dread inside me. It required a certain proportion of my energy and my will to prevent me from focusing my thoughts inwardly on that dread. I did not want to know of what I was afraid. I tried to distract myself with the comings and goings of the street.

Lights came on in the shopfronts and bars up and down this minor Cainon thoroughfare. Streetlights lit up on top of their poles like tree trunks, and threw out impalpable spheres of brightness as foliage. The passing cars became pimpled with glowing dots of red and white.

The sun set entirely, and it was dark. We were sitting there in the cone of light cast from a lamp-pole a little way behind us.

'I don't understand,' said Mark Pol in a state of increasing anxiety. 'What is happening? I'll try entering again ...' and he bustled off, his eye stalks quivering. But once again he was repelled at the door.

'This is—' he said, in his metal-tinged voice, 'a—*most—provoking—thing*—' His distress, and his anger, were comically intense. What, I wondered, was making him so furious? 'Why doesn't she come? Has she abandoned us?'

'If she has,' said Gymnaste, 'then we have no reason to complain, or rebuke her. She accompanied us through the desert. Perhaps that was enough. Certainly she owes us no obligation – she did not before, and she does not now. We should be grateful that she spent any time with us, and leave it at that. Perhaps she has simply walked out of the back door—'

'Without,' fumed Mark Pol, waving his right hand in the air although his left lay in his lap, 'without saying *farewell*? Without so much as an—?'

For once Gymnaste raised his voice, and squashed Mark Pol's complaints into silence. 'Perhaps she has slipped through the back door, and if she has then *that is that*. Maybe she felt awkward wishing us farewell, and preferred to slip away quietly. We should be grateful she was with us at all, grateful that she attended to us after our decapitations – recall that no one compelled her to do this. Grateful that she kept company with us for as long as she did.'

Mark Pol was silenced. But I could feel, within me, the edges of a terrible anguish. 'But,' I said, fumbling the words through my speech machine, 'what shall we do?'

'We are three adult men, though we are headless,' said Gymnaste. 'Do we need Siuzan Delage to lead us around like children?'

'I suppose not,' said Mark Pol, in a deadened voice.

'We must find work, I suppose,' said Gymnaste after reflection. 'We need food and drink. Also, we should find a chemist prepared to serve us, for we need now, or soon will, as Jon here has discovered, pharmocopies of certain hormonal chemicals. Perhaps we can find a hostel for people such as us. I, for one, am disinclined to carry on sleeping under the open sky. It is cold enough now, but in a few months it will be winter.'

But this stream of practical advice fell upon my mind as a series of monstrous irrelevancies. The dread that lurked subterraneously in my thoughts was becoming clearer to me now. It was that I should never see Siuzan again. It was that I was in love with her, as hopelessly and as bitterly and as demeaningly as ever I had been in love with any person – or more so, much more, because my previous romantic infatuations had always been *achievable* things, whereas this was clearly fated never to be. She was so very far above me, and I was so patently unworthy. It was all so very evidently impossible that the ferocity of my emotion was almost a rebuke to my yearning self. Impossible! But the thought of never seeing her again was intolerable. It was worse than losing my head. The passion in me, it led, through its dignity-corroding twists, to my conviction and my punishment. I wanted to cry out.

'Well then,' said Mark Pol, who seemed, to my supersaturated sensitivity, to have grown calm with suspicious rapidity, 'perhaps we should walk on.'

'But,' I objected, 'what if Siuzan has been delayed for some trivial reason, and hopes to meet up with us again? What if she comes outside the chemist hoping to see us and we have gone? Should we not stay here, until we are sure she is not coming?'

'And for how long would you have us wait?' snapped Mark Pol. 'We have waited here half a day. Is that not enough? Let us be going, as *Sieur* Gymnaste says, to make our new way in the world.'

'At the least,' I continued, clutching straws, 'at the very least we should leave some message for her, some means whereby she can communicate with us in the future, should she wish to meet us again.'

'Your suggestion is impracticable,' said Mark Pol. 'Should we graffitise the wall behind us? This would be merely criminal. And where would we tell her we have gone, since we do not yet know ourselves?'

'We could ask the chemist to take a message,' I said, leaping to my feet. Now it was I who was agitated with a furious nervous energy that overcame my former feelings of sickness. The prospect of losing Siuzan after so short a space, after barely having known her – it was too much. I was beyond reason now.

'He would hardly accept a message from us,' Gymnaste pointed out.

And I concede: you may, reading this account, consider it beyond absurdity for a headless man to have daydreamed so far as even to contemplate, howsoever hazily, the prospect of marriage with a woman so young, beautiful, so widely adored, and virtuous. But this is to ignore the enormous force that Love applies to the coal of the everyday as it crushes out its unique diamonds. Moreover, as I told myself, it was not altogether unprecedented for a headless man and a headed woman to unite in marriage. Naturally it has never been a common occurrence, but there is at the least nothing in law to prevent such a marriage. And (for now my desperate mind was contorting itself) Siuzan had shown herself much less prejudiced against the headless than most. Perhaps her devotion to such fallen individuals as ourselves was not merely motivated by religious piety. Perhaps there was (I could not be sure of this, but I hoped) some *fascination*, even some level of *attraction*, at work there. And with enough time was it not possible for her to come to know the person who still lived inside the truncated body? The fable of Beauty and the Beast is very ancient, and speaks to a very deep need in the human soul. Only the shallow fall in love with mere physical beauty – I felt confident in asserting this, because for my adult life I had been one of these shallow types. A preener, a vain fellow, hypercareful of my body, sparing no expense on toiletries and beauty enhancers. I had flitted on the surface of society. I had told myself that I was a romantic adrift in a rigorous world. But it was precisely as a romantic that I believed in people *unlike* me, who cared for the soul rather than the body, who judged by the content of character rather than beauty of appearance. This spectral romantic, lurking inside me still, insisted that Siuzan was such a person. And so it was imperative that I spend more time with her, in order to permit this inner knowledge, this fated-to-be love, to blossom.

I do not seek to convince you of the truth of this absurd reasoning. I seek merely to explain to you the state of mind in which I struggled. Of course Siuzan could never marry me, or any other person marked by the shame of headlessness. Of course not.

'Leave a message with the chemist?' repeated Mark Pol disdainfully. 'I invite you to try such a lunacy. You will be repelled, as I was, by the policeman at the door.'

'The policeman,' I said, uttering the word stupidly. 'The policeman.' He was standing in front of us.

Six

He was not alone. There were two colleagues, also in uniform, standing beside him. Their transport was parked on the pavement a little way along the road.

None of us knew what to say.

'Under the powers of the Social Order Promulgation ...' he said, without smiling. He did not bother uttering the remainder of this sentence. He held out what, in my agitated and illogical state, I took to be a handgun. This he aimed at my chest, perhaps because I was sitting on the far left of the three of us. I suppose one must start somewhere.

He pulled the trigger.

A threaded dart launched out, popped through my shirt, scratched my skin and was snapped back into the device. The policeman repeated this action on Gymnaste and Mark Pol. I was so startled it took me several moments to realise what the device was.

After our DNA had been flagged up, the fellow addressed us each in turn. 'Jon Cavala, Mark Pol Treherne, Gymnaste Peri. You will be surprised, or not, to learn that I am permitted in law to apprehend all three of you.'

Mark Pol was immediately indignant. 'On what charge?' he said, getting to his feet. 'Though headless we have nevertheless certain legal rights.'

'Indeed you do,' said the policeman. 'There is no charge. I am permitted, by the law, to question you about certain matters. You are invited to attend questioning, but you *will* be compelled to attend questioning if you decline this invitation.' He turned his back on us and addressed his companions, that they might recognise us. 'Treherne,' he said, 'is the one with the neck-mounted stalk eyes. Peri is the fat one. Cavala the other. So now you know.'

We were led to their police transport and locked into one of the compartments at the back. Here we stayed for several hours. Sometimes we were aware of movement, as the transport was driven; sometimes the van was motionless. It was difficult to be sure what was going on outside our windowless compartment. No amount of Jon Cavala hammering on the side and giving voice to his ourage with as much volume as his device permitted, no amount of his demands that he be heard, or released, or financially compensated for his inconvenience, produced any response from the police.

Eventually the door was opened and we found ourselves outside the front of Cainon's main police station. We were removed from the transport and led up the flagstone-laid ramp of the building. This imposing building, like a colossal upended desk-table of marble and concrete, was enough to silence even Mark Pol.

Inside we passed into an entrance hall and down a corridor. We were taken to a room, and there we were left.

It was a fairly comfortable room, as police rooms go, and not a cell: upholstered seats for us to seat ourselves if we wished, a screen in the corner of the ceiling relaying the News Channel to distract us, even water for us to drink – and being thirsty after our long wait we all of us drank freely of this. It was a pleasant room in many ways, although of course the door was locked. The News Channel was crowded with stories from the Sugar War on Egafredo and on Athena, which seemed very distant to most citizens on Pluse, and doubly distant to the concerns of the headless on Pluse. Mark Pol paced up and down. Gymnaste and myself sat very still.

'This is something serious,' said Gymnaste.

'I have no doubt,' Mark Pol pronounced as he strode, 'that this is but a taste of the oppression and random harassment which we must come to expect as our daily chore, now that we are headless. Have we not paid for our crimes, paid a price higher than required of any bank fraud or common thief? Does society not owe us the chance to live as others do? It may be true that we have transgressed, but the guilt of that infraction has been cut away from us. It is outrageous! It is an outrage! I shall,' he declared with sudden force, hurling himself down onto the seat, 'I *shall* start a campaign to highlight the injustices which the headless must suffer. I shall write a manifesto. I shall recruit the young from three continents, those who care about justice and—'

'There have been such campaigns before,' I reminded him, somewhat crossly. 'It was such a campaign that involved the technologies which now support our consciousnesses in the process. But no campaign has ever shifted the opinion of the people as to the fundamental justice of the beheadings.'

'Boh,' sneered Mark Pol, literally snapping his fingers at me. His fidgeting fingers crackled before my face like dry sticks in the fire. 'I shall change things. Things are not like this on other worlds. Why must they be so on *this* world? You should pay attention to what I am saying, for you will see how I shall make the changes happen.'

'This matter is something serious,' Gymnaste repeated. 'They have not gone to such lengths merely to harass a trio of newly arrived headless.'

At this moment the doorlock snapped and slid free. A policeman entered. He had a chiller looped in at his belt, but was otherwise dressed as any worker or civilian, in a dark blue jacket and meadhres over a pale blue shirt. '*Sieurs*,' he said.

After the confinement in the transport, and our insolently lengthy wait in the room, this honorific seemed merely facetious.

'My name is Mag Bonnard, and my preference would be that you address me as *Chevaler* Bonnard.'

'My preference,' I blurted, 'is that you do not call me *sieur*, for I do not deserve the title.'

Bonnard looked at me for a long moment in silence. His was a long face, a sharp chin bone visible perking at the skin of his face and pulling his cheeks into irregularly shaped ovals. His eyes were close-spaced and though not deep-set yet they were so forcefully hemmed in by thick black eyebrows above and bruise-coloured half-moons of tiredness below as to appear sunken. His smile had a sourly feline quality.

'Very well,' he said. 'You are Cavala? I find it difficult to tell one headless from another, even though I am very experienced in the doings of your kind. My only information is that Cavala was the one neither fat nor with expensive and gaudy prostheses.'

'I am Cavala,' I admitted.

'And you Gymnaste? And you Treherne?'

'Yes,' quiet and 'Yes,' surly.

'Very well. To be brief: Siuzan Delage, whom of course you know – Siuzan Delage has been taken into legal confinement.'

I listened to this sentence, and understood it. Then, in a distinct and subsequent moment, I reacted – 'No! Impossible!'

Bonnard ignored me. 'Because of this act of arrest by the police, it has become necessary to question the three of you. But I will say at once that this is an unusual questioning.'

'Siuzan in legal confinement?' I cried. 'How can this be? This is some mistake or error. It *cannot* be.'

'Please, Jon Cavala, restrain yourself,' said Bonnard. 'Allow me to talk. This will be, as I was saying, an unusual questioning. I shall tell you my opinion, although it at the moment remains unsupported by proof. But it is the opinion of a senior *chevaler* of the police, and worth something for that reason. Though I say so myself!'

We waited for the opinion.

'Well,' said Bonnard. 'My opinion is that one of you has committed an act of rape upon Siuzan Delage.'

'No!' I yelled. 'Never! None of us!'

'Nonsense! Obscene nonsense', blustered Mark Pol, talking simultaneously with me.

Only Gymnaste was silent.

The word itself, so ugly, polluted the air. It polluted my thoughts. That it could be coupled with the name of the woman with whom I was in love was monstrous. It jangled echoes in my thoughts. No!

'Has Siuzan laid a legal complaint against us?' Mark Pol demanded. 'Against one of us? In which case, which of us? Why are we other two being kept in confinement?' He swivelled his torso just enough to make it plain that he was looking at me.

Astonishment gripped me, but enough of my wits remained for me to understand his implication. Treherne was informing the police that *I* must be the guilty party. It was difficult enough absorbing the revelation that Siuzan had been assaulted in this hideous way. To hear myself accused of the assault was too appalling.

'Stop,' I said. 'Wait – Mark Pol—'

'It is my legal obligation to inform you, *chevaler*,' Mark Pol went on, 'that my companion Jon Cavala was decapitated for *precisely this crime*. Rape I mean, and nothing else. Clearly *he* must be the suspect, until DNA can confirm his guilt absolutely. But my other companion and myself, there is surely no need for us to remain here.'

'Traitor!' I snapped. 'I had nothing to do with – There's not a scrap of truth in what he says about—' 'Has,' said Gymnaste in a loud voice, 'Siuzan laid a legal complaint of rape?'

I spoke over the first half of this question, and Gymnaste had to repeat it. But I stopped talking once it had been asked. My thoughts were in turmoil.

'She has not,' said Bonnard.

'In that case,' said Mark Pol eagerly, 'no crime is inferred, and we must be released at once.'

'Wait,' said Gymnaste.

'Indeed,' said Bonnard, smiling and fingering his chiller as if it were a bauble or a toy. 'There indeed *has* been a crime. It is simply that we, as police, are not certain which crime it is.'

'I don't understand,' said Mark Pol.

'It is simple enough. A medical examination reveals that Siuzan Delage has been the recipient of penetrative sexual attention, and that this illegal act has happened within the last two days. The examination suggests, furthermore, that this penetration was neither solicited nor enjoyed by Siuzan Delage. There are, without being too graphic, certain bodily symptoms that are highly suggestive of this circumstance.'

I felt a sickness in my belly. A shudder shook through me at these words.

'But she has not made a legal complaint about . . .?' Mark Pol asked.

Bonnard, in possession of vocal chords, a mouth, the subtleties of the human power of speech, brought this reedy metallic sentence to a halt by interjecting, loudly, 'Do you think us fools?'

We all sat up straight on our seats.

'Do you think,' Bonnard continued, 'that *we*, the police, have been unable to patch together a picture of the last few days? We know what you and this woman have been doing. We have contacted our people in Doué, and also our people in Lacon. We have consulted the legal records on each of the three of you. *Sieur* Treherne? *Of course* we know about the reason for Jon Cavala's decapitation. How could we not? The police in Doué and the police in Cainon are allies, after all. This much we know: Siuzan Delage entirely misfits the profile of a criminal. She is a devout and genuine person. All testimony confirms this. The worst that might be said of her is that her piety leads her into a rather *over-innocent* idealism, the sort that encourages a beautiful and talented woman to waste her time helping beheaded criminals – even going so far as trekking with them through the desert, without chaperone or protection.'

'And yet,' said Gymnaste, speaking in a low voice, 'you have taken *her* into legal confinement.'

'Indeed. And so I must talk to you three . . . individuals. That she has had sexual intercourse cannot be denied. If she has been raped, then no fault, legal or moral, attaches to her, and our duty as police becomes simply to apprehend and punish her rapist. The punishment being, as you three all know, and as one of you has greater cause than most to know, decapitation. Saving only that a man may be beheaded only once, and the rapist who is already headless must be executed.'

None of us replied to this.

After a while Bonnard continued:

'Which is the man? This is what I must ask you. You might think that the easier path would be to ask the victim. This we have done.'

He paused again, and looked at each of us in turn.

'She refuses to tell us the name of her attacker, although I am certain she knows it.'

He paused again.

'It is the sentence,' he said, eventually. 'This, I think, explains the reticence of Siuzan Delage. For she knows that to identify her rapist and lay charges will lead to that person's death. Such a thing, though it seems to me justice, and greatly to be desired, perhaps does not seem so to her. Maybe she believes that such a thing should not be allowed to happen.'

We remained silent.

'She feels she must protect her attacker. It is misguided, but I suppose it's what she believes. So the question I have for you three is simple. I ask one of you, whichever one is guilty, to confess to the crime now. Your confession will mean your death, I am afraid. But such is justice. And at least your words will save Siuzan Delage from shame and beheading. You, Jon Cavala.' He pointed at me. 'Have you repeated your former offence, and forced yourself sexually on a woman?'

'I have not!' I replied indignantly. 'And if you have consulted the records on my case, as you say you have, then you must know that I have *never* forced myself on any woman. I pleaded guilty to the charge of rape, in that former time, so as to *protect* my lover, whom otherwise would have faced the rage of the law for indulging her physical love with me.'

'A common defence,' said Bonnard, without heat. 'Though much less often true, I find, than it is asserted. But I am not, at present, interested in your previous crime. I am interested in *this* crime. Did you have sexual relations with this woman, this Siuzan Delage?'

'No,' I said.

He turned his head. 'You, *Sieur* Mark Pol, did you—?'

'Certainly I did not,' said Mark Pol hotly. 'Most certainly, no.'

'And you, *Sieur* Peri? Did you commit this act with Siuzan Delage?'

'No,' said Gymnaste.

'I appear to have exhausted the list of suspects. She has been in your company, and yours alone, for the last three days; and it is certain that the act occurred during that length of time. Accordingly, one of you is lying.'

'It will be a simple matter,' said Gymnaste, 'for you to discover from DNA which of us is the guilty one.'

'Indeed. And yet, not so. For Siuzan Delage refuses to lay a criminal charge against her attacker. As I say, I believe she *does* know which of you assaulted her – although perhaps she does not, for it can be difficult to distinguish one headless from another. But in that case, if she were unsure which of you had assailed her, she could most certainly lay a *general* criminal charge. Doing so, she would be treated as a victim and we would investigate the crime. This would, as you say *Sieur* Peri, be a simple matter, the extraction of DNA from the materials left inside Siuzan Delage to match it with one of you three. But she refuses to lay a criminal charge. She refuses, in fact, to cooperate. Under these circumstances it is not possible for us to obtain the necessary DNA – forcibly to do so would, indeed, constitute sexual assault under the law, and render us liable to prosecution!' He chuckled at this. 'Us – the police ourselves!'

'You extracted DNA from us,' Mark Pol pointed out indignantly, 'without our consent!'

'Ah, but you were being investigated for a specific crime. The law permits us to extract your DNA in the course of this investigation.'

'Siuzan Delage is being held in confinement on suspicion of a crime . . .' I said.

'But not the crime of rape,' said Bonnard. 'Accordingly we are not permitted to extract such DNA as may be found within her inner uterine cavities. We may, of course, extract *her* DNA, and so confirm that she is indeed Siuzan Delage. But how would this advance the case?'

'She has permitted herself to be examined,' said Gymnaste, 'to the extent that you were able to determine that sexual congress had taken place.'

'She had been . . . wounded in that portion of her body,' said Bonnard. 'This wound happened, presumably, as a result of the assault.'

I was shuddering. A nightmarish sense of the appalling intimacy of this crime, a consciousness of how beautiful and innocent was the woman who had suffered it, was tormenting me. I also felt a hard anger growing in me, a desire to find the man who had perpetrated such a foul act and punish him – to kill him.

'She applied to the chemist for medicines to aid her. The chemist, learning of the part of the body concerned, declined to examine Siuzan Delage himself. Quite properly he called a doctor. She (the doctor I mean) examined Siuzan Delage in the chemist's diagnosis room, and naturally informed the police, as the law required her to do. At this stage, I might add,' and Bonnard leant forward as he spoke 'she was weeping copiously, was *Chère* Siuzan. Weeping! A woman in considerable emotional and mental distress. But by the time I arrived, to commence my investigation, she had, perhaps, thought through the fullest consequences of her situation. When the doctor asked to take a DNA sample from her she refused permission.'

Bonnard paused, and smiled. The effect was sinisterly predatory.

'Now, perhaps,' he said, 'you may understand the dilemma we, as lawmen, face. For the law cannot comprehend that a woman, once raped, would wish to protect her attacker. As far as the law is concerned, a woman proven to have had sexual intercourse becomes guilty of that crime, unless she complains of forced congress. Now, the punishment for illicit sexual congress is—'

I could not bear it. 'You would not behead an innocent woman!' My voice was distorted by the emotional pressure that forced it through its synthesiser. 'A woman you *know* to be innocent of!'

'Jon Cavala,' he said. 'Be quiet now. You think it is the business of the police to make exceptions from the law? It is not. Illegal sexual activity has happened here. Either this activity is rape, or it is illicit-consensual.'

'Surely,' said Mark Pol, 'Siuzan may declare that she has been raped, and yet refuse to name her attacker?'

Bonnard placed his hands palm uppermost, a manual shrug. 'This would be one course of action. The law does not require her to know the identity of her attacker, after all.'

'Well then!' said Mark Pol. 'She should do that. Declare that she has been raped but she knows not by whom.'

'She does not do this,' said Bonnard. 'Nevertheless.'

'I do not understand,' said Mark Pol. 'Does she *wish* to be beheaded?'

'Not that,' said Gymnaste, 'but she knows that we three are the only suspects. If she complains of rape, then she must surrender such DNA as is inside her. She knows that to lay a criminal charge is to kill one of us. Evidently she would rather face beheading than condemn, by her words, one of us three to death.'

My thought processes were slipping and scratching. I could not focus them. 'The law cannot condemn an innocent ... it is monstrous – you, *Chevaler* Bonnard, you would not permit an innocent—'

'It is not a matter for me,' Bonnard said. 'My duty is to explain the circumstances to you. Siuzan Delage, out of what is, to my mind, a misguided sense of duty, refuses to speak the words that will execute one of you three. But she need not say those words. If one of you – the guilty one, of course – if *you* confess to the crime, then she will keep her head.'

He looked, in turn, at each of us.

'I have asked you once, and I shall ask you again. I will not ask you a third time. This second time, however, you are all apprised of the weight that attaches to your reply.'

'I certainly,' blustered Mark Pol, 'I *certainly* did not force myself upon this poor woman. I reiterate my innocence of this crime. I insist upon it. I am not guilty.'

Bonnard looked at him. 'Very well. *Sieur* Peri?'

Gymnaste was silent for a long time. There was a peculiar shiver to his flesh, as if he were cold. The material of his shirt was darkening in patches, at his underarm, where sweat was soaking in. Eventually he spoke, and the voice synthesiser gave his tone a level calmness not consonant with these physical symptoms of his inner distress. He said, 'I cannot lie.'

'I certainly do not wish you to lie,' said Bonnard smoothly.

'It is my curse,' said Gymnaste.

'Indeed?'

'It has cost me my head, and now I fear it will cost sweet Siuzan Delage hers as well. But I cannot lie. I simply – cannot. To lie would – break me, would collapse the person I am. I did not have sexual relations with this woman, with Siuzan Delage.' He was pressing his hands together, knotting the fingers, drawing his forearms apart with his fingers still snagged together, stretching and contorting himself. 'I wish,' he said, 'I wish I could claim this crime and so save her head! I wish it more than anything – but I cannot lie!'

'You are not, then, guilty?'

'No!'

'Very well,' said Bonnard, and he turned to me. 'Jon Cavala, I ask you the same question. You have answered it once already, and answered it in the negative. Now how do you plead?'

My mind was sprawling and spindling like a drunk. 'But,' I said. 'This is – this is monstrous! You know the woman to be innocent!'

'Did you force yourself upon this woman? Did you injure her, physically and emotionally?'

'I,' I said. 'This is – you ask me because of my previous conviction.'

'I ask all three of you. The other two have answered.'

'Just as Gymnaste cannot lie,' I said, 'so I cannot – hate – a woman. The man who would do this thing to *any* woman, let alone to a woman as pure as Siuzan Delage ... that man must hate womankind. But I do *not* hate womankind. I cannot hate womankind. I know my shame, and I bear it. I must, for the sake of the woman who—' I stopped. The pressure of that moment, of the shock and trauma, had unbalanced me. Of course it was merest idiocy to say these things to a serving policeman. Of course, and despite my conviction and punishment, to indicate that the woman regarded in law as my victim was in fact a willing accomplice in our sexual transgression – this could serve no positive aim, and might bring the anger of the law upon her. I had sworn to myself never to reveal the truth of my so-called crime. I had resolved to accept on my own, naked shoulders the sole guilt for our love affair. But here I was blurting the truth.

I stopped myself.

I considered the lie. And yet I found I could not utter it. It would create a world in which I had harmed Siuzan Delage, and this I could not do. You, reading this account, may say that this created world would be merely a world of words, but it would also have been the world of law, of general perception and public attitude; a world as real as the world of matter.

And then again, I thought to myself: this policeman *knows* Siuzan to be innocent. He could not – he would never – allow her to be beheaded. Naturally he was telling us that he would allow this to come to pass, but this was obviously by way of a strategy for the extraction of a confession. He could never force the issue so cruelly.

'I am innocent,' I said.

Bonnard sat back and blew a sigh of frustration through his teeth. 'So,' he said, regarding us, disdainfully, each in turn again. 'As the Bibliqu'rân says, *Skin for skin, everything that a man hath he will give for his life.*'

'I resent that remark,' said Mark Pol. 'If sexual assault happened, then one of these other two is guilty, and I refuse to be accused of—'

'It was *you!*' I said, turning on Mark Pol with a crashing sense of realisation. 'Whom else? It *must* have been you who... injured Siuzan in that unspeakable way! Torn her flesh – there's no love in *that* action, it's pure malice. Gymnaste I do not believe capable of such a thing, but *you*, you are a bad fellow. You are capable of it. You were beheaded for a violent crime ...'

'Be quiet,' retorted Mark Pol. 'You fool! What do you think you are doing? Be quiet. I am innocent, I tell you. Before you throw such accusations at me, consider your own history. I have no predilection for sexual crime, whereas you have already faced the judgement of the law for rape. If you could rape once, then why not again?'

My thoughts finally fell into a whirlpool of rage and fury, and I launched myself at him. My leg muscles, still weary from the long walk of the previous days, tensed and projected me up. My arm muscles were still strong from the old days when I had exercised them assiduously.

I hurled myself at him.

I felt my fingers grasp the fabric of Mark Pol's shirt, and through that the texture of his flesh: like raw chicken, or old rubber. 'Confess,' I said, as the two of us tumbled from the couch. 'Tell the truth, Mark Pol!'

His reactions, startled by my suddenness, were poor. He tried punching at me, bringing his fist up against my stomach, but the blow was weak and did not hurt me. 'Leave me, get away, get off,' he was saying, jerking both his knees up. We were rolling on the floor, now banging into Gymnaste's legs in all this commotion, Gymnaste did not move, not even to lift his legs out of the way of our brawling bodies.

I reached up with my right hand and found the eye stalk on the right of Mark Pol's neck. The fury was very fierce inside me now. With a jabbing blow I punched his ribs with my left hand, and his throat valve clicked open. Then with my right hand I pulled as hard as I could on the eye stalk. 'Ah! Ah!' Mark Pol was saying. I had the satisfaction of feeling the prosthesis yield, and pull away, and the sticky slickness of blood, before Bonnard intervened with his chiller.

I felt the moist nose of the device, like a dog's, on the skin at the base of my back – I suppose my shirt had ridden up in the fighting – just above the ordinator, and then, at once, I felt the jarring pain of the discharge. It felt something like an electric shock, although it was not: a griping sensation of intense cold, like burning on the outer skin and like paralysis and frost running hurriedly through the muscles. My back spasmed and arched, and I lurched clear of Mark Pol. I fell onto the ground, my arms and legs spread wide.

Despite being convicted as a criminal I had never before been struck with a chiller. I had never, except on the one occasion that had lead to the loss of my head, been in trouble with the police. Had I experienced the chiller before I do not believe that I would have risked it on this occasion by brawling with Mark Pol, for it is deeply painful and unpleasant, much more so than I can convey to you with these words of mine. The worst of it was the clenching sense of being unable to move at all, not even to heave the chest to draw air into the lungs; although close behind this was the sheer pain, as if the whole branchéd bristling tree of my nerves had been hollowed out and acid pumped through those channels instead. My vision was whited through, a blindness of pain. A childish panic filled me that I would never breathe again, and had I possessed the ability to do it I would have kicked and struggled. But, of course, my muscles were held in an absolute grip.

Then, with the first relinquishing of the effect of the weapon, my limbs shuddered, my neck valve clicked, and air was sucked into my chest. I exhaled raggedly, my speakers producing a weird musical moan, and sight began to return, hazily, dark forms against a light background.

There was a flicker, as of a cloud going before the sun. Then, distantly and unreally, I felt something collide with me.

The breath went out of me again, forced out by impact, and again I struggled to inflate my own chest. But, in the muddle and brightness of my pain, and still unable to move properly, I was aware of localised intensities of hurt that flared at multiple sites. Finally I realised what a less dazzled consciousness would have deduced at once: that Mark Pol had thrown himself onto my fallen form and was punching me in the chest and midriff.

And, for a second time, Bonnard applied his chiller, and with a high-pitched electronic whoop Mark Pol's limbs locked. I was barely aware that he had stopped punching me, or that Bonnard had called other police into the room, or even that Mark Pol's rictused body was being hauled off me. I was concentrating my whole mental energy on drawing another breath, and then another one after that, and then another.

Seven

The effects of a standard chiller blast, if applied centrally to the torso, can cause all the body's muscles to lock for many minutes. There is then anything between three and six hours of debilitating after effect, depending on the person. The device is designed to overstimulate the nerve pathways such that pain registers throughout the whole body. A glancing blow – on a hand, say – will immobilise that limb and produce a devastating sensation of pain throughout the entire body. Centrally applied, for example to the spine, it will freeze the largest and most muscular of bodies into solid agony. The device has less effect on one of the headless, because (although this sounds like a facile thing) he or she has less muscle to clench. Nor can the headless suffer the side-effects of the device, such as inadvertently biting through the tip of one's tongue, or dislocating one's jaw, because we lack those things. Moreover, I have heard that a headed individual will usually suffer a severe headache after being chilled; this does not happen to the headless. Nevertheless it was an intensely disabling and agonising experience for me to feel the touch of the policeman's device. Indeed, because I had spent so much time in the gym, I possessed larger and better defined muscles than the average man. Accordingly it was many hours before I was able finally to coord-inate my motions again, and sit up from the bed on which they had placed me. I discovered that I was alone in a tiny police cell.

I stayed there for a long time. Lights were turned off, and I tried to sleep, something I managed only fitfully. Lights came on again – the whole three-metre-square ceiling shone bright neon – and I woke again. Some pap was served me, the bowl popping through a tiny hatchway in the wall. I was given no water, but the pap was fairly fluid and I was not thirsty.

My ribs were a little sore, but I paid that no mind. Indeed, my ord-inator-mind was not as adept at maintaining consciousness of pain as an actual brain; the sense data, which registered as pain to begin with, soon wore the sensation recognition programming into a diminishing neural loop. The pain shrank away.

I sat on the bed and stared at walls that my vision software registered as yellow, but which might have been any colour from grey to brown. I found my mind reverting, hideously, to the ordeal that Siuzan Delage had suffered. I parsed the possibilities. Could the legal system in Cainon truly punish a woman clearly innocent? Could so virtuous a woman be beheaded for a crime she so very obviously had not committed?

I told myself no. I said to myself no, never, but my heart told me that it could indeed happen. Men like Bonnard would tell themselves: *This will send a warning to the whole of our world that sexual immorality cannot be tolerated.* He might perhaps have said to himself, *It is indeed a shame that Siuzan Delage must suffer, but perhaps her plight will prevent future women – lovestruck, or hamstrung by misplaced pity – from protecting their assailants.* I could imagine it only too well.

I resolved to confess to the crime, regardless of the consequences – regardless of the shameful death that would follow for myself. But then I thought of Mark Pol. My confession would free him, and he would walk away, possibly (no, I told myself: not possibly but *certainly*) to attack other women. He was a man with corruption and violence in his soul. My sacrifice might save Siuzan Delage only at the cost of other women. Could I do this?

Like Gymnaste I could not lie in this matter.

Perhaps, I told myself, perhaps Bonnard could be reasoned with. Surely there were ways he could apply pressure to Mark Pol? Were there no drugs he could be forced to take to compel him to confess? I tried to think of the ways Bonnard might be made to see that Mark Pol – and only Mark Pol – must be the criminal in this case. As a policeman Bonnard must surely want to see justice done.

On occasion, during this monotonous process of mental rotating and sifting, I would find myself, without intending to, making odd little mewling noises through my speech software. After a while I realised that these noises were all that remained to my body of the ability to cry.

After a while I was visited by a police doctor. He told me that, where before I had been merely 'being questioned', now I had been taken into legal confinement. 'On account of my physical assault upon Mark Pol Treherne,' I said, expecting confirmation. But the doctor claimed not to know the reason. 'I am not told the charges,' he said. 'I perform my duty regardless of such business.' He was a fellow made of globes, a round face with big round eyes set very wide, a plump round torso, round thighs which chafed one against the other as he moved, round calves, even round little hands with plump fingers. His skin was an olive-drab colour, and his hair was very black and shiny as if just out of the shower, although it was not wet.

'And what is your duty?' I asked him.

'Since you are in legal confinement certain legal obligations devolve upon the police. One is, within the bounds of what the law calls reasonable expectation, to maintain your health.' He examined me to determine whether Mark Pol had injured me with his punches. 'Some bruises,' he said. 'The bones are not broken.'

'Good news.'

He took some blood in a pepperpot-shaped device and left the cell. Some time later, perhaps half an hour, he returned with a different coloured pepperpot device, blue where the former had been green. 'Your hormonal levels are perilously low and unbalanced,' he announced. 'This is a particular danger for the headless.'

'I am aware of this danger. I attempted to purchase a new purse of pharmocopy hormones at a Cainon chemist, but he refused me service.'

'People in Cainon are suspicious of the headless,' he said in an uninflected voice. 'Suspicion is fuelled by the proximity of the Land of the Headless.'

This surprised me. 'Is Cainon so close to Montmorillon? I had not realised.'

The doctor placed the blue device against the skin of my neck stump. 'It is a hundred kilometres or more,' he said. 'Here, also, is a purse of long-release pharmocopies. Please swallow it.'

'I have no water.'

'I will ensure water is supplied to you.' He turned to leave.

'A hundred kilometres,' I said, 'does not seem to me close.'

'It is close enough for the people in Cainon,' he replied, without turning back to face me. 'It is too close. We pride ourselves on the exactness of our devotion to the All'God, and the civilisation and superiority of our culture. To live so near to a bandit land is unsettling.'

He left before I could ask him anything more.

The water was delivered. I pushed the purse of pharmocopies down my throat hole and poured the liquid on top.

The lights went out with a clang. In the darkness I fell quickly asleep. I did not dream. The headless do not dream.

I awoke, in the dark, with a strange sensation in my body. It felt like that hopeful tingling children feel on the morning of their birthdays; or, more poetically, like that continually shimmering pattern of interlocking thorn-shapes that sunlight makes on the surface of pond and river. I was tingling with sudden insight.

I saw it, then: the way out of my dilemma. There was one way, and only one, that would save Siuzan and punish Treherne – to save Siuzan, yet not allow Treherne to escape scot-free to prey upon further women. I must *murder* Mark Pol. And as soon as I had done this I must hurry to the police to confess the crime. Once Mark Pol was dead I would also 'confess' to having harmed Siuzan – my execution was assured for this latter act, and since I could not be executed more than once I would suffer nothing for the former. The thought was clear and pure as a bubble of glass. My only consequence would be to face the All'God and explain my action to Him, the All'God in whom Gymnaste disbelieved. But how could He fault me? The All'God is Justice tempered with Clemency. My self-sacrifice would balance the sacrifice of Mark Pol. This would be justice.

Naturally I would first have to release myself from police confinement; for I could hardly murder Mark Pol from within a police cell. Indeed, I could not yet confess to the assault upon Siuzan Delage, or I would be detained by the police and I would not be able to act justice upon Mark Pol. So I must make whatever reparation was required for my hot-headed brawl with that fellow – a trivial crime, surely, since neither of us had been seriously injured – and get away from the police station. Then I must locate Mark Pol and punish him. And, most clearly, I must act rapidly – for if I delayed too long then Siuzan would be beheaded.

As I lay in the darkness my delight was tangible to me. As I look back, now, I may speculate how much of this feeling of new well-being was a result of the police doctor's medical intervention, and the rebalancing of my hormones. Perhaps it was this, but I do not believe that this diminishes the purity and joy of that period in the dark.

There was only one thing for which I yearned, now that I had resolved that I was shortly to die. I wished Siuzan Delage to know what I had done. This was vanity, of course; yet it was the vanity of love, and as such is perhaps the least despicable of vanities. For my love for her was immense and precise, and all the women I had loved before Siuzan Delage – the women I had *thought* I had loved, or to whom I had vainly told my love – became all accumulated into the force that pressurised my love from soot to diamonds. I would doubtless never see her again; yet this thought made the lithium flame of my love burn brighter in me. There is a truer love in selflessness, and in sacrifice to others, than in romantic ditherings and courtships. Siuzan Delage had sought to help us selflessly, and her charity had been abused. To make amends for this, selflessness was required, and my own life a very small coin indeed in the addition.

Nevertheless, my fear was that Siuzan would come to believe that it had indeed been I who had assaulted her. I tried, although my mind revolted from the thought, to picture the scene. It must have been dark, in the deserts south of Cainon. She must have been sleeping, unprepared, when a torso with gripping arms and covering legs climbed suddenly on top of her. Perhaps he had stifled her mouth. Would she have seen the eye stalks in the darkness? Could she had *known* it was Mark Pol? Perhaps she remained, to this moment, uncertain which of the three of us had assaulted her. If so, then would not my confession root the certainty in her mind that it had been I? This was the hardest sacrifice to make. I was content that the rest of the world, those people I had known before my decapitation, those people who had known me only through my poetry, all of these – I was content that they would despise me as a double rapist. But to think that Siuzan Delage *herself* would despise me! It was almost too much.

I consoled myself with this thought: I might be able to deliver a message to her, assuring her both of my love for her and of my innocence, that I was sacrificing myself to preserve her. This, surely, would be possible?

And if it were not, then I would have to pay the price. There are, let us be clear, two varieties of heroism: the feat performed before an audience of admirers, and the hidden and secret heroism, the hermit's heroism. This second is of course the more glorious.

I was lying awake, pondering in this fashion, when the ceiling startled brightly on, and the sight of close walls seemed to burst tight upon me. The novelty of consciousness reawoke in my ordinator mind the actuality of the bruises in my side. I tried to examine myself, but lacking a mirror, and lacking a flexible neck with which to reangle my vision, I could see nothing. I pressed my fingers against various pad-shaped patches of pain on my torso.

The door juddered in its frame and flew wide. In stepped *Chevaler* Bonnard, wearing what seemed to be the same suit of clothes as before. He was alone. I had been sitting on my bunk, but I stood up, smartly as if I were in the army and he my superior.

'Jon Cavala,' he said. 'Please step this way.'

My eye was drawn to the chiller, dangling from his belt, seemingly so insignificant, yet potent enough to start a hare-gallop in my heart muscles. 'Of course,' I said.

Bonnard strolled nonchalantly in front, his unprotected back to me, talking loudly without turning his head. I walked unsteadily behind him, my arms at my side. In this way the two of us passed down a long corridor, marked with a number of narrow doors at regular intervals.

'At first,' Bonnard was saying, '*Sieur* Treherne insisted upon charges being laid against you. He said he did not feel safe, and that you might attack him again. He insisted the police prosecute you. He said we had a duty to protect him.'

'I am indeed sorry that I attacked him,' I said.

'As you should be. Physical assault, even where one can demonstrate provocation to the satisfaction of the court – physical assault may involve up to three years in prison. But I have persuaded Mark Pol not to force legal charges against you.'

We emerged from the corridor into a large room, staffed by several policemen. The quality of the light was different; not a whole ceiling lit, but three rose-shaped hangings that cast shadows in an interlocking series of blocks from desks, chairs, datascreens, people. The colour of the light registered on my vision software as a warmer though still pale yellow.

'I am,' I said, 'pleased to hear that I will not be prosecuted for this attack.'

'Of course you are pleased,' said Bonnard, still without looking at me. He stepped through a doorless space in the wall and into a further room. I followed; it was a bare space, with nothing on the wall and no furniture save a desk made apparently of a single block of plastic and two chairs. Bonnard took a seat on the far side of the desk. At a gesture from him I sat in the seat on the near side, but my lack of a head meant that the vision from my epaulette eyes was occluded by the block. It was surprisingly tall. Unlike a table this object, dark grey or dark blue, seemed solid throughout. I sat up, but still could see only the top of Bonnard's head.

I stood up.

'Do you wish to know how I was able to persuade Sieur Treherne to relinquish his legal right to insist upon a prosecution?' Bonnard asked me.

'It does not seem to me,' I said, 'like a characteristic action on his part.'

'No. But I informed him that if you were to be charged for assault, then so would he.'

'Assault?'

'He leapt upon you when you were immobilised, and struck you several times. Of course, once again, the court would doubtless take into account any provocation – and his lawyers would be able to demonstrate that he had been provoked much more substantially than had you.'

'I will only say ...' I began, but Bonnard stopped me by raising the little finger of his right hand. I stopped speaking at once. I need hardly say that I respected his chiller much more profoundly than I respected his finger, even as a symbol of his innate authority.

'Nevertheless,' Bonnard went on, 'it would be a prosecution. He, as you, would be forced to remain in police cells until trial. When this fact was pointed out he, after some protest, agreed to drop the charge of assault.'

'It seems I must thank you,' I said.

'I do not require thanks.'

'Has Mark Pol been released from legal confinement?' I asked. 'I should like to meet him again, and apologise in person for my behaviour, which was disproportionate.'

'He has been released.'

'Was he met by Gymnaste? Did they leave note of any address at which they would be staying?' I was, I realised, too eager. I controlled myself. 'We have walked a long way together, and I do feel I should apologise in person.'

'He has been released,' Bonnard said. 'There is a criminal charge outstanding, however, which prevents us from releasing *you*.'

'What charge?' I was suddenly afraid that I was to be charged with the assault upon Siuzan Delage, and that I would therefore be prevented from finding Mark Pol. A moment's thought would have reassured me how unlikely this event was, but my ability to think clearly was impaired by my unusual circumstances, and by the chiller I could still see in the belt of the man sitting in front of me.

'The charge is theft,' said Bonnard.

'I do not understand.'

'You broke off one of *Sieur* Treherne's eye-stalks,' he said affably. 'It was inside your fist when we carried you to your cell. Yours,' he added, 'is an unusually large fist.'

'But I do not understand,' I repeated. 'Is this a joke? I have spent days in my cell. I do not have Mark Pol's eye stalk. I never stole it. Search me – you will not find it about my person. This is absurd, to claim that I have stolen this thing.'

'Naturally you do not have it about your person,' said Bonnard, smiling. 'We confiscated it from you whilst you were still unconscious –

unpeeling your fingers from it much as a man unpeels the skin from a pomegranate.' This analogy seemed to please him, for he chuckled to himself.

'But what can you mean?' I pressed. 'Is this a joke? It can hardly be argued that I stole this eye stalk. Why would I want such a thing? I did not steal it, and do not have it.'

'We placed the disputed item in police security, as material evidence in a theft prosecution.'

'There is no sanity in this,' I said.

'On the contrary. It is the way of the law. I told *Sieur* Treherne that I would gladly prefer his complaint against you for theft. This pleased him, for he was eager to see you punished for your assault upon his person. He is, in my judgement, a man very precise in assessing exactly the extent to which his pride has been offended.'

'What court will prefer this ridiculous charge?' I asked. 'I am happy to concede that my intention was to hurt Mark Pol Treherne, for reasons that—' But again I stopped myself. 'But I had *no intention* of stealing his eye stalk. If I broke it off, I did so in anger, not in attempted robbery. Why would I steal such a thing? What good would it do me? It is hardly compatible with my own vision software.'

'As to whether the stolen item would benefit you or not,' said Bonnard, 'this is a matter the court will consider, of course.'

'You smile,' I pointed out.

'Jon Cavala,' he replied genially. 'Can you expect me to deny my pleasure? Why should I, a man who has devoted his life to the upkeep of the law, *not* enjoy the discomfiture of one of the headless? You are individuals who have, to a man, broken the law. You can't deny it!'

'Is this consonant with the objective and unbiased performance of your duties?' I tasked him.

'I believe it is. Not a jot or tittle of the law shall pass away, you know. The Bibliqu'rân itself mixes legal prescription equally amongst its narrative and lyrical exhortation. I shall stick precisely to the meaning of the law.'

'Is this why you are prepared,' I said, becoming heated, 'to allow the beheading of a woman, Siuzan Delage, whom you know to be innocent?'

'In this matter of Siuzan Delage,' he said, 'a case unrelated to the matter in hand, I shall be guided by the law, as in every other case.'

'How can you say this case is unrelated to the matter in hand? Why else did I attack Mark Pol except that he is so clearly the one responsible for the attack upon Siuzan Delage ...' My fury tangled my words, and my speech software juttered and stalled. I composed myself. 'Instead of preferring Mark Pol's ridiculous prosecution of theft against me,' I said, in steadier tones, 'you would do better to investigate him for the assault upon Siuzan.'

Bonnard looked at me for a while, but the smile did not leave his lips. 'The fact remains,' he said, 'that *Sieur* Treherne's charge has been referred.'

'It is an absurdity!'

'Indeed. In fact, he himself came to regard it as such. I told him that he was free, and should leave the police premises. He insisted upon being given his broken eye stalk, and the money necessary to have an engineer repair it. I told him that it was not the duty of the police to give away money to any headless beggar who asked for it. This offended him.'

'I am not surprised.'

'He pressed the point. He said that at the very least we must give him back his eye stalk. He claimed that his mono-vision was disorienting, and distressing.' The expression on Bonnard's face suggested that he regarded Treherne's distress as rather a delightful thing than otherwise. 'I reiterated that he was now a free individual and must leave. He became aggressive, and demanded his eye stalk. Of course I did not accede to this request.'

'By what law did you keep his eye stalk from him?' I asked.

'I am surprised to hear you take *Sieur* Treherne's part in this matter,' Bonnard said languidly.

'I do not take his part. Only, it seems to me, you take a perverse delight in tormenting the headless. I wonder if it is something legally sanctioned, or whether you indulge your hobby regardless of your declared precision of legal observance?'

'Your ignorance of the necessary processes of law is comical,' said Bonnard. 'How can a prosecution for theft proceed without the evidence? Naturally it cannot. The police must hold the evidence in trust until, *after* the trial, it is restored to its rightful owner.'

'You explained this to Mark Pol?'

'He was disinclined to wait until the trial was completed. He asked, several times and in a disrespectful tone of voice, *but how long will this take?*'

Since this question also touched closely on my own future, I reiterated it. 'And how long will it be? Did you answer his question?'

'I told him,' said Bonnard, looking away and waving his hand evasively, 'that, given the relatively low priority of this prosecution – the small monetary value of the stolen object, the low status of both victim and alleged thief – it would probably be a year or more before court-time could be found for it.'

A year or more. I scratched at the bruises on my trunk, which were intermittently making themselves known to my consciousness as localised shines of pain. The whole affair seemed unreal to me. Once I was released on bail it would matter to me not in the slightest whether they delayed this joke trial a year or a decade; I had to enact justice upon Mark Pol, and declare myself to the police in good time to save Siuzan's head. But a year! It occurred to me to wonder, indeed, why Bonnard was wasting his time (valuable time, I assumed) upon such games; except that evidently he derived a rather juvenile enjoyment from the banter.

'A year,' I repeated. 'This seems understandable. I suppose I could short circuit this lengthy time by confessing to the crime, and accepting whatever punishment the law determined.'

'That would indeed shorten the time-frame considerably,' agreed Bonnard. 'And it would mean that *Sieur* Treherne would receive back his eye stalk much sooner. But I am surprised to hear that you wish to help *Sieur* Treherne in this way.'

'I wish,' I said carefully, 'to meet with him, as I mentioned before. I wish to apologise to him, face to face – or, perhaps I should say, trunk to trunk. My attack upon him was . . . improper. Since I had no intention of stealing his eye-stalk, I can have no reason to prevent him being reunited with it.'

'But this is the opposite of a confession of theft!' laughed Bonnard. '*Since I had no intention of stealing his eye stalk . . .*'

'*Chevaler* Bonnard,' I said frankly. 'Please enlighten me as to the purpose of this business. It puzzles me that a senior policeman is spending his time on so trivial a matter.'

Bonnard nodded, as if I had spoken nothing but good sense. '*Sieur* Treherne,' he said, with the tone of somebody finishing a long-delayed story, 'became most agitated at my estimation. *A year?* he cried. *A year? A joke! I demand my eye stalk now! Or if, as you say, it must be preserved in police store as evidence, then I demand I be given the money to purchase a replacement! I demand! I demand!* It was truly comical to see how insistently he demanded. I told him that what he demanded was impossible. *In that case*, he said, *I withdraw the charge against Cavala. There is no theft here, and no reason to keep my eye stalk from me.*'

'So there is no charge against me? He has withdrawn it?' I asked. 'And I am free to leave? I ask only for clarification.'

'An understandable wish. Clarification will shortly be forthcoming. I told *Sieur* Treherne, in a tone of voice more angry than not, that he was becoming a severe nuisance. I told him: *Be quiet. If you withdraw your charge I shall prosecute you for wasting police time.* This is what I said to him. I do not think he believed me at first, but after some more bluster he calmed down. And in all honesty–a headless, making wild charges, withdrawing those charges, demanding and blustering: how could this be conceived except in terms of wasting police time? Finally he left the police station. He was in no good mood.'

'He has left? Where has he gone?'

'I have no idea.'

'*Chevaler,*' I said. 'Do I understand you correctly? It was *you* who insisted upon this ridiculous and footling charge remaining in place? Am I to understand that I am indeed to be prosecuted for stealing Mark Pol's eye stalk?'

'You are to understand this,' said the policeman.

'But—' I said. 'I do not see the sense in it.'

'A philosophical statement questioning the validity of the law?' said Bonnard. 'Or an expression of personal ignorance?'

'Very well', I said. 'At what is the bail set for my release on this miniature charge? One totale? Fifty divizos? I shall pay it and return a year from now for the trial.'

'No bail is set.'

I began to understand. 'No bail?'

'No.'

'What,' I asked, 'is the financial cost of the item I am alleged to have stolen?'

Bonnard shrugged. 'I do not know.'

'You will not deny it cannot be more than a totale.'

'Most probably not.'

'Then why has no bail been set?'

'That is the prerogative of the law. There is no *requirement* to set any bail, even in the matter of a petty crime such as this. Bail is a matter of the convenience of the law, not a matter of right for the criminal.'

I was silent for a while. '*Chevaler* Bonnard,' I said, eventually. 'I believe you have some purpose in mind, and I request you, respectfully, to tell me what it is. This verbal fencing and dancing – to be frank – infuriates me.'

'Jon Cavala,' said Bonnard. 'What is it to me that you are infuriated? Do not assume that I care. I do not like you, not in the least. I have no concern for your well-being, or anything of that nature. I do not like you. I *know* of you. Know that I am a personal and a long-standing friend of Georgis Benet.'

'I see,' I replied, too quickly.

Bernardise Benet, daughter of Georgis, was the woman for whose sake

I had lost my head. The Benet estate was in Cainon, and they owned a town house in Doué, out of which Georgis supervised the trading of the goods he grew on his estate through the Doué port. I had first met Bernardise at a party in this house – a tall thin structure, six or seven storey high but barely fifteen metres across, located in a curving cul-de-sac not far from the seafront. *Chère* Benet, the mother, liked to supervise a sort of salon, in which poets and painters, musicians and sculptors and gamers congregated. My invitation came after the publication of my book *The Slur.* Those of you interested in my writing – and whom else would read a narrative such as this? – will know that this book, though not my first success of popular estimation, was the first to percolate into the more general consciousness of the literary culture of Pluse. Or at least (since I have sworn to be strictly and exactly accurate in this memoir, howsoever poorly such accuracy reflects upon my own status) I should say, into the consciousness of the literary culture of those countries bordering the Mild Sea. On the other continents I am still little known.

Yet I was celebrity enough to be invited to *Chère* Rehab Benet's day gatherings and soirées. And it was here that I met and befriended Bernardise. And now, despite what I say in the previous paragraph about an absolute strictness of honesty in my writing, I must pull closed a form of curtain. Honesty does not mean an obsessively whole truth, including descriptions of every private act or bodily function. The beautiful Bernadise is still alive, and she merits her privacy as much as anybody.

This is as much as I will say: charges were laid against me of rape, and I acceded in these charges, even though it cost me my head. Some may say I did so because I am a rapist. Others may believe I did so to spare another party from a gruesome punishment whose crime was nothing more than an excess of love and attachment. I must say nothing on this matter now.

But a man as strict, religious-devotional and backward-looking as Georgis Benet would have been more disgusted with a daughter willingly engaging in sexual intercourse than with a daughter raped. Either way he, of course, could do nothing but despise me. And of course his friends followed his lead. He was a powerful man, a trader in hemps and flaxes who had made many millions of totales, and brought tax wealth to the land from many overseas locations.

Hence, when Bonnard announced his long standing friendship with the man, I said *I see* too hurriedly.

And yet, at the same time, my love for Bernardise had been pure enough, and whole enough, to have brought me trekking through four desert days and three nights simply on the chance, the small chance, that I might see her – from a distance, perhaps; stepping out of a family car and going into a shop, or walking with her friends in a Cainon park. The love of men and women draws people to extremity.

'You wish to persecute me,' I said to Bonnard.

'Persecution,' said Bonnard, 'is not a very legal-sounding term.'

'Then you want ...?'

'*Your* position,' he interrupted, 'is awkward. I am within legal rights to hold you in confinement for the whole year, for however long it takes for this matter to come to trial.'

Something occurred to me. 'I do not believe a sitting judge would allow a case to languish for a year, knowing – as he must know, for he must be informed – that the defendant is not on bail but is in confinement.'

'That is perfectly true,' agreed Bonnard. 'In these circumstances trial may happen within the month. Or perhaps two. And so you must return to your cell for the foreseeable weeks.'

But this was no use to me. It would surely be too long – Siuzan would lose her head within such a timescale. I needed to be released before sentence was passed on Siuzan, to perform justice on Mark Pol and still have time to make my false confession. 'And,' I asked, trying to remain calm, 'is there no other option?'

'As it happens there is,' he said. 'Your other option is military service.'

'I have no military training,' I said. 'Before my beheading I was a poet, and I lived a life according to aesthetic and religious parameters. I have never been violent to a single person, never in my life. Though active, as the muscles on my body attest, I created these solely by gymnasium exercise. Not, for instance, by boxing or—'

'Training is provided as part of military service.'

'Am I to understand, by what you say,' I asked cautiously, 'that you wish to *press* me into military service?'

'Press,' said Bonnard, lingering on the word, 'is no legal term. No, Jon Cavala. Of course I know you for a poet. I have read your poetry.'

He said this in so disdainful a voice that my writerly pride was smarted, and I could not help saying: 'It is designed to be sung, rather than read.'

He ignored this. 'You were a wealthy man.'

This seemed to me a *non sequitur*. 'I was,' I said. 'But my wealth was my family's, not my own. It has now been removed from me. I have no money except some poor coins in my wallet, and even that has been taken away.'

'It will be returned to you upon your release, at whatever date that might be. I ask after your wealth because, in my experience, it is those who were formerly wealthy who are the most ignorant about the usual fates of the headless. Poor people will likely meet and know at least some headless individuals. The rich not so.'

'You are saying that I am an ignorant man.'

'I say that you are relatively ignorant of the paths taken by many headless. Otherwise you would know that enlisting in the military is a common choice for headless of both genders.'

'I discussed this very possibility with my fellow headless,' I said primly. 'Upon our journey here, to Cainon. A journey completed, as you know, upon foot, since we lacked the money to travel any other way.'

'And in your discussions of this possibility,' said Bonnard, 'had you decided to follow this path?'

'Not I.'

'You had alternate plans?'

'None of any precision. I hoped, I think, to take work here in Cainon.'

'Not in Doué?'

If I had still possessed a face I would have blushed. I could feel the skin of my chest warming. 'We all three resolved to leave that city, since it had been the location of our crimes. We did not wish to' – and I paused as I spoke this sentence – 'embarrass our victims, or the families of our victims, with our presence.'

'How strange then,' said Bonnard, 'that you have come to the very city to which your victim has removed herself?'

I am ashamed to say that, at this point, I lied to the *chevaler*. 'I was not aware that the Benets lived in this city.'

'Indeed?'

'I mean,' I said, compounding my lie, 'I knew that Bernardise's family owned estates in the north of the country. But I did not know exactly where.' Then, feeling the lie too transparent, I sought to plaster over it with more lies, although of course by doing so I merely made the lie more patent. 'I believed that she planned to continue living in Doué. I sought only to avoid her company.'

'I do not believe you,' said the policeman.

My heart was scuttling now as if trying to knock through my ribs and flee the scene. It was ashamed at my mendacity. There is no sensation so uncomfortable as being discovered in a lie. 'I am sorry that you do not,' I said.

'My belief is that you came to Cainon specifically to be near the young *Chère*, Bernardise Benet.'

'I cannot help what you believe,' I said.

'It is a common thing amongst rapists, this yearning to revisit their victims.'

I flinched. I was sweating. 'Please,' I said, 'use that revolting word with care. If you have read the accounts of my case, then you must know—'

'Please, let us have no cant here,' he said. 'I have many decades experience with criminals of your type. They divide, I may say with authority, into three sorts. The first, and most dangerous, is the type who knows what he has done, and relishes in it, for he specifically wishes hurt and death upon all people, and all women in particular. He makes no excuse for his action because he knows that there is no excuse. You do not belong in this type.'

'I am glad you say so.'

'The second type is bad, but not as bad. He does make excuse for his action, but his excuse is that women deserve such treatment, that they are prostitutes or criminals themselves, they "asked for it", they had it coming. This sort of criminal believes, or he tries to make himself believe, that violence is the proper way of dealing with women.'

'I do not see how they differ from the first type you mention.'

'Oh, the first type does not bother itself with justifications of *any* kind. But then there is the third type, the Romantic criminal. He is self-deluding, and in a way the most dangerous and pitiable type, for he does not even realise that he has committed a crime. Instead he folds the violence into an invented category of his own, *passion*, and he constructs an elaborate personal mythology in which it is better to be passionate than law-abiding or devout, in which to indulge in sexual congress is equivalent to love, and moreover that this base, self-gratifying love is the supreme virtue.'

'There may be a fourth type,' I said, 'of which you do not speak. It is those who were accused, and perhaps even convicted, of rape, yet who accepted the charge only to save their lovers from suffering at the hands of the law.'

'A very romantic notion,' said Bonnard. 'But not a very convincing one. In my many decades as a policeman, and with experience of scores of rapists who have claimed this as their justification, I have – genuinely, truly – only encountered this type once. And I am not talking about my acquaintance with yourself, *Sieur* Cavala.' He smiled coldly. 'But I am forgetting,' he said, although clearly he had done no such thing, 'that you prefer to deny yourself the honorific, believing yourself unworthy of it. An acutely romantic affectation, Jon Cavala.'

I sat very still. 'You wish me to enlist?'

'It is useful to a policeman, such as myself,' he said, settling himself back in his chair with the air of somebody happy to have guaranteed somebody's complete attention. 'It is useful to establish for himself such leverages and bargaining items as he may, for dealing with such circumstances as present themselves as possible threats to the law. In this case, Jon Cavala, I do not especially blame you for attempting to catch a glimpse of, or perhaps even wishing to meet and talk to, your victim. Do not misunderstand me. I *do* blame you for your crime, for which I consider beheading barely punishment enough. But yours is a common enough psychological profile, a post-traumatic transference of emotional urgency and yearning onto the object of your previous desire. But although I understand your motivations I cannot permit them to come to pass. The law does not allow me simply to expel any headless from the city, much as I might welcome such powers. But the law *does* allow me to hold you for trial on this matter of the stolen eye stalk, for as long as it may take to arrange the trial. And, after that, to hold you on whatever other infraction you commit.'

'I will commit none,' I said proudly, but even as I spoke I remembered that I had resolved to commit murder and perjury. But that, I told myself, was in the cause of a greater justice.

'That will prove harder than you think, given my very exact understanding of the law. But why should you put yourself through this difficulty and privation? Take another path. Enlist in the army.'

'I could promise to leave the city,' I said, thinking of the necessity of keeping my liberty to the extent of locating Mark Pol.

'I would not trust your promise. Nor could I enforce such a promise in a court, should you elect to stay. No, the choice is starker than that. You must enlist, or you must return to the cells.'

'Your zeal in persecuting me,' I said, 'though energetic, is misplaced.'

'On the contrary,' he said. 'Were my zeal truly energetic, it would result in your execution. I regret I am unable to ensure that. But perhaps, if you join the army, you will be sent into a combat zone and killed.'

'How charitable!' I said.

'Do you deserve charity?' He asked this thoughtfully, as if it were more than a rhetorical question. 'When we consider what you have done once, and most possibly twice?'

'You *cannot* really believe I assaulted Siuzan Delage!' I cried. 'I did not – indeed I am innocent of this crime!'

'So you have asserted twice before.'

'My words carry no weight with you.'

'They do not.'

'Surely you can see, given the many years of wisdom of which you have just been speaking – *surely* you can see that Mark Pol Treherne presents a far graver danger to others than I?'

'Surely I can see this?' Bonnard shook his head slowly. 'Indeed not. Certainly *Sieur* Treherne is proud, after the manner of the petty-proud; and he is vain; and he is quarrelsome. But he is not, I think, capable of very great evil, or premeditated harm.'

'You do not know him as do I,' I said.

'You do not know him at all,' he retorted.

I struggled, inwardly, to find a way of communicating to this strict and literalist policeman the fact that I would gladly confess to the assault upon Siuzan Delage if only Mark Pol were prevented from harming others. Force *him* to enlist in the army, and I would go to my death happily to save Siuzan! But honest haggling over this matter was out of the question.

I could see no way out. 'Very well,' I said. 'I agree to enlist.'

'Wise,' said Bonnard, getting to his feet.

'What now?'

'Collect your belongings from the captain, in the adjacent room,' he said.

'And the charge of theft?'

'The value of the stolen object, being less than one totale, falls at the discretion of the presiding officer in charge of the case. I shall advise *Sieur* Treherne to litigate under civil legislation to recover the item, or its value plus legal costs. Which is to say, I shall so advise him if and when he applies to me. Which I do not expect him to do any time soon.'

'I am free to go?'

'You are free to go into the military.' He walked round the bar and smoothly out of the room. Those, indeed, were the last words he spoke to me at that time.

Somewhat disoriented, I came through into the central space and tried to identify which of the several policemen there was the captain from whom I might collect my belongings.

In so far as I had a plan, it was to search for Mark Pol, to kill him, and thereafter to return to the police building. I assumed that there would be enough time in between my discharge from the station and my supposed enlistment in the military – which I by no means intended to follow through – in order to accomplish this.

But I had not reckoned on the rapidity with which the police can funnel convicted men and women into the army. I asked two policemen before discovering which was the captain, and after a second DNA test to confirm my identity I was given my wallet back, and also a small blue plastic object with a plastic knuckle at one end, like a fingerbone from a plastic robot. It took me a moment to realise what this was.

'This does not belong to me,' I told the captain.

His was a large, wide, long face, very flat on the front, although the skull was rounded and indeed rather knobbled behind. His eyes were like cuts in a drumskin, pulled tight over cheekbones large as knees; and his lips – according to my unreliable vision software – were a purply colour, almost black, set in lemon-coloured skin. His eyes, black as blackberries, peered at me from between their tight lids. He looked at his datascreen. 'My instructions are that it is to be given to you,' he said.

'But it does not belong to me.'

Again the captain consulted the datascreen. 'There is a note, personally inserted by *Chevaler* Bonnard,' he said, 'that insists you be given the item.'

'And if I refuse to take it?'

The captain stared at me, saying nothing, and I picked up the eye stalk and placed it in my pocket. 'Goodbye,' I said.

'They will be here soon,' the captain said. 'Perhaps you would like to sit down until they arrive?'

'My understanding,' I said, 'having just come from an interview with *Chevaler* Bonnard himself, is that I am free to go.'

'The file, on this very datascreen, states,' said the captain in a dogged voice, 'that you are to enlist in the military.'

'Such was my agreement with the *chevaler*,' I concurred. 'I fully intend to enlist at the earliest opportunity.'

'Then you will be pleased to hear that they will soon be here.'

'By earliest opportunity,' I clarified, 'I meant tomorrow morning.'

The captain unhooked his chiller and rested it on the desk between us, leaving his right thumb draped over the shaft of it.

I sat down. Ten minutes later (I counted off every minute by the large oval clock over the main entrance) two individuals, a man and a woman, both headed, both in the dark blue military uniform of the Pluse Defence League, stepped smartly in. My opportunity for escape, if ever it had existed, was now gone.

PART TWO
Of Revenge

One

During my induction into the military I was concerned with only one thing: to escape from the compound in Cainon. I planned to discover whatever place Mark Pol had gone to, to go there and kill him, and afterwards to return to the police building where I could confess and save Siuzan's head. This was the means by which I would atone for my failings: for my craven failure to confess when Bonnard gave me that opportunity. For failing to protect Siuzan from Mark Pol on the journey itself. For lusting after her in my own mind, to my very great shame. Blood would atone; I would take Mark Pol's and give my own.

I hope I do not shock you with the violence of my ambition. It is true that I planned a murder, but I did it without venom, without heat, as a purely judicial killing. Your good opinion is important to me, and so I hope you understand my motivations. Nobody should be prepared to kill, I believe, unless they are at once prepared also to die. The one life must balance the other. Nobody should kill with hatred in their hearts. Now this was a principle which, though I believe it true, made my decision difficult; because, of course, I had no love for Mark Pol. But my thoughts were not on personal revenge; they were on the *necessity* of this murder, and the countless women I would save in the future from his depredations.

There is another consideration. My thoughts were in truth focused on practical, rather than ethical, matters. I needed to provide myself with enough time before enlisting in the army to achieve my goal. I needed to find Mark Pol, and then execute him in some manner although I had no gun or knife. I pondered these matters, and thinking about them left me with no time to consider the rightness or wrongness of my aim.

I walked meekly enough behind the two PDL officers, through the main entrance of the police building, down the ramp, and to a waiting military van – its wheels, though narrow, as tall as the chassis and angled slightly at an upwards taper.

It was a bright morning. I had lost track of time inside the police cell. The sky was blue.

'Where do we go?' I asked.

The man replied: 'You must address me as "Superior".'

'My apologies, Superior. I have no previous experience of the army ...'

'I am not interested in your experience,' said the man abruptly.

I climbed into the back of the van, and sat myself meekly down. The two PDL officers sat, one on either side of me. My thoughts chiefly turned upon the possibility of escape, of slipping away. I wondered how long I would be able to absent myself before being noticed. In this my lack of experience of the military life was a handicap; for I was vague as to how security would be enforced at camp.

The truck rolled into motion. 'Superior,' I said, addressing myself to the man. 'Should I address you by your name, or will "Superior" by itself suffice?'

'There is no need for names,' he responded curtly.

'Very well, Superior. Thank you, Superior. Superior – I have a question.' He sighed briefly, an aggressive noise. 'What?'

The woman interjected, 'You'd be better to lose this habit of questioning,' she said. 'There's no place for that in the military.'

'Nevertheless, Superior,' I said. 'Am I to sleep in the camp tonight?'

For a while it seemed as if he would not reply. Then he said, in an impatient voice, 'The army is your home now,' and turned his face away.

'I only ask, Superior,' I said, 'because there are some small matters, some personal matters, to which I must attend before I can properly devote myself to my new life as a soldier.' Neither of them said anything, which emboldened me to continue speaking. 'Perhaps if I reported for duty tomorrow? The very first thing in the morning. I am quite used to rising early. This would enable me to tie up certain loose ends, and—'

'Quiet!' said the female office. 'Your old life is dead to you now.'

'But with respect, Superior—' I said.

'Nothing more,' the male officer said. 'No more words from you.'

I was silent. The truck rolled on. 'Superiors,' I tried again. 'Pardon me, but my mind is full of questions ... who is the commanding officer at camp? To whom should I report?' My thought was that I might be able to persuade this person that it was imperative I be given a space of time – perhaps no more than a day – to arrange my affairs. But neither soldier spoke to me.

*

The truck stopped, rolled forward for a while, stopped again. Without windows it was not possible to know what was happening, except that I could see my two escorts readying themselves to disembark and in this way I knew that we had arrived.

I climbed out of the truck, and was taken to a waiting room in which four other headless sat silently. I did not attempt to talk to any of these. My escorts left me there, unattended.

After a quarter of an hour or so of silent sitting, I decided to try slipping away. I got to my feet and walked about the room, as if inspecting the walls (they were tiled: a motif of blue tiles in a knight's-move pattern repeated and rotated upon a white ground). I looked at the posters attached to the wall: one was an animated scene of an apparently endless stream of glum-looking cartoon headed people stepping smartly into a recruitment office and emerging from the far side of the building in cartoon pale uniforms looking happy. Then I made my way to the door. It was unlocked, and opened to my hand.

Outside the sun was shining. My software blanched, and then adjusted for the change in levels of light. I could make out a wide space – a parade ground – at the far end of which, very distant, was a wall. It looked like a low wall at this distance, but there were some people walking in front of it, and it was twice the height of a man. There were some buildings, blocky halls with sharply white walls and slanting orange tile roofs, to the left and to the right was a very tall hanger constructed, it seemed, of sheets of metal crinkled like gigantic corduroy. Behind and to the right of this an enormous stone platform was just visible, and parked upon it three spacecraft: the real thing, vessels for travelling through space. Sculptures in silver of giant creatures from an impossible mythology, half bat and half bird.

Beyond the wall the mountains stood very tall, as if pulling themselves up to their full height. They wore sharp-creased white cowls covering their heads, perhaps so as to intimidate this encampment of men at their feet. There was a powdery precision to the details on the flanks of these mountains: pale cream and darker brown stretches etched with scraps and chinks of black for two thirds of the height, and the upper third looking as if the artist has not yet coloured them in.

And above the overwhelming mountains – so high up that, as I angled my torso to see properly, I tripped and had to stumble backwards to regain my footing – was the sky. It registered as a single shade of bright blue on my vision software. Half a dozen sheaf-shaped clouds stood to the right, as if parcelled neatly away. The rest of the view was bright blue.

I could not see a main entrance to the camp, and walked around the building from which I had recently emerged to check out the other side of the compound. Here I was met by a man in the pale blue uniform. 'You!' he barked. 'Headless – you.'

'Superior,' I said, coming to a halt and standing up straight.

'What are you doing wandering about out here?'

'I was looking, Superior,' I said, truthfully enough, 'for the main gate.'

'You don't need the main gate,' said this man. 'You're a recruit.' This was not a question. 'Go back inside.'

'There are certain matters,' I said, 'to which I have to attend – one loose end, in particular, from my civilian life, which must be tied before I can devote myself properly to the military calling.' Then, as he gawped at me, added, 'Superior,' and angled my torso down in a bowing gesture.

'You headless all look alike to me,' he said.

'My name—'

'I am not interested.'

He stepped up close to me, stepped smartly all the way around me. 'Your ordinator,' he said, 'has been modified by our Medical Officer?'

'By no means.'

He peered closely at me. Then: 'you are not *authorised*,' he barked. And, grasping my shoulder, he hurried me through the door and sat me down.

I was back inside.

The wait stretched. I attempted to quell my anxiety by reviewing my options. If possible I would slip away later that day – perhaps at night, when most of the camp, presumably, slept. Alternatively I would try simply to bluff my way past the guards, telling them that I had been ordered to go into the town. But if this proved impossible, and if I could not on any terms escape from the camp (or if I did get away but was unable to find Mark Pol) then one ultimate possibility remained. I could let Mark Pol go, and trust to providence that he would be apprehended in the commission of some later transgression. I would simply present myself to the camp Magister, and confess to him that I had assaulted Siuzan. He would turn me over to the police, who would release Siuzan Delage from her legal confinement. I would take the shame from her, take it clean away, and instead drape myself in it. My death would be a small price for a great gain. It would be a bargain.

Having access to this last resort calmed me a little. I found my thoughts wandering, returning to memories of Siuzan. I tried to picture her face with an absolute precision; her white skin, her blue eyes, the weight of her dark hair. But the memory was elusive in its detail. I could not be sure of the exact path taken by the swivelling line that defined the profile of her nose. I knew it was tightly plump. A pert nose. But, with an upsetting vagueness, the face I was remembering would not stay pinned and fixed, but would wobble as though it was under flowing water. The nose would swell snoutishly, or shrink to a spine. I tried to remember her lips, so richly coloured my visual software had sometimes interpreted as black. But thin? Or thick? Plump and curve-kinked in their smile, or thinner, straighter lines? I tried to fix my thoughts on her mouth, but I could only see it wide and open, as if she were screaming noiselessly. This upset me; I felt the sparkle and shiver go across my skin, a tremor in my fingers, which I was coming to associate with the tears I no longer had the capacity to shed. Love means a supersensitivity to the hurt of the other, and she had been so gravely hurt. I felt it, acutely, in my own self.

'You shouldn't have done that,' said somebody.

I brought my attention back to the present. The headless man sitting next to me had leant sideways on the bench a little way, and was talking to me.

'That?' I said. My vocal tone was not wholly under my control.

'You weren't been in the army before?'

'Before?'

'Before you lost your head?'

'No,' I said. I swivelled my shoulders, back, forth, to take in the view of the room. The other headless were all sat as motionless as corpses.

'I was,' said this other man. 'I served three years as a headed soldier. On release I got into bad ways – hence,' and to complete his sentence he slanted his right hand through the space where his head had once been. 'Nothing for me to do now but re-enlist. I won't be a soldier any more; I'll be nothing more than a carcass, but better a carcass than a gasping labourer outside. Or a beggar. My name,' he added, holding out his right hand, 'is Syrophoenician.'

'A curious name,' I said, grasping his hand. 'I am Jon Cavala.'

'You shouldn't have done what you did just then,' he said again, in a more kindly voice. 'Allow me to advise you, drawing on my previous experience of the army.'

'What is it I shouldn't have done?'

'Got up and wandered out. You should wait until the Medical Officer has rummaged through your ordinator.'

'Will I be permitted to walk about after he has done so?' I asked, genuinely interested.

'Oh Jon Cavala, *no*,' said Syrophoenician, as if amused. 'Quite the *reverse*. It will render such wanderings quite beyond you, I would say. We are all criminals, here, after all. I confess it to my shame. I was beheaded for murder.'

'Murder,' I repeated.

'And you?'

I turned a little away. 'For adultery,' I said.

'Ah!' he said. 'Rape?'

'The circumstances,' I said, 'were complicated.'

'They often are. They were for me. I lost my head for killing a man. Yet in the army I had served in half a dozen wars and killed howsoever many men – I have not kept count. Some do, some do keep count, but I reason that the All'God will keep the account for me. So – is not this a strange circumstance? For killing this man in the prosecution of the Sugar War I am given a strand of gold braid for the breast of my uniform. For killing that man in the prosecution of a fight in the Willow Quarter of Cainon I am beheaded.'

'As you describe it,' I said, 'it appears certainly – unbalanced.'

'These complications,' said Syrophoenician, as if dealing in profound wisdom, 'are the entanglements of civilian human life. No, no. It is not good. But there are no complications in the military! *Do as you're told* is the height and the breadth and the width of the law. Do as you're told by those in authority over you. There are no complications in the service of the All'God either.'

'You are clearly a devout man,' I said.

'It has always seemed to me,' Syrophoenician said, becoming more garrulous, 'that serving in the military and serving the All'God are—' But then, suddenly, he stopped, and sat upright and still on his bench. I wondered only for a moment at his behaviour, until I saw what he had seen, a shadow on the floor at that place where the sun painted its door-shaped rectangle of light. A moment later an officer stepped through into the room.

'You, carcasses all,' he called. 'To the Medical Office.'

We were led through the sunlight and into another complex of buildings, and again told to sit down on benches. But from here we were, one by one, ordered through to an adjacent room. When my time came I was told to strip naked and lie face down on an examination couch. The Medical Officer, a hound-faced man with dark skin and a swirled, grained mass of hair on his head, was brusque. He spoke into a data machine, recording my details.

'Name?'

'Jon Cavala. I was a—'

'Nothing more, name alone. Reason for beheading?'

'Adultery,' I said, flinching despite myself.

He seemed unconcerned. 'A good musculature,' he told the data machine. 'A recent decapitation. Within the last month, I'd say. Type three eye and ear prostheses. Acceptable. Type three neck cap.' Here he tapped at my neck valve and setting with some sort of small hammer. 'Thyroid largely present, still functional, I'd say. A moment,' he said, apparently to me, 'and I'll replace this cap. What sort of hormonal supplement are you taking? When did you last augment it?'

'I was in police confinement,' I said. 'The police doctor examined me and gave me a pharmocopy pouch – two days ago, I believe. It may have been three days.'

The Medical Officer was clearly unhappy at having to listen to so lengthy an explanation. 'I don't have all the world's time in my supply,' he snapped. 'You'll receive fortnightly military pouches with the other members of your cohort. If you received a police pouch only a few days ago, I won't bother with one now.'

He pressed a cold metal tip against my shoulder blade and withdrew it. There was a wait, whilst he busied himself at something – presumably checking the DNA he had sampled.

The next thing I knew he was tapping at my ordinator with two long needles, like metal chopsticks. 'Type three ordinator,' he told the data machine. 'Standard procedure. Soldier, I'm going to switch off your pain receptors to remove your neck-stump cap and fit you with a military model. This won't take long.'

I felt a series of points of pressure inside my ordinator that related, slightly out-of-synch, to sensations of invasive pressure upon my body. Then there was a peculiar sense of hiatus. I was aware of a series of tensions and forces moving in my shoulders, not unlike as if I were being massaged; and I could see the lower body of the Medical Office moving about. There was a wrench, and my body juddered. I began to feel that something wrong. This feeling was not pain, exactly; but rather an apprehension of something out of place, like a dislocation in some bone so deeply inside the body that no nerve endings go there. I did not like this sensation at all. I began to breathe more deeply, but instead of the neat click and snap of my neck valve there was a slobbery spittish sound. My neck valve was gone, and my neck, a wetly red bundle of cut tubes and severed lines, was exposed. 'Doctor,' I querrelled, 'Doctor, I must report, Doctor, I must say.'

'Be quiet,' the Medical Officer said.

There was a sequence of pushes and pressings, heaves and needlepoints at my neck. Soon the operation was completed, and with a twist to the needle still inserted in my ordinator the Medical Officer told me I was finished.

I stood up, and then (a delayed reaction of some kind, I assume) the sensation of pain washed through my consciousness again. I felt the ragged rim of my neck like a scalding ringlet. Later – several days later, in fact – I stood before a mirror and saw the military model of neck stump with which I had been fitted. The valve was more complex, goitered about now with a layer of filter and machinery, inset with ingenious curving reservoirs to enable me to breathe even should the air be poisoned, or even for a short time in the vacuum of black space. This is one of the ways the military prepare their headless soldiers for sundry malign eventualities.

I was told to pick up the bundle of my clothes and pointed in the direction of a door in the far wall, and through this I wandered, naked as a new born calf and almost as unsteady on my legs.

Here was another officer, standing behind a broad low plastic unit. He took my clothes, and riffled through my pockets with a practised hand. He found my purse and put it down on the unit. He also found Mark Pol Treherne's eye stalk, the strange fingerbone of blue plastic. 'What's this?'

I considered telling him, exactly, what it was; but I had come to the quick conclusion that the military were undelighted with lengthy explanations. 'A talisman,' I said.

He shrugged his eyebrows. 'Soldier,' he said. 'The regulations permit you one lucky charm. It must be worn about the neck on a cord. Do you have enough neck for that?'

'I believe so,' I said.

'Address me as "Superior".'

'I believe so, Superior.'

'So – if you hang it around the neck and lose it because you lack enough neck to retain the cord,' he said, 'you will not be permitted to obtain another lucky charm. Do you understand?'

'I understand, Superior.'

'The lucky charm may also be worn at the waist.'

'That will not be necessary, Superior.'

'Do you have a cord? Regulations require that it be a bonded plastic strand of no more than a millimetre in thickness and strong enough to support ten kilograms.'

'I have no such cord,' I said. 'Superior.'

He stepped back, and consulted his datascreen. Then he picked a laser from his pocket, a device no larger than a cigarette lighter. Holding the eye stalk at arm's length he drilled a hole in the end of the object. He retrieved a length of plastic cord, of the sort he had just described, from a drawer and placed both cord and eyestalk on a pile of dark blue cloth. This whole armful he placed on the unit. 'This is your uniform. The cost of it, together with any prostheses fitted by the Medical Officer, will be deducted from your yearly pay at a rate not exceeding twenty per cent of said pay. You understand?'

I nodded.

'Dress quickly. Report outside to the parade ground. Your fellow headless are waiting.'

The uniform fitted me perfectly. I reflected, as I pulled on the meadhres and the smooth cloth shirt, all very dark blue, that the Medical Officer had evidently loaded my measurements into a database, and a machine had immediately tooled these clothes for me. I tucked the talisman underneath the shirt, and pulled my jacket about me. Finally I pulled on buskin socks and plastic overshoes, and stood up. Another headless, naked, had come into the room. I left, stepping through a door into the outside.

In the sunlight outside my software bleached, paused, and then slowly filled the detail of the view in again. A row of headless soldiers, all in their uniforms, was standing to attention. I joined the end of this line.

Two

We all stood as still as we could manage. Slowly the new recruits filtered out through the door, many still fixing their jackets. We lined up, one after the other; watched at all times by two headed officers. Standing still for such a length of time was no easy matter. There was a great impatience in my soul. Come the nightfall, I thought to myself, and dressed in my uniform it would be a much easier matter to slip away from the camp. My uniform would surely camouflage me amongst all the others who were coming and going, such that there would be less chance of me being challenged. I could probably walk straight through the main gate.

I stood as still as I could, but I desperately wanted the sun to set. I wanted to rush out and find Mark Pol, to turn myself over to the police. I thought of Siuzan in legal confinement; I wondered what she was doing at that very moment. Probably in prayer – certainly attempting to prepare herself for decapitation. The thought of her living in this dreadful apprehension was sharp misery to me. I wanted, pressingly, as a matter of the most extreme urgency, to save her from this state of mind. I wanted her to be relieved.

One of the two officers was coming and going, leaving the parade ground and then returning to it at intervals. The other remained statuesquely, glowering down upon us.

Slowly, the sun moved round. From shining obliquely upon the north-easterly facing flanks of the mountains, it shone directly from above, gouging more and longer black wedges and trapezoids of shadow from the pale brown and white flanks of those peaks. Then it moved over and the mountains took on the tint and dye of shadows; delicate mauve overlays.

Finally the whole cohort of headless soldiers was assembled.

'Soldiers!' cried the taller of the two officers. 'You will address me at all times as "Superior". Today is your first day. In an hour you will march to your barrack. Tomorrow we will begin your training. But today there is one important demonstration to which you will pay close attention.

For some of you – the wise ones – it will be the last time you will need to pay attention to this experience. For others – the stubborn and the foolish – it will be repeated many times. Reply!'

'Yes, Superior!' from some, just 'Superior!' from others.

'Respond with *Superior*!' he bellowed.

'Superior!' we all called, in an approximation of unison.

The taller officer began marching along the length of us; reaching the end, wheeling and marching back down. The other pulled a short stick out of a holster and held it before him.

'Your ordinators,' the first officer boomed, 'have been altered. We have patched a program into your ordinators that interrupts the reception and perception of pain. In *battle*,' (he positively shrieked this word), 'we will *dampen* your pain. This will make you *better soldiers*. Respond!'

'Superior!' we all shouted.

We were capable of much greater *volume* in our voices than had been the case before. This, I suppose, was another military adaptation, perhaps to enable soldiers to communicate over the din of battle. It was surprisingly liberating; more so than you might have thought. To be able fully to *shout*!

'Some of you are murderers,' the officer continued. 'For some the murderous impulse is very close to the surface. During your training, you will come to hate me; doubtless you will come to hate all your superiors. And yet we are not afraid. We carry no weapons when we are with you. Do you wish to know why we are unafraid?'

'Superior!'

'It is because we have the truncheon.' The other officer held up the stick. 'In a moment I will show you how it works. Once the demonstration is over with, I will use the truncheon only on malefactors, on cowards, on deserters, on those who disobey orders. Do you understand?'

'Superior!'

'Good. Just as we will dampen your pain in battle, so we can switch your pain *on* in training. And so you must, as quickly as you can, acquire the habit of respect.' With this last word, the second officer flourished the truncheon.

What happened next was an experience far worse than the police chiller. I would not have thought such a worseness existed, but the truncheon proved me wrong. Every nerve in my body blistered and clenched at once, as if flayed along every length. I screamed, but my screams were swamped by a general roar or bellow or agony from the whole corps. My legs crumpled, jellied, evaporated. I smacked onto the ground and rolled, kicking and thrashing my limbs in an anti-ecstasy. I was hammered and destroyed by the downpour of pain.

And then, suddenly, the pain ceased.

'Get on your feet!' the officer was screaming. His voice was hoarse at the edges with the sheer volume of his yell. 'Get to your feet, all of you! Are you soldiers? Are you men? To your feet! At once – to your feet or you'll feel the truncheon a second time!'

Dazed, nauseous, I stumbled upright and fell straightaway over onto my knees. Besides me I heard the click of a neck valve followed by the spurt and splash of vomit striking the ground. I struggled up again, staggered. I endeavoured to pull myself together.

I had never, until that moment, known what pain actually was. I had suffered broken bones in my youth; I had suffered decapitation; I had endured the touch of the chiller, but these amounted to nothing by comparison.

'You miserable carcasses!' the officer was screaming. 'You *toy* soldiers! Fall over at the slightest touch of the truncheon? Roll in the dust? Disgrace! Disgrace! Respond!'

'Superior!' came from several wobbly throats, including mine.

The officer went up and down the line, hauling headless men up with his own hands. 'Disgusting!' he screeched. 'Disgrace!'

'Superior!' we cried, louder, in greater unison.

'Again!'

'Superior!' more heartily. But my eye was not on the screaming man. It was on the officer holding the truncheon. His face was impassive, as if he had done nothing more than switch channels on a television set.

I surprised myself with a thrust of the purest hatred, right through the core of my thoughts. I was close to stepping forward and tearing at his neck with my fingernails, forcing my forefinger into his eye socket. The urge to hurt him was almost overwhelming; but that small peg, the truncheon in his hand, was enough to hold back the avalanche of my passion.

On the walk to Cainon I had wished for a staff to help me walk. Now I longed for a staff to use as a weapon: to pay him back for the pain he had caused me.

I took a hold of my emotions.

'Better,' the taller officer was saying. 'A little better. You disgraceful carcasses! Do you understand the truncheon now?'

'Superior!'

'Then understand this. Follow every order given you by an officer, at once, without dissent or question. Or feel the truncheon. Put your heart and soul into the fight, on orders, and risk your life without flinching.

Or feel the truncheon. Over there' – he waved to his right without looking – 'is the launch ground. Three spacecraft are sitting there, with the infinite patience of the thinking machine. The *Heron*, the *Shrike*, the *Swallow*. On one of those, when your training is complete, you will leave this camp. You will leave the camp in no other manner. Do you understand?'

'Superior!'

He began marching up and down the line. 'Some of you are thinking of deserting, of running from the camp. Some of you are hoping to escape from the military life that you have chosen.'

At this, my whole nervous system still twanging unpleasantly from the memory of the truncheon, I started. It was just such a desertion that I planned.

'I would advise against this,' said the officer. 'Passing through the gate or past the walls will trigger your ordinators to register total pain, just as you have felt it.'

But this was terrible news! All my plans at escaping, at tracking down Mark Pol, sublimed away at these words. I did not doubt that the officer was telling the truth. The truncheon had, it seemed, paralysed my capacity to doubt.

My mind jittered and spun. There was now no option. I had hoped to visit justice upon Mark Pol before sacrificing myself for Siuzan. But now, it seemed, that would not be possible.

I resolved to confess the crime at the first opportunity. I would leave Mark Pol to providence – and perhaps, also, to the workings of his own conscience, although in this I had little faith. I resolved to turn myself over to the police.

'Very well,' said the officer. 'You will now form up – *smartly!* – into two lines; and you will march – *orderly!* – to your barrack. Do not tempt us to use the truncheon again! Taste it a second time and I guarantee you will strain everything in your power to avoid tasting it a third.'

We formed up, eager to please the officer, and marched a little raggedly, trying to keep in step, across the parade ground towards one of the many two-storey buildings. The sun was now standing exactly between two peaks of the mountain range, like a scarlet gong hung there and waiting to be struck. Our headless shadows stretched away beside us.

We were installed in a bunkroom, and ordered to remain there for the rest of the day and the night. 'You carcasses do not eat with the regular soldiery,' the superior told us. 'Pap will be delivered to your barrack here. Because you are newcomers, you will be inspected by an officer at irregular intervals. You may talk,' he continued, 'but at no louder volume than thirty decibels. Once I have left the room any headless soldier talking at louder than thirty decibels will trigger a sonostat response.'

'Superior?' asked one of the men, standing to attention, 'May I be permitted to ask: what is a sonostat response?'

As soon as he asked the question he dropped to his knees and banged forward onto his front. It was as if he had been poleaxed from behind, despite his lack of a head. The officer brought his truncheon into sight. His thumb was on the switch at the end.

'You carcasses,' he said, 'are not here to ask questions. You are to answer when asked. To obey without questioning.'

The prone man was stirring, drawing his limbs in like a stabbed starfish.

'To your feet, carcass,' shrieked the superior. 'There are many truncheon settings, and your was a minor one. Do you hear me?'

'Yes, Superior,' mumblingly said.

'Would you prefer,' asked the superior, in a parody of an insinuating tone of voice, 'to lie on the floor and feel the truncheon again, or to get to your feet and attempt to recover your dignity as a soldier?'

The headless man struggled to his knees, and tried to push himself up on quivering knuckles; but his legs were wobbling badly. 'I will stand, Superior,' he said.

The superior's hand went to his belt, and without sound or flash the headless threw his arms out and banged down upon the floor again. It goes, I daresay, without saying that none of us made any offer to help him.

The superior turned and, unostentatiously, left.

At last a few headless went over to the trembling figure on the floor and lifted him to a bed. 'No louder than thirty decibels?' somebody whispered. 'How loud is that? How loud – precisely?'

'We must assume,' rasped another headless, whose name I did not know, 'that the sonostat response involves the same technology as the truncheon; and that, if one of us makes too loud a sound, all of us will suffer.'

'Perhaps,' I asked, emboldened to my speculation by the thought that I would not be staying in this place for much longer – indeed, that within a short while I would be dead – 'perhaps it would be worth our while to test this warning?'

We were all of us huddled around the bed of the one who had been truncheoned for asking his question. At my words several people hissed 'No! no!' and then somebody else rebuked the hissers saying, 'Do not all bicker at once, or our combined volume might trigger the sonostat!'

We all fell silent.

'I only mean to suggest,' I said, in a whisper, 'that perhaps this business is a test of our mettle. Perhaps there *is* no punishment for speaking loudly. Would the army be content with meek soldiers, too timid even to try the water and see how hot or cold it is? Perhaps the superior will punish us tomorrow for pusillanimity because we sat here in a huddle whispering all night – instead of singing martial songs at top volume?'

'The army may not want meek soldiers,' said another, gesturing with his right hand for us all to remain quiet by pushing down with his palm several times, 'but the army certainly wants *obedient* soldiers. As I see it, the officer gave us an order, and we had better follow that order.'

'That is well said,' said somebody else. 'Do you desire to feel the truncheon again? Do you want to be like *him*?'

We all looked down at the figure on the bed. He had stopped trembling; but without a face it was impossible to see whether he was fully recovered or not.

Belatedly I realised that this figure was the same Syrophoenician who had spoken to me before the medical examination. 'Syrophoenician,' I said. 'Are you well?'

'Tolerably so,' he replied, speaking not in a whisper but a low voice. Several of the people gathered around him flinched; but his voice did not trigger the sonostat – whatever that might be.

'Your experience of army life,' I whispered to him, 'did not stand you in good stead.'

'Indeed,' he replied. 'A regular soldier may ask an officer a question, provided he does it respectfully. Indeed, ah – I regret I have forgotten your name ...'

'I am Jon Cavala,' I said.

'Jon Cavala. Yes. Well, Jon Cavala, as a soldier I was *encouraged* to ask questions – in a mood of proper respect of course. But, it seems, they regard the headless troops as lesser creatures than headed warriors.'

'So you have discovered to your cost,' I said.

We spent the rest of the next hour in a cowering frame of mind, each of us claiming one or other bunk, none of us prepared to argue the case for fear losing control of the volume of our voices. Half an hour later an officer stepped through the main door and marched up and down the central aisle. He was a different fellow to the previous ones, but was possessed of no sweeter temperament. 'Stand by your beds when a superior enters,' he shouted. 'Present yourself neatly.'

From this I deduced that whatever device governed the sonostat response disengaged when an officer was present. If the device even existed.

The superior left, and shortly thereafter an automated bin rolled in with a soupy sludge in its central container. There was one ladle, but no bowls, plates or spoons. After much anxious whispering amongst ourselves, which occasionally pushed the volume dangerously high, we determined the order in which we were to share the ladle.

We ate, each of us spooning a full ladle into our neck valves. I was, perhaps, halfway along the line; and although all taste and savour was of course absent from my meal the mere sensation of warmth, and the gloopy texture of the pap as it slid down my throat, was enormously satisfying. I was hungry. Little clenching pains had been passing along my gut and shivering my stomach, and it felt exceedingly good to eat. Immediately afterwards, as I handed the ladle to the next man, it occurred to me to marvel at how thoroughly I was adjusting to my new condition. Those criteria that, formerly, distinguished good eating from bad, as savour, smell, spices, sweetening, and even the look, had all gone; but my consciousness was now finding in quite other qualia (the texture in the throat, the warmth, the sensation within the belly) grounds for judging a meal good or bad.

But when the last man stepped up to take his turn he discovered that all the soup was gone.

'What is this?' he hissed furiously. 'You greedy fools! You have all taken more than your share – and now I must go hungry?'

'We took no more than a ladle each,' said somebody.

'Evidently the officers omitted to tell us,' said Syrophoenician, sagely, 'that, to divide the soup between all of us, we must take a little less than a full ladle each.'

'This is another of their little tortures,' hissed a man called Geza. 'It seems we can discover the truth only by suffering.'

'By *my* suffering,' said the hungry man.

'Apologies, friend,' said Syrophoenician. 'Your name?'

'Garten.'

'Garten, you must take the first helping of tomorrow's first meal.'

There were murmurs in the group at this as a fair solution to the dilemma. But it did not sweeten Garten's temper.

'What use is that to me now? My belly is empty *this moment* – now, not later. You,' he turned on the fellow who had been before him in the queue. 'Who are you?'

'I am Costra,' said the man. 'My name is Bil Costra.'

'You *must have seen* that there was only a ladle's worth of soup left in the bin. Why did you not take half a ladle, and leave me some?'

'Everybody else had a full ladle,' Bil Costra objected. 'Why should I have less?'

'Why should *I*?'

'You were behind me in the queue.'

'We drew no lots,' said Garten. 'My position as last was not fairly chosen.'

'We did not know, ahead of time,' Bil Costra pointed out, 'that one must go without.'

'There was no need for *me* to go without,' retorted Garten, 'if all of *you* had not been so greedy – a spoonful less for you, each, and my belly would be full now!'

Tempers were clearly fraying.

'Friend,' said Syrophoenician, attempting to make peace. 'We all regret your position.'

'Regret is facile on a full stomach,' snapped Garten.

'At the least you may scrape the remnants from inside the bin,' I offered.

'Oh, scrapings,' said Garten, hissing sarcastically. 'Why thank you *sieur*, and thank you.'

Nevertheless, of course, he stepped over to the automated bin to salvage what he could. He put the ladle in its slot and attempted to open the lid; but it had sealed itself, as presumably it was programmed to do when empty. This was too much for Garten. 'By all that is holy in this world ...' he shouted, striking the top of the bin with his fist.

So it was that we discovered the nature of the sonostat response. All of us fell directly to the floor, as if choreographed to fall in perfect unity. The pain was not so intense as it had been on the parade ground – I say so in retrospect, but at the time I was consumed by the sharp agony of it; it dazzled and sparked along every one of my nerves. It drove my limbs apart, and it forced a howl through the flute pipe of my neck.

This, indeed, was the worst of it; for as long as we howled, so long did the truncheon-like sonostat effect continue. To begin with this was a matter of sheer and agonised astonishment – amazement at the wholeness and utter penetration of the pain, and amazement that it did not come to an end. These varieties of amazement are, I suppose, actually the same; any pain we experience bewilders us in duration simply by virtue of the fact that it has dared trespass into our bodies at all.

It is also true what they say: that pain stretches time. One flayed-out second gave way to a second, and then a third – for there was a clock fixed above the door, that we might know the time to reveille and sundry other duties, and from where I lay on my back it fell within my field of vision. The second number shimmered from five to blankness, and then shimmered back into existence as a six, and at all times my nerves body screeched like fingernails drawn down a blackboard, and burnt like scalding acid was running along its veins.

One of us (afterwards we discovered it was Geza) mastered himself sufficiently to shout, 'We must all – be quiet – to stop this pain—'

Several of us stifled our screams. I fought mine down. But three or four continued to whistle and pipe mindlessly.

'Stop–the–*screaming*–' cried Geza, 'and–*the–pain–will*—'

One by one the screaming people quietened; several by smothering their neck-stump valves with both hands. The last person gulped in, sucked a long breath, and instantly the pain ended.

Precious seconds. Then one of the headless belched and vomited out his potage upon the floor, and, like an aftershock, a glass fragment of pain cut lengthways through our bodies again. The vomiting did not last long, and soon all was quiet.

Shivering, moaning only in whispers, we picked ourselves up by ones and twos. I gathered myself, and moved on jellied legs to my bed, upon which I collapsed. Then, desperate not even to breathe too loudly, I lay until the last memory of the actual pain had drained from my body.

Syrophoenician had taken the bed next to mine, and he reached it by crawling and pulling himself up. But not even an experience as severe as this could silence him for very long. 'As a regular soldier I was never treated so cruelly,' he whispered. 'The officers respected us as warriors. And when a man had to be punished – I never was, but sometimes a man would be – he would be beaten a wooden staff. A proper punishment which, though painful, was not undignified. But this – this is infinitely worse.'

'Or better,' I said. 'For although it is unpleasant, this pain does not damage our bodies at all.'

'I suppose not,' said Syrophoenician. 'It's all in the mind, as the phrase goes, except for us the phrase is a literal truth. 'Course, it *feels* very much as if it were all in the body. It feels so very much like that.'

I could not disagree. Soon after that the lights went out.

I was in no mind to sleep, and neither, I think, was anybody else. All of us revolved our new fate in our minds, pondering with what fortitude, or with what desperation, we might face it in the months to come. All save me: for the thought that was most insistently in my mind was how glad I was to be leaving this place very soon. I pitied these men that they faced years of this treatment. Death, even a shameful death such as the one I faced, was better.

'I will tell you,' Syrophoenician whispered to me, 'what I miss most now that I am a headless man. It is the sense of smell. I had a very keenly developed sense of smell when I was headed. The aroma of a rose, or a desert lily. Stone-filtered coffee when it is fresh in the cup. The smell from grass when it has been cut and watered.'

'My own sense of smell,' I returned, 'was never well developed.'

'But how deprived you were! Without a fine sense of smell there is no fully developed sense of taste, and the best foods are—'

'Be quiet,' hissed the person at the next bunk along. 'With your talk of fine smells and delicious flavour – what do you do, except torment a room of people who are deprived these things for ever?'

There were murmurs of agreement, which ceased abruptly as the murmurers became, all together, fearful of raising the volume too high.

After a pause I said, 'It is possible to purchase smell receptors, as prostheses. Our ordinators are perfectly capable of processing the sense data of smell, I assume. And even, I suppose, of taste.'

'Hoo hoo,' whispered Syrophoenician, as if amused. 'And are you so wealthy, as to be able to afford these things, *Sieur* Cavala? The wealthy do not often end up in the army. How did this come about, that you are now a soldier?'

'My personal history,' I replied, after a pause, 'is complicated.'

'It seems we have a wealthy man amongst us!' whispered Syrophoenician to the room. '*Sshhh!*' returned somebody out of the darkness.

'I am as poor as anybody here,' I said. 'My purse is underneath my pillow – shall I show you how many coins it contains?'

'Oh a totale or two, I'm sure,' said Syrophoenician. 'I don't doubt that you've lost much of your former wealth when you lost your head. But you *were* wealthy . . .?'

'I,' I said, shortly, 'was a poet.'

'A fine profession. And not one that tends to hurt the back with heavy lifting, or blister the hands with harsh use. A poet, were you?'

In the bed on the other side of me was Geza, who broke in now with a carefully hissed: 'I used to read poetry.'

'Another wealthy man,' said Syrophoenician, amused.

'By no means. I was an accountant. But sometimes I would read poetry. Your name?'

'Jon Cavala.'

'I have never heard of you.'

'My fame was, perhaps, limited.'

'Speak one of your poems, *Sieur* Cavala,' urged Syrophoenician. 'Only whisper it, lest your words be words of fire to us!'

I was silent for a while. 'I am not convinced that you truly wish to hear my poetry.'

'Come now,' said Syrophoenician. 'Don't be coy. That is unbecoming.'

And so, whispering the words through my speakers, I spoke:

> *It's good you've learned to smile*
> *And no one looks for traces*
> *Of tears about your eyes:*
> *Your face is like most faces.*
> *It's good you've learned to smile.*

There was a silence. 'Is that all?' said Syrophoenician. 'That is barely enough poem to fit inside a ring.'

'It is brief,' I agreed.

'Do you catch my meaning?' said Syrophoenician eagerly. 'I meant, as it might be, to write a charm inside a wedding ring, such as *my love my life.*'

'My poems were mostly brief,' I said. 'If you want an epic you must go to another poet.'

'If you whispering *sieurs* will quieten yourselves,' said Geza, turning on his side, 'I would like to sleep now.'

We all slept. Then, all at once, we were all woken.

I was startled into a terrible wakefulness by the sensation of clenching pain up and down in body. Everybody was awake at once.

There was a greater degree of self-control about the group on this occasion; we stifled our cries, and blocked the more involuntary hooting from our neck pipes caused by spasming chests and lungs. Very soon the pain passed, but we were all sharply awake now.

Afterwards, clustering together in a group and exchanging angrily whispered words, we agreed that one of us had cried out in his sleep, moved unconsciously by some nightmare or provoking dream. Yet no one would admit to being this person; either concealing the truth for fear of reprisal, or else perhaps genuinely unaware that they had been the one.

'If I had a head,' hissed Geza, 'I would tie a scarf tightly around my chin to hold my mouth shut and prevent myself from barking out in my sleep.'

'Yet there is no equivalent for the headless,' said somebody else.

We returned to our separate beds; but it was very hard to fall asleep after that.

Three

There is no need for me to delay this narrative excessively with accounts of military training. That is not my purpose. This is not, properly speaking, my story after all: it is Siuzan Delage's, of the dreadful thing she had suffered and the more dreadful danger that we three, through our selfishness, had placed her in. It is about my resolution to make atonement to her for those things.

Indeed, as I stood at attention beside my bed in the morning, I did not expect to spend another night in the barracks. A police cell, I resolved, was infinitely to be preferred.

A superior inspected us. 'First, breakfast. Then you will form up on the— what? What is this?' He was standing by the spatulate spread of vomit upon the floor. 'What *stink* is this?'

None of us wished to be the one to answer the superior's angry question.

'You,' he bellowed, pointing his truncheon at me.

'It is vomit, Superior.'

'Is it yours?'

'By no means.'

'You revolting pigs,' he cried, swivelling on his heel so that the truncheon, like the barrel of a gun, swept past us all. 'You disgusting dogs! You think that because you can't smell the rest of us are prepared to sniff up your stink? Why did you not clear up this disgusting mess?'

None of us replied.

'One of you,' he screeched, 'will reply to my question, or I will give *all* of you're a taste of the truncheon.'

'We had no cleaning materials, Superior,' said Bil Costra.

The superior clacked across the floor to Bil. 'None? No mops, no buckets, no water, no detergents?'

'No,' said Bil, in a nerve-charged voice, 'Superior. There is only the toilet, and in that room there is not even a sink.'

'You have,' asked the superior levelly, 'hands?'

'Of course, Superior.'

'You were beheaded, not behanded?'

'Yes, Superior.'

'Then *use* your hands. You! You! You!' (singling out three at random), 'scoop up every *peck* of that vomit, take it round the back of the building and rub it into the dirt. Now!' With three little nervous hops the three chosen men scurried to the mess, wiped and scooped it up in their hands, and hurried outside. Whilst this was going on, the superior marched down the aisle between the bunks. 'Whose was it?' he asked.

Nobody spoke.

'You think, perhaps, you are protecting one another. But this is to misunderstand the logic of your situation. If the vomiter does not make himself known, then I shall punish you all with the truncheon. If he does not make himself known after that punishment, I shall do it once more. And if this does not prompt him to come forward I shall do it again—'

'It was I, Superior,' said a headless.

The Superior walked over to him. 'Your name?'

'Steelhand, Superior.'

There was a moment of silence. Then the three headless came trotting back in from outside.

The officer raised his truncheon, and tapped Steelhand's shoulder with it. The headless man flinched. But the superior did not flick its switch, and instead he hooked it back onto his belt and stepped back. 'You must learn to control yourself, Steelhand,' he said. 'You three, back to your position.'

The three stood by their beds. Two of them were rubbing their dirtied hands against the fabric of their meadhres.

'In a short while,' the superior announced, 'the breakfast bin will roll through. After breakfast you will assemble upon the parade ground.'

I spoke up. This took, perhaps you can believe, considerable courage on my part. The memory of the pain from the truncheon was in my bones and muscles as well as my mind. Yet, I told myself, I must go through with it.

'Superior!' I said.

The stillness in the barrack was so complete that the mumbling of Garten's empty belly sounded like a drumroll.

The superior stomped over to me. 'What?'

'I have something to report, Superior.'

He peered at me, leaning forward a little. I could see his hand reaching down to where the truncheon was dangling from his belt. I could even

97

see the little circular button, on the flat end of the handle, which, I presumed, triggered the response. My heart was trilling. I felt an urge, almost impossible to squash down, to start running and run as far as fast as I could.

'Report?' he said.

'Superior, I must speak to the Magister,' I said. 'There is a vital matter I must report to him.'

This provoked a laugh from the officer, a series of little nasal snickery sounds. Indeed, he was so amused that he took his thumb away from his truncheon. 'The Magister, is it?' he said. 'Why, certainly not. Most certainly not. The Magister of this camp would not waste his time speaking to *me*. What chance is there of him talking to a carcass such as you?'

'Then a captain, Superior,' I said. 'I beg of you.'

I could see that my attitude puzzled him. He fingered the truncheon again. Perhaps he was telling himself that since I had experienced its effects more than once I could surely not be engaging in a deliberate levity or insubordination.

'Report to *me*, soldier,' he said. 'I am your superior.'

This was the hardest moment of all. Even after only one day, my treatment had gone a long way towards conditioning me to obey without question. Yet I felt I needed to speak to a higher ranking officer.

'Superior,' I said, 'if you order me to report, I will. But I believe your captain will want to hear my report himself, and not at second hand.'

The superior glowered at me. 'This is,' he said, 'a serious matter?'

'The most serious, Superior.'

'Concerning this camp? You should report any matters to do with the camp to a superior.'

'Not camp, Superior.'

'Then what is it?'

Again I hesitated. 'I could tell you, Superior,' I said. 'But all I say is that it may be the case that your captain would prefer that I report it directly to him.'

The superior pondered this for a long time, evidently debating within himself whether he could afford to ignore what I was saying. Presumably he decided that he could not. 'Carcass,' he said, in a slightly distant voice, as if going through the motions of warning me, 'if you are wasting the army's time, the army will not be pleased.'

'Superior!'

He turned and marched out of the barracks, and I, feeling trepidation even at so minimal an act of personal decision-making, fell into step behind him. We passed across the parade ground, round a wide, single-storey and windowless building, and finally across a lawn of what appeared to my eyes to be blue grass. The building on the far side, towards which we walked, was pilastered and painted white – of a different sort to the others in the camp: three storeys, windows shining in the morning sun, a Pluse pennant – as long as the building – slinking and undulating effortlessly in the wind.

Up the ramp and inside. I was nervous, a condition exacerbated by the superior stopping, pointing at a door and saying: 'If you're are toying us, you'll pay for it, believe me.'

'Superior!' I barked.

I knocked at the door.

At 'come in' I opened and stepped through.

The captain was standing at a chest-level desk. He appeared, at first sight, to be consulting a datascreen, although from where I was I could see that the screen was not switched on. There was a pile of slim plastic ovals on the desk before him, irregularly piled, each no bigger than a palm; perhaps medals, or music players, or simply plastic ornaments.

The captain was clearly surprised to see us. 'Greenwood?'

The superior stood forward. 'This headless recruit insists upon talking to you, Captain.'

'Insists?'

The superior ducked his chin down, but did not reply.

'Well,' he said, turning to me. 'What is it?'

He was the sort of man termed handsome by other men, but with that style of male beauty women find forbidding rather than beguiling. He wore a moustache, as black and glistening as if recently dipped in ink. This moustache followed the downward bowing contour of his upper lip, and was clipped into a precise tapering bow. His eyebrows (or his single eyebrow, for they were joined over the bridge of his nose into a single line of black) formed a larger upper echo of this shape, arcing over the whole face. His nose was straight and symmetrical, with a sculptural curl to each of his nostrils. His eyes were small.

'I must report, Captain – confess, Captain.'

'Confess?' he said.

'It is a burden upon my conscience,' I said. 'I must confess I have committed a crime.'

The captain did not change his expression.

'It is a serious crime, Captain,' I said. 'I regret to say – regret for my own sake, for the punishment will be my death. But I must confess that I ... attacked a woman.'

99

'Attacked a woman?'

'A virtuous woman, whom I assaulted in the ugliest manner possible.'

'Rape?'

'Captain,' I said, tipping my torso forward. 'It is indeed that word. I am ashamed. The police questioned me and I denied the crime, hoping to save my life. I escaped into the army with the same aim. But the crime will not permit my conscience to settle. The attack happened a little way south of the city, in the scrublands.'

'I'm truly, genuinely surprised by this,' said the captain, speaking slowly. 'I mean, surprised that you reckon this confession might interest me.'

I considered his response. 'Captain,' I said. 'My shame is greater that I must disappoint you.'

He put his head a little on one side, with a tender expression on his face. 'I'm afraid my position does not permit me the leisure to be concerned either with your shame, nor your crime.'

'I ask you, respectfully,' I said, 'to deliver me to the police.'

'That's perfectly impossible,' he said, turning away from me. 'There is only one crime that interests me here, and this is wasting the time of a superior officer.'

'Rape – which is to say, criminal adultery—' I pointed out to him. 'This is one of the three most serious crimes in ...' I was, I think, merely puzzled at his reaction, thinking he had not understood my confession.

He said: 'No, no.'

'Captain,' I said. 'Forgive me for pressing you on this matter, but—'

'The crimes you committed in the civilian world do not interest me in the least. You are new. But you will soon learn that the least infraction of military orders – let us say, stepping accidentally upon a newly watered lawn, or failing to address an officer as "Superior" – is infinitely more serious than rape, murder and heresy in the civilian world. That's always been the way in armies, ever since men have walked without drawing their fists in the dirt as they go. You've nothing more to say to me.'

'Captain, a moment more, I beg of you,' I said. 'There is more at stake here than simply my life! My victim is herself at risk of beheading. A virtuous woman—'

The Captain put his head on one side again, with a tenderly curious expression upon it. 'But why should she be beheaded if she was the victim of your assault?'

'She refused to lay charges against me, knowing that it would cost me my life.'

'Foolish of her,' said the captain.

'By making my confession to the police I would be saving her head.'

'Some whore in the city,' he said, his tone of voice not changing, 'and I should care about her head? Let her lose her head. It won't affect her trade. It may increase it.'

'With respect, Captain,' I said, becoming agitated, 'she is not – that thing you name, but a virtuous woman.'

'Whore or fool, I don't care.'

'Captain, so much depends upon me confessing the truth to—'

'Carcass!' the captain snapped, his voice suddenly hardening. 'Back to your barrack with you. I shall *not* hand you to the civilian police. You're to be a soldier.'

With a thunderous sense of horror, that came upon me all at once, I recognised that he meant exactly what he said. He refused to report me to the police. These words from the captain were, in effect, sentencing Siuzan Delage to beheading. My terror and fury got the better of me. Much of this, I later reflected, was a fury at myself, for I had been given the chance on three separate occasions to confess and save her head, and I had not done so. The first time was from fear and a base instinct for survival. The second came about because I could not (believing that the law would never behead a woman it knew to be innocent) allow other people to see me in so vile a light – I who loved women above all else, to be thought a woman-hater! But this was merely pride. And the third time because I had decided my duty was to prevent the real culprit from committing more outrages before sacrificing myself. In all these three self-justifications I now saw only one thing: the despicable desire to clutch my miserable life to me, a cowardly refusal to accept the necessity of my death.

I gathered myself. I must be a coward no longer. My task was clear: to make this captain understand the urgency of my need – the hideous injustice of any woman, but especially of so pure a woman as Siuzan Delage, suffering on my account –

Stepping forward I blurted: 'Captain, I beg that you *must* understand—' The sentence was broken off by the sensation of my shins and thighs, my spine and ribs, flaming with overwhelming agony. I felt the thud of the floor against my chest. My arms jerked out. I quivered and jerked upon marble tiles. The horribly scintillating pain completely filled my body.

Then, after too long, it ceased. I lay front-down on the floor. My breathing was very rapid. I heard, somewhere else in the room, the captain saying, 'He screamed through the whole of that.'

'He's new, Captain,' returned the superior. 'He has spent merely one night. It hasn't been conditioned out of him yet.'

Later, reflecting on this, I came to understand one purpose of the sonostat, to condition us to swallow our screams when pain happened to us. But, naturally, this is a secondary function. The first is the same function as all torture. To ensure we know our inferiority. 'Up, carcass!' snapped the superior. 'Or you'll feel again the—' But I was already on my legs, jittery though they were, up before he even finished his sentence. This was the effectiveness of the truncheon as a motivational device.

Four

The superior marched me back to the barrack, leaving me at the door. There was to be, it seemed, no further punishment.

Stepping inside I discovered that breakfast had been entirely devoured. 'In your absence,' said Syrophoenician gaily, 'we were all able to take a full ladle of porridge. Even Garten has ceased complaining.'

I slumped onto my bed. 'I am cursed,' I said. 'I have brought disaster upon a pure and undeserving woman.'

'What's that you say?' asked Syrophoenician.

'I will not train,' I said. 'I will lie me down on this bed, and not rise from it. They can kill me. I don't care if they do.'

'This poet seems a glum sort,' said Bil Costra, coming over.

'Come along, Jon Cavala,' said Syrophoenician. 'You mustn't speak this way. What was it that so burned inside you that you had to speak it to the captain, anyway?'

'I went to request he handed me over to the police,' I said, my stomach griping and swirling with the sense of horror of what I had done – by which I mean, of what I had done to innocent Siuzan Delage.

'A strange request,' said Bil Costra.

'I can indeed see why the captain refused it,' agreed Syrophoenician.

'You fools!' I cried. 'You idiots! A beautiful and innocent woman has been raped!'

'I do not understand the connection of this fact with your previous statement,' said Syrophoenician.

'Don't joke, don't *speak* about this matter in that way,' I cried, in an agony of remorse. 'She was assaulted, assaulted sexually, but to preserve the life of her attacker she did not report him to the police.'

'Preserve the *life?*' asked Syrophoenician.

'The attacker was headless,' said Costra.

'Ah!'

'But this does not explain why she would wish to preserve the life of a man who assaulted her in such a vile fashion,' said Costra.

'Because she is pure!' I said. 'Because she is devout, and does not wish the death of another man – even so vile a man – laid upon her conscience!'

'Is it you?' asked Syrophoenician. 'Were you her attacker?'

In my convoluted fury and bitter self-devouring rage I could have plunged my hand into the fool's chest and pulled his heart straight out. But I did not. I rolled, upon my bed, in a series of jerks and spasms. 'No, no, no!' I cried.

'Yet you want to be given to the police.'

'I wish to confess to the crime to save her head – not because I am guilty, but to save her head. I wish to save her, because I love her! I love her!'

Neither man said anything to this. Eventually Costra said, 'I see.'

'An unfortunate situation,' agreed Syrophoenician. 'The captain – he refused your request?'

'I tried to explain to him,' I said. The words did not come smoothly, but rather with fluttery little lurches from word to word that accentuated their artificial, electronically-vocalised tone. 'But he would not listen to me!'

'This doesn't surprise me,' said Syrophoenician. 'He prefers military justice to civilian.'

'But,' I said, sobs breaking up my words completely, 'she will lose her head, because of me, and because of my foolish delay! She is the purest and best of women! I love her! I love her!'

'Well,' said Syrophoenician, drawing the word out. 'If I were you, Sieur Cavala, I would hold your love at arm's length.'

'To do so,' agreed Costra, 'might remit your suffering a little.'

'What do you mean?' I cried.

'Only,' Syrophoenician said, in a whiningly pious voice, 'that it sounds as if this love between you and the woman is not a permitted thing. What, after all, does it say in the Bibliqu'rân? Does not Solomon himself say, in the Book of Light, *Corrupt women for corrupt men, and corrupt men for corrupt women; but pure women for pure men, and pure men for pure women. Is not the purity of a woman like a pearl?*'

'*The mouth of a virtuous man is a wellspring of life, but violence covers the mouth of the wicked man,*' said Costra, completing the quotation.

'Do you mock me with scripture?' I cried.

'What's this yelling? You must learn to temper your voice come nightfall,' said another man, coming over to the bed. 'No matter your distress. Keep your howling quiet, or we'll all suffer'.

'My distress is such that I will die of it,' I claimed. 'Before the night comes I shall be dead.'

'Nonsense,' retorted a chuckling Syrophoenician, perhaps attempting to jolly me out of my self-concern. 'Nonsense. You'll overcome this little setback, my friend. You're strong.'

I screamed. I believe I did, although the memory of this morning is hazy to me now. Perhaps I merely moaned. Certainly the others left me be, and I rolled and thrashed upon my bed. I couldn't believe that I was trapped in this hideous existence. I couldn't believe the persistence of my misery. It circled and circled violently inside my head, a great serpent of thought biting its own tail. I had caused the woman I loved to be beheaded. In her innocence she had been beheaded. I loved her. I was the cause of her mutilation. I could have saved her. I had not saved her. The intensity of the emotion inside me was enough, I felt certain, to snap my spirit into two. To break it like a green bone held between two gigantic fists and bent savagely until it splintered in two.

But this did not happen.

I was, I think, vaguely aware of the entry of a superior into the barrack; but I was utterly rolled up into my misery. I was unreachable. I had taken my knees in my hands, and was lying curled like an ampersand upon my side, producing a double-noise, an electronic warble from my chest speakers and a tuneless hooting through my neck stump. I do not know whether the superior ordered me to my feet. I was unaware. Perhaps he did, perhaps not. It hardly matters. The next thing I knew my sight had switched to whiteness and I could hear nothing. Pain shorted up and down my body as if I were a man-sized electrical wire being overloaded with a constantly reverting shock. My bones were glass. Fire flowed through the glass and shattered it all to powder, and the powder retched and ground against my flesh. No. I can't express to you the intensity and duration of this agony. Think of the worst physical pain you have suffered, imagine it intensified and prolonged, and fill in this space in my narrative with that memory. The pain flayed skin from flesh, flesh from bone, and left behind only a Hiroshima shadow that was nothing more than a flattened layer of pain upon the bed.

Finally the pain – stopped.

I became aware of

—myself gasping, a forceful series of expulsions of air from my lungs almost like coughing.

I was lying on my back, my arms and legs starfish straight.

'Off your bed, soldier,' said the superior.

Still gaspingly breathing, I tried to roll myself sideways, to plant feet on the floor and stand up. Instead I collapsed to the floor. I felt the smack of it against my two palms at once. I heard the noise of this smack. If I had eaten breakfast I would, at this point, have vomited it up. Instead I forced my willpower down my spine, like a pump forcing water along a very thin pipe, to my legs, willing them to work. I pushed back and tried to stand, but my muscles were cramped from the severity of the contractions the truncheon had forced them into. The floor slapped my palms again.

'Soldier,' said the superior, in a warning tone. I could picture his thumb hovering over the button of his truncheon.

With a monumental effort I pushed back again, and compelled, strenuously and effortfully, my legs to hold me up. I was on my knees. Everything in my universe had shrunken down to this: to get to my feet, to stand, and so to avoid the truncheon. There was nothing else: neither future nor past, not Siuzan Delage being fitted with an ordinator prior to beheading, nor me facing a lifetime (however short) in the army. Not my comrade headless, not even myself. There was nothing except the superior and his truncheon; nothing except my recalcitrant body. I reached back, because my hands seemed more under my control than my lower body, and found the mattress. Placing my hands upon the lip of this I pushed myself up, and slowly, shudderingly, and with a series of juddering aches running up and down them, my legs began to do what I so frantically wanted them to do.

I stood.

The superior was in front of me. I recognised him, although I did not know his name (it was not Greenwood, who had taken me to the captain, but another one). He was looking at me. All my will was focused on not staggering, not falling, on holding myself steady.

He turned away from me. I do not believe that anything, in all my life before or since, has been such a relief to me as that turning away.

'To the parade ground, carcasses,' he said. It appeared he was no more interested in the reasons for my display upon the bed; that once I had stood up, his interest in me ceased. I trotted out onto the parade ground with all the others.

Five

My misery was resilient, and returned to me. But the conditioning power of pain and discipline was more resilient. In those two sentences you have the nub of my military training.

That day was spent prancing up and down the parade ground to the barking commands of the superior. We might have been troops training for Alexander's army, or Patton's, or al-Hattim's, so timeless and basic was this process. This elemental process, teaching the body the useless clockwork yoga of marching and standing, is the most ancient portion of military training, as ancient as farming, or religion. It is beneath thought, and as such it is almost soothing. To begin with my mind fell into the rhythms of this regimentation, and coordinating my limbs occupied all my thoughts. Slowly, as my body learned the routine, my thoughts poked their head out from the shell into which the truncheon had driven them, I began to think again of Siuzan.

At first this produced merely a sapping sensation of despair, such that I stumbled and nearly fell; and had I fallen I would surely have lain on the dirt and cried. But my will was strong enough, just, to keep my feet moving.

Then the thoughts returned in less debilitating form, although as painfully as before. I cursed myself for allowing a pure woman, so beautiful in body and spirit, to come to this terrible and shameful end.

But as I thought this I marched. I stood. I raised my arms and lowered my arms, in unison with the entire block of headless troops, as the superior ordered.

Soon a new sensation, of bodily fatigue, began to overblot my repetitively self-lacerating round of thoughts. We marched, we wheeled and marched back under the impassively spectacular scenery. The mountains, like an impossibly vast curtain of rock petrified in the middle of billowing, withdrew from us. Our suffering had nothing to do with them.

After half an hour my stomach was cramping with hunger. After an hour these gripes went away. I marched on.

We could see other soldiers, headed men, coming and going. Cars, shiny and finned like fish, drove round the perimeter of the camp on the stone road, coming and going on obscure military business. A headed troop jogged out through the main gate, and several hours later jogged back in.

Steelhand fell to the floor. 'Up!' screeched the superior, running over. 'Superior, I can't,' he pleaded. 'Exhaustion, it is ...' But the superior's hand was on his truncheon, his thumb fidgeting on the button, and with a yelp like an animal, before the button could be pressed, Steelhand scrambled clumsily back to his feet.

We marched on.

Finally we were told to return to our barrack for lunch. Inside a bin of soup was waiting for us; and we clustered around it, too worn out even to talk.

This time we made sure that each of us took a ladleful and then poured away a little from the top, so that there would be enough for all.

'This is the same soup as yesterday. Do they intend never to vary it?' Bil grumbled, as he held his ladleful in front of his shoulder-mounted eye.

'I'm surprised you can be sure it is the same,' said Geza, taking the ladle after him, filling it from the bin and pouring a little back. 'It is not as if we can taste it.' He downed his share and passed the ladle to me. 'I do not doubt that it contains all necessary nutrients and vitamins.'

I filled my ladle, poured a little of the sludge back into the bin, and tipped the remainder into my neck. It hit my stomach like molten lead – so much so, indeed, that I had to sit down after passing the ladle on. I felt the warmth, and felt nauseous, but held on to the contents of my stomach. After a while the sickness went away and I felt a little better. The muscles in my legs were achy, but not impossibly so. I felt strength coming back to me, and with it a slender hope, skinny as a sliver of new moon. Siuzan still possessed her head. In my own case justice had waited more than a week after conviction for my appeal to be heard, and a further day after the genetic materials test before my beheading. It was possibly the case that Siuzan, dizzy (who knows?) with dreams of martyrdom, would not make this legal appeal; but even in that even-tuality I still had several days. Even if the trial happened that very day, and sentence passed, Siuzan would retain her head for thirty more hours.

I had to deduce some way of escaping the compound. Perhaps, I thought (although I flinched as I thought this) I could simply leap from the wall, and run – push on through the pain of the truncheon-effect in my ordinator. It seemed unlikely to me; but perhaps, I reasoned, the effect would cut off after a while. There must be some overload, surely; for the notion that a consciousness could endure such pain for longer than a few moments was impossible to entertain. But contemplating this, I decided it was more likely that the pain would be continuous; and that I would lie in the dirt just beyond the wall until my heart seized and killed me.

Alternatively, I thought to myself, perhaps it might be possible to disable this truncheon effect. I could not think how, and did not assume that it would be easy, or else prior generations of headless conscripts would have discovered it and escaped. But there might be a way.

A third possibility suggested itself to me. Perhaps I might communicate my confession to the police some other way than in person. If somehow I could get to a radio or some other form of ansible, and contact the police, I could confess the crime. I could tell them that only the fact that the military were not prepared to hand me over stood in the way of prosecution. Would that be enough for the police to suspend prosecution of Siuzan? They could hardly raid the camp and arrest me. But perhaps pressure applied, as it were, from one branch of the government to another ...

My attention was redirected to the present by a commotion at the pot. It transpired that, even though we had all assiduously poured back a portion of our ladlefuls, there was still nothing left in the pot for the last man ... in this case Syrophoenician. 'You idiots!' he groaned. 'You greedy idiots, you have taken it all and now I must do without!'

'It appears that they have reduced the ration,' observed Garten dispassionately, 'without informing us.'

'We were not to know,' Geza pointed out. 'It was reasonable of us to assume that the ration would be the same amount as it was yesterday – or the same as it was earlier today, at breakfast.'

'Easy for you to say,' Syrophoenician complained. 'You have a full stomach!'

'Hardly *full*!'

'Fuller than mine!'

'I recall,' Garten said coolly, 'that when this same thing happened to me yesterday, you advised me to be philosophical.'

'What use is your babbling?' demanded Syrophoenician, gesturing theatrically with his arms. 'Your *words* can't fill my empty stomach!'

'What if they reduce our ration every day?' asked another man. 'Eventually we will all starve.'

'It must be some sort of test,' said Steelhand. 'They expect us to pull together and face down adversity.'

'Either that or they just enjoy torturing us,' I put in.

'It is hardly torture,' said Bil Costra, sitting on his bed with his hands folded in at his lap. This was, perhaps, unwise of him.

'You say so, do you?' cried Syrophoenician, going over to him. 'As you sit there with a full stomach? Are you saying it's a *comfortable* thing, going hungry?'

'I only meant that, compared to the truncheon—'

'Is the truncheon the only torture?' squealed an outraged Syrophoenician. 'I say *not.* Are there *other* forms of torture? I say there are.'

'The torture,' I put in, hoping to avert a fight, 'is the uncertainty these actions of theirs create in our minds. It is that uncertainty, rather than any person missing a meal, that is the torture.'

I averted a fight, but only because Syrophoenician left Bil and veered towards me. 'Another headless idiot uncaring of my empty belly, eh?'

'Do not forget, *Sieur* Syrophoenician,' I said sternly, 'that I went without breakfast this very morning.'

Syrophoenician stood very close to me, leaning in with his wide torso, as if to intimidate me. Then he stepped back and wailed, 'Oh how can I spend the rest of the day marching and marching on an empty belly? How can it be done?' He threw his arms into the air, making himself into a Y-shape, a theatrical or operatic gesture.

'You are a comical fellow,' said Garten.

The mood became less fraught, and more comradely. We gathered together in a huddle and discussed how we might determine the number of ladlefuls that were in any given soup bin before we began scooping. One obvious way would be to count them out, emptying each ladle into some second receptacle or tureen; but we had nothing that could serve in this secondary capacity. We discussed the matter at length. One person suggested we each use one of our shoes as a makeshift bowl, but this idea was raucously dismissed. 'We may as well block the toilet bowl with a blanket and pour the soup in there,' shouted Syrophoenician.

'I have a different question,' I said. 'I am very keen to disconnect, or otherwise unprogram, whatever device it is that creates the truncheon effect in our ordinators.'

The group considered this. 'It is surely impossible,' said Geza.

'Why do you say so?'

'Even if we could do it – and which of us would not wish the threat of truncheon-agony lifted from us? – but even if we did it the military would discover what we had done, and would punish us severely.'

'I do not ask this for everybody,' I said. 'But only for me, that I might escape from the camp and give myself over into police custody.'

Several headless murmured at the propriety, or possibility, of this thing. Some insisted that we should consider ourselves as bondsmen; others insisted that we had chosen service freely and that therefore there was no bond. Discussion was cut off by the reappearance of a superior. He ordered us outside.

That afternoon we marched and marched, this time over rough terrain rather than in the parade ground. For the first hour the food inside me, and my resolution somehow still to save Siuzan from her fate, gave me energy; but as the forced exercise was prolonged I began to sag. Clambering up steep and abrasive rocks, that bruised and cut my fingers when I grasped them to obtain purchase for the climb: this quickly became a very disagreeable business.

We climbed the artificial hill. We clambered down the other side. We climbed back up. We climbed down again, such that we found ourselves where we had been before.

'Now,' said the superior, 'you will all turn your headless backs on the hill. Turn about! Sharp!'

We did as we were told.

'You will climb the hill, *without* turning around. Anybody turning around,' yelled the Superior, 'will feel the truncheon. Do you understand?'

All our voices were as one multi-tracked voice. 'Superior!'

'After you have climbed, you will descend. Again you will descend without turning. I will watch carefully, and anybody turning – even for a moment to gain their bearings – will feel the truncheon. Standing, back to the drop, on this irregular slanted surface is *not a place*,' he bellowed, 'where you want to feel the truncheon. Believe me. Perhaps, falling, you might not break your skulls, since you lack those. But you would break other bones. Do you understand?'

As one: 'Superior!

'When you are down on the other side you may take yourself away to the barrack. Begin!'

And so we began the arduous business – really quite astonishingly arduous, much more so than I would have believed. I backed up to the first block, and hopped up onto it as I might have slid myself, sitting, onto a tall table. But then, standing, I could feel nothing behind with my hands, and I had to kick with my heels, and explore by lifting my left foot. Eventually I stepped up, and then nearly unbalanced as I drew my right foot up.

I do not wish to prolong my account tediously. Climbing the artificial hill backwards was a tiresome process of feeling each step of the way. I could see, looking ahead of me, several less rapidly ascending headless stumble on steps, or taking them very slowly. The only reason that I knew I had reached the top was because I very nearly fell backwards in my repeated attempts to feel the next backwards step-up, first with my hand and then with my feet. At this point I sat down.

I tried to prepare myself, mentally, for the downwards journey. Descending *backwards* a chaotic and irregularly arranged staircase, very steep and precipitous, is a difficult thing when you are not allowed to look behind you, or even to angle your torso. Sitting is no good. You must stand, and tentatively run your toe down the step behind you, lowering yourself as far as you need to on your other leg as the toe probes the way down. I alternated my legs, but nonetheless my thighs were stabbing with cramp and pain after only half a dozen steps. Sometimes the steps were very short. On several occasions, on the other hand, I was forced to lie flat on my belly, clutching at what I could with my hands, whilst my dangling feet searched for a base.

At one point I heard a scream, and could not help pulling my shoulder back to give my eyes a glimpse of a headless body – Bil Costra, I later discovered – cartwheeling down. It was an alarming sight, made worse when the screams ended abruptly in a solid noise of collision out of my sight.

Eventually I made it to the ground. The fallen man was on his back on the dirt. His arm fitted into the torso oddly low against his body.

A superior was standing over him. He gave me no specific orders such as *go away* or *return to barracks*, and so I stood and gawped.

'Why are you not on your feet, carcass?'

'Superior, it is my shoulder. It is a cold pain.' I recognised Bil Costra's voice.

'Dislocated,' said the superior, matter-of-factly, and touched his truncheon.

Bil thrashed and groaned on the dirt, so vehemently as to kick up spurts of smoke-like dust. Later, in whispered discussion in the darkened barrack, we decided that the superior had used the truncheon deliberately in an attempt to jerk Costra's dislocated shoulder back into its socket. This might, I suppose, have worked (perhaps the superior had had success with this brutal strategy on previous occasions); for the random lurching and fitting might lever the joint back in. But then again, perhaps this was simply the instinct to punish a soldier lying on his back when a superior was addressing him. It might even, conceivably, have been nothing sadistic, no torturer's instinct. It might even have been a sort of habit. I have thought about this often, in the years since that time – I mean, thought about the superiors' casually brutal attitude to us in general, of which this was one example – and I have come to the conclusion that few superiors used their truncheons maliciously. They had no access to or experience of the sort of pain they were causing their victims; there was nothing comparable for them. I daresay they watched the floppings and writhings of headless men with the same dispassion that anglers watch a fish on the wooden slats of the pier. To them it had, through continued use, become merely a habitual thing.

But in this case the thrashing about, encouraged by the agony that Costra was experiencing, did not reconnect the shoulder bone in its socket. When the superior switched off the truncheon Costra was still twitching on the floor, still moaning, and his arm still seemed connected to his shoulder too low down, a positioning accentuated by his lack of a head. Orders for him to get to his feet had no effect. A second bout with the truncheon produced a markedly more listless thrashing, and then nothing at all. I watched as the superior stood over the body of Costra flicking the switch of his truncheon on, off, on, as if testing an electrical connection. Then he spoke into a lapel microphone, and shortly afterwards two purple-uniformed men came running over and pulled Costra away by his heels.

I made my way back to the barrack, and went through to the toilet at the back. There was no sink, taps or soap in this small room, for it was deemed that the headless needed no such luxuries. If our hands were dirty, then so what? Nobody would touch us, and we had no mouth, nose or eyes to contaminate with restless fingers. Some of the troop would run outside the main door after depositing solid waste in the toilet and rub their hands in the dust to clean them; others were less scrupulous.

But though there was no sink there was a toilet bowl, and in this bowl was water; and after a full day of sunstruck exercise we were all so thirsty that we were no longer fussy about drinking such water. A slender trooper called Cash was in the toilet before me, scooping water into his hands and feeding it, inefficiently, into his neck valve. I followed him. There were people waiting behind me.

After this I lay on my bed and contemplated the muscles in my legs and back, which were shivering with ache and fatigue.

Syrophoenician collapsed onto the bed beside me. 'May the All'God have mercy and compassion in his plan for me,' he wailed. 'For I am about to give up the ghost.'

'What a theatrical fellow you are,' I said.

He rolled onto his front. 'Well, I am, But the way I see it: life needs colour. It needs vividness. What is life without vividness?'

'That's mere tautology,' I said. 'Life and vivid being the same word—'

'Were you a poet or a pedant?' he said.

I laughed. 'They're not so different to one another, I agree.'

At this Syrophoenician sat up. His blue shirt and meadhres were black with sweat, the fabric heavy and sluggish with the weight of his water. 'It is good to hear you laugh, my friend,' he said.

I was very struck by this: partly at his concern, partly at the fact that he considered me his friend. Indeed, it is almost shameful for me to record that it was only my lack of a head that prevented me from crying. I felt the goosebumps rise and fall in a great swathe across my skin, as wind moves and strokes patterns into a field of corn, from my neck stump down to my hips. For moments I could not even speak.

'You are a good man, Syrophoenician,' I said, when I was able.

At this *he* laughed. 'By no means,' he said. 'A good man would have a head. A man without a head is *by definition* not a good man'.

'There is a great deal of honour in you using that word friend to describe me,' I said. 'Friend,' I said, 'I have a favour.'

'Ask it,' said Syrophoenician, putting his arms wide, as if he had the world to give and I need only request it.

'I told you of the woman—'

'Ah,' said Syrophoenician, folding his arms into a self-hug, 'the woman you love. Love is a glorious thing, *Sieur* Jon. For does it not say in the Bibliqu'rân—?'

I interrupted him, to stop him running into a lengthy scriptural digression. 'Your piety is indeed creditable, my friend. But my request is an urgent one. Let me assure you that the woman I wish to save is as pious as you – in fact, she is much more so, indeed—'

'So I should hope!'

'—she is innocent of any crime, yet prepared to suffer beheading rather than send a Headless man to his death. I cannot allow her to do this. The man she would save—'

'You?'

'No, no,' I said, crossly. 'It was not I who assaulted her in that disgraceful manner. But the man who *did* has gone. He is beyond justice.

And by confessing to his crime I can at least save her.'

'At the cost of your own life?'

'A small cost, I think.'

Syrophoenician thought about this for a while. 'It sounds noble, I agree. And that appeals to what you are pleased to call my theatrical soul. But I have a worry. Don't your actions amount to suicide? The Bibliqu'rân is very clear on this matter. Suicide is impermissible.'

'It is an arguable point,' I said. 'For mightn't it rather be considered an act of martyrdom?'

'But you are seeking your own death.'

'I am not,' I said. 'If I had a head to lose I would lose it for this crime. If the justice system decides to spare me I will be glad. But that is not the important thing; the important thing is to save Siuzan from—'

'Ah,' said Syrophoenician, leaning back luxuriantly against the pillow of his bed, 'so her name is Siuzan? My first tender passion was for a girl named Siuzan. I was only a lad. How pure was our dalliance!'

'My friend, I feel I must leave the camp tonight. Since the captain will not hand me to the police, I must go myself.'

'Impossible! To step outside the camp would bring the truncheon down upon you. You might lie in the dust in agony – how many minutes of that suffering would be enough to kill you?'

'I believe you are right,' I said. 'But' – and here I turned my back on him – 'please examine my ordinator. Is there some addition to it, some prosthesis that might be broken off or pulled out?'

I heard Syrophoenician rise from his bed behind me, and after a pause he said: 'Nothing. The modifications they have made must be internal.'

'Is there nothing you can do to—?'

At this point in our conversation the soup-bin trundled in, and Syrophoenician broke away. Then there was a lengthy discussion. 'Bil Costra is not with us,' said Garten. 'I say we can all take a full ladle.'

'But what if they have again reduced the ration?' asked Steelhand. 'What if they have accounted for the absence of Bil and given those that remain less than a ladleful each?'

'In that case,' said Syrophoenician, stating the obvious, 'the last man would go hungry.'

'You should be that man,' said Steelhand, pointing at Garten.

'I went hungry yesterday,' returned Garten. 'Somebody else must go at the end of the line today.'

'Not I!' declared one headless. And then everybody was twittering or whispering 'not I!', 'not I!', 'not I!'

'Let us all take half a ladle,' suggested Geza. 'That way we can be sure, or reasonably sure, of all getting something.'

'That will surely leave a surplus in the pot,' Garten said. 'And how can we distribute that?'

'Let us address that matter after we have eaten our half portion,' urged Geza.

'Perhaps the most needy could be given first access to the surplus?' suggested Cash.

'Most needy?' returned Syrophoenician? 'That would be me! I went hungry at the last meal.'

'That is a mere temporary thing,' said Cash. 'I'm talking about constitutional need.'

'And how should such neediness be defined?' Syrophoenician pressed. 'Do you mean yourself, *Sieur* Cash, because you are so skinny? But why not argue that the larger men have a greater need – since they have larger bodies to feed, and need the nutrient more.'

'Such logic is deficient,' said Cash petulantly.

'Perhaps one ladleful each, from which we return *two* spoonfuls?' suggested Steelhand.

'There is greater risk in that,' opined Garten. 'Would *you* be prepared to be the last in line?'

'Provided two spoonfuls from each ladle are returned to the pot,' said Steelhand, 'then I would.'

'Very well!' boomed Syrophoenician. 'A solution! Let's eat.'

There was a scurry of activity as we took up positions, and Garten was at the head of the line. But he immediately discovered that the soup-bin had closed its lid and could not be persuaded to open it again.

'Infamy!' cried Syrophoenician.

'We spent too long bickering amongst ourselves about portions,' wailed Geza. 'The machine thinks its meal is unwanted.'

And, as if on cue, the bin's motor whirred and the device rolled back and out through the door. Several of the headless ran after it, smacking its top in a hopeless attempt to get at the food within. But they stopped on the threshold, for a superior was there, with his truncheon in his hand.

'To bed,' he called. 'Come eight, and lights out, and you must all be in bed.'

We clambered, weary and starved, into our beds. The numbers on the clock over the door mounted towards eight, and with a snap the lights went out.

I listened, and heard the retreating crunk of the superior's boots on the dirt outside. Everything was quiet.

'Syrophoenician,' I hissed. 'Syrophoenician.'

'*Sieur* Jon,' he replied in a weary whisper. 'I am extraordinarily fatigued. I must sleep.'

'My friend,' I hissed. 'It must be tonight. I *must* do what I can – and do it tonight – to save Siuzan's head. Will you help me?'

He groaned, very low. 'Don't ask me, *Sieur* Jon,' he said. 'I need sleep.'

'It must be tonight,' I said.

'Be reasonable,' he returned. 'You cannot leave the camp. Five minutes after stepping outside – five minutes of unimaginable agony, lying outside the camp wall – and your mind would collapse. You would surely die.'

'Then I must stay *in* the camp, but find some sort of communicator or radio with which to contact the police.'

Syrophoenician made no reply to this, beyond another low moan, but Geza, from the bed on the other side of mine, spoke up. 'I will come with you,' he said.

'Thank you,' I whispered.

We got up and crept to the door of the barrack. It was locked. 'What if there were a fire?' I hissed. 'Would we all simply burn to death?'

'Would the superiors care?' replied Geza.

'Hush,' hissed somebody from the nearest bed.

'I'll try the lock,' said Geza, in a lower voice. For several minutes he fiddled, but to no effect.

'There is a window in the toilet,' I whispered.

Carefully we picked our way along the aisle between the beds and into the toilet. There was the window. Through it the moon, sliced diagonally in half like a silver fruit, gave out its light, cold and strong. It printed a parallelogram of white upon the dark floor, which shape intersected the edge of the toilet. Standing on the seat I could reach the window, and doing so I discovered that it opened perhaps half a metre. 'Is it enough?' hissed Geza.

'I think so.' I pulled myself up to the lip, and wriggled through the space, at every moment half expecting the truncheon to hit me. But it did not, and I dropped, clumsily, to the floor. I landed with a painful impact, but already I had learnt not to call out upon suffering pain.

Geza emerged soon after me, and I was able to catch him as he fell.

The camp looked austere in the moonlight. The mountains had sheathed themselves in a close-woven tessellation of blacks and purples that only added to their grandeur. Though the sky was dark the air was still warm from the day. The perimeter fence was illuminated with blobs of dim purply light at regular intervals, each blot of light standing like a head upon a pole. Buildings, at various locations about the place, were imprinted with lines of orange-lit squares from doors and windows. Otherwise the whole place was deep-sea dark.

We pressed ourselves against the wall and crept round the vertical rim of the barrack. Across the parade ground the nearest buildings were perhaps a hundred metres from us: bright windows like dealt cards placed in an orderly line beneath the bar of a low roof. We stopped. From the shadows we watched a car growling its way along the perimeter road, its headlights sweeping the road like a snout sucking up crumbs. It stopped at the gate. The timbre of its engine faded as it idled. Voices were distantly audible, but no words could be distinguished amongst their buzz, musical as blue-flies. The gate opened and, with a little scurr of acceleration, the car drove through. The gate closed. Silence settled its blanket again on the camp.

Very faintly, beyond the walls, cicadas rang like distant phones.

'Where are we going?' asked Geza. Now that we were outside we were, of course, free from the barrack's sonostat, and there was no need to keep whispering, but nevertheless we continued to do so. Fear had habituated us.

'I suppose – over there.'

There were no spotlights inside the camp perimeter, but the moon made the run across the parade ground a dangerously exposed business. We trotted, trying not to look conspicuous but of course failing in this. It was luck, only, that nobody stopped us. Reaching the block on the far side unchallenged we hunkered down in the shadows at the side of the main ramp. Voices floated in from somewhere, one laughy, the other more level. It was not possible to distinguish individual words, but the tone of the exchange was clear: cheerful, lighthearted. Perhaps there was a window open somewhere above us, and two men inside that room. Eventually the voices stopped. Another car passed, this time coming into the camp, its motor revving up and then fading away as it drove past.

'We must go inside this building, I suppose,' said Geza.

'We must.'

I offered up a silent prayer to the All'God for success, reminding Him that it was not for my sake that I prayed, but for Siuzan, a devout and virtuous woman. But as I did this, it struck me as foolish and impertinent, for the All'God knew her virtue, my intentions, and everything else. The All'God knows everything in the whole echoing, sunbleached cosmos. How puny we must seem to Him; specks crawling on the face of specks circling dots of life. How subatomic our concerns and passions and agonies must appear, from His perspective!

'I suggest,' whispered Geza, 'that we do not skulk into the building, but rather walk up purposefully, as if we have been ordered to come.'

'Very well,' I said.

'That will look less conspicuous, I think.'

'I agree,' I said.

And so we did. We walked straight up and inside. There was nobody on the ramp, and nobody in the hall through the main door. Inside the building we were faced with many doors, all painted the pale blue of the military.

'Where?' I asked irresolutely.

Geza pointed. We stepped towards a door. I felt my stomach tighten. Siuzan's redemption might be on the other side of this door.

It opened on a darkened room, and a wave of my hand before the light pad summoned a yellow glow. Inside were a dozen or more datascreens.

'This is perfect,' I said, hurrying over to the nearest and turning it on whilst Geza closed the door behind us. Its screen flickered blue and white and snapped into focus.

The door opened again. I looked up, and a superior was standing there.

If this officer had come into the room only minutes later than he did, I am certain I would have had time to send my message to the police. I could, conceivably, have typed the whole message, located a sending destination, and processed it in a very little time. But the superior chanced upon us before I had typed a single character.

Geza stood to attention. I, sitting down, rapidly calculated the odds. Everything depended on this, I reminded myself. Siuzan's whole future had distilled itself into a single gleaming droplet of time. Everything that mattered to me, love and honour and the hope for atonement, was now bounded inside the 'o' in the centre of *now*. There were only two possibilities, no others: I could try to bluff my way, to convince the superior that I had legitimate business in that room. Or I could try to type my message, as rapidly as possible, and hope that Geza detained the superior long enough for me to complete it.

Perhaps I should have attempted the first strategy. But I ask you to consider two things: one was that, even in the short time I had been there, the superiors had conditioned me to be automatically and servilely subordinate to them. I regarded them as powerful beings, more powerful and knowledgeable than me. This feeling had already been deeply rooted in my psyche by the truncheon. It did not seem to me likely that I could hornswoggle them. And, secondly, there screen was *there*, in front of me: lit. I needed only type my name and details, and call up a send-address screen, which (surely!) would list all relevant police and civic destinations. It might not even take me two minutes. It might take me—

'What are you carcasses doing in here?' demanded the superior.

—one minute, or perhaps less, and my fingers were already on the keys, and I was scrabbling at the words, mistyping, returning the cursor, retyping.

'Superior!' Geza said. 'I respectfully inform you that we have received orders to—'

'Be quiet!' snapped the superior. 'You there – step away from that datascreen.'

'We have received,' Geza tried again, but the sentence finished with a grunt, and a double thud as he collapsed to the floor.

'You!' said the superior again, at me.

I was halfway through the message. My name was down, my location, and the fact that I confessed – but not yet the crime to which I confessed. I felt the panic bubble inside me. Should I send the message as it was? Would it be enough to call the police to the camp to investigate further? My finger stumbled on the keypad like feet on an icy pavement, and a menu spooled down – containing nothing but military data addresses. I could see no civilian addresses at all. But there *was* a search box. My fingers formed themselves over the keyboard to type 'police'.

My fingers flew up from off the keyboard. My legs kicked straight out with a clatter as they knocked the wall. I grunted, and clamped down upon my pain, even as I was toppling sideways out of the chair.

I knew nothing else, then, except pain.

A little later I stood stiffly beside Geza, and even the fear and proximity of the truncheon could not blot out the realisation that I had failed, for the message remained unsent on the datascreen.

The superior marched us from the room, and gave us over to the custody of another officer. Soon after this, we were marched outside. It struck me that we were at no point interrogated; nobody seemed interested in our motives, or in what we had been up to. I was given no opportunity to plead my case, to urge upon the humanity of the superiors the injustice of an innocent woman losing her head on my account.

A treacly, tar-pit sense of despair was clogging my spirit. I repeated silently to myself the woeful mantra *this can't be happening*, over and over. I tried to convince myself that it was a dream – I had fallen asleep in the barrack, and now I could wake and be given another chance to reach the outside world and save Siuzan. But the sensation of the night air, its temperature dropping away from the heat of day; the sounds of feet on dirt, the quiddity of my experience, all these things were such that I could not truly doubt that I was awake. I wanted very much to disbelieve my senses, but they must be believed. I had failed. Siuzan was doomed.

I assumed, in my broken soul, that I was being marched to execution. Even this belief failed to stir anything in me. If I could not save Siuzan then death was the least that I deserved.

But of course we were not to be executed. In fact, and by the standards of the camp, our punishment was mild: we were hanged upside down, by a rope attached to one leg only, from a frame not far from the barrack. I barely cared. The headless, lacking a head (pardon me for stating the obvious), cannot feel uncomfortable from the sensation of blood rushing there. Instead, batlike, I was a pendant of deadening despair. I had failed Siuzan. Physical discomfort did, eventually, intrude upon my thoughts, but this had the effect of intensifying my self-loathing and misery. The problem was in those of my limbs not actually suspended. The left leg, circled at the ankle, was supported. The right one either folded down so that the knee touched my chest (a most uncomfortable position), or flopped the other way, behind me (which put a painful strain upon my hip); or else I tucked my right foot in behind my left one, which brought relief for a while but which soon enough brought on cramps and sparkles of agony. My arms were easiest if they simply flopped to the side, but this too became unbearable after a while, and I was forced to move them about, fold them against my upside-down chest, or lift them so that they ran along my sides towards my hips. Sleep was out of the question.

But I could not have slept, even had I been tucked into the most comfortable of beds. I was filled with both a brute, acidic fury and a monstrous unhappiness. Or perhaps the fury was the unhappiness, or perhaps it was the unhappiness that took the shape of fury – an impotent and inward-turning fury. It burned me as a fuse, or as a candle-wick, drawing the clogging sour wax up through my inverted body to sparkle into the black sky as stars, silver braided night-black clouds, and the coin-sized sliced half of moon and, eventually, a much larger conflagration just out of sight beyond the eastern horizon that made the eager angles of the mountain range shine and glow like neon. By the dawn I had lost all sensation in my left foot, and had grown used to the continual aching and straining in my body; but the fury in my head was a fresh and flaying as ever.

Geza, dangling three metres from me, said nothing but: 'I am sorry', which phrase he uttered early. I was too consumed in my tormenting self even to answer him. I should have thanked him, for he had tried selflessly to help me and was now suffering on my account. But I was grieving Siuzan. There is nothing more selfish than grief, except perhaps self-hatred, and that too is a form of grief.

Six

The sun had been up an hour or more when two officers came by, released the ropes and dropped us, sacks of meal rather than men, to the dust below. We both pulled ourselves up until we were sitting, and spread our legs before us, rubbing and chafeing the skin to allow the blood back into its former channels.

'Breakfast,' said one of the superiors, and that was all he said. Indeed, at no time then or afterwards were we interrogated, or questioned, as to what we had been doing. I still do not know what the senior staff thought of it – perhaps they assumed it was a prank, or that we were trying to send a message to family, or that we hoped to access illicit or pornographic images of women in underclothing. I don't know. I assume they didn't care. The issue, to them, was whether we obeyed orders or not, and nothing more. A very clarifying perspective on the universe.

Haltingly, we limped into the barrack to find the porridge bin already there and people helping themselves to ladlefuls.

After a night of no sleep, and of furious self-accusation and internal strife, I was exhausted. There was another day of marching and drilling to get through; and I managed to do this. I am not quite sure how: for I was not awake, nor yet asleep, through most of the physical manoeuvres. But for this type of drill the higher mind functions are not only unnecessary, but a positive disadvantage. A soldier with nothing more than a spinal cord could, in a manner of speaking, drill; and this is what I was. I marched. I lay down when I was told to and wriggled under netting on my belly. I trotted back to barrack with the others and partook of soup. I came out again, half-alive, and performed all the physical actions required of me. But my conscious thoughts, of the sort that constitute one's self-aware *I*, were fission-hot and ugly. I relished my bodily discomfort and fatigue and the near hypnotic state in which I worked through the orders, because this is what I deserved for my betrayal of the woman I loved to a shameful execution.

The thought of what I had done, or failed to do, was nettles growing inside my mind.

That evening I returned to the barrack and ate again, but did not take part in the conversation with which the others eagerly filled up the time before the lights went out. They were pleased with themselves for finally having determined the way to share the portion from the soup bin fairly, irrespective of how little, or much (and the portion was, presumably deliberately, very changeable) we were given. Each man took a half ladleful; then the ladle was filled from what remained and passed round everybody who took a single sip before passing it on to his fellow; and the ladle was filled again, if this was possible, until everybody had eaten a whole half-ladle and as many sips as were in the pot. Some inevitably received more sips than others, but we all took turns to move from the front of the line to the back, so over time this evened out.

'We've scored our first victory!' declared Syrophoenician, hand clutching hand and wagging over his head at the ends of his upreaching arms – an absurd, and comical, yet characteristically theatrical gesture of triumph.

I rubbed my forefinger slowly around the anklet of purple that lay, beneath the level of my skin, all around the bottom of my left leg, where it connects with the foot.

Save I alone, everybody was laughing at Syrophoenician's mummery. One or two even cheered, and then the number above the door flipped to 8:00 and the sound was instantly gone.

Day followed day. I buried thought, or at least I tried to do so. I was only intermittently successful. The rote of training helped me. One day we had to walk underwater. 'The ladder is laid along the bottom of the lake,' the superior of the day declared. 'You must walk by tucking your toes under the rungs of this ladder, and in this fashion proceed to the far side. Anybody who floats to the surface will feel the truncheon.' Knowledge of this last detail concentrated the mind very effectively upon tucking under one's toes, and creeping forward through the murky water. The purpose of this exercise was for us to become used to the facts that our new army-issue neck valves contained a ring of breathable compressed air, and that it was possible to relax the metal sphincter such that we could breath underwater – or, we were assured, in space vacuum. It was a strange experience. A quarter of an hour, or maybe a little more, of breathable air had been sequestered by the device from the general air, but it did not feel, as I worked my lungs and hooped my chest inwards and outwards, the way that actual air does. It felt thin and unsustaining, and part of the mind rebelled against the sensation. For some of my comrades this sparked panic; but not to me. I had found, as I moved my feet through the awkward ballet of snagging underwater rung after underwater rung, an ideal correlative to my misery. I was breathing the very air of misery, barely enough to keep life in me. Depression, you see, is a sort of asthma of the mind. It is a strangulation of the emotions. I could not see my feet. I could only see my hands if I tucked them in at the elbows and presented them, directly, to my visual receptors. Everything was particulate and grey.

I emerged from at the far side of the lake, and the heat and light broke over my head like a cosh. It was better in the gunmetal-coloured murk of the lake. That was my element now.

Bil Costra returned to us after his time in the hospital, but a querulous yearning for self-protection had become entwined with his nature. He was over-cautious, which in many of the training exercises proved more dangerous than boldness or even recklessness. He always seemed to be bruising himself. Once he ran at a trench, ordered to leap it, and instead of running hard and trusting his legs to the leap, he stuttered at the edge, and fell, barking his chest against the lip of the far side and snapping his collarbone. For more than a fortnight after that, and despite the intervention of the medical officer (who implanted a staple to link the bones), Costra spoke no words except words of complaint. 'How it hurts,' he would say. 'The edges of the bones rub one against the other. Oh! Oh! Oh!' It was a tedious business listening to him.

I escaped serious injury during training, although I was often bruised. On occasion – though much more rarely than at the beginning – I would receive the blow of the truncheon, as would the others. But where pain continued in hideous freshness for Bil Costra, it became stale and tedious to me, and I paid it little attention.

When I thought of my great failing, things were much worse. Prompted by some oblique association, or chain of associations, Siuzan Delage's face (say) would reoccur to me, and this would provoke the remembrance of what I had done. That would be a bad day. I became fixated upon the illogical conceit that, lacking eyes with which to cry, my tears were building up within me in a reservoir of grief. I knew this was not physiologically possible, for tears are created in the same head that vents them, but it expressed some truth about the way I felt.

Syrophoenician, in his clumsy and bright-coloured way, tried to console me. One time he told me 'What's done is done; it can't be undone. There's no road backwards in time.' But this was no consolation, for it reminded me of the terrible implacability of my action, or rather of my lack of action. If I could go – not even travel myself, but merely send back a voice to myself in the police cell, I would say to my earlier self, *Confess now! Your chance will not come again!* This fantasy played itself through my thoughts many times.

Other times Syrophoenician would say, 'Think how things might have been worse! She will still have her life, even though her head has been taken.' But I knew that, for a person of Siuzan's purity and perfection, a shameful life – a life of headless ignominy – was much worse than death.

On none of these occasions did I reply to Syrophoenician's attempts at consolation. For several weeks I talked to nobody, except once, in a small voice, to thank Geza for attempting to help me, and for enduring the dangling punishment with me. But otherwise I was quite silent, and the troop seemed to accept that I had withdrawn from the world of conversation. They included me, as much as they could; and some evenings before the lights went out it was almost warming to sit in the circle with them all and listen to their chatter. But I did not take part. I had been severed from the world. Or I had severed myself by my cowardice.

In the daytime I pushed my body harder than any of the troop, throwing myself into whatever the Superiors ordered. This won me no plaudits, and did not distinguish me in their eyes; they were not, after all, interested in distinguishing any of the headless, but merely in rendering them efficient machines for prosecuting war. But I found a solace in the blanching fatigue of it, in the bruises and scratches, in the deep creaking ache inside my muscles.

Sometimes I thought of the two companions who had walked with me to Cainon: of Gymnaste and of Mark Pol Treherne. Of the former I could not think with kindliness; the memory of his over-fastidious veracity was acid to the twisted metal sheet of my mind – for he also could have saved Siuzan, if he had chosen, by confessing to the crime, though the confession was a lie. His 'truthfulness' was, to me, nothing more than an absurd and prideful impediment to the saving of Siuzan. Of course I can see now that this simmering fury at Gymnaste was simply a transferred version of my fury at myself. For if Gymnaste could have confessed to the crime, even in his innocence, then how much more true was it to say that *I* could have confessed – asked three times, like Peter the apostle, and denying her three times too. Moreover there had been a greater motivation for me, for it was not Gymnaste but I who had loved her.

Now she was wandering Cainon headless. Some nights I would lie in my bed and ponder where she was; had she returned to Doué, or remained in Cainon? Perhaps she was living amongst other headless continuing her mission, but now as one of the afflicted instead of a saintly headed helper. Perhaps she had made her way to Montmorillon, the Land of the Headless. Perhaps she had been made its queen.

Several of us, myself included, developed clenching, painful guts and a loose and flowing stool, evidently from drinking from the toilet, which was not a clean source of water. Of course, once the diarrhoea started nobody wanted to drink from the toilet any more. The urge to defecate would possess me, and I would become no better than a cow producing its gushing cow-flop. If I were in the barrack I would run to the toilet. If it was occupied, as sometimes it was, I would find myself compelled to pour my lower guts upon the floor, and afterwards I would have to scoop it up with my bare hands – painstakingly wiping away every mark and streak with my fingers – or risk the truncheon in the morning. This was a filthy business, which I would perform completely naked, and after (if I had enough uninterrupted time) I would wash my body with toilet water and flush the last of it away. If I felt the telltale griping in my gut during parade, I begged permission to excuse myself. Sometimes this was granted; but if the superior were not in the mood this might result in me soiling myself and the ground beneath me. Then I would have to dig a bowl out of the dirt to contain my effluent and cover it over, and could only clean myself after with dust. My meadhres, hideously caked on the inside, I would clean in the toilet later when the chance arose.

There were several other of the troop in the same position as I. But I alone secretly revelled in my degradation. This was what I deserved.

'We have been foolish,' Syrophoenician complained. 'We ought to have reserved the toilet only for drinking, and not polluted it with our bodily wastes.'

'Perhaps,' scoffed Garten, 'you feel we should have held inside all our waste matter, by holding our breath and crossing our legs?'

'But,' Syrophoenician insisted, 'we might have gone outside and dug holes in the dirt in order to—' But before he could complete this sentence Syrophoenician was compelled to run moaning to the toilet, where he stayed for long minutes.

'Our preacherly comrade forgets,' said Costra, to nobody in particular, 'that the barrack door is locked at night. What must we do in that circumstance?'

Eventually our guts restored themselves. Nobody risked drinking from the toilet after that. We were often thirsty, but it seemed that there was enough fluid in our soup to keep us alive.

Several weeks passed for me in a sort of purposeless, unfocused agony, the only release from which was the mentally uncoupled business of drilling, of training. Depression is a silting down of thought, a sliming over of the pebbles that constitute the course of thought's bright flow. It is a cumulative thing. It becomes a habituated state of mind.

Every two weeks we were ordered to line up in the Medical Officer's anteroom. We were not seen singly; instead a nurse came out – white-uniformed, but with the pale blue armband of a regular officer. Each fortnight he gave us each our pharmocopy pouches, and plastic cups of clean water, and we gobbled them down.

Outside the brightness of the sunshine was like a form of bleach; it overloaded the information processing capacities of my software. The height and near-palpable weight of the mountains beyond the perimeter seemed, somehow, a specific rebuke to me.

We learnt to fight without weapons, the forceful ballet of punches and hand strokes that might disable or kill an unarmed enemy. 'I do not believe,' declared Syrophoenician one evening, 'that we will ever encounter an unarmed enemy. We will have guns, as will they. We should concentrate upon mastering guns. This training is fruitless.'

'I disagree. I may use it,' said Geza, 'upon my comrade headless, if he becomes too preacherly.'

'And *I* may use it,' laughed Syrophoenician, 'to defend myself against cowardly assault.'

It is not possible, I daresay, to maintain the full intensity of rage on any subject for more than a few weeks, even on such a one (*The woman I loved! The one woman in my life I was fated to love above all others! The perfect woman – violated and beheaded!*) that touched me so completely. Fire, being a combustion, is always in the process of rendering itself inert. I found that my fury became a feature of my existence, like a leg or a lung. What I mean by this is that it became something that only very rarely intruded itself on my consciousness. It did not fade and it did not vanish, but it ceased to occupy the centre of my thoughts. What is inside a volcano? Is it the fire and gleaming lava that washes the face with heat? Or soot and black dust, choking hillfuls of choking ash? Or perhaps the question should be: which quantity outweighs the other? This is a difficult mathematics.

I settled.

My misery became habitual to me, and therefore a matter of indifference. I suppose, had I thought about it, I might have preferred my medium to be happiness rather than misery; but I did not think about it. Thought was no friend. Better was the drill.

Then there was a moment that crystallised my fury, as if the pressure that my continuing to live had subjected it to was now, suddenly, producing diamond. This revelatory moment came when our superiors gave us our first weapons. This was nothing more than a basic needlegun, although in due course I handled all the weapons that one person can carry: from enormous club-guns and frock weaponry down to suckers, shunt pistols and projectile pistols. But our training had to begin somewhere, and so it began with needleguns on the firing range within the camp.

We fired the weapons on the range at flat targets that lurched and scurried on robot mounts. Eventually we were even taken outside the camp (the truncheon pathways in our ordinators disabled I suppose) to dance the gun-dance, shoot-dance, spot-the-target-dance, amongst the boulders and jetsam of the lower mountain slopes. Here our targets were automated to shoot back at us, although with pebbles rather than needles. But of course to be struck by a fast-flying pebble was bruising and potentially bone-breaking, and so we danced the dance as our superiors instructed us. Roll and duck, leap and run, boulder to boulder.

Aiming, since both the binocular vision and the single-eye sightings of the headless are equally vague, involved pointing the weapon where the target was, and then adjusting the aim as the little screen on the top of the butt advised us. 'For those of you who have talent for this,' a superior announced, marching behind us as we pinged and ta-tatted away, 'will be given better weaponry – guns that plug into your ordinators directly, such that your visual software can interpret the muzzle camera data directly.' He offered this as if it were a great prize.

But I had discovered a greater prize. For the first time in my life I had a gun in my hands. And the target I was shooting at was, to my mind, Mark Pol. All the associations of him that fed into my mind printed out the same word: *revenge*. It was he who had violated Siuzan – which, given her exacting purity and piety (which caused her to deny the assault to save the life even of one as unclean as him), meant that *he* was the one who had struck off her head. I swore a great, though silent, oath: I would survive whichever campaigns the army sent me on, and then I would return to Pluse and I would find Mark Pol and kill him. With each twitch of my finger, and each friendly tap of the butt upon my shoulder, with each squrling puff of dust from a target hit, the fantasy of *revenge* bedded down inside me. I had planned to kill Mark Pol and then save Siuzan. It was too late now for the latter; but the former portion of my plan could still act as pole star to guide me through life.

I fingered the eye stalk, my fragment of him, my holy relic. This was the most precious thing I possessed.

Seven

The weekly trips to church on Holy Day and the fortnightly doses of pharmocopy pouches marked the time away. Eventually our food became more amply provided, and a separate bin brought us clean water. The earlier experiences had been part of the army's strategy for breaking us before reassembling us according to their template. Truncheon punishments became rare. Every now and again, it is true, one or other of us in the barrack would cry aloud at night – at a nightmare, perhaps – and all of us would be woken by piercing rods of agony filing up and down our long bones. But on these occasions we never shouted with the pain. Even the man who had provoked the sonostat would silence himself when he felt the pain inside his body. We had been conditioned.

The life rhythm of the camp became second-nature to us. We watched the headed soldiers being trained, although we never interacted with them. There were two other troops of headless being trained at the same time as us, one who had begun the process six months before us, and one that had come in after we had mastered the basics. We had some exchanges with these individuals, on such occasion as we ran across them, but mostly we kept ourselves to ourselves. Now, when the new recruits first arrived in camp, I made it my business to go amongst them (as none of the more experienced headless had done with us, on our arrival). But I did this because I was interested in one thing only: whether Mark Pol had joined, or been recruited, or otherwise press-ganged into the army. It seemed to me possible, that a shiftless man, prone to violence and marked as shameful by the lack of his head, would enter the military. But he was not in that batch of recruits, and neither was Gymnaste.

I waited. I was spiderlike. The gravitational centre around which my life rotated was now revenge. It might seem that I was hurtling away from Mark Pol, but I would sweep round and soar back, a comet bringing disaster to his life. This was a vow that I made.

From time to time we would hear the huge clanging, repeat-explosive sound of a spaceship lifting off. We might be on the parade ground, or training with weapons, but the sight of the great whale-shaped craft hammering itself into the sky would stop us wherever we were. It is a splendid sight, the kind of thing of which a person never grows bored. On occasion a ship would land. This produces a very different set of noises; a growing, frictive screeching noise, and sonic boom, and finally a great roaring that crescendos like the final movement of a symphony. After landing the craft would sit on the kilometer-wide concrete circle and do nothing but produce enormous creaking and snapping sounds as its superstructure cooled.

Over time the people in the troop became more like themselves, as if perfecting stage roles which they had previously played only as amateurs. Syrophoenician became more circus-ringmasterish as the time passed. Geza became more contemplative. Garten more insistent – indeed, and although he was *prideful*, as the chief of my old Masjud used to put it, none of us thought badly of him. We pardoned him his pride, not because we were charitable, but because he was a comrade. Bil Costra became more obviously cowardly, always attempting ineptly to preserve himself from harm and thereby making the injury worse.

I was chosen as gunman, and an input was added to my ordinator so that certain weapons could be plugged in by optical cable. Doing this had the effect of giving me a third eye, which, by triangulating the field of vision (and by virtue of the fact that military technology of this sort was of a higher calibre than civilian prostheses) gave me a much sharper and more vivid field of view. I saw details at great distance; things appeared rounder, deeper, more crisply demarcated against their backgrounds. I could also, by willing it, call up a variety of targeting patterns that appeared, like spiderwebs of luminous dew, over my field of vision.

Then, one morning, a superior stepped into the barracks just behind the porridge bin. We all stood at attention by our beds.

'You are,' he announced, without preliminary, 'the Thirtieth Troop of Cainon Headless.' We had not, before, been given a troop designation.

'Superior!' we sang, in absolute unity of voice.

'Your training is complete. You are soldiers now. Some of you were soldiers before, and you'll know that, on completing their training, headed soldiers receive the congratulations of the captain. But you headless do not merit congratulation. No matter how well, or badly, you have completed your training, you have not yet atoned for the crimes that truncated you.'

He paused, and we filled the gap with a loud, bright shout: 'Superior!'

'But you will have the chance for atonement. Tomorrow you ship offworld. There is no drill today.'

He turned and left.

It was a startling thing. We ate our porridge, and then we gathered in a huddle. Our experience had taught us not to make decisions singly, and now, as a troop, we had to decide what to do with the day. 'Safest,' said Costra, 'just to stay in our barrack.'

'I may,' announced, Syrophoenician, in an excessive luxuriant tone, 'sleep all day!'

'Do you suppose the sonastat will be off?' asked Garten.

'*Sieur* Garten,' said Syrophoenician gaily, 'we may sing and dance and shout the roof to splinters if we wish!'

And, indeed, something of Syrophoenician's gaiety infected us all that day. It felt as if shackles had been uncoupled from our limbs. 'Of course,' Geza pointed out, 'many of us will go to our deaths. We are to be sent to fight in the Sugar War, I suppose.'

'What are soldiers for,' asked Syrophoenician, 'if not war?'

'The Thirtieth Troop of Cainon Headless,' said Steelhand, trying out the phrase for its grandeur and resonance. 'Is it prideful to take pleasure in this?'

'By no means,' I said.

'For in the Bibliqu'rân, does it not say—' Syrophoenician began pompously. Laughingly we shouted him down, and several of us leapt playfully upon him, to stifle this preacherly affectation. It was in no way an act of disrespect to the Faith of the Book, but rather an expression of the high spirits of the moment.

We sat about talking, or sleeping, or playing hand games (such as gun-stone-paper, or finger-wager) for the whole of the morning. The sense of luxury was so intense it almost soured the enjoyment. The soup bin came by at lunch, and we ate. After this half a dozen of our number stepped out of the barrack, to make their way to the church for prayer. I slept for an hour, the food in my belly pulling me down into slumber.

Later it became clear that the group was becoming restless. Unused to inactivity, the novelty had passed off and left behind only a restless sense of the wrongness, almost the sinfulness, of doing nothing.

'Come *Sieur* Cavala,' boomed Syrophoenician. 'You were a singer-poet – this we all know. Yet we have none of us heard your poetry!'

'Not so,' I objected. 'My last recital received only a chilly reception.'
'But sing us something now! We'll surely be more appreciative.'

I demurred. I knew no songs except my own, and they, I insisted, would not be appropriate to the occasion. But the rest of the troop joined Syrophoenician in insisting, and eventually I sang, unaccompanied:

> On the cold hill and under the sky,
> Standing alone in fall weather,
> Lonely winds passing by
> As I and my sorrow walked together.
> Then gone, gone.
>
> The swallows were swinging themselves
> Through the sky over my head,
> Flitting in sixes and in twelves
> Repeating what my sorrow said,
> And then gone, gone.
>
> My whole self, my body and spirit:
> To keep, or cast aside?
> To claim or disinherit,
> Or do as the winds decide?
> Gone, gone, gone.

The mood after this recital was subdued. 'Well,' Syrophoenician said. 'That was no war chant.'

'That does nothing to make the blood pump more vigorously,' agreed Geza.

'You asked, and I obliged,' I said, feeling snubbed. 'I am going to lie down and try to sleep.'

'Does anybody else know a song?' asked Syrophoenician, in his penetrating voice. 'A more *cheery* song?'

'When you are this troop's first casualty of the Sugar War,' I told him, 'I shall compose your lament, and *that* will be a jolly ditty.'

He laughed. 'Since your rejoicing is indistinguishable from your lamenting,' he returned, 'I may thank you in advance for the elegy.'

'You are a cardboard fellow ...'

'And you,' he returned, 'are the soldier of the doleful countenance.'

'Come!' I cried, breaking into laughter myself. 'Let us play finger-wager, you and I.' My spirits, unaccountably, were suddenly high. I told myself: once the training is over, then to war. Once the war is over, then back home and to my revenge.

Eight

The following morning we were ordered to an equipment shed, and fitted with body armour, made from some chitinous and matt material. After this we marched to the huge blasted concrete circle from which ships landed and launched.

We filed over to the arching side of the craft, where it curved up and away from us like a smooth mountain overhang. We mounted the ramp. I felt the childish urge to reach out and touch the hull as I passed through the hatchway, for I was strangely moved by the thought that *this structure had been in space*, but I restrained myself.

The notice over the hatchway gave us the name of the craft: the *Heron*.

We trooped along and through to our hold, and here we had seats. Excited, we bubbled with conversation and speculation. Laughter passed through the group infectiously.

The hatch to our hold was closed from outside. We settled ourselves and waited. After a while we heard the engines growl into life, the noise swelling. The floor lurched. Those of us not in our seats hurried to occupy them. Then the craft leapt into the sky. With a tremendous vehemence that shook us like dried peas inside a rattle, the jackhammer drive punched the ship forward. We were squeezed into our seats, and then flopped forward; another explosive burst and we were squeezed back, and then flopped forward. I felt the porridge, still in my stomach from breakfast, threaten to bulge up into my throat.

We jerk-hurtled on, a great hammer striking against the anvil of the sky and always falling through it to reach higher.

The last of the explosive thrusts passed, and there was a period of silence and weightlessness that seemed to last a very long time. Then the engines growled to life again, and a more continuous thrust brought a half-gravity to the hold.

We were silent for a while, but conversation soon started up again.

Naturally we were nervous, and uncertain as to what the future held for us.

'It seems to me futile to assert,' said Syrophoenician, 'as those beheaded for blasphemy attempt to assert, that there is no God.' He slapped the wall panel beside the pallet upon which he was sitting. 'How else is this craft powered?'

'You are making a schoolchild's error,' said Geza.

Syrophoenician walked forward and pressed his torso against the torso of Geza – had he still possessed a head, he would have glowered intimidatingly down upon him. But Geza was unintimidated. He pushed the other man away. 'You think the All'God pilots this spaceship?' he said disdainfully. 'You think as a child thinks. Does the All'God have a white beard, a long white beard, as he sits in the pilot's seat?'

Syrophoenician notched his volume up. '*Does* this craft move faster than the speed of light?'

Geza declined to answer.

'Is this *possible*, in our material universe? To travel faster than light? Answer me!'

'Simply because the particle is named as it is ...' Geza began.

'*Can* this ship achieve the impossible? It *can!*' boomed Syrophoenician. 'Does it operate according to the logic of the natural world? No, it operates according to the supernatural! It is, in my view, heresy to assert otherwise.'

'Be quiet with your preaching,' grumbled Garten. 'We were none of us beheaded for blasphemy.'

'This one', (Syrophoenician threw his arm out theatrically to point at Geza), 'denies the divinity of the God particles pouring from the nose-cone of the—'

'Be quiet,' called Garten again. 'You old bladder – quiet I say.'

Syrophoenician sat himself back down. God particles have anti-gravitational properties, possessing also anti-momentum, and they leech backwards along the track of time. The *Heron* aimed a blast of these particles forwards, and these in turn acted upon the minutely porous texture of spacetime in a certain way – which way depends upon how you best like to think it. You may wish to think of them as reversed in their momentum and therefore *pulling* the ship after them, backwards in time and *therefore* faster than light – for travelling against the line of time must, necessarily, involve travelling through space faster-than-light. Why must this be? Because only thus do we roll the correct way, the *only* way, down the gradient of cause and effect. Or, if you prefer, you may wish to think of them as cutting through the texture of spacetime, opening an elongating and receding pocket of no-space, or true-space, or what you will, through which the ship slips. Or, if you prefer something else, you may wish to think of God particles as the aura of the Holy Spirit, or Jibreel, or the All'God Himself, and that by conjuring them from the three lenticular generators the Heron is touched by the tip of the little finger of the All'God, or nudged by the breath of His nostril, or winked away by the slicker of His eyelid (I have heard all three of these idioms used) into beyond-*c*. Each of these three explanations is a way of talking.

'If our spaceship is not powered by the God particles pouring from its nose,' said Syrophoenician, evidently in an argumentative mood, 'then perhaps you may explain to me, *sieur* soldier, how is it that only the godly may travel this way?'

'Another fallacy,' retorted Geza.

'You assert that the ungodly travel through space?'

'Indeed they do.'

'But not *faster than light* – only faith in the All'God permits travel that is faster than light.'

'You are wrong.'

'Solider!' barked Syrophoenician, in imitation of a superior, with a metallic and sneering edge to his words. 'Your words are rotten and decayed, because your mind is rotten and decayed. Everybody knows that only the godly may travel faster than light.'

'A popular fallacy,' said Geza knowingly, 'is still a fallacy, for all its popularity.'

Everybody in the compartment was now paying close attention to this exchange. Some were laughing.

So Syrophoenician, playing up to his crowd, adopted the tone of a popular preacher of the sort that is seen sometimes upon television. 'My son, you stray from the truth. It is well known that God denied faster-than-light travel to the ungodly so that the colonisation of the universe might be accomplished by believers, whilst the unbelievers stagnate and remain in Mondial-Earth.'

At first it seemed as if Geza, being made the laughter object by Syrophoenician's extravagance, was going to refuse to answer. But he could not resist the provocation. 'I concede,' he said eventually, 'that *most* of the colonised worlds are part of the congregation of the Book ...'

'... and worship the All'God ...'

'But there *are* secular worlds. Such places exist. Worlds colonised by the nonbelievers.'

'Devil worlds!' chuckled Syrophoenician. 'And now I insist that you listen to the *true* history of space exploration.' And here, despite inter-jections of protest from Geza, he related a cartoonish account of the first wave of settlers from the Mondial-Earth – all, he said, devout believers in the Book, fleeing the corruption and secularisation of a world gone to the bad, leaving behind an infuriated secular population prevented, by their lack of faith, from utilising God-particle drives.

'No! No!' Geza could not help himself. '*God particle* is only a manner of speaking – this particle is simply another elementary particle, like the others, except that it has certain unusual properties ...'

'The *God* particle,' said Syrophoenician, holding up his hand, as if by simply restating the common name he was making an irrefutable point. '*The* God particle.'

'We would better call it the gluonic photino – serious scientists do not refer to it as ...'

'I'd say,' interrupted another soldier, whose name was Hoppier, 'that you have lost the argument, Soldier Geza. Don't be a carcass. Accept your defeat!'

'You are arguing not against me,' said Syrophoenician piously, 'but against the All'God.'

There was general laughter.

Geza, puffing and clicking at his neck stump, moved across the floor away from the main group, and sat down next to me. I do not know why he chose me; perhaps my silence led him to believe that I did not share the mocking hostility of the others. In this he was half-right; for I felt neither hostility nor warmth towards him.

He lectured me for a while, myself remaining unresponsive, about how, whilst the majority of settlers who left Mondial-Earth in the first wave of settlement belonged to the faith of the unified Book, many groups of settlers came other faiths, and some from no faith at all. 'It is peasantry, and ignorance, to believe, as this carcass does, that only believers can travel faster than light.'

Something in his despairing outrage touched me. 'Perhaps,' I offered, 'Syrophoenician does not truly believe so simplistic a thing.'

Geza sat in silence for a while. 'And he says so ...?'

'Perhaps from sheer delight in contention.'

'But of course this,' said Geza, in a bleaker voice, 'makes me a double fool. Once for being bested by him in argument, and twice for falling for his raillery.'

'You should not trespass upon your own self-esteem over so small a matter,' I suggested.

For a long time he was silent. There was a growl from all the walls of the thrust engines increasing their load, and then the floor angled by about five degrees, causing much slipping and staggering and accompanying merriment amongst the soldiers. The *Heron* was turning, the shift in its accelerated gravity revealing a last-minute adjustment.

The floor straightened again.

'Preparing to travel faster than light!' somebody cried. 'Have a care, Geza – you'd better firm up your faith, or we'll leave you behind!' Everybody laughed. Their laughter, it seemed to me, masked a nervousness. Few of this crowd had ever travelled through space before; nor had I myself. In the face of the unexpected we blustered.

'The irony is,' said Geza, angling his body towards me and speaking low, such that only I could hear, 'is that I *am* a devout man, probably more so than soldier-carcass Syrophoenician over there. I attended the Masjid of Saint John, a famous school. I stayed there for three years after the end of my basic education, to learn more about the nature of the faith. And yet it offends me to hear science and religion muddied in this manner.'

'Speaking purely for myself,' I said, since it appeared that some response was required, 'I would say ...'

I stopped. I had no idea what I was saying. For a moment I could not remember what we had been talking about, or even to whom I was speaking.

'What was I saying?'

'I don't know,' said the headless man sitting next to me. 'What were we taking about?'

'I am Jon Cavala,' I said.

'Geza,' said the headless man.

'Those individuals – headless, all,' I said. 'They were laughing. Were they not?'

'We,' said Geza, as the realisation dawned on him, 'have just been projected through space faster than light.'

But of course this was it. One cannot travel faster than light without also travelling, in effect, back in time; and the effect of this backward temporal motion, woven intimately with the relativist consequences of moving so rapidly, is that any journey, no matter how lengthy, takes literally no time at all. But it takes no time because it travels forwards and backwards in time at the same rate and at the same time – or more accurately, because time is simultaneously dilated forwards and reversed. And this in turn interferes with any mental processes that are tagged to time, such as memory. It is said that fleshly brains cope with the aporia better than individuals whose minds live inside mechanical devices.

Computation inside an ordinator is literally parcelled out by timing devices, and these are muddled by such an experience.

I do not know how much of my conversation with Geza was lost to my memory by the passage faster than light. Eventually the mind fills in the gaps, draws on long-term memory (it being less temporally marked), and a picture of the whole passage settles into a mental narrative. But in the immediate aftermath we were confused. The headless who had been laughing stopped in mid laugh, and looked around in puzzled surmise.

'We have arrived,' somebody said portentously.

There was no announcement made, either before or after the faster-than-light passage. Why should headless be kept informed of what was going on? Nobody said, 'We have arrived at the world of Athena, and will soon be entering orbit.' I daresay that headed passengers were kept informed; but what point was there in talking to the headless?

Time carried on. Some of the headless switched on the television inset in the wall of the quarters and watched various programmes. Others lay their truncated forms down and slept.

As for me, I lived again the memories with an uncomfortable freshness, as they returned to me, of my betrayal of Siuzan Delage, the woman I loved – my stupidity and delay, offered two chances to save her with my confession and rejecting them both. I considered the fact that she was now certainly headless, and living a shamed life on Pluse. All this, with a little mental effort of recall, was still clear in my head. And recalling these things brought back some of the anguish I had felt before. Yet there had been a breach in the continuity of my emotions. Travelling faster than light had jarred the thread of my depression, perhaps had even *broken* it, even if only for a moment – and try as I might I could not gather it up again so as to experience it as I had before.

Don't misunderstand me: I felt no relief from my own shame, and I didn't curse my stupidity any the less for poor Siuzan's undeserved fate. But somehow my mood was less severe. I chatted with my comrade headless. I felt a curious feeling, close to elation, at the prospect of descending to the surface of Athena, and facing battle for the first time. Perhaps this paints me in a fickle light. But I cannot, in a memoir dedicated to rigorous truthfulness, disguise the fact. Perhaps I *was* fickle in this matter.

The first we, in our quarters, knew that the ship had gone into orbit about Athena was a change in the tone of the thrust engines, a slew of changes of direction in the arrow of our pseudo-gravity, and finally weightlessness.

At first we soldiers mostly laughed and frolicked in the weightlessness. It seemed a fine sport; and, lacking inner ears, none of us felt in the slightest bit nauseous. But after a while it palled. This same lack of an inner ear meant that a headless man can orient himself in empty space only very poorly; we floated not like swimmers or ballet dancers, but as clumsy men, banging and knocking our bodies. Soon most of us had strapped ourselves down to our benches, and lay or sat sullenly, waiting for the next stage.

Food and drink was delivered. The television, as our only mental distraction, remained continually switched on. People, imperfectly remembering their former friendships, chatted nervously. 'Do you remember what the war is about?' 'Do you remember what the war is *called*?' 'Which side are we fighting on?'

'It is called the Sugar War,' said Geza.

This prompted our memories. 'Yes – that is it.' 'Yes of course.' 'I remember the name.' And so on.

I fingered my talisman; my blue knuckled stalk of plastic. It meant something to me, but for a moment I could not remember, exactly, what.

Nine

We had been dropped onto the world Black Athena. I did not discover, in my time there, whether the 'Black' was part of its official name, or was simply a nickname, or unofficial designator – for the world, such as I saw of it, was black indeed. In the night-time no stars were visible, and the world's three moons were all so small as to be nothing more than sliding points of light, distinguishable from the lights of orbiting battlecraft only by the fact that they were a pale cream colour instead of the reds and mauves of the artificial lights. And in the daytime the sunlight barely penetrated. So much polarising agent had been pumped into the air – in the area of the battlefields at least – that a very little smoke blackened the air completely. Flares were often launched into the air, to provide light for assaults, but they merely added to the problem by contributing more smoke to the environment.

Fighting in this medium was like fighting in a black fog, except that the polarising agent did not deaden sound. All the crashes, the violin screeches and high-pitched whistles, all the sub-base rumblings, all the screams and shouts of wounded and dying men – these remained egregiously audible throughout.

We were shipped forward, and left in a warehouse building. A superior inspected us. He was wearing battledress: the rubbery-textured leggings and armings, the stiffer material of his torso guard, and a strange multiple-panelled helmet the design of which was new to me, with many baffle wedges and fins upon it, like a strangely petalled flower a metre high. His face – eyes, nose, mouth – poked from the midst of this protection through the triangular slot into which, in combat, a guard plate was slotted.

'Headless,' he said. 'You will shortly be shuttled to the attack zone. Prepare yourself! Your training has brought you to this place – and glory and atonement wait those who fight bravely.'

'Superior!' we cheered.

'You will be joining, and reinforcing, the Fortieth Troop of Doué

Headless and the Seventh Troop of Didion Headless, so as to press again the attack. It is vital we take this objective.'

We were given three bins of food, and left to our own devices. We slept. We were ordered up, and went outside to a dented and rather dirty transport, thrumming its engine impatiently in the darkness – it could have been the middle of the night, or perhaps the middle of the day. We bundled in.

The ride was a bouncy one, and various strange sounds – clucks and knocks, keening noises and sudden bangs – were audible through the porthole-less walls. At the far end we were unloaded and hurried into a dirigible building, an oval-arching warehouse space. Here were the other troops of which the superior had spoken.

They were in their battle armour, and were clutching their weapons, gathered in knots of two or three people about the place. We, the Thirtieth Troop of Cainon Headless, moved amongst them; but they seemed unexcited to see us. 'Hello!' I tried, settling myself on one man. 'I am Jon Cavala, of the Thirtieth Troop of Cainon Headless.'

'Harsent, of the Fortieth Troop of Doué Headless,' he replied in a dull voice.

'You have already been in battle?'

'I have. I returned with my life, to spend an hour coughing my lungs free of the hardfoam – no pleasant business, I can tell you. Have you been in combat before?'

'No,' I said.

'But you feel yourself well trained, and prepared?'

'Indeed.'

'Perhaps you are even excited?'

'I am glad,' I said, 'to have finished training. I am eager to get past the war. I have business on Pluse to which I must return.'

'You must not think me unfriendly,' said this Harsent without pause. 'I wish you luck in battle, and I hope you do not die. I hope, indeed, that you return to Pluse to complete your business. But I cannot befriend you.'

'This is abruptly said,' I pointed out.

'Indeed. But if I befriend you and you are killed, as is more likely than not given your inexperience, then I suffer the pain of losing a friend. This I am disinclined to endure.' He stood up, hoisted his snub-gun, and walked away.

I made my way back to my own comrades, and found Syrophoenician complaining of the inhospitality of these troops. 'It approaches treason, in my opinion. My friendly advance was rejected imperiously.'

'The same has happened to me,' I said.

'Leave them be,' suggested Geza.

We newcomers sat in a ring, talking intermittently, and sometimes stopping to listen to one or other sound effect – a whizz, a bang, a drumroll, or the interspersed silences which assumed the palpable intensity of anticipation in this context. Below all these noises there was a strange throbbing almost-sound, an ultra-low base note that swelled and receded, but which never departed.

Within the hour three superiors entered. We stood to attention in a dozen rows. All three of them were wearing the strangely finned and petalled helmets.

'Troops!' said the first superior. 'The assault will take place in one hour. Fortieth and Seventh, to you I say: with the new reinforcements of the Thirtieth Troop of Cainon Headless we will press again at the salient and be successful.'

We – the Thirtieth – cheered 'Superior!' in unison. The soldiers from the other troops did not speak; although they were standing smartly enough at attention.

'To you,' said the superior, turning in our direction, 'I shall say what the Fortieth and Seventh already know. It is usual in battle for headless troops to be commanded by superiors. For strategic reasons, this is not possible in the current assault. Accordingly, your battlefield commander will be Aolis of the Fortieth. He has your orders, and you must follow him unthinkingly.'

A headless stepped forward. He marched over to us, and spoke. His words emerged slightly doubled, once in muffled form from beneath his torso armour, and once from an amplifier set upon his neck stump. I assumed that this was so we could hear his commands clearly.

The superiors were leaving, walking with loose strides towards the entrance. 'Salute the superiors!' shouted Aolis.

'Superiors!' we yelled.

They did not look round as they exited.

'Very well,' said Aolis to us. 'You may as well sit yourselves. I will attempt to prepare you for what is to come.'

We arranged ourselves in rows, sitting cross-legged. Aolis stood. His torso armour, I could see, was banded with gold stripes, to identify him as our point of command in the murk outside.

He began without preliminary and spoke without force or emphasis, as if reciting words from rote. 'Are you trained in specific weapons, or are all trained in all?'

None of us answered, since he had not addressed any of us in person. 'You,' he said, pointing to somebody in the front row – Garten, as it happened.

'All are trained in all, Superior,' Garten replied. 'Though some have been given software augmentations for sniper work.'

'Do not call me "Superior",' he said blandly. 'I am no superior, but a battlefield officer and nothing more.'

'Then what should be call you?'

'You should call me Aolis.'

It seemed, to me, strangely indecent for a subaltern to address a person in authority baldly by their name. But this was what was ordered, and this is what we did.

'You,' he made a sweeping gesture with his arm, 'will collect needle-guns. You,' picking some further back, including myself, 'will collect club-guns. And you at the back, pick out frock weaponry – all save you...' He was pointing now at Syrophoenician.

'My name is Syrophoenician,' said Syrophoenician

'I do not care to know your name,' Aolis said without emotion. 'By tomorrow, or the day after at the latest, many of you will be dead. I choose not to clutter my memory with the names of people I won't need to remember hereafter.'

I thought to myself, *This is a poor way to plump up the morale of soldiers about to go to war!* But of course I said nothing.

'As soon as I am finished speaking go fetch your guns. You will need them outside – I mean, or course, that you will need them for fighting, but just as important you will need them as eyes. It is murky, and you will need the guns to help see your way.' He stopped, seemed to be thinking. Then he said: 'Your pain sensitivity has been tuned down. They cannot turn your pain off wholly, or you lose coordination and sensation and become useless. But they have turned it down, so you will not feel the pain as badly as otherwise you might.'

'I am not afraid of pain, Aolis,' said Syrophoenician grandly.

Aolis angled his torso to look at him, but said nothing.

'Our salient is a hill, well fortified. There are no enemy troops there, so the defenders are all distance-remotes and automates. But there are very many of these, and more are being shipped-in all the time. The battle resolves itself into destroying as many of these as possible, until such time as we are able to break through and destroy the salient.' He thought some more, and even turned back to his comrades away on the other side of the warehouse, such that several of us thought he had finished and started getting up to go and fetch our weapons. But then he turned back and said: 'We have our own remotes and automates, of course, but they are as sluggish and dim as the enemy's. If we left the battle to the machines it would be like . . .' He dried, unable to summon words. He rubbed his hands together, and then had a thought: 'It would be like watching two computers of equal processing power play chess together, a thing seemingly endless, and bound eventually to be drawn.' He seemed pleased with this analogy.

We all started getting to our feet again and then Aolis turned back to us. There was momentary confusion, some of us sitting down again, some standing up properly; but he stood before us until everybody had sat down again.

'You'll know me on the battlefield,' he said, 'by these stripes.' And he put a thumb to his own chest. 'Then there's the boomshell. It's that on the hill.' He fell silent again.

'Are our orders to destroy it, Aolis?' asked Syrophoenician.

'Of course!' For the first time Aolis spoke with some emotion, sounding a little peeved. 'Naturally! But you do not know what a boomshell is. Do you know what a boomshell is, soldier?'

'My name,' said Syrophoenician, puckish, 'is Syrophoenician. And I do not know what a boomshell is.'

Aolis still had his thumb on his chest. He dropped the hand to his side. 'Syrophoenician is an unusual name,' he said. 'I fear I shall remember it even though I do not wish to. The boomshell is the reason why there are no headed officers with us on this assault. It is the reason why, before we step out, we must pack our lungs with an aerating stiff foam. The operative will give you your wadding.'

'What is wadding?' asked Steelhand.

'It is not comfortable,' replied Aolis, as if this answered Steelhand's question. 'But it will transfer oxygen to your bloodstream, and will soak up carbon from your bloodstream. It is oxygen rich,' he added, as if this was explaining matters, 'and configured chemically in such a way as to be able to transfer the oxygen to the blood in your lungs. It is not comfortable, but you will get used to it.'

He fell silent again.

'Aolis!' said Syrophoenician loudly. 'I do not understand.'

Aolis looked at him. 'You are simple-witted?'

'By no means, Aolis,' returned Syrophoenician, evidently enjoying the unusual liberties this situation granted him with respect to the officer in command over him. 'It is the case, rather, that your explanation was deficient.'

Aolis looked at Syrophoenician for a long time. My heart was hurrying, wondering whether Aolis had been given a truncheon, and whether he was about to use it on Syrophoenician. But instead he started speaking, with more force and urgency. 'I apologise, soldier,' he said, sounding like somebody waking up for the first time. 'I forget that you know nothing at all. The boomshell lays down a wide sonic footprint. It is a deeply discomforting thing, and worse than discomforting – it will collapse the brain of a headed soldier. I mean the physical organ, the skull; it will clench that cavity inwards and squeeze the brain. The brain cannot be wadded. It is like a jelly, very vulnerable.'

'This is some manner of sonic projection?'

'A very low frequency. An anti-sonics. It cannot harm *your* skull cavities because you have none. But it will try to collapse your lungs. Without wadding you would die; and so, uncomfortable though it is, wadding is better than nothing. The worst,' he added, as an afterthought, 'is coughing the stuff up after each raid. That is a rasping and drawn-out process.'

'What of the other cavities in our bodies?' asked Steelhand, alarmed.

'It will give you pains in the gut, and possibly flatulence and diarrhoea, but this will not kill you, and it will pass when you are out of range of the weapon.'

'Does it not collapse the cavities of the heart?' asked Geza.

'It does.'

'Your pardon, Aolis, but is this not a fatal circumstance?'

Aolis seemed to contemplate this. 'It is not comfortable,' he said slowly.

'But even a headless soldier needs a beating heart to ...' began Syrophoenician in his best theatrically-outraged voice.

'For the heart is designed to collapse,' said Aolis. Then he said: 'All your arteries will collapse too, or they will try to. But blood – water, you see – is incompressible. By trying to collapse this network of vessels the boomshell will move your blood about your body as effectively as any heart. And the heart recovers when you move out of the weapon's range. But there has been enough talking now. We must all go to war in a moment. Go fetch your weapons.'

After we had plugged in our guns, and opened the eyes in the barrels, we spent a minute or more accustoming ourselves again to the more vivid visual inputs. Then we formed a line, and one by one we presented ourselves to an operative, who fed a tube through our neck valves and down to our lungs. 'This feels diagreeable, especially the first time,' Aolis announced. 'It feels as if you cannot breathe. But you can. Five minutes, and you'll get used to it.'

The headless from the Fortieth and the Seventh received their wadding foam without demur. But the first of our troop to take it – Garten, as it chanced – jerked and threw out his arms. It made no difference that he resisted; the pumping tube was lengthy and flexible, and was locked in at his neck stump, and no matter how he danced, or how he wrestled with the join, it filled him up. After it was withdrawn he danced awkwardly away, his hands over his chest or fumbling at his neck as if suffocating. But he was still alive five minutes later, and ten, and by the quarter hour he had settled down.

'I apologise,' he said, to nobody in particular, or to everybody. 'I acted with a panic unbecoming a soldier.' He was, of course, able to speak, since a headless's voice depends only upon his will and the speakers mounted in his body, and not on his lungs.

By this time I had experienced the same discomfort as he, and although I did not react so outrageously I was far from happy. As the tube slid in there was some small discomfort; but it was trivial compared to the drowning sense of fear that I felt as the foam packed itself into every alveolus. I held myself straight, and afterwards staggered a little distance away; and it took many long minutes before my body got used to the idea that it was not about to choke and asphyxiate.

Aolis said only one further thing, and that was after we had come to terms, as far as we each were able, with our heavy filled-in lungs. He said: 'If we can destroy the boomshell then headed troops will be able to move in and secure the ground, and that will end our work for the day.' Then he reminded us of the signal for retreat.

Then he formed us up in ranks. The Fortieth and the Seventh, or what remained of them, were in front of us by the doorway, each with their own headless battle commands.

We waited.

There was no signal that I could see, but at one moment the front troop moved forward. They pushed the button to open the door and trotted out. We followed.

This, my first experience of battle, was a clammy and choked experience, the fog all about me leeched fighting spirit; it was a grim combination of shadow and blackness with occasional misty patches of bottle-green or with red glows like coals. Even when I opened the eye of my gun it was hard to make out any details. Through my gun-eye the texture of the fog became highlighted, a bitty, swirly semolina-thick quantity. I could glimpse only oblique hints of the things that the fog hid.

It was also the case that the compact density of the matter filling my lungs oppressed me. The cough reflex was useless in the face of so complete a stimulus. I later discovered that the mucus inside the lung began a chemical reaction that started breaking the foam down. This was a process that took about three hours, whereafter the foam started to emerge in gobbets and tight spirals and strands of phlegm, and coughing became the body's main activity. But until then it was as solid as expanded polystyrene inside.

It angered me. I became more angry as we trotted along zigzag paths that seemed, perversely, to be taking us the longest way about. I did not see why we were made to move two hundred metres to the left and then two hundred to the right to move forward only fifty, when the bare land we avoided seemed perfectly traversible – a little parched and black and dusty, but firm and uncluttered. But we followed the path, single-file, and I, eager to get to the battlefield, kept knocking into the man in front of me. Receiving these repeated checks stoked up my fury. I shuffled forward, under the dun and black sky, and in my eagerness to fight the whole frustrating, infuriating experience became caught up with my resolution for revenge. Mark Pol was, by some unclear connection and a new logic, associated with the enemy. By killing them I would be killing him.

Finally we came to the breaklands. These were thick walls, remnants of some baffling architectural project that interpenetrated the upward and downward swells of the black hills and so provided cover. Defiles were cut through these structures, and it was via such insets that we were to move through and begin the assault.

There were no headed soldiers of any kind in this place.

Aolis gathered us and gave us our orders. 'Through the defile and over the hill. You'll start feeling the boomshell soon, but do not be distracted by it. Press on together. Do not fire upon *our* automates – they have green lights upon their rears. But fire upon every enemy machine you see.'

I expected to burst through the defile and begin using my gun, but this was not what happened. Instead I followed Geza through and emerged onto a gently upsloping black hill. We sprinted forward, leaning into the upward incline, purple dust kicking up beneath our heels. The brow of the hill was visible through the murk as a frowning line above which the blackness was tinged with a dimly glowing red. But this colour was very dimly constituted indeed.

I came up over the top of the hill, and saw a cluster of machines to my near left. The man in front of me dropped down, and began firing, and I followed suit. I shot a club that collided with the superstructure of the machine, but it pulled back and clanked away into the murk seemingly unhurt.

After that the raid became frustratingly stop-start and unfocused. I ran hither and thither over the far flank of the hill, occasionally crossing paths with my comrades. I caught glimpses of our own remotes, sea-green clusters of light swaying as they stumbled along. Once I ran into a tangle of metal wreckage, striking my shins against it and falling forwards. I felt very little pain, although later I discovered I had cut my skin deeply enough to expose bone.

It was not clear in which direction the target was to be found.

I ran to the left, jumping over corpses and wreckage. The dead bodies were all headless, but they excited in me neither pity nor fear. Something in the black dust, I believe, reacted with the flesh to shrink and wizen it; some military weapon or other, I assumed. After a few weeks the flesh desiccated completely and only brittle body armour and corroded weapons remained.

I soon encountered the effect of the boomshell, as the ubiquitous rumbling sub-base noise suddenly swelled, or intensified, something felt in the fabric of the body rather than heard as such. It felt, I might say, like a fist trying to squeeze me; or, to be more precise, and since the pressure came not from the outside but was felt internally, it felt like a sucking from some visceral black-hole. It was intensely unpleasant. But it was not debilitating. The worst thing was the stuttering spasming sensation in the midst of my chest. It felt much as I imagine a heart attack must. But, after the initial surprise, I became acclimatised to it quickly enough.

An automate loomed up from the fog, very close to me, and I dropped to both knees to fire a club at it. This struck home in a visually spectacular but utterly silent chrysanthemum of lights and dazzle. The boomshell swallowed all sound. The machine reared up, deformed its wheels to long ovals and stalked away on them, again weirdly silent in the swamping throb of the boomshell. I fired off another club, and struck it again, but this also failed to fell the device.

The boomshell reduced in intensity, and then passed away. It was replaced by a series of high-pitched squeals, feedback noises, and then, as my heart relaxed, pulsed and relaxed, the ordinary sounds of the battlefield became audible again.

Shortly after this I saw Syrophoenician running up the hill towards me. 'The retreat has been ordered,' he called.

'But our objective remains uncaptured!'

'Come along, my friend,' said Syrophoenician, grabbing me. Together we ran up the hill, down the near side and in through the breaklands.

We made our way back to the temporary barrack, and slotted our guns into the general rack, through which the central processor could download data from our gun-eyes. 'They'll find nothing useful from *mine*,' said Geza, in digust. 'I did nothing but run up and down like a wet hen.'

'A curious idiom,' said Syrophoenician.

'I too accomplished very little,' I said. 'I fired twice upon a machine, but failed to destroy it.'

'At least,' said Aolis, in a weary voice, 'we sustained no casualties.'

My sense was of mere anticlimax. I had anticipated the assault heroic, and instead I had experienced a frustrating and occluded hour of scurrying.

Soup bins trundled in, and we gathered to eat.

'Why do we not simply blast this boomshell machine from above?' asked Geza, as we took our soup together. 'There must be funnel nukes or pruning missiles that can reach it.'

'It is very deeply set, under the ground,' said Aolis. 'Nor is this merely a matter of protection. It uses the ground as a sounding board to focus its attack.'

'So we must, eventually, crawl through tunnels in the dark and the cramp, to get to this beast?' Syrophoenician complained, making a contorted shape with his two arms to express his dislike of this notion.

Aolis, unused to Syrophoenician's theatricality, was puzzled at our general laughter. 'We shall do as we are ordered,' he said sharply.

'At least,' I said, 'we shall not bang our heads upon the low ceilings.'

'It is also the case,' said Aolis, ignoring my levity, 'that the polarising agent makes it almost impossible to coordinate any attack from above.'

At this point I discovered the injury to my shin, and spent ten minutes bandaging it. By the time I had finished most of the others had fallen asleep. I joined them. I was, I discovered, immensely tired.

I woke myself up with coughing. The wadding in my lungs had turned to sludge, and although it still possessed aerating properties my body was rejecting it. I sat up, leant forward and spat quantities of the stuff through my neck valve and onto the floor. It was a remorseless and uncomfortable business, especially towards the end of it, when I was coughing up as much of my own phlegm as I was foam. But eventually, and after many sips of water, my chest settled itself. It felt peculiar, and not particular enjoyable, being able to draw air into my lungs again.

Later, when I became used to the effect that the fringes of the boomshell had upon my body – the asthmatic tightening and spluttering it produced even when it passed glancingly and at the extreme edge of its effect-iveness – I came to crave the solid sense of a filled chest.

Ten

The pattern into which the fighting was to fall soon became apparent to me. Every six or seven hours we scurried through the defile, and spread out over the forward hill like ants. Our objectives were never very clear to me, except to shoot upon such enemies as we encountered. This we would do until the time came to scurry, like ants, back through our slot and to our barracks: eat, perhaps talk, sleep. Then we would do it all again.

Sometimes we would be ordered to swap our guns about. Upon encountering one of the lumbering great automates, a club-gun was the most destructive option, although needles and projectiles could do a surprising amount of damage if they happened to strike the right portion. But the enemy would vary their defensive attacks, sometimes pouring hundreds of small remotes at us, in which case the heavier ordnance was worse than useless. Indeed, and since we were ordered never to discard our weapons, but always to return them so that their data could be processed, the bigger guns tended only to hamper resistance.

With the remotes we were at least spared the boomshell. Their handlers were headed, and needed to be relatively proximate to their drones. But they were nimbler and more deadly, two metres tall and possessing human-controlled reflexes rather than the lumbering ones of automates. At one point I was standing shoulder to shoulder with Garten, both of us firing needleguns into the approaching mêlée, when a scyther cut him into two pieces: three quarters of a body falling forwards from below the cut, a wedge of chest and shoulders and two arms tumbling backwards above it. There was a great deal of blood, but, though I was messed by this, I was otherwise unharmed. I fled that scene.

So much for Garten. He had been my friend.

After several days fighting we learned the best way to tackle remotes was for several of us to target their metal heads. Here was where the sensors were located, and destroying those produced a painful feedback in the handlers, plugged in to their sensornets. Presumably (I never discovered for sure) the screams of one handler back in the handling facility discommoded the morale of the others, for after destroying a remote in this manner it was often the case that the remainder would flee the scene.

The boomshell created unpredictable dislocations in air pressure that made it difficult for planes to fly. But, when it was not operating, aircraft would sweep through the blackness above us dropping sheet-ordnance or localised bombs upon us – or upon the enemy, if the planes were ours, although the weapons made no distinction. The murk disoriented attempts at precise targeting. Bil Costra and Cash were killed by overhead bombardment, and Syrophoenician was nearly crushed by a falling plane – caught by the boomshell, and perhaps clipped by shrapnel, ploughing with enormous speed into the hillside, carving a broad road-like furrow, flipping over and over, shedding great spinning chunks of fuselage, and finally exploding into white skimming light, all (Syrophoenician later said, with many theatrical gestures) utterly silent, save only the thrum of the boomshell. 'How strange it was,' he said, as we picked fragments of metal out of his stomach and legs, where they had shredded through his armour, and bandaged him, 'to see this enormous wreck happen, silently, directly before my own artificial eyes.'

I took up a needlegun, and scurried forth to make my pointless antlike runs over and over the hillside. I ate, I slept. I exchanged my weapon for a club-gun, and ran forth again. One sally brought us up against a solid wall of automates, flaring their nozzles and spewing glass shot towards us. It was on this raid that Aolis was killed. Upon his death Syrophoenician was appointed battlefield officer. But the relentless pressure of repeated raids was starting to dent even *his* enormous liveliness. He paraded about the barrack as we ate our soup shouting, 'None of this intimate name nonsense with *me*!' and, 'You carcasses had better call me "Superior", or I'll truncheon you to jelly!' and such like. But his heart was not really in it.

Sleep was our only balm, and we all took refuge in it.

Once again I awoke to a space filled with retching and coughing men, and once again I joined them in retching and coughing. We had, in the absence of specific instruction from superiors, agreed a rota, such that we took turns to sweep away the mounds of sludgy foam and spittle that were the result of this mass lung-clearing. Indeed, we so rarely saw a superior these days that we began to forget what it was like to receive specific orders from a headed man.

*

On the next raid, as had been the case on my very first, I encountered almost nobody on the hill. Our own automates had pushed forward, and only occasionally did we encounter an enemy machine, alone and fleeing. I ranged widely over the black and dusty space, and in fact pushed right to the bottom of the hill. Here there was a broad and irregular pathway of stones, perhaps a dried river-bed, on the other side of which was the start of another upward slope. Three comrades were here, pausing and scanning the darkness with their gun-eyes. 'This is it,' I cried. 'Should we attack?'

'My orders are not clear,' replied Syrophoenician. 'Now that you are here, Cavala, we are four; but surely this is not a large enough force to go clambering through the tiny tunnels and—'

The boomshell started up, and his remaining words were swallowed. He waved us back and we made our way to the breaklands and base.

At soup there was a new excitement. 'Have we cleared a path?' Geza was asking. 'Perhaps now this endless skirmishing can end, and we can push through.'

'A superior is coming here to advise,' said Syrophoenician. He had become uncharacteristically subdued since assuming battlefield authority, and a new caution had entered his manner. 'He will tell us what we must do.'

'For my part,' I said, 'I hope we can rush the boomshell and destroy it. I am sick of this tentative probing forward, all this insect-like scurrying here and there. I want to force a way *through*. Give me a path, a straight line, a *goal*.'

'You are thwarted. You wish to give expression to the passion in your nature,' said Steelhand.

I was struck by the wisdom of this. '*Sieur* Steelhand,' I said. 'You put it very well. For what good is life without passion?'

'This expresses precisely *my* philosophy of living,' said Syrophoenician.

'A man may be passionate in his work, or his love, or the way he takes his pleasure,' I said. 'As soldiers, we should be passionate about our fighting.'

'But – passionate about killing?' said Steelhand, without conviction. 'That doesn't sound so praiseworthy a passion.'

'I am no coward,' said Geza. 'But I am *most* passionate about my self preservation. I hope to survive this war.'

'I want only to atone for what I have done in the past,' I said.

'To atone passionately,' said Geza, laughing.

'And does it not say, in the Bibliqu'rân ...' began Syrophoenician.

'We must mutiny against this canting preacher!' cried Steelhand, leaping up. We bundled upon Syrophoenician, and our laughter was the first for a long time.

Two superiors arrived, in their bulkily petalled helmets, with a new set of headless. The taller of the headed men made a brusque speech.

'Troops!' he shouted. 'The new assault will take place in one hour. To the Seventh, the Thirtieth and Fortieth, I say to you: fresh blood and heart comes in the form of the Eleventh Troop of Gable Headless. With these reinforcements, and with the battlefield largely abandoned by the enemy, we will press again at the salient and be successful.'

The new troops cheered 'Superior!' in unison. The rest of us were silent.

'To you,' said the superior, turning to the men of the Eleventh, 'I shall say what these others already know. It is usual in battle for headless troops to be commanded by superiors. For strategic reasons on this battlefield this will not be possible. Accordingly, your battlefield commander will be Syrophoenician of the Thirtieth. Follow him unthinkingly into the corridors of the salient, and destroy it! Once it has been eliminated our armies will flood through the gap in the enemy defences. The war will soon be over.'

Syrophoenician stepped forward and made his way over to the new recruits. When he began to address them he did so without levity or jokes.

Eleven

We embarked on the next raid in high spirits, expecting to swarm down to the dried river and then press up. But, instead, we ran straight into a large deployment of remotes. The men of the Eleventh Gable, still awkward and skittish with the wadding in their lungs, and unused to combat, charged directly at them, and were blasted with scythers and glass shot. Fully a half of them tumbled, dead, to the ground. This was very disconcerting to the rest of us. We scattered back up the hill to the various obstacles and potholes, well known to us now, behind or within which we might find cover. Once there we returned the weapons fire. From where I was, behind a box of fallen girders still corseted with the remains of some of their metal ribbing, I saw Syrophoenician and two of the new soldiers harassed in a foxhole by a dozen remotes. They were crowding all about the space, yet had not taken their chance to destroy the three headless. But their danger was very imminent.

Having only a club-gun I was poorly armed for engaging a large number of remotes, but I did what I could. I aimed my weapon carefully, hoping that a well-placed club might skittle away enough of them to grant Syrophoenician and those others time to kill the rest. I fired. My club struck a single remote, on one of its legs, and detonated upwards, blowing its clamshell-shaped head high into the dark. But this did nothing to dishearten the other machines. I saw Syrophoenician leap up from his hole, attempting physically to bundle through the circle of attackers, and two of the new recruits – bravely – followed him. But the bodies of the remotes, of course, were charged, and all three men staggered back at their contact. This shock must have been fiercely painful, a sensation, even with dampened pain reception, of electric muscle-shredding. But despite it I saw Syrophoenician turn about and raise his needlegun. The entire scene lit up in a glitter cloud of crossfire.

All this happened before a second club was able to slot itself in the breech of my weapon. I aimed again, and only realised too late that three remotes had come up rapidly on my left.

I swung my weapon, or began to, but I knew that this was my own moment of death. Accordingly, I feel I should report to you something of my state of mind at this point. I feel I should report, for instance, whether the prospect of imminent death was alarming to me, frustrating, terrifying, or whether I felt that deep and philosophic calm and certainty of a new life in the All'God of which divines sometimes write. But this would be a feeble pretence. You are reading my account, and so you already know that I did not die. All I can say, to be consistent with my aim in this memoir of absolute truthfulness, is this: had I known, then, that I was about to be taken prisoner by the enemy I would relate to you my state of mind at this prospect – fear, relief, whatever it might be. But I did not realise that. I assumed that I would die. And when, with a bright apparition in my right-side visual sensors of the looming electric-light-encrusted face of a remote, my consciousness abruptly cut-out there was just enough time for me to think: *This is the very moment of death! The thing itself!* And to be pleased with myself that I had kept enough of my wits to be able to recognise this moment. A dazzle, a crunch, and nothing after it.

PART THREE
A Brazen Head

One

I did not expect to wake. But I woke. What then? When it occurred to me that I was indeed waking up, I suppose I expected to find myself inside a prison. But I was not in prison.

When I opened my eyes I could see a pale wall, a shelf with books upon it. I could see the edge of a door. I turned my head a little and saw the trappings of an unluxurious but comfortable room. I was lying upon a bed in the middle of this. The sheets felt like cotton, clean and fragrant. I turned my head, and saw a square of lit blue sky. Bright sunlight came washing through this window, dousing all the objects on the floor, saturating everything.

I could see much more clearly and distinctly than was usual for me. Even when my sight had been augmented, for instance with a gun plugged into my ordinator, it had never been as sharp and lively as it now was. Everything in the room picked itself out with unusual clarity. I recognised my shirt, where it lay discarded on the floor, patched with triangular and rectangular blocks of shadow from the various kinks and ruffles in the cloth. But these patches of shade were so darkly distinct that I at first thought, in my half-awake state, that they were actually marks upon the clothing – wine stains, perhaps, or dye patches. I had to rise from the bed and shake the shirt in my right hand to confirm for me that the marks were indeed only shadow. The motion scattered all the black triangles and rectangles away like a conjurer's trick, revealing only a forked, white stretch of cloth.

I sat back down upon the bed. It was disconcertingly hypervivid. 'My mind,' I observed, to myself, 'is not itself.' The words, spoken aloud, chimed a different timbre to the usual sound of my voice.

I was still wearing my meadhres. I stood up, and put my arms into the sleeves of the shirt, fumbling the buttons closed with my right hand. I resolved to explore this place.

Through the door led me into a short hallway, at the end of which was another door. Inset in this was a bright-lit panel. Only as I came towards this did I realise it was glass, lit by the outside sun, rather than being some manner of artificial light.

The door opened easily.

I stepped outside into a warm afternoon. The heat was very tangible on my skin. The heat of pine and lavender. A clean and clear heat.

What could I see?

There was a headed man sitting beside a swimming pool. He was sitting upon a white plastic recliner. Light, reflected up from the undulating surface of the pool, wrigglingly caressed his face. Behind him was a low wall fashioned from a warm-looking yellow stone, and beyond that a pale-grassed hillside rising to the left of my field of vision. The texture of the honey-coloured grass on this hill was very clear to me. I could hear the occasional rustle, like a percussive zither, as the wind moved over these dry strands, and then was still. The sky behind the hill was a very dark blue.

I blinked. I shut my eyes, and opened them. Strangely vivid; intensely vivid. Its intense lifelikeness was so pronounced as to give the scene an aura of strangeness.

The man waved to me. He was smiling. His wave said *come over here!*

I walked over to him. As I walked across the warm patio my point-of-view rotated. To the right, down the precipitous khaki hillside, a whole landscape turned into my sight. Directly below the land on which the house was built there were trees, still carrying full heads of dry and rather metallic-looking leaves. Further down the hill were other houses. At the bottom was a bright blue lake, and on the far side of this was a small lakeside town, and another towering honey-coloured hill behind *that*. I did not recognise the landscape; neither in its particulars, nor as being consistent with the sort of landscape I had previously seen on this world. But, I told myself, surely planets contain a wide variety of different climates and landscapes, and it was more likely that the enemy had flown me to some other part of Black Athena than that they had shipped me wholly offworld and to another planet. And of course, I reminded myself, the polarising fog could hardly have been disseminated across the entire world.

It was clear enough, however, that I had been captured; and that this man, sitting so blithely alone and unarmed, was my enemy. I tried to prepare myself. But how could I prepare myself? I had quite literally no idea what was going to happen.

As I came closer to him, the man spoke. He said: 'Hello, my friend!'

I was walking along the side of the pool now. The sunlight threw fat webs of light through the water and onto the swimming pool floor, where the ropes of light shifted and swayed as if blown by an underwater breeze.

'Don't fall in!' said the man brightly. 'You're looking rather wobbly on your pins.'

I came up close to him. He indicated a second recliner and I sat myself on this.

The man was perhaps forty, perhaps fifty years of age. There were creases cutting into both side of his face, as if the skin had been removed and folded upon itself and only imperfectly flattened before being refitted to the skull. The hair on his head, grey and black, was close-cropped. His eyes were green. The bristles of his beard, several days old, stood out on his chin and cheek with almost hallucinatory vividness, like those thousands of tiny scores and marks an engraver makes upon a metal plate to indicate the shaded areas of an illustration.

A gust of wind moved through the air around me. It rummaged briefly in the leaves of a fat-headed oak growing just beyond the wall, making a sound exactly like a flurry of rain. Then the air was still again. There was an uncanny quality to the silence.

'Welcome to my eagle's eyrie, *Sieur* Cavala,' said the man, in slightly accented Homish. He waved his hand over his shoulder, indicating the view down the hill towards the lake.

'Your name?'

'My name,' he said, smiling, 'is Levitt Dunber. You and I are alone here, my friend. I trust myself to you – for you are a trained killer, and I could not defend myself if you decided to attack me. You see how trusting I am?'

'What have you done?' I asked. The noises were coming from my mouth, rather than my chest. Belatedly I realised, consciously, what my body had realised as soon as I woke: that I had a head. I put my hands up and fumbled my fingers-ends over nose, chin, cheek. The skin of the head felt warm but hard, unfleshy.

'It's bronze,' said Levitt Dunber admiringly. 'Oh, I daresay its interior is all plastic connections and neurons and whatnot and who-*knows*-what. That is not my field. But I do know about canons of aesthetic taste, and I'll say that the external bronze laminate has been very stylishly shaped. Do you want to see?'

He fished out a palm-sized circular mirror and held it up before me as best he could, and in that wobbly disc I saw myself. An expressionless, sherry-coloured face lurched up and down, propelled by the miniature tremors of Levitt Dunber's hand. 'May I?' I asked, taking the glass from him. I examined myself more steadily. The nose and mouth seemed carved from solid metal, but an act of miniature will on my part opened the lips and flared the nostrils. The eyelids closed and opened with a distant, dry fluttery sound. I could smile and frown, the metal deforming as the face moved. I let my expression become neutral and looked at the face. They had not reproduced my original face, or even an approximation of it (but of course, how could they have known what my original face looked like?). Instead I had been given a regular and innocuously handsome set of features. The eyebrows were crisscross notches curving over the sockets. The eyes were, strangely, the same colour – whites, irises and pupils all carved from the same bronze. My head-hair was rendered in the rippled solidity of a stone-carved statue's.

I handed the mirror back to Levitt Dunber. Then, feeling an unexpected panic, I put my hands behind me and groped at the small of my back.

'Your ordinator is still there, my friend,' said Dunber. 'We could hardly remove that – that is where *you* are, after all. If you see what I mean.'

'The head?'

'A superior prosthesis? A work of art?' He shrugged. 'And why can't it be both?'

I sat back.

There was a boat on the lake. It was moving slowly, pulling its wake through the water behind it like a heavy robe trailing along a blue marble floor. The sun laid a spearhead-shaped area of bristling shine over the middle of the body of water. The boat inched into this area of lit lake, becoming more silhouetty as it slid through it. Evidently this new prosthesis was visually superior to my previous one.

The far hills, beyond the water, seemed swollen, puffed with their own beauty, beguilingly tall yet gentle in their slopes. Houses, like the one I found myself in, were visible in a slanting zigzag up the side. A single narrow road, taut like a sinew, ran diagonally from base to summit.

I let my eye fall on the town at the foot of this hill. The buildings of it congregated with an intricate precision and clarity; the tessellation of roofs and walls fitting snugly together. In a field just on the far side of the lake I could see a tractor moving across ploughed earth: I saw the oO of its wheels, its square metal parasol roof, the brute mechanic snout of its bonnet. I could, even at this distance, see the driver; the peak of his cap overhanging a bearded face, attention focused on the field. I possessed an extraordinary visual definition.

My hearing was also improved. It felt more like the sense of hearing I had known as a headed man. And what's more I could *smell*: an act of will sucked air into my nostrils, and I became aware of the savour of dry grass, the faint incense of rosemary and lavender, the smell of warm air itself.

'Can it not be constructed,' I asked, tapping my metal head with my fleshly finger, 'so as to appear more lifelike?'

'You are bargaining already?' replied Levitt Dunber, amused.

'By no means,' I said, a little confused.

'There is no need to apologise,' Dunber said. 'It would, of course, be possible to fit you with an *ersatz* head if you preferred it – pink-yellow plastic to mimic skin, milk-coloured glass eyes with blue irises, a little redness at the flexible lips, that sort of thing. If that is truly what you would prefer.'

I looked intently at him. 'Yes . . .'

'But this would look not more but *less* lifelike,' he said. 'You will of course understand why. You'll have recognised the way that, for instance, a fine sculpture in blue stone looks more lifelike than a shop front automaton. Why is this?'

'This is simply a question of respective craftsmanship.'

'I disagree. The automaton, in pink plastic, appears to be trying to fool our eyes, and *our eyes* – which are very acute at detecting the minute verisimilitude of real faces – revolt against the deception. But the blue stone makes no pretence to being real, and so we take it *as it is* and merely admire the artistry.'

'This talk of blue stone,' I said, 'and plastic. It all seems very strange to me.'

'Because you have been plucked from the black fog of battle,' said Levitt Dunber, nodding. 'I understand.' He put his head back. 'Sunset!' he said. 'Sunset, sunset – my favourite time of the day!'

I followed his gaze. The sky over the hill behind us turning orange and pinken. Shrimp-coloured clouds lay overhead in a line that trailed down behind the lip of the summit. Even as I watched the sky seemed to darken with unnatural rapidity; perhaps a function of my new senses, or perhaps simply the way this planet turned.

All about the pool electric lights lit up. Some were mounted on staffs, stubby lamp-poles, some were inset into the wall. Behind me, all the windows of the house were illuminated.

I could hear birdsong, very distant, melodious, like the playing of piccolos. It was a nightingale.

The lake, below me, had assumed a dark blue hue, intermixed in patches with a darker purple. A little later it became perfectly black, something which gave it the appearance of solidity, like a black resin poured into the space between the hills. The boat I had been observing had reached the far side, and was parked alongside its pier. The lights of the little town glinted in strings and clusters along the harbourfront and up the hill. Above me, stars were everywhere, very many tiny droplets of luminous white condensation upon the black-matt dome of sky. Crickets chuckled to themselves in the darkness.

'What do you know about the Sugar?' asked Levitt Dunber.

'The Sugar War,' I said. 'I am a soldier.'

'I'm being tentative,' said Dunber. 'I don't wish to provoke your anger – for as I said before, I am wholly unarmed. And broaching the subject of *treachery* is a delicate matter. It might tip a less self-controlled man into a violent attack.'

'Treachery?'

'Best to call a crime a crime, don't you think? Better to call murder murder, to call rape *rape*.' He looked closely at me.

'Do you insinuate—' I began.

'I'm not making any insinuation,' he said firmly. His foreign accent, difficult to place, gave the word *insinuation* a weird off-kilter emphasis, like a shake. 'It is nothing to me. My view is that the practice of beheading individuals is barbaric, and that the barbarism is barely mitigated by resurrecting the beheaded with technological prostheses to wander the countryside like ghouls. It seems to *me*,' he continued, 'a hypocritical practice – supposedly done in the name of compassion, when in fact it is performed to establish walking deterrence to anybody else who might challenge the political authorities from making any *fuss*. Much like placing the heads of traitors on poles in archaic cities.'

'Crimes must be punished,' I observed.

'Do *you* say so? Perhaps they must. But should consensual sexual congress be punished? Should justifiable homicide, or the free expression of one's opinion about religion – should they be punished in this extreme manner?'

'They order things differently on your home world perhaps?'

He looked about himself. The air was still warm. Lights under the water, set inside the wall of the swimming pool, made the whole juddery rectangle bright.

'They do.'

'Do you wish me to betray my own people?' I asked. 'My comrades?'

He looked quizzically at me.

'I am,' I said, 'only a foot soldier. There is nothing I can tell you that will help your case. It is, I regret, a waste of your time to hold me here. You should have obtained a senior officer, a magister or a president. His betrayal would have served you better.'

Levitt Dunber put his thumb to his unshaven chin. 'So what *do* you know about the Sugar?' he asked again.

It occurred to me, at that moment, whom Levitt Dunber reminded me of: it was Bonnard, the Cainon policeman. There was little physical resemblance between the lean, age-creased man in front of me and the corpulent policeman I had once known, but they both took perverse pleasure in roundabout locution, in game-playing, asserting their own power over their interlocutor. 'Am I being interrogated?' I asked.

'Do you believe that we fly all captured soldiers to *this* location to interrogate them?' he asked, an amused incredulity on his face.

'But I must repeat that I do not know anything that might be useful to you. Believe me when I say that I am not resisting your questions. I will answer anything you ask me. My answers will not be treason, for I know nothing that could help your war effort.'

'It *is* a sugar,' said Levitt Dunber. 'It is a form of sugar. Or – I am no scientist – at least a polysaccharide. Or more precisely still, a deoxyribose saccharide *base*. But a base for what? For some form of life? For something more bacterial, or even viral; not an inert sugar but a living one?' He shook his head, as if unknowing. 'It is somewhat confusing that it has become known as "Sugar", or as it is called by some "*The* Sugar". For this means that other sugars must be referred to with circumlocutions, such as "*conventional sugars*", or "*culinary sugars*". The Sugar is no culinary addition. Believe me when I say you would not wish to place any upon your tongue!'

'*Sieur* Dunber,' I said. 'Humbly and without disrespect I must say: this is meaningless to me.'

'Meaningless?'

'The object of the war is not my concern. I am merely a soldier.'

'The reason I say that you would not wish to place any on your tongue,' said Dunber, 'is that I have seen it done. A small spatula of the Sugar will kill a man, and in an extremely unpleasant way. The tongue – the mouth – all the mucus membranes of the head – dissolve away like melting wax. The body collapses. There is – screaming.'

I tipped my head to one side, thinking that at last I understood the nature of Dunber's game playing. 'Has all this been only a preliminary to torture?' I asked.

At this Levitt Dunber laughed, loud and genuinely. 'No,' he said. 'You misunderstand. What would it benefit us in transporting you here in order to torture you? To this ... perfect place.'

'Perfection?' I queried.

'The ketone ring of this Sugar, or rather the complex of ketones, is very hungry for salts and for certain other minerals. Once it locks enough salt it changes its form. Let me speculate as to what Pluse wants with the stuff. Permit me to speculate about your world. Let us, together, imagine a large enough quantity of Sugar. Let us imagine this quantity dumped into your ironically named Mild Sea. The Sugar would react aggressively with the salts in the water. It would consume any carbo-hydrate or protein it encountered – the fish, for instance. It would consume them utterly, depopulate the sea. But this would be no occasion for grief, because once the whole sea is desalinated then saltwater fish could not live there any more anyway.'

'Desalination?'

'Oh, indeed. Proteins allow the salt-reacting Sugar to breed, and there-fore to lock away more salt. Eventually the protein is all used up, and the Sugar simply accumulates more and more salt. Denser than the pure water it sinks, and beds down as a layer. But it leaves the water above as clean as if it had been filtered.'

'Drinking water.'

'And also for irrigation. *Sieur* Cavala, I think we can see the benefit for your world. Those parched stretches of land, millions of hectares all about the Mild Sea, turned to oases of growth. The greening of the whole land. And this is merely one world. There are planets even more desolate than yours. I know of one world that is covered in deserts of salt; colonisation has proved impossible there because it is so forbidding. But with sufficient supplies of Sugar ...'

'It is for this substance that the war is being fought?'

'Pluse is in dispute with Athena over the trade stipulations. We – by which I mean, the Alliance of the Humane Faithful – appended human-rights protocols to the trade agreements. We urged Pluse, and the other Planets of the Book, to abandon this barbaric practice of beheading. They refused. Attempts were made to enforce trading quotas. Sugar has proved uncultivatable in the necessary bulk outside Athena. And so the war has progressed. Your people insist that they are merely enforcing the terms of a trade agreement upon which we have reneged. We counter that the agreement was never finalised, because of the lamentable abuses against human dignity that your worlds practise.'

'I know nothing of this,' I said.

'But then again' – he shook his head, he looked – momentarily – almost angry – 'is war *ever* fought for such reasons? The leaders persuade themselves that the proximate causes are necessary causes, but they never are. It is a clash of civilisations. Isn't it? That and nothing more. Perhaps this is always the way of war. One part of the corpus humanitas is always separated from another, and the separation itself is reason enough for resentment.'

He stopped speaking, and was silent for a while. Then, brightly, he said: 'Would you like to test the *taste* prosthesis in your new head?'

I was, almost against my better judgement, excited. 'Might I?'

He leapt to his feet and hurried over to a square metal door inset into the wall. Opening this revealed a safe-like cooler, from which he brought out two bottles. 'Beer,' he offered.

I had also stood up. 'But I am not permitted to drink beer,' I said.

'No? I thought you were.'

Was this some sort of test? 'The Bibliqu'rân forbids beer, spirits, and all fruit liquor save only wine. Surely you know this?'

'My congregation,' he said evenly, 'evidently follows a laxer interpretation of scripture than yours.' He replaced the beer bottles in the safe and closed the door. Then, opening it again, he reached in and brought out two very narrow bottles of wine. A flick of his thumb uncorked them both.

I put the bottle to my mobile brazen lips and tipped it back. The fluid gushed into my mouth. It swirled around my tongue. The tang of alcohol, and the rich, darkly violet flavour of red wine, was intensely *there*, inside my mouth. Taste and odour and the physical tang of it. I swallowed. I imagined brazen hoops of an artificial gullet contracting in turn, and speeding the juice into my stomach. 'Will it make me drunk?'

'Naturally it will. It may take longer than it used to. The alcohol cannot transfer into the bloodstream through the roof of your mouth, of course. But into your bloodstream it *will* go, eventually, and a mildly pleasant intoxication will be the result.'

'Why not,' I suggested, 'tell me why you have brought me to this place?'

'It is beautiful, is it not?'

'If you wish me to betray my world,' I pressed, 'then at least tell me how I can do so. What inducements are you offering me?'

He smiled knowingly at this, as if the answer to my own question was obvious.

'Is it this prosthesis?' I asked, tapping the tip of my bottle against my metallic forehead.

'A fine toy, I think you must agree.'

'You think I would betray my people for a toy?'

'I think your people have betrayed *you*.' He shook his head. 'What can *you* do for us, Jon Cavala? The most famous poet of Pluse?'

This wrong-footed me. 'I am hardly that,' I said.

'Jon Cavala? *The* Jon Cavala? Psh.' He closed his eyes, as if consulting the scroll of his memory, and recited:

Flesh slackens when grown,
Plums purple to fall;
Grass lengthens to be mown,
And that is all.

Maturity eradicates
And gives to the air
All known
And death uncreates
The strong, the fit, the tall,
Bodies gross or fair,
Houses of bone.

'Am I, then, so famous on your world?' I asked, startled, but also (I regret to recall) pridefully pleased.

'To behead a poet – a poet of your stature – for mere *sexual* goings-on? Shameful. It was shameful indeed.'

'Do you say a poet of my stature?'

'Oh relatively unacknowledged upon your *own* world, I concede. But widely read, and widely admired, on other worlds.'

'I had no idea.'

'Naturally not, since yours is a closed society.'

'It is hardly that,' I said.

'You are loyal to your culture, which of course reflects credit upon you. But they have stifled your work, stifled it. And yours is work of genius!'

'You seek to flatter me, *Sieur* Dunber,' I said. 'Whereas flattery is ignoble.'

'It is, or it is not.' He seemed unconcerned.

'I remain ignorant how I can usefully betray my own world. Usefully, that is to say, for your purposes. Truly I know nothing at all; I am privy to no military secrets, I can give you access to nothing of any good.'

'Really?'

I took another drink of wine. An image came to my mind. I saw myself touring Levitt Dunber's homeworld. I saw large and admiring crowds. I saw my handsome brazen face on many datascreens and projectors. I saw myself reading my poetry, and also making speeches denouncing the barbarity of the system of justice practised on Pluse. I saw crowds rising to their feet and applauding, fields of wheat through-stirred by the wind, at my words. All this came to me in one moment: the propaganda value of a famous writer, recruiting the opinion of the many against the world that had nurtured me.

It was a powerful vision, made more beguiling by the seeping warmth of wine in my belly. Was this the betrayal that was being offered me?

'As for the Sugar,' Levitt Dunber was saying (as if I cared for the Sugar!), 'there is no desire on our part to *deny* Pluse the Sugar. Nor do we wish to interfere with the consciences of your people, in respect of their religious observation, or freedom to interpret scripture howsoever they choose. The only change we would like is that the Planets of the Book agree to – eh – to certain basic – protocols – on human rights.'

Once again, I must report how flattering it was to hear this man negotiate with me as if I were a great politician or leader. Pride, washing through me, mixed dangerously with alcohol.

'You care so greatly for the fate of the headless?' I asked.

'The headless? I beg your pardon but no – even as you and I talk, *Sieur* Cavala, we are striving to invent new ways of killing the headless. They are swarming over our battlefields this very minute, they are posing a variety of dangers. It is not individual headless that concern us; no, not even one so notable as yourself. It is the *principle*.'

'Principle?'

'It outrages our sense of civilised existence that men and women are treated so. It degrades the dignity of humanity.' He made a little circling gesture with his right hand, as if he could spool forth many similar examples of this manner of speaking.

I pondered. I was conflicted. I cannot deny that I was very strongly tempted by what he offered. But I could not forget what I had vowed to myself.

'Let us say,' I suggested, 'that I do not wish to spend *the rest of my life* upon your worlds, speaking – perhaps – to crowds about the inhumanity of beheading as a punishment. Let us say that there is something else that I must do. That I must return to Pluse to . . .

perform some action. We might even say,' I continued, finding a near-theatrical pleasure in my speechifying (this was the wine, perhaps), 'that, if you could guarantee this for me – that if you could arrange for me to return to my world, so that I could seek out one particular person and perform one particular act ... that for this, for that one thing alone, I would be prepared to betray my world.'

Levitt Dunber was grinning very broadly. 'You *are* bargaining!' he declared. 'I knew you would. But, as you say, what possible use would your betrayal be to us?'

My brazen eyebrows arched.

'I do not understand,' I said cautiously. 'You have been intimating ...'

'Oh, the fame of the poet, yes, yes,' he said. '*Alive* you might be of some use.'

'I would be happy to devote myself to whatever you desire,' I said, 'after I have performed this one act. It has been the guiding star of my life for half a year now. Facilitate it, and I am yours.'

'Alive is one thing,' Dunber was saying. 'Dead quite another.'

'But why threaten me with death?' I asked, genuinely puzzled. 'I have all but agreed to do as you wish, to betray my world. All I am doing is debating the precise terms on which I shall act for you.'

'Threaten? You misunderstand. Ah!' he said, looking about him 'The dawn! This is my favourite time of day here.'

It was as he said: the dark was thinning behind the hills on the far side of the lake, diluting with turquoise and paler shades. As if resolving out of chaos and coming into being for the first time, the lineaments of landscape, lake and town were starting to become visible, paler grey against darker. Many birds in the trees below the house were spirrilling and chirruping their dawn chorus with great vigour.

'How can it be the dawn?' I demanded. 'The night cannot have passed so quickly.'

'The night, with its stars, is my favourite time. The day also.' He looked at me. 'Time moves differently here.'

'Where am I?' I asked.

I should, obviously, have asked that question much earlier in our exchange.

'Isn't it clear to you? I have always felt that the issue is not whether heaven will reject the soul, as some stricter religions claim; it is whether the *soul* will reject *heaven*. What of you?'

'This is not heaven,' I said. I got to my feet. The light was strong enough to illuminate the half-full bottle in my hand, its sloshing black and purple contents. The lights around the pool seemed paler now, challenged by the quickly brightening sky. 'I am not dead.'

'No?'

'This is not heaven,' I said again, looking about me. 'I have *not* come to *heaven* to discover it already in the possession of my enemy. Heaven does not' – I grasped my own metal chin – '*fit souls* with brazen *prostheses*. Heaven makes the soul entire and complete again. Heaven is not' – I slapped my chest – '*bodily*—'

'Be calm, my friend,' said Levitt Dunber. He did not get up. 'Sit down. Heaven, if it is anything, is a place to be calm. Don't you think? Why mightn't your enemy have a house in heaven, after all? Surely that will depend upon how virtuous he was during his life.'

'Tell me what is happening,' I demanded. 'Where – am *I*?'

'You are in my house,' he replied. 'And *what is happening* is the dawn. Here it comes now.'

He was smiling at me. The smile widened and became a grin. Levitt Dunber made a circle of his mouth, stretched his lips as high and wide as they would go.

He was gaping at me, and there was a light inside his throat, a tonsil of illumination so bright I could not look at it, it scorched my brazen eyes.

The light grew. Light was pouring from his open mouth, and the torrent dissolved everything.

There was nothing but light.

Light was vomiting from his open mouth, and there was.

Only light.

The complete whiteness washed around me, outlining my hand as I held it in front of my eyes; and then it washed *through* me. My hand disappeared. My arm. The whole world. My anxiety was scrubbed away. Even my surprise at this surreal turn of events drained out of me.

And then the light seemed to gather, somehow strengthen and tighten, whilst still all about me. And then it burst, into a million neon crumbs that fell through the sky as a firework.

There was a very faint, very high-pitched noise, like a distant flute playing a single, high, quavering note. The note rose in pitch a tone, then a semitone, and then it broke into a violent collision of a dozen loud noises all contending at once.

I tried to focus my eyes. A headless man was above me, leaning forward. '*Sieur* Cavala,' he was shouting, '*Sieur* Cavala, you must get up.' He was shouting so as to be heard over the cacophony of noises, the explosions and clatterings, the stale thrum of the boom-shell in its quiescent mode. 'We're retreating,' he bellowed, 'come now.'

Belatedly I recognised Steelhand's form. I tried to suck in a deep breath, but my lungs were still clogged with wadding. 'I had a vision,' I screeched. 'I had a vision.'

'Increase the volume of your speakers,' bellowed Steelhand, grasping me by my hand and hauling me upright. 'I cannot hear.'

'A *vision*,' I shouted. 'I had a *vision*, of—'

But my flesh jittered into a standing wave and all sound vanished. The quasi-sonic footprint of the boomshell fell upon us. I could hear nothing now. My guts collapsed and clenched within me, and my bones ached. I could feel each lung, distinctly, pressing inward, trying to implode; and I could feel the branched tree-shape the wadding had taken inside my chest. Everything around me was dusky.

It was, as before, hard to think. But Steelhand was stumbling back over the scrub, and I shook my legs and ran after him. The boomshell was present inside me, hideously invasive, making every cell in my body vibrate. My marrow was clenching in on itself inside my bone as if trying to compact itself to chalk. My blood was spurting through constricting vessels. My heart spasmed. It was intensely uncom-fortable; not merely painful (although it was that), but *wrong*-feeling, internally disjointed.

I ran. My mind was instructing my speakers such that I was still in effect shouting 'I had a – a *vision*, a *vision*', but of course no sounds of any kind emerged, or would have been audible even if they had done.

The footprint of the boomshell began to shift away from us, and I was aware of my heart dilating and squeezing again, and of the pain passing off from my limbs. Steelhand, ahead of me, skidded to a halt, turned towards me as he dropped to one knee, and brought up his needlegun. I reacted, turning and dropping into a firing position alongside him. I was carrying the club-gun. It seemed odd to me that this was still the case, after a day and a night and a new dawn – except, of course, that I had not really experienced any such passage of time.

Coming up the low rise, visible through the murk by its cluster of red lights near the centre of its frame, was an automate. It rolled forward, and then deformed its wheels to ovals to walk over a patch of rubble. This gave us a moment, for the extra processing involved would slow its computing time. I hoisted my gun and opened the gun's eye. It all became more vivid. I could even see the particulate grain of the fog, and the blocky layering of the automate's super-structure, the faint white iris-lines in each red headlight. I called up a sighting graphic and willed the trigger in.

The first club hurtled towards the target and cracked it into fizzing sparkles. As I fired, Steelhand's needles were fleeting through the dark, snicking into the target. The device rocked back and tumbled over.

The boomshell had passed away completely. I shut the gun's eye and got back to my feet. Now I was running ahead, with Steelhand a little behind me, although he overtook me as I laboured to the top of the hill. We crested the rise, and then were running down the murky far side of the hill, towards the breakland walls, Steelhand waving his left arm over his head.

I felt a peculiar, near-numinous elation inside me. 'I had a *vision*,' I was yelling, 'a *vision*,' and I was still yelling it as we jumped through the slot in the breakland and were bundled out through the far side of the defile by welcoming hands.

Two

The assault had claimed the lives of a great many people, including Geza and Syrophoenician. My elation from the vision lasted an hour or more and then withdrew, like a tide withdrawing from a shoreline. I stowed my weapon, I ate, I babbled to other headless – to new recruits, whose names I did not even know – I attempted to give Steelhand a minutely detailed account of the vision. But these others were weary and grieving and my mania was alien and bizarre to them.

It fell away from me, and revealed a barren landscape beneath it. On the occasions when other comrades had been killed in battle, I had found it sorrowful to reflect upon, but their ceasing to be had not cut into my own ego. But Geza and Syrophoenician's deaths seemed deeply wrong, a dislocation like a joint out of true. Their loss afflicted me very greatly. I was as filled with grief as a sandbag is with sand. For the first time in the campaign I asked myself questions such as *why*? and *to what end*? I could, at that time, think of no suitable answer. Why had Syrophoenician died? Why had Geza? There was no reason for their lives to have been snuffed out so completely.

The foam in my lungs began to disintegrate and break up, and the coughing and spewing that ensued was a form of weeping for me; physically racking and uncomfortable, all-consuming. Afterwards I took many sips of water, and sat with my back to the wall of the barrack.

But the war did not stop. Superiors visited us, briefly, in their absurd helmets. They went away again.

Steelhand came over. 'I have been given battlefield authority,' he said.

'In place of Syrophoenician,' I said dully.

'Precisely. The irony of it – coward Steelhand given battlefield authority.'

'There's no cowardice in you,' I said.

He sat down beside me. 'We headless need more direction in our attacks, *Sieur* Cavala.'

For a while I was silent, as the iceberg inside me ground soundlessly against my bones. But he did not depart, and eventually I said: 'Why do you ask me?'

'I value your opinion. You have a rapid mind.'

'My mind is in nowise military,' I said bleakly. 'It is a mind for mournful poetry, not for killing and watching friends killed.'

'It is a shame,' said Steelhand, 'that Syrophoenician has died. We must try and limit such fatalities, or soon the whole of the Thirtieth will be extinct.'

'I don't care,' I said.

'Come now. Why cannot we *focus* our attacks? We scurry up and down the hill like ants, but we come no closer to our objective.'

'Because we encounter resistance.'

'With forethought, and a coordinated attack, we could push past the remotes and automates. Human beings are quicker, are more reactive than automates, and even than remotes. Human beings are better soldiers. This is why they deploy us.'

'Send the new recruits in formation,' I said. 'I do not know their names, and care not if they are killed.'

He left me alone. This was, of course, a cruel thing for me to say, and there is no justification for it, except that my grief had made me uncaring and angry. But this was hardly the fault of the new recruits.

I slept, and my sleep brought a vivid dream in which I revisited the strange place of my vision: the blond grass rustling at the touch of occasional breezes, the bright blue lake, the rapid succession of day and night. When I awoke it was because Steelhand was shaking me.

I cannot have been dreaming. The headless do not dream. I must have been suffering some vivid after-flash or memory of my former vision.

'I do not understand,' I said. I was not really addressing him.

'Come,' said Steelhand. 'We must suit up, and take a weapon from the rack. Needleguns this time, my friend.'

We went over to the rack together.

'I don't understand,' I said again.

'What is it,' he asked, 'that you don't understand?'

'I had a strange vision, an hallucination, upon the battlefield.'

'So you told us all when you returned,' said Steelhand as he folded his torso-armour onto his body like a sandwich board. 'You spoke very rapidly, and rather confusingly. A mansion on a hillside, a swimming pool, and dawn following night following day within minutes.'

'There was a man there, who claimed to have knowledge of the Sugar, and the true nature of the war.'

179

'If this was truly a vision,' said Steelhand, 'then perhaps he was an angel. Or a djinn.'

'He told me that he was my enemy.'

'Djinn, then.'

'He said his name was Levitt Dunber.'

'A strange name for a spirit.'

'He reminded me of somebody I once knew, upon Pluse.'

'This sounds more like a waking dream, my friend,' said Steelhand, slapping my back. 'I would suggest that one or other enemy weapon, maybe the boomshell itself, interfered with the working of your ordinator and squeezed a rapid jumble of strange thoughts through your consciousness.'

'This is a possible explanation,' I agreed.

We lined up to have wadding inserted in our lungs. The reinforcement headless were so new that they quailed and thrashed as the pipe was fitted.

On the jog to the breakland my thoughts were on what awaited me. We were told that the enemy had mounted some sort of counterattack, with a great many remotes, and although we had beaten this back – at the cost of many lives – it would surely be renewed. But the prospect of my own death seemed, in fact, appealing. In the manner of the petty thoughts that run through one's mind, I thought: when I die I will be able to disprove the absurd contention of Levitt Dunber that his dream house on that dream hill was heaven! This seemed, somehow, important to me. In retrospect I believe the truth is that I was weary of fighting and lacking in the vital spirit needed for carrying on with enthusiasm.

I rushed through the defile and hurried straight to the top of the hill. The darkness was more complete, and stiller, than usual: the only lights were the ragged green clusters of our own automates, lumbering down the far side of the hill in advance of our assault.

I hurried on through the murk, and reached the stony channel at the base. Here was one solitary remote, picking its way through boulders, and I pinned its clamshell head with two needles before it could even raise its weapon.

Looking behind me I could see a scatter of headless. 'Come!' I cried. 'Would you wish to live for ever?'

'Where shall we go?' one of them shouted in return.

I tried to reply *up the hill* when the boomshell shuddered upon us, shaking the jelly of my body and cramping all my innards. But I was accustomed, now, and the pain did not distract me. I ran on and mounted the far hill.

In the darkness my running became an intimate and alienated thing, as if I were a blind man running on a gymnasium treadmill. I pushed my legs, and strained up the hill. Every now and again a large rock would loom up from the gloom and I would jink round it. After a while it occurred to me that I had gone too far. I stopped, and looked back, but could see nothing. Then on a whim I ran back down the hill for a bit, on a diagonal course. I thought of the hill in the vision, across the lake, with a slant road running straight down it. Was it a dream-translation of my present landscape? One hill, another hill, and the dream-seen path mapping out where I should move? Perhaps so.

A grape-cluster of red lamps faded up into vision as I ran down, and immediately I came upon three small automates standing together. They were, I saw, guarding an inset shaft into the hill. I felt the conviction inside me that this was my target.

I was armed only with a needle gun, when heavier ordnance would have been better. But there was a bleak fearlessness inside me, and I charged on, firing at the machines. One broke into pieces and fell apart. One loomed upon me, gunbarrels aimed, but I riddled it with needles and it froze in place. The third shot at me, and only a painful drop and roll on the stony ground saved me. I slid, and spun, bringing my gun to bear on the target, but when I squeezed the trigger it did not fire.

I could not believe that I had used up my cartridge so soon – but, then again, I had been firing many needles. Perhaps I had lost count.

I jinked again, and dust bullied up from the ground beside me where the automate's weapons hit. There was nothing to do but retreat, and so I started a zaggy sprint down the hill. As if in response the boomshell slackened and faded away. I felt my heart shudder, bell out and start pumping again.

I ran past two headless. 'Back!' I yelled.

'What's happening?' cried one, turning as I passed, and I saw a many fingered blob of black-red, like a coral structure, appear from his chest. Immediately he was falling forward with a hole in his torso, and more blood was gushing. I ran. The second headless turned in the direction of the shooting, and raised his own club-gun; but after holding it there for a short time without firing it he dropped it and turned to run. A dozen automates, of varying sizes, were rolling down the hill out of the black fog.

'My gun!' my companion wailed, as the two of us leapt over the boulders at the bottom. 'It has broken!'

We hurried back to the breakland and through the defile, cursing our weaponry. In ones and twos other headless came back, and the barrage began on the far side of the breakland. I counted three rounds of heavy cannon, and then the bigger guns fell silent.

Engineers – headed men wearing the same elaborate headwear as the superiors – were already in the barrack as I jogged in. Datascreens were connected to the mainframe. 'It seems it is a general malfunction,' said Steelhand.

He pulled off his torso armour, and the two great petal-shaped sheets of it were sopping on the inside with blood.

'What is the manner of the malfunction?'

'All the guns have seized or broken after a few rounds of fire,' the engineer said.

I helped Steelhand locate his wound: a small projectile had passed though the corner of his stomach, in at the front and out at the side. The bleeding made the wound look worse than it was, for I could not have fitted my little finger into the actual hole. I pressed medical insert into the wound and strapped a bandage to his side.

'Why have the weapons seized up?' I asked.

'I do not know.'

'I thought that I had merely emptied my cartridge.'

'A needle cartridge contains a thousand rounds,' he said chidingly.

With no headed officers to report to, the main engineer addressed himself to Steelhand. All the remaining headless – forty men, perhaps – gathered about. The face of the engineer, framed in his oversized helmet, appeared anxious at being surrounded by so many headless soldiers. 'We have uncoupled the mainframe,' he said. 'Your weapons will fire, but the eyes in them will not work. You will have to do without the central coordination of the mainframe.'

I was surprised to hear that there had been any central coordination to our fighting, but I said nothing.

'What has happened to the mainframe?' Steelhand asked.

'A battlefield malfunction,' was the only reply. Though pressed, the engineer would say nothing more. Presumably he did not know.

One of his subordinates, in a state of some anxiety, reported news from one of his datascreens. The enemy had overrun the breaklands. 'We must fall back,' the main engineer announced. 'We are not fighting men.'

And with impressive rapidity they gathered their equipment and left.

The rest of us huddled around Steelhand. 'What must we do?' one of the newer headless asked. 'What should we do?'

'I don't know,' he said.

But this was not what we needed to hear.

'Should we retreat?' suggested one.

'No,' replied Steelhand, drawing the syllable out. Then he said: 'We should stay and fight. Don't you think?'

There was murmuring. 'You must tell us what to do,' I said.

'Very well.' He pondered. 'We shall stay and fight.'

We all of us took two weapons, one in each hand, and gathered outside the barrack. The lights hanging on the side of the building at our backs gave some illumination of the land before us, but the prospect was a foreshortened one, detail soon disappearing into darkness. 'If they have broken through the defiles, they will be bringing automates over the breaklands,' Steelhand announced. 'But first of all I suppose they will send troops through.'

'Remotes?'

'Surely they cannot send remotes so far from their base,' I said. I was talking as if I were expert in such matters, although this statement was nothing more than a guess.

'It will be troops then,' said Steelhand. 'We must ready ourselves.'

We manoeuvred such heavy machinery as we could, hauling it out to provide ourselves with cover, and aimed our guns at the land in front of us. Soon figures emerged, running rapidly towards us out of the black.

'Fire!' cried one of the newer recruits, and a volley was discharged, dropping several figures, before Steelhand's voice crying 'Stop! Stop!' halted us. The running men were the headless who manned the breaklands. We had been shooting at our own.

We gathered the dozen or so survivors behind our cover. 'Our weapons will not work!' was their complaint. We sent them into the barrack to rearm themselves.

'They're right behind us,' one of these newcomers said. 'It is headed troops.'

Almost as soon as he had spoken we heard the rumble of automates, and soon we could see the lights of the big machines as they rumbled towards us; and, sheltering behind them as cover, I saw my first human enemy soldiers.

After so many weeks of dutifully jogging along the zigzag paths between the barrack and the front, weeks of resenting that I was not permitted simply to run straight forward – I at last discovered what it was about the dust in between that obliged us to circumvent it. The nearest automate rolled over the path and detonated a dust cloud that spurted up about its wheels. It groaned and whirred, tried flattening its wheels to pinched ovals and walking its way out, but the dust sucked it down.

Troops darted from behind the stalled behemoth and dazzling firework flashes spouted from their weapons. Shrapnel burst upon us in a cloud of glitter. We returned fire, but human troops were much harder targets to hit than the machines with which we were familiar. A second and third automate rumbled to a halt, but the troops, in a series of weaving interlocking runs, continued advancing upon us. They were much more accurate with their weapons than the remotes. Many of the headless fell.

I summoned my resolve. Surely, I told myself, this was as good a place to die as any. And, telling myself this, I yelled and broke cover. Perhaps startled into action by my lead, eight or ten headless shouted and followed me.

My intention had been simply to die, because I was weary of living and fighting. But my impromptu charge had quite another effect. The sight of a dozen headless men running towards them discommoded the enemy soldiers, unused as they were to so outlandish a sight – headless men, ghouls, monsters, firing weapons. The forward mass of enemy broke and ran. I chased, screaming, until I reached the nearest automate and observed its guns levelling on me. Then, without passion, I fired my club-gun twice and disabled the thing.

'We must retreat,' Steelhand was yelling.

I ran back, and the group of us retreated through the barrack and along the supply road, half of us covering the run of the others, then swapping positions. This was tiring work, and dangerous too, but at least it occupied the mind and prevented us worrying too greatly at the prospect of likely injury and death. The headed troops had seemed remarkably jittery at the sight of us. Perhaps we were too monstrous for them to bear. But there were too few of us to press this advantage and drive them from the field.

It is the nature of a polarising fog that vertical lines of sight are much more closely muffled than horizontal ones. A balloon might have been hanging ten metres over our heads with powerful arc-neon lights angled down, and we would have seen nothing. But this fog cannot muffle *sound*, and so we heard the approach of planes coming from behind us. There must have been many of them, but I do not know how many. There was only a multiple wailing noise that steeped sharply to a steam-whistle intensity right over our heads. The screaming hung above us, and then was starting to pass away when piercing bright light ovalled out from a hundred places low against the ground, behind us, to our left, to our right, in front of us. My visual software blanked, and for a moment all I could see was a virtual cursor blinking as the system struggled to reinitialise. Then the grey screen darkened, and became populated with shadowy lumps, headless men, picking themselves up, stumbling on. I felt clogs in my skin where shrapnel had lodged, and there was painful sense of dislocation in several of my ribs. I paid little attention to this, and I ran for cover before planes made a second pass. Both my boots were full of blood and they squelched comically as I lumbered.

We had almost reached a single-storey building whose roof had gone and whose profile presented an undulating rubble line. Crenellations fashioned by the instant erosion of war. But the screaming was coming across the sky again and we had not yet made the cover when the planes again blanked my visual software with their fiat lux. I felt the light as intense pressure and heat and then I felt nothing for a minute or more.

A dozen surviving headless were all who recovered consciousness after this second raid. We gathered on the far side of the broken wall of what had once been a barrack, or warehouse; I knew none of them by name. Steelhand was somewhere behind us, lying unbreathing amongst the black dust.

The others crowded around me and pressed me with questions, because to them I was the veteran, and the leader. The very idea! I told them to take position and hold off the advance, but although we waited for a long stretch with our guns poking over humps of rubbled concrete and through gaps, the assault did not come. The sound of planes, mercifully far distant, was still audible, and from time to time the horizon would gleam with brief splotches of light.

The roofless space in which we took cover was littered with all manner of junk, including quantities of drink and food. This latter had been intended for headed soldiers, but we were able to break it and feed it into our neck valves. No matter how we searched, though, we could not discover any pharmocopies. This was a matter of concern for me.

Soon enough we began coughing up our wadding, and for a while all that could be heard was the hawking and screeching of a dozen headless. Afterwards we found apple juice in a large vat and made cups out of folded cardboard to drink it.

One soldier approached me. 'What should we do?' he asked. I did not know his name. I did not ask him it.

'I have no idea.'

'Should we stay here? Are our orders to defend this place? Should we push back?'

I examined myself. Blood from eight or ten small wounds had flowed under my armour, down into my meadhres and boots. Two of my ribs were evidently broken, and the fingers of my right hand, where they still clutched the handle of my weapon, were scorched and purple. None of the men now under my command was in a flawless physical condition.

'No,' I said. 'We'd better pull back.'

'Are you sure? Are you sure?'

'Somebody must assume command,' I said. 'Shall we debate it?'

'*You* must assume command,' said the soldier.

We cleaned up as far as we could, using supplies of army-issue mouth-wash to rinse wounds. Then, in reasonably good order, we made our way out of the back of the building and along a kibble-strewn road into the darkness. Coming out we straightaway encountered an automate, one of ours, lying at a forty-five degree angle. Its leg-wheels were broken and much of its infrastructure was melted and torn, but some of its lights were on, and it swivelled a gun barrel at us as we passed. Either it was out of ammunition, or else it recognised us as friendly troops; but either way it did not fire.

Soon we saw our first headed corpse, lying across the road with his face in a puddle. Then we found ourselves stepping over dozens of similar bodies. I do not know how so many troops had been killed so far behind the front line. Perhaps they were casualties from earlier air raids. We passed by this scene. Seeing headed soldiers killed and discarded, amongst them many superiors, was queerly upsetting. This seemed somehow a distortion of what was right and expected. That this many were dead still possessed of their skulls, whilst we limped along alive headless, implied an unhealthy cosmos, a fungal decay at the roots that ought to nourish, a rottenness that twists and buckles the tree above into monstrous shapes.

'What must we do?' said my soldiers anxiously. 'Should we stop and bury them? Should we at least recite the relevant scripture over their bodies?'

'No,' I said. 'We'd better push on back.'

Finally, after long slog, we saw lights and came straight upon an armed encampment: a fence of wire and behind it a bright-lit barrack and warehouse. The guards did not fire upon us, for they recognised our profiles as headless. Instead they waved us through and we came inside the building into a bright-lit space. There were many soldiers here, all headed, lying and sitting, talking, eating, praying. These men stared at us as we came in, their expressions not welcoming, for to them we were criminals and desperate men. This hostility acted upon us as a defining pressure, gathering us into a tight little group.

I tried to find a superior to whom I could report, but nobody answered me when I asked where to find one. Eventually I spotted a captain, and, weary and sore, my skin stiff with my own blood, I summoned my courage and approached him.

'From where?' he asked. He was a handsome man, smooth-skinned and pale-haired with sharp blue eyes; but his face was sucked-in with tiredness and the skin beneath his eyes was crimped and hollow. 'From the front? The breaklands?'

'Yes, Captain.'

'I can't help you. Have your men eaten?'

'We have, Captain.'

'If I were you,' he said, turning away, 'I'd gather them out of the way. The men here are unhappy. They are startled by the turn events have taken. Don't give them a reason to become angry with you.'

I took his advice, and led my eleven followers to a quiet space behind some large cases. I did not ask why they might be angry with us, of all people; I assumed it was the natural order that we would receive their cuffs and contempt.

Here we sat, and some of my headless took the chance to sleep. I did not. I fingered Mark Pol's eye stalk, still on its cord about my neck. I explored again the ridges and length of it. I thought about Pluse, about my former life. I thought about my vow to revenge myself upon Mark Pol Treherne. Never before had all these things seemed so utterly distant. It was a complete distance. I say *complete* in the sense of being unbreachable, although the word has other meanings. Every breath, every click of my neck valve, brought welling soreness in my chest, but that was the least of my concerns.

Three

A number of hours later the captain came behind the crates and addressed himself to one of my soldiers. 'Are you the leader of these headless?' The man did not reply.

'I am the man you are looking for,' I said, standing up.

He turned to me. 'You – you are the one to whom I spoke earlier?'

'I am.'

'You all look alike to me,' he said. 'Come along.'

Across the barrack the headed troops were gathering their material and preparing to move. I stepped through the groups of them feeling, for the first time, intimidated; these men all towered over me, all aggressive and sour. I readied myself, with some weariness, to fight them if I must do, but of course the mere presence of a superior was enough to recall to me the effect of the truncheon, and to make me pliable. I do not believe, as I look back, that he was even carrying a truncheon.

At the back of the open space were several smaller inset rooms, and it was to one of these that I was brought. 'The magister wants to have a word with you,' said the captain. 'Have you ever spoken to a magister before?'

'No, Captain.'

'Don't be intimidated. Or, perhaps it would be better to say, don't be *overly* intimidated. Address him as "Magister".'

'Yes, Captain.'

'In.'

Inside the small space were half a dozen headed people hurrying about, busy with unimaginable tasks. The room was filled with datascreens and processing equipment, some of which was being dismantled, some packed away.

The magister himself was a short bald-headed man, dark-skinned. The end of his nose was divided into two little lumps by a central crease, like a coffee bean. He had no eyebrows, not even eyelashes, and his mouth was very wide and mobile. He saw me. 'Visions?' he snapped at me. 'Hallucinations?'

I was very disconcerted. 'Magister?'

'Have *any* – of your *men* – reported visions?'

'Yes, magister. I myself have—'

'Visions of what?'

I could feel my heart galloping. 'An encounter with a man in a country mansion,' I said. 'A conversation. The too-rapid succession of night and day.'

The magister nodded. 'Where were you stationed?'

'Magister, I regret to say I do not know. We were attacking a boomshell installation set in a hill – up by the breaklands . . .'

'You're a fool,' he said. 'All my headless troops have been attacking boomshell installations, *of course*. To break through the boomshell line is the *point* of the whole – boh – why *talk* to you?' He snorted in anger and turned to say something to a subordinate. I felt my bowels jellify within me. He turned back to me. 'So you don't happen to know *which* boomshell you were attacking? Seven? Nine-A?'

'Magister I regret to say that I—'

'Off you go now,' he said.

I left at once.

The captain was still outside, and walked alongside me as I made my way back. We went in silence for half a minute, and then he asked abruptly, 'Are you well?'

I was disproportionately touched by this small verbal politeness.

'Captain, yes,' I said.

'You're trembling.'

'I have never before,' I said, 'encountered a magister.'

The captain laughed, a brief low laugh. 'He is only a man, he is only an officer. He is, admittedly a high-ranking officer. But to think of one of the fearsome headless trembling at meeting an officer! I had thought you all practically devils. I'd thought you were monsters who roar and devour human flesh!'

'Is such our reputation, Captain?' I asked, genuinely astonished to hear this.

'Indeed. But you seem quietly spoken, even timid.'

We walked on for a while, and returned to the corner of the barrack where the headless were all, save one, asleep on the floor. The captain loitered, talking to me for a while; and I was emboldened to ask him: 'What has happened here?'

'I am not sure,' was his reply. 'There have been reports of visions from several of the fourteen salients. It is puzzling.'

I was silent. Then the captain said: 'The mainframes are firewalled, and the guns are firewalled. But *you* are not firewalled. I believe that is the matter here.'

'I do not understand, Captain.'

'Your ordinator, I mean. What would be the point in firewalling your ordinator? Why would anybody try to load a virus into *your* consciousness? And, in the usual course of things – in peacetime, I mean – if they did, why would anybody be concerned? That matters might be different in war: well ... I suppose that didn't occur to anybody.'

I saw then what he meant. It felt like a wave of exhaustion, as if everything was suddenly too much to bear. I wanted to go to sleep. I was unconcerned whether I would even wake up again. 'The visions ...'

'*From* individual headless, I suppose, into their guns. The guns cannot be hacked externally, for they are designed very carefully to be proof against such attack. But connected to you they become part of your consciousness, of the – how is the phrase? – of the *simulation software*. I suppose the thinking is that if a virus could be installed into *you* ...' He shook his head. 'Then corrupted *guns* download corrupted data into the mainframe and in turn corrupt them. It was all very well co-ordinated. Dozens of headless have reported visions. Conversations that delayed them, spooled out the time, until the viruses could be loaded. Then – snap back to consciousness and back to barracks, and ...'

I held my peace.

'We shall counter-attack,' he said, drawing himself to his full height. 'We will get things up and running, of course.' He spoke with genuine confidence. 'Their software skills cannot be so very far ahead of ours. That cannot be. But the feeling here is ugly, and men who have lost friends and honourable soldiers who feel victory curdling into defeat would need little provocation to turn on your kind. Perhaps,' he said, as he went, 'it is only your fearsome reputation that prevents them from falling upon you here and now. That and our orders.'

Soon afterwards the headed troops all pulled back, leaving that place and hurrying away. We were told to stay and defend the installation from enemy attack. We were twelve bodies, no more, and nobody could say how many thousands of enemy soldiers were advancing upon the position. But to think in those terms was, of course, to miss the point of the orders.

We took up positions in the dark outside the building. Behind us the barrack was full of the noises of men and materials being packed up and marched out. Eventually it fell silent. I sent one of my men (*my* men! – to think I had arrived in such a position of authority!) back into the now-empty space to recover any supplies of food, drink and anything else that might be useful.

We sat and lay at our positions for long hours. The air was sometimes troubled with distant noise, and sometimes there were flickers of peculiar light in the distance, piling upon the horizon like tree-rings and then instantly vanishing into blackness again. There were no signs of encroaching soldiers.

I grew dozy. It occurred to me that it had been a great many days since my last pouch of pharmocopy. Given the nature of war I was not able to recall precisely how many days, but in the solitary dark I tried to remember. But my memory was like a hand from which fingers had been blown off. I could reach clumsily into the past – my life as a poet, the walk to Cainon, my training as a soldier – but I could not manipulate the finer details, or pull anything over towards me for a closer look. I could not remember precisely how many days since the last pouch, or the exact order in which my friends had become casualties. Or the precise delineation of features upon Siuzan Delage's face. I tried to visualise her, this woman whom I loved and whose life I had ruined, and I could not even remember that. This struck me, in that dark place with sleep starting to rust the metal of my wakefulness, as the most appalling thing of all. I had been prepared to die to save her, and now I could not even picture her face. A melancholy gripped my thoughts, and in an interior fug I pressed at the memory, pushed and pushed my thoughts as if by sheer will I could conjure up her face. I tried to evoke her eyebrows, the colour of her eyes, the precise tuck and trim of the shape of her lips.

I had a dark revelation. I could not remember her face because she no longer possessed a face. My love for her was such – it was so finely attuned to her – that it had jettisoned her beautiful face as had the headsman. This made me sadder. I could barely hear the noise, like a buzzing, of rhythmic repetition. But it persisted, and I concentrated upon it, and eventually it came into focus as Jon followed by Sieur Jon, repeated over and over. Jon – *Sieur* Jon – Jon – *Sieur* Jon—

It was one of the soldiers. 'What?'

'*Sieur* Jon—?'

'What is it?' I snapped. 'What do you want with me?'

He pointed, and I turned my torso to follow the line of his arm. Glinting in the polarised dark were many red lamps, and the scurrying shadows of enemy soldiers. They had advanced silently, and now they were very close to our position. Perhaps I had dozed.

Infuriated I gave the order to fire, and our puny force let loose a number of volleys; but remotes swarmed forward to soak up the barrage and under their cover a large troop of human soldiery rushed us from the left. Hindsight tells me that, of course, I should never have allowed them to slink so far round to the left. But this is what they had achieved, and in minutes they had overrun us. In the last frantic moments I ordered my men to pull back, but this was fruitless. Five of us lay dead; one more refused to give up his weapon and was shot through the chest. Those of us remaining, a ragged half dozen, were wrist-strapped with binding plastic and marched into the empty barrack behind us. I do not believe we inflicted a single human casualty upon them.

They took all our names and wrote them on a data tablet. Why did they take our names? I don't know why, except that I have heard it said of the Congregation of the Humane Faithful that they take excessive delight in making lists, gathering facts, constructing taxonomies and so on. This is their culture, and there may be little point in quoting at them the Bibliqu'rân to the effect that *the spirit keeps alive where the letter kills*. This is not their way; they read the sacred book differently. They logged us, and sat us in a line against one wall whilst a great many troops passed into the captured space. We watched as several automates lumbered in, and settled on their creaking wheel-haunches to undergo field services.

A captain came up. He was, or seemed to me, extraordinarily young; but there was no mistaking his rank. He spoke to us with a surprising informality, and his Homish was so heavily accented as to be, on occasion, incomprehensible. 'You are leader?'

'I am.'

'You are Jon Cawa?'

'Jon Cavala.'

'You sign docimentation? You sign docimentation accepting *your* men in surrender of me?'

'You are a captain?' I asked. When he looked puzzled I said: 'Your rank? You hold the rank of *captain*, yes? You have command here?'

He put his head on one side. 'Sure, but my name is Haward Fulliof, call me Haw, or sometime Haw-Haw.'

'Your rank,' I said, speaking slowly, 'is such that you may order me to sign whatever you choose.'

He furrowed his brow as he pondered my words, blond eyebrows bowing to one another across the spiky bridge of his nose. His pink cheeks moved as if he were grinding his teeth. 'No,' he said eventually. 'Jon – OK? I an *enemy*.'

'Nevertheless,' I explained, 'as captives we become bondsmen and you have authority over us.'

'I to prefer if you sign free, free-ish.' He shut his eyes, opened them. 'Free-*ly*.'

'I shall do whatever you order me to do,' I said.

He released my hands from behind my back. From his pocket he brought out a data tablet and stylus. The document I signed was tri-lingual, and one of the languages was Homish. I signed it – of course – because I had been ordered to do so. Afterwards Captain Haw-Haw asked me, with too many *pleases*, to turn round and he refastened my wrists in their plastic cuffs. This pulled on the muscles over my chest which increased the pain of my broken ribs. But that was nothing. I tried pushing my hands down so that they might slide over my hips and thighs and come up the front of me, but the shackle was too high up my wrists to permit this. It did not matter.

We sat for a long time, watching the men coming and going. The barrack was a forward point, and at one point a great stream of fresh soldiers poured in, loitered for ten minutes whilst they were re-armed, and then poured out of the other side to prosecute the campaign. The automates, repaired, squeezed their oval wheels thinner to stand up and clanked out. Many of the enemy soldiers rolled out mats and lay down upon them. On occasion a few soldiers would glance in our direction, and talked amongst themselves at the oddity of our appearance. But soon enough we were just one more fixture in a large space filled with things and we were ignored.

The plastic wrist binds were not too tight, and the plastic was soft, but of course it was uncomfortable to sit with my hands strapped together in the small of my back. I rebuked myself, silently, that I had allowed my mind to wander and so be captured. It would not have been too difficult, I reasoned, to have put up a fierce defence and died in the fighting. It was shameful that I had not. It is a feature of shame that it can fill a person brimming as water in a jug, and yet when more shame is poured in it does not spill over the lip but rather sinks into the depths of the jug, thickening the fluid. After everything that I had done in my life, or failed to do, this final failure was nevertheless painful.

The bustle and noise in the barrack died down. I cannot say how many hours we had sat silently against that wall. The lights were dimmed across half the space, perhaps to permit the soldiers the better to sleep.

I concluded that I had the stomach for more shame, after all.

I stood up. I walked, without hurry or delay, to a rack of lances not far from where we were.

I brought my bound hands round from my back to my front. If you, reading this, have a head, you may not understand how easy it is for a headless man to accomplish that mild contortion. My hands were twisted backwards on themselves at the wrist, but a certain range of movement remained in them. After this manoeuvre my hands were still bound, and now bent backwards, but in front of me. The lances were, of course, locked in their rack and all of them were lacking their firing chips, but I was able to fumble a test code into one keypads with the backs of my numb fingers. The tip of a lance heated, and I pressed the plastic of my handcuff to it. Naturally the heat scorched the backs of both of my hands, but this was a pain I could handle easily enough.

In a short time the bonded plastic of my handcuff gave way.

Nobody had noticed me doing this.

I slipped behind a stack of storage boxes and waited there for a while. Watching round the side of this I observed the enemy soldiers: most of them asleep, some of them awake and sitting in groups. Every now and then one might glance over at the line of tied-up headless enemy captives, but they did not register that one of this number had slipped away. My men were canny enough not to draw attention to the fact that I had freed myself.

My options were limited, but after half an hour I was able to insinuate myself close enough to a rack of handguns to lift three weapons. The enemy had omitted to alter the keypad codes, or perhaps they had not yet got around to that task, which was fortunate for me. I primed the weapons.

I slunk back to the wall and my men. A hand weapon was not the best tool for cutting their bonds. Nevertheless I reasoned that it would not be possible to lead them all one by one to the heated tip of the lance. We would surely be observed. And if, in shooting off their cuffs, I shot away one or two of their fingers, then this, though unfortunate, would not prevent them from fighting afterwards.

I slipped back into position amongst my men, with the three guns in my hands behind my back. I did not need to tell them what I had done, or what I planned; nor did I need to spell out the risk to themselves. They understood, and acceded.

I waited until I judged that things in the barrack were quiet. Then I placed the mouth of one gun, its little 'o' mouth of metal surprise, against one of the plastic cuffs, and squeezed out a single round. As I pulled the trigger I hoped that it would not make too loud a noise.

It cracked like a snare drum as it fired, and thumped into the stone floor like a whomper. Naturally this noise attracted attention.

Heads turned. I was forced to swap surreptitious action for haste.

I grabbed the next man and pressed the gun against his bond. A sneeze of blood sprayed down with the shot. Of course, he did not complain, but when he lifted his hands they were, I decided, too bloody to hold a gun.

People were shouting.

I would not have time to free all of my men; but since I only possessed weapons for three of them this was, perhaps, no bad thing. I tried once more, attempting greater precision in my positioning of the mouth of the gun against the centre of the bond. I fired. The plastic snapped apart.

'I have only three weapons,' I said to the two remaining captives. 'You are lucky in that you shall not be compelled to violate your position as bondsmen.' From my left shoulder eye I saw several soldiers hefting their weapons into firing positions. There was no more time.

Two of my freed men picked the handweapons from the floor, and the third fellow with bloody hands stood up. He could have stayed, of course, but he chose to come. I held my gun with both hands and began firing into the mass of enemy troops. There were so many of them that it was hardly possible to miss. Each shot sent a headed man sprawling.

There was enormous confusion.

We darted backwards and looked for cover. There were several varieties of weapon that the enemy could not risk firing in the enclosed space of the barrack for fear of injuring their own; but it was not long before files of men were being assembled with more suitable ordnance.

The nearest exit was in the corner of the building. I sprinted for it, and ran smack into a man who was hurrying in from outside to see what the commotion was. This impact momentarily winded me, but one of my men was able to shoot the enemy down. Three of us were though the door, with the bloody-handed fellow almost there, when the sound of scores of volleys of needles filled the air behind us. I did not see, but can imagine, what happened to the men still wrist-tied against the wall. The man with bloodied hands staggered outside to fall into the black dust with a burr of needles in his back. The three of us did not look back.

Four

We three ran into the darkness. Of course we were pursued. Needles
flickered past us like flaws in our vision software. Our good fortune was
that the land rose half a league south of that camp, so that by hurrying
up the incline we disappeared into the murk. The dust was thicker here,
sometimes swallowing my legs to the mid-shin like a maw, but it had
not been primed as a dustmine or with a clogging agent and so was easy
enough to move on. My two men were close behind me.

We came across a repair-automate, a machine so huge its top was
invisible in the smirr. It had been broken, perhaps by enemy action, and
had lowered its box-girdered belly into the dry dirt, and it was in amongst
this twisted scaffold that we took temporary shelter. We rested our guns
against spars and made careful observation of the land over which we
had just come. Nobody was directly behind us, or at least, nobody that
we could see in the murk.

'What are your names?' I whispered to the two headless with me.

'Grande,' whispered one, and 'Kym Field,' the other.

'I am Jon Cavala.'

'We know,' said Grande.

There were noises below us, and we fell silent. Presently a cluster of
remotes came labouring up through the darkness. They stopped before
the prow of the fallen automate, spun their clamshell heads left and right
and then passed by climbing higher. This was a sharp moment, for I did
not like the idea of permitting the enemy to get behind me. But I liked
less the idea of revealing our position to remotes by firing at them, for
they would transmit our location to the enemy mainframe and surely
after that would come attack from the air that would crush us. Besides,
I told myself, the land all around us, behind as well as in front, was
surely filled with enemy anyway.

Shortly after this three headed soldiers came up. Again we held fire,
and lay silently. The soldiers examined the ruined hulk, poking through
it unsystematically, and they failed to uncover our hiding place. After

this desultory search they put up their weapons and sat on the ground not far from us. Then they removed their helmets to share the smoking of a curved cheroot.

We were perfectly quiet, unobserved.

The enemy soldiers spoke amongst themselves in low voices, chattering in their own tongue, which I could not understand. Then they fell silent. One pointed with his finger down the hill, and the other two looked in that direction. There was a dim fold of light gleaming down there somewhere, a damp-looking pearl-coloured line half a degree of arc in length: will-o'-the-wisp, or refracted light from some more distant explosion, who knows what it was? Whilst their attention was distracted, and their helmets were off, I took my aim and cut bulleted-channels through two of their skulls with two rapid shots, such that those two men slumped forward and fell on their dead faces. The third got to his feet, but with a weird slowness, not at all what you would expect: not a rapid leaping *en garde!*, but an almost leisurely uprise. Kym Field shot him in the side of his head as he turned towards us.

We tried to take their guns, but they would not work. They were keyed in some way to their owners, perhaps. They did, however, have rations in their belts, and these we took and devoured at once.

'We must find a storage facility,' I told my two. 'I have not had my pharmocopy in several weeks, and the lack of necessary hormones is impairing my ability to fight.'

'Where must we look?' asked Grande.

'I do not know.'

'Let us wait here for a little,' suggested Kym Field. 'And then explore over the far side of this hill.'

'Yes,' I agreed.

We lay in the dark. I believe the two others fell asleep, but I could not.

After a while I roused my men and the three of us climbed to the top of the hill. Creeping through the dark. Grande came up to me. '*Sieur* Cavala,' he said. 'I am troubled.'

I did not reply. As we started down the far side of the dark hill the ground was broken into craters and gouges, and we had to tread carefully. There was a great deal of litter mixed in with the black dust.

'There is,' Grande said, after a moment, 'a certain shame in breaking our duty as bondsmen.'

'Not for you,' I replied. 'For you and Kym Field were following my orders, as was proper for you to do. The shame, which – I agree – is great, is mine alone.'

He was silent for a while. Then he said, 'I find myself disinclined to die.'

I understood what he meant. 'I too,' I said. 'But this by itself, merely wanting to live, this is not inherently shameful. For life is the gift of the All'God, and we must not squander it.'

'Is this a *decent* philosophy for a soldier?' he asked. 'Are such thoughts *proper*?'

His question annoyed me. 'Your philosophy should be to follow my orders,' I retorted. 'That should be enough for you.'

We roamed the hillside for a long time, on two occasions dropping into the dust as noises clanked past us. At the bottom of the hill we found a road, its paving slabs cracked and dislocated as if the tabletop on which a domino-game was laid had been kicked heartily from beneath. Except that the domino tiles were all three metres long and one wide. Lights glimmered on the far side of this road and we made our way cautiously.

The lights belonged to an open truck that was moving, awkwardly through the dust towards us. A dozen headed troops sat in the back. But the foolishness of it was that I did not realise that this is what the lights meant until we were almost upon it. Blinded, perhaps, by the urgency of my need for pharmocopy I told myself that the lights were a building, a storehouse, a medical supply facility, and I hurried towards them. And so it was that we blundered suddenly into the headlights of the approaching vehicle.

The surprise of our appearance, and the ferocity of our reputation, was perhaps of service to us. The engine noise rose and the truck accelerated towards us as if to run us down. But it was a simple matter to step aside, myself and Kym Field on one side, Grande on the other. And then the sides of the truck moved smoothly from right to left before us, with the heads of the troops visible above the board, such that it was like a fairground test of marksmanship. We fired and fired again, and the mass of men on the back was thrown into confusion, huggle-muggle in panic. Needles flashed out from them in all directions, but they were poorly aimed and none struck us.

The truck lurched away from us, and I tapped Kym Field on the flank and ran past Grande, who followed. In moments we came upon a low wall, broken in many places, and behind this we took cover.

*

We stayed where we were, listening to the noise of shouts and the retreating engine roar. Then the noises changed. The engine stopped, and the shouting sounded more purposeful. Troops formed up and perhaps came looking for us. We stayed where we were.

Then we heard the sound of fighting, the snick of needles and the distinctive clump of clubs being fired. Then, without warning, half a dozen soldiers came piling through the gap in the wall. It was so startling that I almost did not realise that these were as headless as I. My weapon was up and my finger almost pulling the trigger before I saw.

Their weapons, likewise, were on us. 'We are headless,' I said.

There was a pause, and then weapons were lowered. For a moment we all listened to the noises on the far side of the wall. They swirled and chattered, and then they began to recede. 'They are going away,' I said. 'They are chasing us in the wrong direction.'

'Who are you?' hissed one of the newcomers. 'Why are you not wearing your armour?'

'We three are what remains of the Thirtieth Troop of Cainon Headless. Or I am. I don't know which troop these two belong to.'

'We are the Sixth Troop of Rotier Headless,' said the leading headless. 'Where are your weapons?'

'We were captured,' I said. 'Then we escaped capture.'

He stood, silent, for a while to think about this. For a moment I thought he might turn in disgust and move away. But then he spoke. 'I was a restaurateur,' he said. I waited to see where this non sequitur might lead. 'A man died in my kitchens – an undercook. His family insisted I be prosecuted, as responsible for his death, and so I was.' He paused again. 'Since being beheaded, and since joining the military, many things that were previously certainties to me have become unsettled.' I understood him to be saying that the fact that we, though bondsmen, had broken from captivity was merely one more such unsettlement. 'But,' he added, as if testing the idea, 'was it well done?'

'We fought,' I said. 'We killed some of the enemy, and those of us who died doing it went to the All'God with clean souls. I believe it was well done.'

'War is a strange time,' said the former restaurateur.

'Your name?' I asked.

'Causta.'

'If I may suggest, *Sieur* Causta,' I said. 'It might perhaps be overscrupulous of you to reject us from your troop on the grounds that we violated our duty as bondsmen.'

'I have no desire to reject you. But I confess I am uncertain what our strategy may be.'

'I assume we must fight the enemy until a counter-attack reconnects us with the main body of Pluse troops.'

'This is what I have been assuming,' said Causta. 'But I have doubts.'

'We must find pharmocopy,' I said. 'I need a purse of it immediately, and if you do not need one now you soon will. We must find a store and obtain a supply.'

'This seems a sensible aim,' he agreed. 'But where will we find it?'

We spent two days – perhaps a little more or less, for it was difficult to keep time in that unchanging dust-dark – in one another's company. For a long time we did nothing more than stumble through the dark, taking cover where we could and when we chanced upon the enemy, killing some. Kym Field had received a needle in his thigh when he and I and Grande had chanced upon the truck, and we did not have pliers or any similar necessaries to remove it. He could still walk, limpingly, and he could still fight; but over a day or so the motion of muscle in his leg made the wound much worse, and soon he was bleeding so heavily that no quantity of bandaging could prevent it. We lay him down beside a road and left him. I do not know what happened to him afterwards.

We came across much rubbish. There were many empty containers, all of which we searched for useful things. In the dark, once, I stumbled over a wheeled wire-mesh trolly, of the sort that supermarkets provide to their customers to port their shopping about the store. It lay on back with its pitiable little wheels up in the air. I do now know what it was doing there. We found a hubcap. We found an artificial leg, its motor broken, and many folded pieces of paper, and strips and scraps of rag. We found a roll of wrapping material, brand new: that variety of wrapping material in which transparent plastic is covered in myriad blisters of transparent plastic. Another time I found a surfboard, patterned in red-dotted purple, like a giant's severed tongue: a strange sight indeed amongst all that endlessly dry and war-scorched dust.

I was feeling increasingly ill, and desperate for pharmocopy. When we at last discovered a warehouse I was recklessly eager to storm it.

'The enemy possess it,' Causta pointed out.

'A raid,' I insisted. 'Surprise – suddenness – for there are only a few guards.'

'You are too hasty.'

'Pharmocopy,' I urged, 'is more to us than food. For we can fight without food for weeks, but without our purses we will sicken and die.'

He thought for a time, and then agreed. But our attack, when we mounted it, was impromptu and ragged. One of Causta's men fired a club into a fuel bin, causing it to explode. But there was only a second of fire, and then the flame was replaced by oddly blocky clouds of smoke pouring out, rising and billowing like black sacks filled with hot air. Grande and I rushed the main entrance, shooting without precision at the three or four headed enemy. They returned fire, but I ignored them. I shouldered the door open and had time, just, to see that the space inside was filled with soldiers – hundreds of them, all armed, all starting up. My rage at the hopelessness of it was more painful than either my broken ribs or my lack of necessary hormone.

I tried to lift my handgun, but I caught the barrel of it against the doorframe and it jarred from my grip. This, perhaps, seems improbably clumsy to you. Perhaps you consider my actions to have been subconsciously motivated by a desire to surrender and save my life. I do not know. All I can say is that, at that moment, any motivation must have been subconscious, for I was aware of no conscious thought at all.

Five

The enemy had learned a lesson from our previous escape. Now they bound us tying left wrist to left ankle, right to right. We sat with our knees up and our arms forward for many hours; it was not a comfortable position. My ribs were hurting more than they had done before. The pain was tolerable, but I was certain I could feel the point of break in the two ribs, the rough ends of the fracture, settling out of true. Though it's silly to admit it, it was the aesthetic of this that bothered me more than anything else. Would my chest become distorted if the bones set badly? In the event, they did not; but I worried over the question for a long time.

'You are not in your proper uniform,' said one enemy soldier to me.

'I am not.'

'Did you discard it? Was it taken from you?'

'The latter.'

'So you were in captivity,' he said, starting back from me. 'You are one of those—' Realisation had made him fearful. He hurried off to find his captain.

I did not greatly care. The question that most concerned me, at this juncture, was whether we were liable to execution for breaking our duties as bondsmen. Death would surely have been the natural consequence of such action on Pluse, but I spent a long time wondering whether the same protocols would govern the actions of the enemy. I needed to know in order to decide whether I should prepare my soul to meet the All'God or not. And if not, what I should do.

Finally an officer came over to us. He was holding a data tablet. He spoke Homish fluently. 'I must ask you certain questions. I must ask your names.'

'We are men of the Thirtieth Troop of Cainon Headless and the Sixth Troop of Rotier Headless,' I said.

'Are you in command?' he asked me, checking some details off from his data tablet.

'Syrophoenician,' I said.

He looked up sharply. 'Is that your name?' he asked.

This was a moment about which my whole life shifted and hinged.

Though I was tired and ill, lacking pharmocopy and drugged with defeat, nevertheless I had a flash of insight. I deduced that this man was holding in his hand data about our troop disposition. This must have been derived from the same database that the enemy had infiltrated with their virus. They had of course downloaded our data, including perhaps names and ranks.

And I realised, at that very moment, that he was looking for the soldier Jon Cavala who had breached a signed agreement to subsist peacefully in captivity, causing the deaths of such-and-such number of men. Of course *that* was why he was questioning me. And of course he would punish this Jon Cavala. Even the Congregation of the Humane Faithful must punish such wrong-doing.

Now, the thought uppermost in my mind – as of course you will understand – was one of *shame*. It is shameful to lie, and very shameful to preserve oneself from rightful justice by lying. But, I reasoned, I had filled myself so fully with shame that an additional quantity would settle easily into that mass and barely even be noticed. If by pretending to be Syrophoenician I could escape the punishment allotted to Jon Cavala, then why should I not do so? And so I resolved to impersonate Syrophoenician. My thought was this: that this would confer some *meaning* upon my friend's death, for by freeing up his identity he had made it possible for me to live. It was, in other words, as if he died to save me. Perhaps this thought was mere rags to hide my shame, but it was my thought for all that.

'*Is* that your name?' repeated the officer.

'Syrophoenician,' I said, gravely, and then, almost too late – with the sudden, thundering understanding of what the enemy database would include – I added, 'was my commander.'

Three words, there, a mere three words that preserved my life, and enabled the composition of this narrative (for a dead man cannot write his memoirs). There they are. They were added as a frantic afterthought. It is by such mutterings that the thread of this or that story is severed, or allowed to continue.

'He's listed here as dead,' said the enemy captain, tapping his data tablet with its stylus.

'Just so. I took command of the remaining troops upon his death.'

'And your name?'

'Steelhand,' I said.

He consulted his tablet. The data upon it had evidently been assembled from the data stolen from our processors *at a certain time*. When I had logged my weapon, after witnessing the death of Syrophoenician with my gun's eye, this information had been loaded into the machine; such that when the machine was corrupted, and made accessible to the enemy, this information was part of what they seized. But I hoped that the things that had happened subsequent to that data meltdown were unknown to them.

He seemed to spend a long time looking at his screen.

'Very well, Soldier Steelhand,' he said eventually. 'Your people, the people of the Book, are renowned for truth-telling. Is that so?'

'The Bibliqu'rân tells us that the All'God hates a lie, and a liar,' I said. 'As you know.'

'You won't lie to me?'

'I cannot lie to you.'

'Very well. I don't wish to create a division of loyalty here, Soldier Steelhand,' said the captain. 'But we wish to apprehend one soldier, a man called Jon Cavala.'

'You wish to apprehend him?' I asked levelly.

'He has committed certain crimes, beyond the actions legally sanctioned for a soldier in wartime. He must be tried, I am afraid. I shall not press you, if you choose not to answer, for you have rights as a prisoner under our code. But I will ask you nevertheless: do you know this man?'

'He is dead,' I said. 'I know him well – he served under me. I was with him when he died. You will,' I extemporised, 'probably find his corpse a league or so north of here.'

'It would be fruitless for us to look,' said the captain, drawing symbols in the face of his data tablet. 'You headless devils all look alike to me.'

I have, of course, thought a great deal about this lie of mine in the years since. One question that recurs, in such a way that it is impossible to avoid it, is the *why* of dying. For what purpose did Syrophoenician die? Or Steelhand? There have been times when I have almost convinced myself that Steelhand did indeed perish in order to save my life, leaving his name free for me to take. And thinking so, of course, gives shape to what might otherwise be a chaos of meaningless grief. But on the other hand: is it not an act of egoism to declare that one life – mine – is valuable enough to deserve the death of another? This seems to me hard to justify.

Fortunately, perhaps, it is not given to me to justify this thing.

PART FOUR
Faces

One

I was a prisoner of war for a year. The enemy did not put us to work, the imposition of slave labour (as they considered it) being contrary to their ethics. This was, if anything, a cause for regret; as a bondsman I would have been more comfortable working than sitting in a cell with four other headless with nothing to do but talk and fall silent; nothing to do but sleep or wait to sleep.

My ribs healed.

They provided us with pharmocopy, although via mist-injections through the skin rather than in purses to be ingested. This they did, I am sure, out of a rigid sense of the strict application of humanitarian codes, for that was the sort of people they were.

We five, in that large but low-ceilinged cell, had nothing much in common beyond our headlessness and the fact that we had all served as soldiers. We none of us talked much about ourselves, but only of what we fancied was the on-going news of the war. This was a subject that fascinated us mightily, perhaps because we were given by our captors no information at all about the war's progress. Naturally we speculated. We could not assume that our enemy had suffered utter defeat, for in that case we would surely have been freed by our own people. But neither could we attribute utter defeat to our side, for our minds revolted at such a thought. So, perhaps, the fighting was still going on, perhaps it would always be going on, army clashing against army with the endless reverberations of a repeatedly struck gong.

Breath pulled into the lungs, and breath pushed out again, and this bodily momentum marked always by the tick-tock clicking of five neck valves. There was something insect-like in the interlocking mark of these sounds, but of course after a while we ceased to register it.

A great deal happened during those months, as will inevitably be the case between five people over a long stretch of time, even if those people be confined to a small room. But this is not the place to detail all those happenings, the berries and the thorns of that time that inevitably intruded as our personalities grew wild into one another's, like brambles. It is not that I consider the narrative of that time irrelevant, or beneath notice; on the contrary, I consider it a more worthwhile story than many others that eagerly foist on the public their drab exotica. I do not pass over this time because it was monotonous, although it was. I pass over it because it is about me, and I am not the point of this story.

As you will have gathered now, my reader, this is the story of Siuzan Delage, who lost her head to save my life. Steelhand lost his *name* to save my life, but his was a lesser sacrifice since, being dead, his name was something for which he had no use. Siuzan, on the other hand, gave up everything. I had come to love her more completely than I had ever loved any other person, and moreover – perhaps which is more important (for this realisation came to me during my captivity with great force) – more even than I loved myself. I had stolen Steelhand's name, and poured shame down my throat and into my belly, but I had not done this to preserve my life for its own sake, the mere relentless accumulation of breath upon breath. I had done this thing for *her*. I lived now for one purpose: to return to my home world and try, in whatever way I could, to make amends to her.

Our speculation about the progress of the war outside our cell was answered when we were moved to a much larger and less secure prison. Here we mixed with, and received cuffs and abusive words from, headed troops. But we did not stay there long, for one day we were told to assemble in the main hall where the tannoy announced that we were to be released. The war, we were told, was over now.

Rather than simply release a large mob of ex-enemy soldiers in one great group – and since they made no provision for repatriation, careless as to how we made our way – they let us go in small batches over a number of weeks. We emerged from the gate and were pointed in the direction of a tram. This (it was the only free ride I enjoyed in the whole of my time upon Athena) rolled, automatically driven, along the tracks from the woodland in which the camp was located. We boarded and it rolled on. It passed through fields and suburbs and finally into the central station at Gryke-Ashland, a major town in Dunmore, itself a major country in D'Or, one of the six continents of Athena. It was strange to see the fields, the tractors and people, and stranger still to see tall buildings of the city braving the sky itself: strange after months of fighting in the fog, followed by months of staring at the walls of our cell. The polarising fog had been dispersed, or else had never settled in this place. There were few signs of war-damage, for I suppose a year is enough time for a properly technological world to restore its farmlands and cities – except in the woodlands, where I did see many gaps and split, wrecked trunks of trees lying prone like dead men.

The tram stopped at every stop: small villages first, or (once) in the middle of damp fields with not one building visible. Later we rolled into the fringes of the conurbation, stopping at a number of suburban stations: deserted platforms under slate-concrete roofs. Some few of our number, prompted by whim, or perhaps by something they saw that appealed to them, got up and walked off the tram at these points. Some went singly, others in pairs or knots of three. One place, I suppose, seemed as good as another.

The sky was the colour of faded denim.

When the tram came to a complete halt there were eight ex-soldiers remaining in the compartment, I the only headless amongst them. I was sitting at the far end of the tram away from the other seven. I walked out last, and strode into the spring sunshine in an alien city whose language I did not speak, and where I knew nobody. I was not downhearted. I had, I told myself, survived the war. Many had not, better men than I. But I was alive. That was something.

The general style of building in this city was blocky and grey, with wide gaps at the joints of most of the outer walls and inner walls visible through these in blue and red. It was very unlike the architecture of my homeworld. The railway terminus appeared to have been built from colossal grey biscuits leant together, the constitutive stone a type of crumbly looking concrete. I walked onto the concourse outside the station and gazed at the buildings, and they looked to me like a child's drawing of buildings. But perhaps this had been the deliberate intention of the architects. The people were almost all dressed in black and blue, and they were mostly hurrying, dropping into subway entrances that sat starkly into the ground like grave mouths, or rising up from them; zipping on pedplatforms or striding along. Some of them looked at me, but their glance tended not to linger, monstrous though I must have appeared to them.

I walked on. I walked the city that first day and slept that first night under a blue-mauve sky littered with a glorious broadcast of unfamiliar stars. Night-butterflies twisted and floated and rose in the darkness all about my head as I lay there. In the morning I rose contented. I felt, almost, holy; as if removed from the material pressures of ordinary living. I found food discarded in waste tubs and left out for the dogs and cats of the city – perfectly good food, which I took and ate very happily. There were public water fountains whenever I was thirsty.

I approached people in buildings, shops and workshops, randomly at first but later, as I learned, more purposefully, to ask for work. I was rebuffed, or ignored. Sometimes I was offered charity, which of course I accepted. More often I was told to go on my way.

Eventually I found a job. A grease collector called Hollis paid me a clutch of divizos a day to travel with him and haul tubs of used cooking fat and other organic grease from restaurants and schools, from hospital canteens and other places. Collecting the grease was easy. Processing it back at Hollis's workshop was less pleasant, and the worst of it was that there were no washroom facilities, so I finished each shift sodden with oily running sop – and stinking, I have no doubt, although of course that was nothing to me. But I took to bathing in one of the city's fountains, and sleeping underneath the parked buses at the bus station. The water in the fountain was as cold as vacuum under the blue-dark sky, and bristled goose-bumps onto my flesh. It made me feel alive. The drive shafts of the buses radiated heat for several hours after they were parked; I was not the only vagrant to sleep there.

My aim was to earn enough money to buy passage upon a spaceship to Pluse. I hoped to return to my homeworld and devote myself to searching for headless Siuzan, to apologise to her and make such amends as I could. Nor had I forgotten my vow to take revenge upon Mark Pol Treherne. But such passage is expensive and I had, at first, no money at all.

For a while my chief worry was obtaining pharmocopies of the necessary hormones. Lacking a population of headless, Athena's shop owners did not carry preparations of these necessary chemicals, and when I asked, respectfully, that they be made up out of existing stock I was either ignored as a sight too freakish even to acknowledge, or else gruffly dismissed. My health suffered. Begging – an activity legal upon Athena, as it is not upon Pluse – enabled me to gather enough divizos together to buy some drugs. Necessity forced me to mix and swallow them in approximation of the pharmocopy purses upon which I had relied in the army. After a fortnight I fell in with a company of released war prisoners, all headed men and all Homish, who adopted me almost, as it might be, as a mascot. But they tired of me quickly when they discovered that the reputation of the headless for savagery was unsupported in my personality. After that I worked at minimum pay at a waste shop – a small business that sent devices into the sewers to collect deposits of congealed fat thrown down the drain (illegally) by restaurant and domestic kitchens. These deposits built up quickly, and needed to be dismantled, and I worked for a while in the confined spaces of the city's waste channels. The machines that quarried the fat were stupid devices, and my job was to prevent them clogging up, or digging into the walls by mistake, it being cheaper to buy stupid automates and then pay me to service them than it would have been to buy more intelligent machines. Through this employer I discovered that there were a dozen or more similar or related enterprises in this city alone. I worked at several of them in due course.

I discovered many things, and one thing in particular that haunted me. Only rarely did I enter into conversation with the natives of Black Athena, and the most that any such folk would say to one such as myself were bald instructions to do such-and-such or go to such-and-such a place. But there were exceptions. One or two headed Athenians approached me, out of curiosity or pity, to discover more about my condition. After several such conversations it dawned on me that my name, Jon Cavala, poet, was wholly unknown to them. It surprised me then, and it still surprises me as I look back upon that time, that this discovery upset me as much as it did. But of course the reason is obvious enough: it was nothing but the wounding of a bad pride.

Two brief exchanges. The first with an employer, who was curious as to what I had done before the war, and whether losing my head would interfere with me resuming that former occupation (for I think he assumed I had lost my head in the fighting). I told him I had been a poet. He told me that he also read a great deal of poetry, 'Television for the story, poetry for the shiver in the spine,' he said. 'My wife always says that, and she's right.' He was a tall, wide-built man and he ran a fat-recycling unit with his wife, who was small and forceful. His most characteristic posture was question-mark shaped, huddling over and angling his ear as if always fearful of missing something from below his line of sight.

'But what did you *do*?' he asked again.

I told him, again, that I had been a poet. It dawned on him that I did not mean that I had enjoyed reading poetry, but that I had been employed writing it. He looked confused. I attempted to clarify by saying, 'My name is Jon Cavala. I have heard that my poetry is popular here on Athena ...' But the blankness of his face made it clear that he had never heard of me.

I don't remember being concerned about this conversation at the time. But the capstone was a second conversation with a bookseller. The idea had got inside my mind that many copies of my poems were being sold on this world, but that I had received no royalty payments. I remembered my time as a headed man, and the small sums that accrued from my publishing, and I was certain that there had been no offworld monies. Working long hours for low wages to accumulate enough to buy passage home, the thought came to me that, perhaps, an approach to whichever house was publishing me on Athena might persuade them to pay me something. I assumed that my work, selling widely on several worlds, had made them a deal of money. I fantasised a bagload of totales; a rucksack filled with scrip.

The first task was to discover which were the publishers to whom I should make application. To this end I stepped inside a bookshop one morning before work. The shop was a single room, eighty yards high and lined on every wall with books. It smelt of wood dust and ink. In the middle was a man behind a desk, with a round cranium clear of hair and a flame-coloured face, and he was reading.

'I beg your pardon,' I said, in my accented but (by now) fluent enough Ellaish. 'I have an enquiry concerning a poet.'

The man looked up at me, and stared. I have noticed that people with faces feel uninhibited at staring at those without. Presumably their unembarassment is a function of the fact that, lacking a face on which to register our humanity, we headless seem to the subconscious of these people a kind of furniture.

'Excuse me,' I prompted him.

'Name?'

'Jon Cavala.'

'Is that your name? Or the name of the poet in whom you are interested?'

'It is.' I said, cautious after breaking my bond, 'a poet's name.'

He scratched his nose and put his book down. 'Spell it,' he said, picking a datascreen off the floor. I told off the letters, forgetting the Ellaish names of several of them, but giving good enough approximations for him to type it in.

'We do not have him. He is not published here.'

This was a shock. 'I beg your pardon one final time,' I said. 'But could you clarify? Has he ever been published here?'

'No.'

'Never been published in Ellaish translation?'

'Never been published at all. I have never heard of him.'

The thing that first confused me about this, as I walked away from the shop, was the intensity of my disappointment. On reflection it seemed logical to me that the Levitt Dunber individual, during my sojourn within the virtual house on the virtual hill – it seemed logical that he had lied to me about my eminence as a poet. Perhaps this had been a misdirection designed to keep me, unsuspecting, in the virtual reality long enough for the enemy to upload whatever virus it was uploading. Perhaps there had been no Levitt Dunber, and he had been nothing more than a figment of my own imagination conjured by the peculiar circumstances in which I had been located. In that case my fame had been a projection of my own vainglorious and lamentable pride. This question bothered me for a long time.

And since I do not think I shall return to this question in what remains of my narrative, I shall record my conclusion, namely that I consider the latter explanation the more likely. My first thought had been that I had been captured and rendered unconscious and then my ordinator had been connected to some Ellaish mainframe, into which the virtual avatar of the real Levitt Dunber had entered. But this fact omits the observation that many headless were hacked in this fashion, and that I do not believe that the enemy mainframe would have been able to identify each of them with so much personal and specific information. Rather, I believe, a holding virus, reactive to my interaction after the fashion of computer algorithms, appeared to me as 'Levitt Dunber'. Most of what this individual said was taken from my own mind, including the recitation of the poem about the inevitability of decay, and was an echo chamber, as it were, of my own obsessions, my anxieties and vainglories. The object of the exercise was merely to distract me long enough for the virus itself (I remembered how vivid had been the light that emerged from Levitt Dunber's gullet) to establish itself in my subroutines. And the most worrying feature of the whole episode is that this virus, whatever it is, must still exist within my mind. It has not manifested itself, so far as I am aware; but I suppose it might at any time.

Two

I eventually accrued enough money to buy passage upon a ship called
Thumbscrew. The ticket officer would not sell me a ticket to Pluse –
which world contained only ramhammer ports, the *Thumbscrew* itself
being a balanced-momentum craft – but he assured me that once we
were upon a world that pledged direct allegiance to the Book it would
be easy to purchase extra travel. This was not a very satisfactory arrangement for me, since the price of the *Thumbscrew* ticket was more than
forty totales, a sum I had hoped would get me all the way home. But it
was my best option, and I told myself that I could earn some more
money upon whichever planet I ended up. There were other spacecraft
that flew direct from Athena to Pluse, but they were more expensive
than I could afford at that time.

My berth was in the general hold, and since transit was no more than
a day I was content with no finer surroundings. I shared my particular
square mattress with another headless – we two the only headless in all
the craft. His name was Latour, and his experiences of war had jarred
his sanity.

Within moments of me introducing myself to him, he made great play
of confiding in me. He told me all manner of incriminating details. At
this point the *Thumbscrew* had not even lifted off. 'I beg of you,' I told
him dispassionately, 'control your confessional urges. You do not know
that I am to be trusted.'

'Headless, like I,' he pointed out. 'We are members of an exclusive
brotherhood. Adultery, this was the cause of – the cause of my – and
you? *You*? You?'

I angled my torso away from him; but he was insistent.

'Regret, regret, that's the tone of my life now,' he said. As he spoke to
me he rolled up his sleeve and began picking at the flesh of his left arm
with his fingernails. Old scabs marked that flesh, like a map of black
volcanic islands in a pale sea. 'I hoped the All'God had written my death

into the war on— but, no. So I have a plan, a plan. I shall make up for my past crimes.'

'It is good to atone,' I said. 'And it is good to have a plan.'

'Indeed, indeed, but this is better than that. I have been trained, a soldier, to take life.'

'That,' I said, as to a child, 'is *not* good.'

'Listen to me, brother headless,' he said. There were blotches of blood upon his arm now. The blood was sliding down his arm and dripping to the floor. 'Listen to me, I shall seize the ship.'

At this I concentrated my attention, to determine whether this was merely the braggadocio of a deranged man or a genuine threat to all of us.

'Now, friend,' I said, speaking carefully. 'Why would you wish to do such a thing?'

'There is a time machine,' he said.

'How so?'

'It is part of the functioning of any ship. A time machine.'

'In,' I conceded, 'a manner of speaking only.'

'I shall seize it. Then I shall force the ticketman to take me back in time, until before my attack upon Marthe, poor Marthe. Then I shall prevent the attack, and my head will not be taken, and I will not have to see Brownjean and Gunn and Alain killed.'

'The ticket officer will be unable to oblige you,' I said.

'Why so? If he tries to resist,' said the fellow, leaping up, 'then I'll force him. Do you think I've never killed? You think I lack will? Why do you doubt it?'

'I don't doubt it,' I said, also getting to my feet. 'But you misunderstand the nature of the time machine. It cannot take you back to the time of which you are talking. This is contrary to the rules of physics.'

He sat down and began again picking at the skin of his arm. 'Do you say so?'

'Such time travel as happens,' I said, seating myself, 'is a function of the very high velocities at which the craft moves. The effect of the particles which ...' But it is hard enough to explain the nature of faster-than-light travel even to the most intelligent listener, let alone to a crack-brain. 'Time dilates as we move faster than light, but the God particles ejected from the nose have, amongst other things, the effect of inverting this dilation.'

'God!' he said, as if in derision. 'God particles!'

'Such time travel as there is,' I said, 'amounts only to the effect that the ship which leaves this star at noon arrives at its destination at, precisely, noon, and not many millions of years in the future. But in order to arrive at its destination at a time *before* noon, as you desire, it would have to travel *faster* than an infinite speed, which, naturally, is impossible.'

'Nothing is impossible for the All'God,' he said slyly.

I tried again. 'You misunderstand the situation if you believe that there exists a time machine upon this craft,' I said. 'It is, instead, that one of the properties of the stream of drive particles that—'

'I know all this,' he snapped. 'Do you think I didn't go to kindergarten? Do you think I don't know *physics*?'

'Well, then,' I said in a placatory voice, 'you know that the derelativist effects of our drive is no time machine.'

'Time machine!' he scoffed. And then, 'The ticketman will know how to operate it.'

'Remember what we have just discussed,' I suggested.

'You think I won't be *able* to persuade him,' growled Latour. 'But he's only a ticketman. He has not seen fighting, such as I have seen, upon Black Athena.'

I made my excuses, went forward in the *Thumbscrew* where I reported him as a dangerous party to the RO officer. It took less effort to persuade this officer than I had thought it might. 'I *remember* telling the ticket-officer,' the fellow said in accented Ellaish, 'that he was too eccentric a fellow to take with us. I have seen war do this to many people. But he was stubborn. The ticket officer was stubborn. He has a quota of sales to meet, and if he does not meet it his commission is reduced. This makes him reluctant to turn away custom.' He was not a native Ellaish speaker, and his accent gave his fluent sentences a *wah-wah* cadence. I could not guess what his original tongue had been.

'What will you do?' I asked.

'I shall arrest him, on suspicion, as the terms of the AHF provisions for the portage of enemy aliens permit me to do.' Then, smiling, he said something complicated-sounding in his native language, of which, of course, I understood nothing at all.

'I speak only Homish and Ellaish,' I said apologetically.

'There is no need for an apology,' the RO officer told me. 'Take me to this fellow, identify him for me, and I shall arrest him.'

'There is not need for me to identify him for you,' I said. 'He is, apart from myself, the only headless man aboard.'

'Nonetheless the law requires that the complainant identify the person complained of.'

'Very well.'

When I went back to the general hold, with the RO officer a few paces behind me, Latour saw us coming. He leapt up, and began complaining loudly that he was being persecuted, that he had done nothing wrong and so on.

'Be quiet now, Latour,' I advised him.

'*You* have betrayed me,' he cried. '*You* are a traitor. What price the solidarity of the headless? What price the unity of the congregation of the Book?'

'Be calm,' I said. I could see the other portage-class passengers watching in alarm, or, some, in amusement at this scene.

'I have come to arrest you.' the RO officer told Latour, 'under the terms of the AHF provisions for the portage of enemy aliens. I may, since we have yet to depart, eject you from the craft; or I may confine you in a cell for the duration of the journey. Which do you prefer?'

'I must return to Pluse!' Latour cried. 'Do not put me off the ship! I shall choke in the vacuum!'

'We are not in space,' said the RO officer. 'We have not yet left the planet. But, since you request it, I shall confine you aboard for the duration.' He stepped forward. Latour brought out a knife. All weapons were supposed to have been stowed before coming aboard. It later transpired that this knife had been laser-cut from a bone to avoid the metal-detection devices. But, though made of bone, it certainly appeared sharp enough. The RO officer brought out a chiller from a hip holster and spoke harshly, and, in an instant, the man's resistance vanished. He dropped his knife and wailed. The chiller was returned to its holster. 'I am ineffectual!' Latour cried. 'I am weak!' But the RO officer paid no mind to this, and strapped his elbows together behind his back.

'I'm glad at least,' he told me, as he dragged the fellow away, 'that he indicated a desire to stay on board. Had I ejected him we would have been legally obliged to refund him the cost of his ticket, and then the ticket officer would have been furious with me.'

As I said earlier, this is not my story; it is the story of Siuzan Delage who lost her head to save my life. The minutiae of my voyage home are not relevant to that story. The same is true of the six weeks I spent upon Forward, the first planet upon which the *Thumbscrew* stopped from which it was possible to buy passage to Pluse. It is enough that I worked there, and ate little, and slept out of doors regardless of weather – slept outside in the cold, dark-coloured rain showers and the mauve snowfalls and the bright cloudless nights that were the coldest of all, wrapped in scraps of fur like a caveman from the dawn of time. I worked first in an animal skinnery, and then in a sewage facility catching rats. I earned more totales, and eventually I was able to buy a ticket to my home.

I can add, now, that this detour – though infuriating to me at the time – was a 'fortunate inconvenience', the *felix incommoditas* of which theologians sometimes speak. For I later discovered that all travellers from Athena direct to Pluse were taken aside, questioned, and tested for DNA by the authorities. I would have been logged as Jon Cavala, returning to my home. Once entered as such on the police database, *Chevaler* Bonnard would certainly have continued his persecution of me – reporting me to the army as a deserter, perhaps, or arresting me and trumping me up for false trial. Had this happened, I would never have met Siuzan Delage again, and my story would have had no point to it. This very story, the one you are reading now, would have had no conclusion. As it was, though, arriving from Forward I was not DNA-checked, and accordingly I could come back to my own world under the assumed name of 'Steelhand'.

I set down on Pluse far from my destination, on the island-nation of Man Pasio, at the port of Nize. Having travelled trillions of leagues in days it took me months to travel the last few thousand back to Doué. This, of course, is one of the ironies of travel in this, our modern world. But I got to Doué eventually. There, still bearing Steelhand's name, I stayed for a month, working in the docks with a gang of seasoned headless. We packed and unpacked containers, and slept on bales in the main warehouse.

But I had no desire to stay in Doué. I believed that Siuzan was still in Cainon. It might have been possible, of course, that Siuzan had come back down to this town; but my instinct was that she would still be in the city where she had been punished. Of course I wanted to go to her.

It was strange to walk streets that were so familiar to me, to count the lime trees along Straight as I had done as a child; to pass the library and the State Temple, and yet to see all these things with artificial eyes as a stranger and alien, lacking even my true name. Sometimes I walked past people I had known very well in my youth – people who had clasped me and called me best friend – and, of course, they walked straight by without a glance. How could they recognise me? Quite apart from the lack of a head, I was a different person to the one I had been in almost every way.

I contemplated walking north to Cainon, as I had done before, but though the hardship would have been nothing to me as I now was, yet the memory of the last time I had walked that way was too painful. To think that I had walked with Mark Pol and Gymnaste and with Siuzan herself – to think that she had been assaulted in the foulest manner, only *yards* from me, whilst I slept – and that she had said nothing! It had the logic of nightmare.

To think of the woe that is in memory.

I could not walk across that ground again. Accordingly I worked in the dock until I had saved enough for an airbus. The price of the ticket was eight totales. It would have cost me more for a regular ticket – twelve totales and fifty divizos, more than I remembered from my younger days – but I was refused the sale of such a ticket. I could fly with the cargo or not fly at all, this is what I was told; and I took the cargo place without rancour. The hold was chilly and only partially pressurised; but I was not too uncomfortable, and the flight lasted only an hour.

And so, after my long detour, I returned to Cainon. I rode a bus from the airport to the centre of the city, where he hasn't got a head. I dismounted and strolled the roads. I saw buildings I recognised, and buildings that I did not (but after all, I had not seen much of the city on my previous visit). It was all very unremarkable, as if I had been anaesthetised to it. I felt no twinge at returning, although in a sort of emotional knight's-move I did feel regret that I felt no regret – it seemed to me that walking the streets of the city in which the woman I loved had lost her head, and done so because of my moral cowardice, *should* have moved me more than it did. But my conscience had become, perhaps, callused like a workman's hand by the war.

I walked the streets. I stood beside freeways where the slab-sided cars of Cainon burlied and dashed, and where the dust went up into the air from their wheels. I loitered outside shops, and cafés and galleries. It felt my way back inside the city.

The strangest thing was being amongst so many headless again without the military context. For there were a great many headless here. Before, when I had still had my head, or indeed shortly after it had been removed, I had simply *not seen* the many headless thronging the roads. Now, of course, I noticed them all the time.

I found lodgings in a dormitory – a former cinema, I believe, that had gone out of business and had fallen into disrepair and had been bought by a low businessman, a dealer in slums. He rented slum-space to headless and other undesirables, and I took lodgings in one such property. He was later accused and convicted of usury and sent to prison, as it happens; but this is not *his* story. It was a large, run-down building on the outskirts of the town. It faced the road with one tall windowless wall, slightly curved, made out of pebble-dashed sandstone and rather resembling peanut-brittle. Round at the side, the wide entrance door had been filled with bricks, excepting only the space in the middle for a galvanised metal door as slender as a postbox. Through this I slipped every morning, coming back from my night-time job, making my way to the room I shared with four other headless, for my day's sleep. A large pan of pap warmed on a stove in the corner; four mattresses thin as velvet were arranged in the middle of the floor at right angles, as if marking out the Hindu swastika pattern. I would eat, and fall directly asleep. In the late afternoon I would wake, and perhaps talk to my fellow slum tenants, or else wander the streets of Cainon under the late sun. The slum was not far from one of the city's many public squares, water misting up in billows from a fountain in the middle, cafés and bookshops hiding their faces under the cap peaks of their awnings on all sides. I often rested there for a while, by the pouring water, before strolling further in towards the centre of town, past the headed throngs in the late afternoon sun, the chalk-yellow and washed-crimson of the low skimming light, where lemon-coloured dust light as talcum was made thickly visible by the quality of the light.

Where was I walking? To a flesh reclamation facility in which, for the first six months, I worked all night in a giant tub filled with bones that sported little tassels and fronds of meat still clinging to them. Many of the items in this ossery were becoming putrid, the marrow exploding from their ends as decay heated and expanded it. Some were like slimy rubber; others were brittle as desert flints. My job – since I lacked nose or mouth to be offended by its noisome smell – was to sort the material. It was delivered through a chute from a trunk in an undifferentiated mass, and the owner of this firm required me to place different kinds of bones into different kinds of processing machines.

This was my work all through the night. My shift finished a little before dawn, and I would rinse myself in the cupboard-sized company shower and then set out back to my hostel. Here I would eat, sitting on my mattress. There was a hole in the wall of our room, large enough (you might think) for a rhino to step through, a ragged oval punched out of the bricks leaving stepped and crenellated edges, and through this I might greet the occupants of the room next door. The paint on such wall as remained was more blister than smoothness, like lime-green bubblewrap, except in those places where it had sheeted away entirely. The beams of the roof were visible above us. The floor of this room had been carpeted, but the four of us had agreed between us that it was too revolting – for it was damp, and patched, and crawling with tiny lice like vermicelli – so we had folded it and burnt it in the yard behind the house. This yard had, clearly, once been a car park, but was now empty except for the brick-shaped rectangles marked out in old paint on the pale concrete.

The rent of this slum took up a portion of my income, including monies that I pooled with the others in my room to keep the pot of pap in the corner filled and cooked. A larger portion was spent on pharmocopies, and vitamins. But I can confirm what some other headless have reported, that the body adapts to the lack of pineal and pituitary organs with surprising success. It stores ingested hormone in the adipose tissue and releases it again – I am not certain how – in approximation to the sensitive action of the missing glands. Although, of course, hormones must still occasionally be replenished from an external source.

Three

To the people in this hostel I was Steelhand. I had good reasons to suspect that going about Cainon under my real name would result in trouble. Of course, since the police had my DNA on record, any simple streetside test would reveal my deception; but at no time was I stopped by any policeman. I was one of the law-abiding headless; working, paying my rent, contributing my mite to the taxman, never harassing, or embarrassing, or even passing one word with the headed who passed me on the streets unbidden. There was no reason for the police to bother me.

But I was not marking time, of course. I was looking for Siuzan. Every spare minute of my time there was given to this task. It was the shape, the horizon, of my whole existence; for I needed to atone.

I did not go to the library to check address records and other official documentation, since to be in the address records she would have needed to purchase a house or set up a business – and how could a shamed and headless woman have afforded that? She could not be in the voter records, for the headless were barred from voting. There were no official records of the headless population; or, if such records existed, they were not made available to the general public.

I asked questions of whomsoever I might. I asked every headless man and woman I encountered whether they knew of her. I went from room to room in my hostel interrogating the occupants as gently as I might.

I pursued this line without panic, or urgency. I considered how many times I had been close to death, and how often I had survived. When I considered these things it was easy to believe that I had been preserved by Providence or (although it approaches heresy to say it) by the All'God Himself, for some reason. What greater reason than to begin to make amends for Siuzan's decapitation? To attempt the impossible atonement, but to attempt it nonetheless? That was my task as I understood it.

Of course my enquiries were often misunderstood. Headless women – proportionately a much smaller group of people than headless men – lived with the shame of their specific crimes and also the shame of general association. Some of them took to harlotry to earn money. Perhaps it was easier for them than for other women, since they lacked that blazon at once of shame and of recognition, which is the face. But it was hard for me to move amongst these poor souls. With every enquiry I made I was sharply aware of the thoughts that would be crossing my interlocutor's mind – that I was wished to seek her out for the pleasures of purchased sex. It would have been fruitless for me to have insisted how pure were my intentions, and indeed would only have rooted the contrary belief more firmly in their minds. So I said nothing.

I asked in my hostel, and at my place of work. If ever I encountered a headless man or (rarely) woman at some other place, I asked them about Siuzan. I walked the city after my shift, simply looking.

Nobody knew where she might be found. None of them had even heard of her. Indeed, after several weeks I began to believe that one of two things had occurred: either she had assumed a false name to mask her shame, or she had left the city at the first chance and gone far away from this place. I planned, I suppose, to travel back to Doué eventually and resume my search there; and after that to search the whole world if necessary. But first I needed to be sure I had searched Cainon thoroughly, and it is a large city, with many inhabitants.

I took to roaming further through the city after my shift, exploring and questioning. I came upon the central police station, and at first I flinched away from it, avoiding it as if it possessed some malign talismanic power to hurt me. But I overcame this foolish fear of the place, and soon I was walking directly past the splendid façade, the ramp, the daffodil-coloured stones of the wall. Once I even saw Bonnard himself – the very Bonnard who had, through his cruelty and his sadistic desire to inflict the letter of the law, decapitated the woman I loved. He was strolling easily down the ramp in company with another man. I was strapped by a terror that he would somehow *know* me – grab me, bustle me up into the police station, lock me away, prevent me *a second time* from saving Siuzan – but of course he did not know me. We headless all look alike to the headed. Nor was it wholly rational of me to think of Bonnard as the one who had prevented me from helping Siuzan: I had, of course, done that to myself. But nevertheless he stood as a dreadful externalisation of the power to hurt innocence. It was as if a djinn, powerful and malign, had taken human form. A devil. I stopped in my tracks and stood like a statue, and he walked past me so close that I felt the stir of air in the wake of his passage. And then he went on, his voice alternating with his companion's in conversation. I remembered that voice, with absolute precision. The mere sound of it was enough to make me tremble.

I gathered myself, and walked to the corner of the station, where the buildings led away in a crescent towards a church.

My mind was still shuffled and disordered by my close-encounter with Bonnard, and so for a moment I did not see her. But there she was. I saw her eventually; and perhaps it was, as I sometimes think, Providence that we were to meet again. The sunlight was pricking out a pattern of filigree lines on the cream brickwork behind her. She was standing in front of the gable end house of a row of houses. A dead root system of ivy adhered to the blank frontage long after the plant itself had died, a huge splash-pattern of dark brown like a sculpture of the nervous system. She was standing in front of this knit of colour, facing me. I knew it was her at once.

You will want to know, perhaps, how I could be so sure that it was her, given that she had no face. You may even expect me to reply that I knew because love chimed in my heart, or that fate dictated it, or that providence recognised its crucial moment. But the truth is plainer: I had lived as one of the headless for a good while, and I had quickly learned to differentiate between people by noting all the myriad physical distinguishing features of the faceless body. There are a great many, certainly more marks of alterity than distinguish one face from another. Soon this process of recognising people by their torsos rather than their faces becomes second nature.

I walked towards her, drawn in, you might say, by the miraculous gravity of her – of her simple existence, in that place at that time. I came within five yards of her before a grit of normality registered in my thoughts: I mean, the inappropriateness of marching directly up to a lone woman, standing on the streets, a woman moreover who had been raped, who had been decapitated rather than betray her rapist to death. It all came back. Everything and all the memory and it almost over-whelmed me.

I stopped myself. I was uncertain what to do.

She was wearing a blue shift, paler than her almost black meadhres. It was a unisex outfit, differing from a dozen others I had already seen that day only in one small detail: the twin collars through which poked her standard-issue epaulette eyes had both been braided with fine stitch-ing, zigzagging tightly in a lip all about the hole like the fine shading of an artist. Perhaps this was her own work, and a very modest, and very affecting, beautification of her uniform it was.

She squared up to me, registering the fact that I had walked so close to her.

'Siuzan?' I said. 'Siuzan?'

'Yes?' She turned her body sharply, to bring me into clearer focus in her epaulette-eyes.

'It is me,' I said, feeling the foolishness of what I said as I said it, but wanting, before anything else, to reassure her.

'Who?'

'Me.'

'How do you know my name?' she asked.

I stepped closer, absurdly protective of my pseudonymity, and lowered my voice. 'Jon Cavala,' I said. 'I am Jon Cavala.'

She barely flinched. 'Jon,' she said. There was no rancour in her voice.

'Siuzan,' I said. 'It has been so long – two years. Perhaps it has been longer.'

'Longer,' she said.

We stood, awkwardly, facing one another.

'I have been looking for you,' I said.

'Really?' Her voice did not sound displeased, but nevertheless she added, 'Why?'

This question – the obvious one – nevertheless caught me unawares. I could have answered it, but not in a few words, and not without opening a larger discourse, love, which would have been premature at this first meeting. 'I wanted to make certain you were well,' I said weakly.

'You wanted to make sure? What do you mean?'

'After what *happened*, Siuzan,' I said urgently. I did not understand why she was so calm. Perhaps I had been expecting her voice to break – perhaps, secretly, I had even dreamed of an obscenely public embrace – a declaration of love. But of course there was none of that. How misleading our fantasies are.

'After what happened? You mean the beheading?'

'I mean that, but also the – things before.'

'Oh,' she said. 'Oh, that. All that. Yes.' She straightened her spine. 'I *have* been well. Life since the ... since the loss of my head has been ... less intolerable than I might have thought.'

'I am sorry,' I said.

'Why?'

'I feel a terrible responsibility,' I said, 'for the loss of your head.' It was extraordinarily hard for me to get this sentence out. I am not sure why: for I had been planning it, or a version of it, for two years, or more. But even so simple a statement came as if wrenched from deep inside me.

'But Jon,' she said, stepping forward and reaching her hand up to touch my elbow, 'it is not *your* responsibility!' She spoke with warmth, and my memories of the old Siuzan, the way she had been before she lost her head, rushed through me.

'You don't understand,' I explained, trying to keep a grip on myself.

'What don't I understand, Jon?'

'I know the sacrifice you made. I spoke to Bonnard ...' (at his name her hand dropped from my arm) '...which is to say, I did not so much *talk* to him. Rather *he* interrogated *me*. He told me that you refused to implicate your attacker.'

'Jon,' she said again. 'There is no blame here. Everything was as the All'God wanted it.'

'But to suffer as *you* have suffered!' I cried, unable to contain myself any longer. 'To be attacked, and then to sacrifice yourself rather than condemn your attacker ...' The words clogged up in my delivery, and I stopped. Had I possessed eyes I would have been crying.

'There was no great hardship in the sacrifice. I am still alive, aren't I? I have only lost a head.'

'Siuzan,' I said. And then I said it plainly: 'Since it happened I have carried around inside me this thought: that it would have been no great sacrifice for me to take your place. That is what should have happened. I would have only lost a life, and you would have been saved.'

'But your life is not yours to throw away,' she said, not unkindly. 'If the All'God has preserved your life, there must be some purpose to that preservation. Has the purpose of your life been fulfilled yet, *Sieur* Cavala?'

'The purpose of my life,' I said, hoping the words did not outrage her, 'is to attempt atonement for your decapitation.'

She was silent for a while. 'I shall not rebuke you,' she said eventually. 'Although what you are saying implies a very great – intimacy between us. Only think, dear Jon, you are not responsible for what has happened to me.'

Indeed she called me *dear Jon*. For three heart pulses I did not hear anything beyond those words.

'I am responsible for myself. We are all responsible for ourselves,' she said.

'What are you doing now?' I said, abruptly.

'I am looking for work,' she said. 'I am looking for somewhere to live. I am presently in a house that – or house is too grand a word. I share a room with three female headless, and they ... or, rather, I am uncomfortable with their—' She stopped in some confusion.

'I understand,' I said, quickly. 'How could you be anything but outraged by their immorality?'

'It is not that,' she said hurriedly. 'It is something else. I have always
tried to live my life according to those words of the Bibliqu'rân, *Judge
not lest you be judged*. And this is the danger I am in: for as long as I
remain in that place, with those women working their carnal work and
taking money for it, just so long do I risk falling into the habit of
judgement. It is the serpent in my own soul that distresses me, not the
work these women are doing. They are kind women, mostly.'

I was very distressed to hear of her living in such a place, although
her experience was common to many headless women. 'You must leave
that house,' I urged her. 'Come back with me now; I live in a house, it
is a large house – there is a room shared by some headless women. They
are virtuous women, as far as I can tell, and I can persuade them to
accommodate you in their room.'

She was quiet.

'I appreciate,' I said, 'that this may seem an improper invitation. Please
do not misunderstand me. You know me, I hope, even if only a little.
You know that my intentions are only honourable. You need a place to
live.'

'I do.'

'Then come live amongst these decent women of my acquaintance.'

Finally she bowed her torso forward a little. 'This is kind *Sieur* Cavala,'
she said. 'Perhaps our meeting is more than mere chance!'

'I hope so!' I said, earnestly.

Then she said, 'You do not mind me calling you *Sieur* Cavala?'

'I was priggish before,' I said, 'when first you met me. My experiences
have taught me not to be so priggish.'

She laughed at this. With her laugh it was as if the whole world levered
about into sunlight on the axis of her joy. Many things which had
been impossible became possible. Is there a better definition of the
miraculous?

I led her back through the city and to our house, and it did not take
much to convince the women in the top room to accept her, provided
only I pay her rent until she found work of her own. Since she was
hungry I took her to a certain café, a place that tolerated headless customers (although in a separate room from others) and bought her some
supper. We talked.

Simply talking to her opened up the universe of possibilities. I was
continually refreshed by the lack of rancour in her voice; after everything

that had happened to her, and her own blamelessness, and her terrible sufferings, after rape and false accusation and decapitation, she was still not moved to bitterness. On reflection, and as I know her now, this is not a surprise. This is consonant with her nature. She has a good soul. I recognised it from the first. It was why I had fallen in love with her. It was why my love was refreshed by meeting her again.

I wanted to ask her about the walk to Cainon, about the assault, but I could not find the words in which to do this. In point of fact I wanted her to confirm that it had indeed been Mark Pol who assaulted her. I didn't doubt that he was the culprit, but I wanted to hear her tell me so herself. For her doing this would add the victim's justice to my vow for revenge. But you can understand: it is not an easy subject to introduce into conversation.

She went back to the house shortly after that to sleep. I, on the other hand, hurried to my place of work. I was several hours late and was not surprised when the owner fired me there and then, neither allowing me back into his establishment, nor paying me the money he owed me for the half-month worked. But this did nothing to dampen my spirits. I had chanced upon the woman I loved. The All'God, or Fate, or Nature, or Providence – whatever the force, a force for *good* – was to permit me to make amends for what I had failed to do years before.

I found another job within the week, working in a fat-rendering facility. This was day work, which suited me better, as it moved the routine of my day into synchrony with the routine of Siuzan's day. She took unpaid work at a church, cleaning and sometimes even giving lectures there to pious headed on the experiences of the headless. The lack of money mattered little; I was happy to pay her rent and her pharmocopy bills, and she accepted my charity with an ingenuousness that only made me love her more. This mixture of child and adult is the most potent of mixes for the loving heart.

We talked. We grew accustomed to one another. This, of course, is the point of the story I am telling you.

Four

Love, just as it involves the coming together of two individuals, also involves the combination of two emotions inside each of those individuals. People may mistake either of these two feelings for *love*, even though each may be severed from the other – and, indeed, previously in my life, I myself had made exactly this mistake. But when actual love comes to a person it grants a commanding perspective upon all former heart trills and self-illusions. You see the past infatuations as trivial things, howsoever absorbing they may have been at the time. You see the actual love as something new.

Actual love came now, as I came to know Siuzan Delage a second time.

This is the nature of the two components of love: one is the recognition of something better, higher, something purer, *more*, something to which the soul feels a tug upwards, more beautiful, more valuable, more talented or essential, and this is the severed half-element of love that I had mostly experienced before in my life. When I had looked on women before, I had gazed much as does the reptile in amongst the leaf-litter who turns his swivelling eye upon a butterfly. This had been my whole former life, I think; living as that cached-away reptile. But this *ideal*, alone, is not enough.

The second element is the recognition of something accessible, something reachable and *graspable* in the other. Do not be shocked in what I say, for the sensual implications of my words, though vulgar, are a necessary part of my meaning. This second thing is something animal as well as spiritual. In saying this I do not mean that the love-object must embody base or lewd desires, and indeed those who know only this kind of love condemn themselves to a living banality corroded by the dull repetitions of hedonism. But in the connection that draws lovers together, in (for instance) the begetting of children, or the creation of that unique intimacy between two souls that is the emotion most like new life, *this* element has its essential part. To love only what one cannot possess; or to love only what one *can* possess *because* one can possess it – neither serves alone. Neither is love. It is only together that they can create true togetherness.

It might be truer to say that I did not *dare* love Siuzan Delage when I first knew her, and this despite the fact that I dreamed of her, that I yearned for her. She was too greatly removed from me. But now that she had been reduced she was beneath the notice of all those virtuous headed men. Through no fault that was hers she had become one with me, with my kind. But since my kind were sinners, and since all men were sinners, all men were my kind.

It enabled love. Habit, which determines most of life, is precisely the thing dissolved by love. I will explain what I mean by this: during those long months in the cell on Athena, in the company of my imprisoned comrades, with all the neck valves clicking and tocking in tumbling rhythms, *habit* was the way this sound ceased to exist for us after only a few hours. Long drawn-out months of this brittle percussion, the putting-together of intricate patterns of noise, sound-waves that registered on my aural prostheses, data that was transmitted and processed in my ordinator, somehow *there* in my mind, and yet wholly unnoticed. This stands, for me, as the type of all habit. What is so remarkable about living with that noise for nearly a year without noticing it is that there was nothing *else* in that cell to notice; no other distractions or occupations of the mind. But the mere habit of that stimulus deadened it nevertheless.

To catch a glimpse of her from behind, the converging lines of her back, in our house, as she stepped from the lowest cracked stair onto the hall floor was enough to balloon my heart with happiness.

We spent almost every evening together, eating and talking.

'I will confess something to you,' I said.

'What?'

'When first I met you, me newly beheaded and you still beautiful in face and form – when I first knew you, you were so far removed from me, so pure and fair, I almost hated myself.'

'Oh, nonsense!'

'Say, rather then, that it made me sink within myself in wretched comparison.'

'Foolish!' she laughed. 'To cast your own psychological weakness out onto me! To make me a tool in your self-dislike! I didn't feel that way about *you* when we first met.'

'But all I'm saying is – that I loved you from the very first.'

'You're saying that your love demeaned you!' She laughed again.

'Not demeaned, exactly,' I said. 'But it certainly brought me a sharp awareness of my own unworth.'

'Worth?' she challenged. 'And who *is* worthy, in the eyes of the All'God? Love comes from Him, as rivers from their source, and so it thrives on the inequality between object and object, for without this gradient love can't flow at all. I would go further. I *might* say,' she went on, 'that it is not *possible* for equals to love. There must be this disproportion to generate love. And, even more than this, the greatest love comes when *both* parties consider themselves far below the other, just as we are with the All'God.'

It saddened me to hear her say this, because it was inconceivable to me that she could ever have considered herself far below *me*. But then I thought to myself that perhaps her shame and beheading had lowered herself in her own perceptions, and I derived some small comfort from this. Does that seem a shocking observation to you? Love can create that level of desperation in a man's heart. But then she said:

'When first I met you – you, older than I, a noted poet, a man enduring sufferings nobly. How could I not feel lower than you?'

'Impossible!'

'Impossible!' she said, as if in agreement.

Weeks came and went. The logic of my days was now shaped about the morning talk with Siuzan before I walked into the city to my work; and about our evening meals together. The rest of the day and all of the night were grey by comparison.

'What is this charm you wear about your neck?' she asked me one day.

I held up the bit of blue plastic. 'Do you not recognise it?'

'Should I?'

'Perhaps not.'

'Is it some memento of your army days? You never talk about the army.'

'The army?' I was surprised. 'Do you wish to hear of it?'

'I don't wish you to keep yourself hidden from me.'

'But the army is hidden in plain view. You know what the army is. It is an organisation devoted to killing. Should I introduce such a subject into our conversation?'

'No,' she said. 'Maybe you're right.'

'I'm not the only one', I said, 'who holds back from talking about certain things. You do not talk—' But she anticipated what I was going to say.

'I know what it is to which you are referring. But I can't talk about *that*. Can't.' She was silent for a moment, and I pondered how much pain and injustice was folded into the single syllable, *that*: all the walking from Doué to Cainon, the assault itself, the walking on through the desert afterwards in company with her attacker, unable even to speak aloud about what had happened. Of course I respected her desire to stay silent. Nevertheless, there was so much I wanted to know about that time. Had she stumbled on in a sort of shock, keeping company with her rapist because she could think of nothing better, until the chemist had examined her and handed her to the police? Or had she purposefully held her tongue, for fear that Mark Pol would attack her again? And what had it felt like, to be taken by the police and treated not as victim but as criminal? I wanted Siuzan to feel that she could tell me the whole of her story. But I was ready to wait. I understood, I told myself, why she could not yet talk about *that*.

Siuzan finally found remunerative work in an ammonium facility, not far from my own workplace. We fell into a routine of meeting for breakfast in the pre-dawn every day, and then walking towards our work places together.

Once, resting briefly during this morning journey, I remarked to Siuzan that she had changed since I had first met her. 'How do you mean?' she asked.

'I don't mean change for the worse,' I said.

'A change in character?'

'Yes.'

She was silent for a moment. 'A change,' she asked, almost sadly, 'in soul?'

'Can one change but not the other?'

'To go through an experience such as mine,' she said. 'To go through an experience like *ours* – how can it not change one's soul? To lose a head! It marks you.' After a moment she asked: 'So, how am I different? I mean, how exactly?'

'Oh, you are not *fundamentally* different,' I said. 'And so, therefore, perhaps it is true that the soul can't be scratched or scuffed by the collisions of life, as you say. But when I first knew you, your faith was a—' I paused, unsure of the word.

'More intensely experienced?' she suggested.

'A more *enthusiastic* faith, perhaps. I cannot speak as to the intensity of it – for you, I mean.'

'My faith is unshaken,' she said shortly. 'It is not my sufferings that have altered my faith.'

'But something *has* altered it?'

'You,' she said simply.

She stood up and walked away from me. It was very early in the morning. We had been sitting on the lip of one of the city's fountains, a shin-high oval wall enclosing a marble structure like a marble stove from which a fine stream of water flew up and misted down. The pallid light of the pre-dawn was in the sky and upon the city but, as yet, inert, the potential of day rather than day itself. The water spouting in a cloud from the heart of the fountain, which sparkled and shuffled rainbows in its mist in the daytime sunlight, was as opaque as milk. The air was cool but contained within itself the promise of the day's heat yet to come.

I did not follow her when she walked away. I did not wish to possess her, or control her actions. I loved her enough to allow her to roam and stride. Of course, I watched as she walked in a wide arc fully about the fountain. And eventually she came back and sat down beside me. What she spoke next had the flavour of a speech she had prepared, and practised as she walked about the fountain, but it had the qualities of truth and directness for all that.

'A thing I had not anticipated about love,' she said, 'is that without *daring* it cannot come at all. I think this is why I am interested in your time as a soldier, although you don't like to talk about it, I know – but a soldier makes daring his job! His career! And I would love to learn that skill. You see, before I met you I believed that all my love should be reserved for the All'God. It seemed so tiny a gift for Him, after the giant gifts he had given me: life, light, the prospect of heaven. I resolved that I must put *all* my effort into loving the All'God. Surely it was a trivial devotion to pour only *some* of my cup of water back into the ocean! A spoonful seemed so inadequate when measured against the entirety of the sea, and so the whole cup must be emptied, and shaken to unloose the last droplets.' She stopped for a while, and then went on: 'Of course the cupful is, in a way, just as inadequate a gesture as the spoonful, when measured against an ocean which is – to speak simply, and literally – infinite. But it was the most I could do. I felt I should do the most I could.'

'I understand,' I said.

'And this is what has changed,' she said. 'I am not putting it very well. I knew that I could only offer a very little, a cupful, or even a spoonful. But I have come to see that when we are talking of the infinite, as we are when we talk of love, a little is enough. Or to put it another way, when we are talking of the infinite a little is everything. For the All'God, I believe now, the little is *more* than the lot.'

She stopped at this point and angled her torso away, so that I thought she had confused herself and I said jauntily, 'You speak like a mystic!'

'No, no,' she said. 'Falling in love with you *has* needed daring on my part, and now that I have taken that risk I understand love better. There are truths that can only be known by bravery. This, I think, is the change in me you recognise. Loving the All'God is an experience of ...' And here, for the first time, she faltered, searching for the correct word. I waited patiently.

'An experience,' she said, finally, 'of homecoming.'

'Yes,' I said. I knew exactly what she meant.

A bird, perhaps a thrush, alighted on the stone lip of the fountain several yards along. Its wings rattled like brittle silk and then folded so quickly away it looked like a conjurer's trick. The bird dipped forward and drank from the water, and rocked back on its pink legs. Its plumage was dark brown and freckled with yellow. It watched us out of the side of its tiny lightbulb-shaped head. Then it bounced up with a whipcracking flutter and flew away into the air. The state of my mind, then, in that place, was as if there was some brief communion between myself and the bird. The whole of the bright sky was my home. I felt that the flow and chatter of the fountain was the pulse of my own blood.

'To understand faith as more than simply ritual and practice is to experience this profound *recognition*,' she said eventually. 'It's to feel the – return. But to love somebody else ... that is to leave home. And that requires a specific courage that loving the All'God does not. For how can you leave somewhere to find the All'God when He is everywhere? My love for you is a – different thing. It does not diminish my faith. It throws it into a more pronounced and more beautiful relief. And I suppose that is why the All'God has made things the way He has. To create beings who can love objects other than Himself does not dilute, but rather intensifies, our love for Him. This is what I mean by the little being more than the lot.'

We sat for a while. I listened to the sounds of the city beginning to wake: the traffic increasing; the café owners about the square opening shutters and rolling out awnings, putting out tables and chairs. 'All the things I have suffered,' I said, 'all my experiences, all the trials – I don't renounce a single one of them. They have all worked together to make me what I am now. And to bring me to this place, here, with you. Perhaps that was the purpose of those things all along.'

We were still alone, although soon enough people would come walking past the fountain; but whilst we were still alone, and despite the fact that we were in a public space, I embraced Siuzan as we sat together. Then we made our way onward to our respective places of work.

How happy those weeks were! Or did you think my narrative would move only from unhappiness to unhappiness? Perhaps you were expecting that – no, or not quite. I discovered something new and gleaming in that city, and the loss of my head and all my suffering were as nothing beside it. Indeed, and since they had led me to it, they were things I could celebrate.

'Let us marry,' I said to her one day.

'Are the headless permitted to marry?' she asked. This, I noticed, was not *no*.

'Of course! We may marry, and we may have children, that's all perfectly legal. I know of people who have done this. Or, at least, I have heard of them.'

'Headed children,' she said uneasily.

'Yes.'

'Would it not revolt a child, cradled in our arms, to look up at two headless parents?'

'I don't think it would,' I said. 'For children take the world as they find it.'

She pondered. 'I am, I confess, a little uneasy,' she said shortly. 'But perhaps not because of the children. If the All'God wills it, children will love us whatever our shortcomings.'

'Then why be uneasy?'

She thought a long time before answering this. 'I am unnerved at the thought of happiness,' she said.

'You deserve happiness,' I insisted, too forcefully.

'I am not used to it. I am afraid of it. Unhappiness becomes so habitual a thing that the thought of leaving it behind prompts a peculiar anxiety. What is the term of it? When a child leaves its parents for Masjud on the first day. Separation anxiety, that's what they call it.'

'Happiness,' I agreed, 'is not a dependable quantity. Not in the same way that unhappiness is.'

'And then,' she said, putting her hands together in her lap, 'there's the question of whether we deserve to be happy ...'

'*You* do,' I said.

'And you?'

'I deserve it,' I said, 'insofar as I make *you* happy. That's my project now: to make you happy. And only if I succeed in that then I deserve to share in it.'

'Perhaps the happiness won't last long,' she said. 'Or perhaps it will be the condition of our lives, and last for ever, and we will live for the rest of our time as happy people. But if the happiness passes away then it will be because it is like any mortal thing. It will be because it has been alive. I would prefer a living happiness that dies to an embalmed ordinariness that does not. I *will* marry you.'

'You say yes!'

'Yes.'

We embraced. This, I can say, was the greatest joy I have known in my life. 'Shall we stay in this city?' she asked, as we separated.

'Let us go to the Land of the Headless,' I said. 'I came to this city not to live here, but only to find you. Now that I have found you, I wish to start a new life. In Montmorillon this newness is possible. I shall take work wherever I can find it – in the mines even. We'll rent a house together, and live amongst many of our kind. We shall have a family.'

'Yes,' she said.

'Then let us go at once,' I said. 'We shall marry in Montmorillon, for that will give us the rights of habitation.'

'We can't go straight off!' she laughed. 'We must conclude our lives here. I must work to the end of the month to collect my salary, for instance.'

'And I,' I agreed. 'We will need the money. But the end of the month is only eight days. And during that time we can prepare ourselves for the journey.'

We embraced again. I felt the press of her body against mine, the pressure of her two breasts squashed against me, her warmth. I thought to myself: this is now no longer illicit, this intimacy. That thought stirred a happiness very deeply inside me.

She pulled away. 'I am going to ask you to promise me something,' she said.

'Of course,' I said.

'You have killed people,' she said.

'Only in the army—'

'Yes,' she conceded. 'But there is still a rage in you against the man – the man you blame for my headless condition.'

'I blame myself,' I said, but weakly.

'You blame another,' she said. 'Your talk has returned to this point many times—'

'You can hardly claim that *nobody* is to blame,' I interrupted.

'Nobody is to blame.'

'Not Mark Pol Treherne?'

'Not him.'

This was the closest I came to asking her directly to confirm that her attacker had been Mark Pol. I took her denial to be an expression of her own principle of forgiveness, rather than as a statement of his material innocence. Perhaps I should have asked her to clarify what she meant at this point. But I didn't. I was already certain of Mark Pol's guilt, you see. This seemed to me confirmation enough.

'You must promise not to kill anybody,' she said.

'Of course,' I said a little stiffly. 'Because you ask me, I shall not kill this person.'

'Not anybody,' she insisted.

'Not a single person.'

I wish, perhaps, that she had not asked me that; or that she had asked it of me at another time. For this, her request that I inhabit *her* realm of perfect forgiveness, that *I* forgive Mark Pol as she had; this request that I relinquish the revenge I had planned for so long, this soured our time together, if only a little. I promised her, but I was unsure whether I would be able to keep my promise. My time in the army had persuaded me that, sometimes, killing must be done.

But after a few days my mood brightened. I had searched the city for Siuzan, and I had found her. And not only had I found her, but I had found her in love with me, and we were to be married. How could I be sad? This reunion, and this marriage, was, evidently, meant to be. Now, during my search, I had *also* been looking for news of Mark Pol. Had I found him perhaps I would have killed him, and so fulfilled the vow for vengeance I made so long before. But I had *not* found him. It was possible that he had left the city entirely, of course. But if he were still in the city, and if I had not chanced upon him in the eight days between now and our departure, then he would live, and my promise to Siuzan would be unbroken. This, I thought likely.

Five

The days went past quickly, busy with work and with the preparations for our departure. I quizzed such headless as were my friends about the direction of Montmorillon – the north-east road out of Cainon, they said; three days' walking, taking such leftward forks of the road as led us towards the tallest peak visible along the crowded horizon. The road went up, through a valley, and finally came to the Land of the Headless itself. It seemed simple enough.

I went so far as to check with an agency of travel as to whether it would be possible to fly, or ride on a coach, to get to this place. There *was* a plane that made the journey, but the agent declined to sell me a ticket. I was neither surprised nor angered by this. I was content to walk. I hoped that the walk would overlay the memory of the previous walk, on which Siuzan had suffered so much, and that this means of travel would supersede all the journeys of the past. Everything was to be made anew.

I was not illusioned. I knew that Montmorillon was no paradise. The authorities controlled it, and many headed people lived there. The proportion of headless was larger than in other places, but many of these were the most lawless of offenders. The reputation of the place in Cainon was as of a nest of bandits and snakes and a continual threat to social order. But it was a new land. It would be the place where Siuzan and I could start again.

I spent much of my remaining funds on supplies for the journey. I bought two pairs of good shoes, one for Siuzan and one for myself. I bought a single backpack in which I planned to carry all our belongings. I bought two staffs, one smaller than the other, that each of us would have one to lean upon as we strode; for walking great distances is much easier with a staff in one's hand. I had taken a walk before, and without a staff, and I remembered wishing that I had had one. That walk, so long ago, that had had so large an impact on my life, for evil and for good. There were many things, then, that I had wished for; and the best of them I now had. And my staff seemed to me a symbol of this: straight and clean-planed and strong to hold me up.

The days counted down. I became aware of a tension inside me, a fear that something would come along to interrupt the smooth passage from my sad old life to my bright new one. Perhaps this was a presentiment, because – of course – something came. And what came was this: I was to be tested against my word.

It happened this way: I was returning from work one evening. In one more day I would be leaving Cainon for ever with the woman I loved. Soon she would become my bride. It was the very edge and lip of my new life.

I made a detour to buy four sealed slabs of sugarcake, which I did to complete my supplies. The first shop refused to serve me, because I was headless, and I was forced to walk further on to find another shop that would. The sun was precisely in the process of setting.

And here was a knot of headless individuals, gathered about a brazier. Here was one, talking loudly and tipping wine into his neck valve, and something about him snagged my attention.

I stepped closer towards the fire. Thin strands of yellow flame struggled upwards from the mouth of the brazier like fluid grass under the action of wind. The sun low in the sky diluted the firelight with its own commanding brightness, but even from many yards away I could feel the heat of the brazier. It was a cool evening, and promised a cold night, but wine and raw fire can make a man feel warm again. The air had that violet quality of dusk that is not, or is not only, a function of colour.

He turned, this man, and was silhouetted against the light of the fire. On the left side of his neck stump was an eye-stalk prosthesis, but his right shoulder was bare.

My hand went to my charm, hanging about my truncated neck. I clasped it.

This was unexpected. I had spent weeks looking for this man and had not found him. Then I had given up the search, and at once I stumbled across him. The remaining day might have passed without me chancing upon him, and then I would have left Cainon for ever with Siuzan to trek to the Land of the Headless. One more night, and one mere day, and I would never have seen him again. Yet here he was, directly in front of me.

I wondered once again whether the hand of the All'God had arranged this. I remembered my vow of vengeance upon him. But I remembered

Siuzan's words as well. Forgiveness was her nature, and mercy was the core attribute of the All'God.

But here he was, drinking and laughing, and he had the right to do neither.

What must I do?

I came up behind him and struck him on the back, halfway between a blow and a slap. He lurched forward and turned about.

'What?' he blustered. 'What?'

'This,' I said, holding up his eye stalk.

The whole little group, half a dozen headless men and women, fell silent at once. Mark Pol Treherne moved his one remaining eye to bear on the object I held. He seemed to have trouble recognising it.

'It is yours,' I said, slipping the cord from my neck stump and offering it to him. 'I return it to you.'

'But,' said Mark Pol, in a voice of realisation, 'it cannot be! This is my eye – Matthea, Senge, look! Here it is – after so much time it returns to me!' He took it from me and held it up like a prize.

'So,' said one of the other headless, 'one-eyed Pol has two eyes again!' There was laughter.

'How did you come by this, my friend,' Mark Pol asked me.

'Don't you recognise me?'

'The light is not good,' he said. 'And I have only one eye. Where did you find my other one?'

'I got it by snapping it from your neck,' I said curtly. 'Do you truly not recognise me?'

'Hah!' he shouted with sudden recognition. 'Really? Is it you?'

'You sound even pleased to see me?' I asked.

'How can I not be pleased, to get my eye back, to meet with an old friend!'

'The last time we met,' I reminded him, 'we were fighting. Old friend? We held one-another in mutual detestation and anger.'

'Ach the old times!' Mark Pol cried. 'I've told you about them often, have I not?' This last was addressed to his friends around the brazier.

'*I* can't recall them with any pleasure,' I said. 'Do you remember Siuzan Delage?'

'Ah, the woman,' he said. 'Yes, the woman. Of course I remember *her*.'

'She was beheaded.'

There was a silence after I said this. Then, in a puckish voice, he said, 'We are all of us here present familiar with *that* procedure!'

My anger almost overcame me. 'Do you make light of it? After what you did to her?'

Immediately he returned anger for my anger. 'I? *I* did nothing to her.' He drew himself up. '*You* are the rapist, not I.'

'This again? You dare accuse me? As you did before, in front of that policeman?'

He squared up to me. 'I did not assault this woman,' he insisted.

'She says otherwise,' I said.

'Then she is lying,' he insisted.

'I should believe you, or her?'

Abruptly he was laughing. 'But this is exactly how we parted, years ago! Bickering over this business! It is as if no time has passed. You didn't believe my protestations of innocence then, and so I don't suppose you'll believe them now. Have you truly met up with Siuzan?'

My mind was half occupied with sizing up this group of half a dozen, and planning how I would fight them off should they come to Mark Pol's aid when I tackled him. 'I have,' I said.

'And she is headless?'

'Yes.'

'Poor woman. She did not deserve that.'

This new tone of his gave me a moment's pause. 'She did not.'

'She showed us great kindness, and was repaid foully. But not by me, *Sieur* Cavala.'

'And not by me either.'

He laughed again. 'When I last knew you, *Sieur* Cavala, you would have rebuked me for using the honorific. You would have said *I do not deserve it!*'

'I have changed.'

'We all have. I am sorry for Siuzan. But everybody here has suffered, and some are as blameless as she. I do not,' he added, 'refer to myself. But some of these others.' I looked about the group again.

'Good day to you, *sieur* stranger,' said one of them. It was a woman's voice. 'I am Matthea.'

'Good day, my lady,' I said.

She laughed at this. 'How pleasant it is to be politely treated,' she said.

'Come, Jon Cavala,' said Mark Pol. 'Let us bury our bygones. We weren't friends before, I know. Perhaps you still despise me, and perhaps I deserve your despite, although not for attacking Siuzan Delage. But I thank you for returning my eye to me. Allow me to repay you with a quarter-hour's hospitality: we have a little food, and a little drink. Sit with us!'

I sat. I shall tell you why. I had resolved, pricked by Mark Pol's infuriating chatter and his shameless self-justifications, to take my revenge upon him after all, then and there. Siuzan would be saddened that I had broken my word, but, on the journey to Montmorillon and in our life together thereafter, I would make such atonement to her as I could for this new disappointment. But, having decided this, I was faced with the possibility that, in killing Mark Pol, I might be compelled to kill some of his friends, or even that they might kill me. They might of course try to protect, or to avenge, their friend. And what, for example, if I killed the woman Matthea? Could my revenge against Mark Pol, which had lived in my mind for so long as a just matter – could that tolerate these other killings and remain pure?

So I sat. I asked myself whether I was merely prevaricating. One more day and I would leave Cainon for ever. One more day, and then nothing to look forward to except a new life with the woman I loved. I could have walked away from that place, and in doing so preserved the integrity of my promise to Siuzan. And yet I stayed.

This was a dilemma.

'So you have met Siuzan,' Mark Pol was saying. 'Is she well? Apart, of course, from her headlessness.'

'She is well enough,' I said. 'Hers is not a constitution well fitted to bear shame.'

'She was always devout, I remember,' he said. 'But there are many devout people amongst the headless. And where have *you* been these years, my friend?'

'I have been in the army.'

'The army! And you've travelled from star to star, in spaceships?'

'I have.'

'It is glamorous. Many headless go into the military,' he replied. 'I have considered it myself, but I fear it's not a choice I can make.'

'I was given no choice,' I said.

'No?'

'The police *chevaler*, Bonnard, compelled me.'

'Him!' Mark Pol barked. 'A foul person. He treated me most barbarously. Cruelly – and it was not as if I'd done anything wrong.'

This peaked up my anger again. 'You hope, by repeating that, to make it true,' I snapped.

He didn't reply. For a while the group of us sat, watching the fire as the flames brightened against the darkening sunset sky. They passed between them the bottle, and also a glass jar of babyfood, taking two fingers' scoop of the latter for each sip of the former. I was neither hungry nor thirsty.

'Now this liquor,' Mark Pol, said, holding the bottle by its neck, 'is a rice wine. I did not know that it was possible to make wine from rice, but it has been managed. And the question is whether it is permitted or forbidden by the Bibliqu'rân. It is not mentioned by name, and therefore perhaps it is not forbidden. But, say some, the only thing permitted is the wine of grapes and so it *must* be forbidden. Therefore the trader who brought this stuff here has been unable to sell it, and so, at a cut-price, it ends up with the likes of us. We, perhaps, are not so fussed as to the precise reasoning of scripture.'

The others murmured. 'My view,' boomed one of them, 'is that rice is a *form* of grape.' He took his sip and passed the bottle round. One more turn around the ring of them and it was empty.

'*Sieur* Cavala,' said Mark Pol in a different voice. 'I fear that you have come to kill me in revenge for this attack upon this woman.'

'You have good reason for your fear,' I replied.

'Do you love her?'

'I do.'

'Are you with her?'

'We are going to marry,' I said. 'She and I plan to travel to Montmorillon. We'll live there as well as we can, and have children.'

'Bravo,' he said quietly. 'I congratulate you, even though it's your love that gives direction to your impulse to revenge. But I ask you: what if I am *not* guilty of this assault upon her?'

'Again with this refrain?'

'Has she accused me?'

'She,' I said, and stopped. '*She* forgives you,' I said, to imply that I did not.

'A moment, for I must press you on this matter,' he said. 'She has said she forgives me?'

'She has.'

'But has she said, without ambiguity, that it was I who assaulted her?'

I did not answer for a long time, but eventually I said: 'No.'

'We were all of us sinners,' Mark Pol said, sounding sober though he must have been drunk. 'All three of us, me, you and Gymnaste too. She forgave us all. It was her nature. Has she told you much about the assault upon her?'

'She has not.'

'It is too painful a matter, I daresay.'

'I daresay.'

'You believed I was the guilty party before,' he said. 'You have believed it for a long time. But what if I am *not* guilty? I only raise the question, you understand. But I am interested in how you would answer it.'

'If not you, then whom?' I snapped.

'There was a third with us on that walk.'

'Gymnaste? Do you seriously propose Gymnaste as the attacker?'

'Why not?'

'It was not in his nature.'

'How can you know what was in his nature?'

I pondered. 'He was a truthful man, beheaded for heresy.'

'He *told* us he was a truthful man. But perhaps he was not truthful when he said this.'

'You,' I said, 'delight in this manner of paradox. I don't believe Gymnaste was the assailant.'

'Then, *Sieur* Cavala,' he said. 'What of you?'

'You are talking nonsense,' I said quickly.

'Perhaps I am. But only you know how much to trust your memory. You have been in space. There is a curious forward-backward time dilation, is there not? It affects the efficiency of ordinators, does it not? Are you certain you can depend upon your memory?'

'I could hardly forget something like that!' I snapped.

'But might you have done it half-awake, as a sleepwalker walks? Be honest with yourself and with me. You desired Siuzan Delage before, did you not? You desired her on that walk—'

'I loved her!' I cried. 'I love her still!'

'And is not the sexual act an aspect of love?'

'You make it filthy with your words.'

'I am only suggesting. You must be *sure*. Ask yourself this: could you have committed this assault upon her, and then denied yourself the memory as something repugnant to you? Is your rage at *me* a transferred rage at yourself for your own appetites?'

'Nonsense,' I said, with less force. 'She loves me. She is preparing to travel with me to the Land of the Headless – she has agreed to marry me, to spend her life with me. Why would she do this if I were her attacker?'

'Perhaps *because* she loves you,' he said. 'Perhaps she has not accused you directly because she *wants* to forgive you. Perhaps she loves your good qualities enough to want to forget about this one bad act. Perhaps she is one of those victims of whom we sometimes hear, who falls in love with her assailant. Human love is a complex thing.'

'It certainly is,' said one of the other headless, staring at the fire.

I must confess that his words threw me into a great inner confusion. My purpose crumbled away. Now, I could not remember attacking Siuzan on that walk. But, it is true, my memory was a patchy thing. And it is also true I had desired her before that attack. I have tried, in this memoir, to be honest; and I have honestly recorded the desire I felt. It was not pure, but men are not pure and we are subject to fleshly desires. All men are capable of this assault. But could *I* have assaulted her?

Could I?

If I had repressed that memory as a repugnant thing then surely there would be some vestigial or fragmentary part of it in my consciousness. I searched, but I could not find it.

Then again, I thought back to the way Siuzan talked of that portion of her past. She was evasive, as if trying to avoid lying whilst also trying to avoid stating a truth directly. What if the truth she wanted to avoid was *my* culpability?

This was a very disconcerting thought.

The night on which the attack had happened. What *did* I remember of that time? I remembered lying on my back upon the cold desert ground, looking at the stars, woken from some bad dream – but what dream? I could not recall. I remembered hearing Siuzan crying out in her sleep ... or had it been her crying out that had woken me? I was not certain. The more I tried to fix the memory, the more friable it became.

Why had she cried aloud in the night?

I had been woken by the cold. Was I sure of that? Did I actually remember waking *because* of the cold, or had I filled that element into my own narrative to explain why I was awake? I remembered that my male organ had been solid, locked with the frost of arousal. I remembered the sense of disgust I felt inside myself at this development – the memory of *that* was sharp and real. But I could not recall the cold which sup- posedly had woken me. For what reason, truly, had I woken? Why had Siuzan cried out in her sleep?

What word had she cried out?

And here is the strange thing about memory. To apply the pressure of mental scrutiny to any given memory is to disperse it. I felt, with the corner-of-the-eye apprehension of something seen and not seen with which you will be familiar, that I knew the word she had shouted out. But I could not bring it to mind. It had been one word, a single syllable. Or had it been longer? Two syllables? A single word, though. But *what* word?

I tried to give order to my confusion. What could I remember? I tried to take a panoptic view of the previous three years. There, as if lining the walls of my inner chamber, were my army comrades, and all the hardships and dangers of training and war. There also, ubiquitous as scent in the air, was my rage. I had spent the whole time since Siuzan's violation in a furious state. I remembered the efforts I had made, the peril and pain I had put myself through, in order to escape the camp, to seek out and kill Mark Pol and take his crime for my own. My whole life had, for a time, become focused into that aim, all my rage flowing through me and showering down upon that point – blows, mentally pre-enacted, pouring down upon Mark Pol's shuddering body, pounding out life and blood and dashing him into a dented stretch of crushed flesh bashed into the ground. That anger seemed very vivid to me.

And here he was, sitting a yard from me, the man himself. And yet the anger did not seem to be able to fix itself upon him after all.

Why not?

And yet – surely – surely – it was not possible for a man to rape a woman and then simply *forget that he had done so*?

A voice chimed inside my thoughts, sounding rather like the voice of Levitt Dunber (but he, surely, could not be *my conscience*). It said: you would remember assaulting a woman you hated, or about whom you felt only indifference. But how could you possibly remember doing such a thing to the woman you loved?

That state in which a person is neither entirely awake, nor entirely asleep.

My memory was porous, unreliable on details. But is not everybody's memory like this? Perhaps, as Mark Pol said, the effect of travelling faster than light, which affected ordinators in ways different to organic brains, perhaps this *had* pulled holes out of the fabric of my memory. But, I revolted: I could *not* have forgotten something so profound. And what of Siuzan? Could she truly have fallen in love with a man capable of such brutality? Would she truly be planning to spend her life with such a man? No, I told myself, and no and no.

I looked over to Mark Pol.

What word had she cried out, that night? I could not remember, but I could (I realised) remember the effect that word had had upon me. The sound of her voice had sent a smack and a recoil through my nerves. Why should that be?

'*Sieur* Cavala,' Mark Pol said. 'I fear we have drunk all of the rice wine, and there is none left. Do you, by any chance, have any wine in your pack there?'

'No,' I said, dull.

'Anything at all?'

'Sugarcake.'

'I used to have a sweet tooth,' said Mark Pol. 'But since beheading I have lost the appetite for excess of sugar. I have lost all my teeth as well. But not because of sugar!' He laughed at this.

'I do not believe what you say,' I said to Mark Pol. I tried to make the words loud, aggressive, but somehow my heart was not in it.

He understood that I was not referring to his appetite for sugar. 'You may believe,' he said carefully, 'or disbelieve. Does it matter what I say? You must believe *yourself*, that is the important thing.'

'I am not capable of such a foulness,' I said, again without conviction.

At this, it seemed, Mark Pol lost his temper. 'Boh!' he cried. 'Of course you are – we all are, all of us men. It is precisely in the nature of men to be capable of such business. No cant, *Sieur* Cavala, not between the two of us. Incapable? Pah.'

'I love her,' I cried. 'We are to be married.'

'Again, my congratulations,' he said. 'How lucky that things have worked to your advantage.'

This pierced through me. 'What do you mean by that?' I snapped.

'And you already know what I mean,' he said, turning away from me. But he turned back, because he could not resist elaborating his imputation. 'I mean that when you first met Siuzan Delage she was as far above you as the moon itself. When you first fell in love with her the most you could hope for in return was her pity. And isn't it insulting to bear another's *pity*? I have always found it. But, miracle! *Now*, after all that has happened, she is beheaded and reduced, dragged so far down that she is prepared to become your wife rather than live in single headless squalor. Is there no benefit to *you* in that debasement? What was it that dragged her down anyway? *You* know.'

'I would – never—' I said. Then: 'Are you suggesting that I assaulted her with designs that she would be . . .?'

'Shamed? Brought to your level? Made accessible to you?' Mark Pol snorted through his neck valve. 'You may, or may not, have planned it as such. The heart has instincts which sometimes it follows. The mind is not always privy to those motivations. You know the commonplaces of policemen: to solve a crime, ask yourself who *benefits* from the crime. Well . . . *have* you benefited? You can answer that question for yourself.' He raised the empty wine bottle as if to toast me. 'Congratulations on your impending marriage, *Sieur* Cavala.'

'No,' I said.

'No? Very well. It hardly matters. I must say,' he added, turning back to his friends, 'much of this stems from our culture's attitudes to the sexual act. Before beheading I was very inexperienced in that matter, for all that I bragged. But since my execution I have become more experienced.'

'You?' I was incredulous. 'Who would favour *you* with such intimacy?'

'Oh a number of women,' he declared airily. 'Matthea here, for example; she indulges me, from time to time.' He pointed with his right arm. The headless woman to whom he gestured put her hands together and wagged them up and down. The gesture seemed, somehow, happy. 'When I can scratch together enough money, of course,' he added, chuckling in his own shame. 'I would not expect her to debase herself out of charity!'

I felt a revulsion swell inside me. I could not sit there any further. I pulled myself to my feet and hurried away. I felt a terrible nausea, a sickness and trembling in my very bones. I had not yet eaten my evening meal and so there was nothing in my stomach to vomit, but I retched and retched. I felt, as perhaps all people do who stumble upon the content of some great secret, as if the answer had been directly in front of me the whole time and yet I had not seen it.

Six

I tried the various little tricks that we all learn to try and recall things momentarily forgotten. I tried thinking about something entirely different in the hope that the memory would pop up unbidden. I tried associative thinking. I tried looking up at the stars, as if that would prompt the thought. But none of this was any good. That one night, on which so much depended, remained hazy in my thoughts.

I asked myself: was that very haziness itself a significant thing? This one night had had more impact on the course of my life than almost any other. Surely it should be crystal clear in my thoughts! I recalled my prolonged fury, years' worth, directed at Mark Pol. And what if I had created him as a scapegoat to my own guilt? Was my rage at him actually a rage at myself?

Back at the house Siuzan was waiting for me. I stood in the doorway and she embraced me, and immediately she sensed something not right.

'What's the matter?'

I went inside and she followed. 'Siuzan,' I said. 'Are you sure you wish to marry me?'

'Of course.'

'You are sure you wish to go away with me to Montmorillon tomorrow?'

'What is this?'

'Siuzan, I'm sorry.'

'Of course I'm sure of these things.'

'But do you *know* me, Siuzan? Are you sure of me?'

'I know you better than anybody,' she replied. 'Love grants a clearer knowledge than other people know.'

'Do you forgive me, Siuzan?'

She stiffened at this. 'There is nothing for which you need forgiveness. Why are you talking in this manner?'

I didn't know how to reply. 'I met Mark Pol Treherne on the way home from work.'

'So this is why you are so late?' Then, with a start, she added, 'But did you hurt him?'

'I did not. I left him well, and living, and even happy. He was laughing when I left. But he said, or he suggested ...'

After a silence, she prompted. 'Suggested what?'

We were standing at the foot of the stairs. One of the other occupants of the house came down, greeting us civilly, and walked past through the door into the night. When we were alone again I said: 'Siuzan, we have never properly talked, you and I, about the walk to Cainon. About the night you were ... assaulted.'

She turned a little away from me. 'I do not wish to talk about that,' she said.

'I understand, but – but it is important to ... Siuzan. Please. I cannot remember the night you were attacked. Or I can remember only pieces of it. My memory is partial.'

'Better so.'

'No, it's not. I don't wish to bury the memory. I must know. I must know this one thing. Was it *I* who attacked you?' It took a great deal for me to say that out loud.

For a while she did not reply. I heard the sound of night insects, tiny as raindrops and scurrying through the air, miniature distant scrapes and clicks that built together into the chorus of the night-time. Siuzan seemed to be thinking very long and hard about my question.

'I don't wish to talk about that night,' she said finally.

'But this is evasion!' I said in a low voice. 'I must assume that such an answer indicates that I was indeed the attacker.'

'You shouldn't assume so.'

'I must *know*, Siuzan.'

'You already know,' she said.

'I don't!'

'Do you know that I love you?' she asked, almost fiercely.

I could not answer.

'Does anything else matter? You – listen to me, Jon Cavala. You *did not hurt* me.'

'Siuzan ...'

'I cannot be plainer than that. Now listen to me a second time: leave these thoughts. Tomorrow I must be at work earlier than usual, for it is my last day and I must work longer before collecting my final salary. I may not see you tomorrow morning, but I will be waiting on the steps outside the house tomorrow evening. When you come back from your work I will be there, waiting for you. When you come back we will start off together.'

'Siuzan ...'

'No, listen now: we will walk through the dusk, and we will be well outside the city by nightfall. We will find a quiet place, away from the road, and eat our supper, we will no longer belong to ordinary society. Then we will roll ourselves into a blanket together to share our heat, and so we will sleep. In the morning after we will walk through the heat of the day, every step taking us closer towards our promised land. That is the only important thing.'

She embraced me again, and then she asked once, and then twice, and then three times, whether I understood her. Finally I said 'Yes', and she made her way up the stairs to her room. And that was how we parted that night.

I went through to mine. I lay down.

Seven

I slept, but the truth of my past was not revealed to me in a dream. The headless do not dream.

In the morning my nausea had passed away, and I ate some pap for breakfast. But my thoughts were still oriented around the hollow place in my mind.

I walked through the city to my workplace. This, my last day in the city, should have been a day filled with the excitements of future possibility. I did not feel that way.

The task we all face is to come to terms with ourselves. Or, to put the matter another way: we must determine for ourselves to what extent we can accept love from another person if we have no love for ourselves.

I stopped at the fountain, in the little square halfway between the house and my workplace, and I sat for a while. The night before she had said, 'You did not hurt me.' Those were her very words. I pondered the possible meanings of this statement. She may have been saying, '*Despite assaulting me* you did not hurt me', as if to say, 'You did me no permanent hurt', as if to say, 'I forgive you'. But this was intolerable. If I were this person, then I literally deserved the death which I had hoped, incompetently, to bring on myself in order to save Siuzan's head. I deserved the death I had planned to inflict on Mark Pol. How could I walk with this pure woman into the desert to start a new life with such an act on my conscience?

But love prompts hope, and I also thought: perhaps she had meant the words literally: 'You did not hurt me' – another way of saying, '*It was not you* that hurt me – it was another man'. Perhaps she had been saying, 'It was Mark Pol', or even, 'It was Gymnaste'. My heart jumped a little at this possibility. Surely one of the duties love brings with it is the necessity of believing the truthfulness of the loved other? Why could I not take her words just as they were said?

But then, a downstroke. What if, in saying, 'It was not you that hurt me – it was another man' she meant only that it had been *an earlier version of me*? Perhaps her words could be construed to mean, 'The *you* who violated me was a different person to the you with whom I have fallen in love'? But this would hurl me back into the pit again. She might consider the two Jon Cavalas she had met, with an interlude of two years in between, to be two different people; but for me those years had been a continuum. If I was capable of such barbarity before, then I was capable again. Was Mark Pol right when he said that all men are capable of this thing?

Words can be very hard to understand.

I do not mean by this that they are incomprehensible. Something the reverse is true, in fact: that there are too many possible meanings, too great a range of comprehension. And yet my future life devolved upon the extent to which I could understand these words.

I resolved: I needed at any rate to get to work, for the money for a month's work was no trivial matter and I would forfeit it all if I missed this day. But after work I would go back to the house and meet Siuzan, and together we would walk from the city. Perhaps then, away from the crowds, when it was just the two of us underneath the stars, we would be able to talk more about this. One way or another she could make her meaning plain to me.

I stood up. There was still hope.

This, insofar as I can express it, was the resolution I reached in my heart: it was not my proper business to *judge* myself. If I could not abrogate this business of judgement to the person I loved, then love meant little or nothing. Could I really insist that my self-revulsion trumped her love for me? Could I pretend that my insight was greater than hers? That would be arrogance indeed.

I thought to myself: this unsettlement in my heart may not be quickly or easily smoothed away. Yet with time and labour it might be smoothed for all that. I thought to myself: was my love for Siuzan, and the prospect of a new life with her, not worth this labour, or this time? Of course it was.

So I resolved: I would swallow my self-disgust.

I made my way to my place of work. Time was tight, now, and so I was in a hurry. Because I was in a hurry I almost did not see her – or if I saw her, perhaps I did not quite recognise her. It's possible I saw her before, and did not recognise what I saw, for my mind was in another space. My foot was literally upon the threshold; I could see the check-in board, and the supervisor standing beside it; I could see one of my headless co-workers tapping the datascreen with his name. It lacked five minutes of the hour. I was at work, and in time, with moments to spare.

But nevertheless I had to pull up my stride. I had to withdraw my foot and step back outside into the morning light.

She was waiting, twenty yards along the road from my workplace. She was waiting at a bus-stop. All the many weeks I had been going in through that factory door every single morning I had not noticed her there before. Indeed I never did find out whether she generally caught the bus from that stop, or whether this was some unusual quirk in her morning routine. Surely it was the latter. *Could* I have walked past her so many times without even noticing? I find it hard to believe, but it might be so.

Everything lurched in my mind. Geologists talk of the occasional upheaval in the orientation of the world's magnetic field, when it switches its planetwide webwork in a great epileptic convulsion and north pole becomes south and south pole becomes north. This was such a moment.

I walked over to the bus-stop. I was shivering slightly as I walked. I felt a weakness in my legs. She was standing there, inside the transparent plastic half-shell.

'Siuzan?' I said.

She looked round at me.

'Siuzan Delage?'

'Do I know you?' she asked.

There was no mistaking her face. It was precisely her full, straight nose, precisely the substantial line of lid and eyebrow about her sharp blue eyes. There had been many times, over the preceding years, when I had tried to remember precisely what she looked like, and had been infuriated by my inability so to do. But to see the face again was, in part, to think, *Of course! This is what she looks like!* She looked extraordinarily like herself.

'Siuzan,' I said again.

'I'm sorry, she said, smiling. 'I'm sure I've worked with you over this last year – please don't be offended if I can't place you. Without the face to prompt us, you know, it's hard for us headed to recognise the—'

'I'm Jon Cavala,' I said.

Her face, still smiling, pondered; her eyes unfocused slightly as she searched her memory for my name, and found nothing. 'I'm sorry,' she started saying, and then, with a little *ah!* of recognition, 'Jon? Jon Cavala? Is it you?'

'Siuzan ...' I said bleakly.

'But we walked together from Doué to – to here! Years ago, how many years, as many as three?' She looked really delighted with herself to have remembered. 'It was you, and those other two – you had all been

254

beheaded in Doué, and we all of us trekked over the desert to Cainon. Now what were *their* names?'

'Mark Pol Treherne,' I said.

'Yes, him! He was a lively character, I remember. And the other one, Gymnoplast, or Hymnoplast ...'

'Gymnaste.'

'Just so. A quiet soul, I seem to remember. Good gracious, what a pleasant surprise! It has been so long. Imagine bumping into you here and now! What are you doing here?'

I looked back at the entrance to the factory. 'I work there,' I said stupidly. What else should I say? I was conscious of a very sharp sense of the ridiculousness of my situation.

'In that place? What does it do?'

'It renders and processes fat.'

'How wonderful that you have found a good job!' she said brightly. 'I work now as liaison between the authorities and headless such as yourself. I mean, I work here in Cainon. When I say liaison with headless such as yourself, I don't mean such as *you*, James, for you have found a good job. More usually I work with headless who find it harder to readjust to society. What were you before your beheading? I knew once, but I've forgotten ... weren't you a—'

'Poet,' I said.

'So you were! I remember now, and a famous one! It seems so long ago. Can it really be only three years? I was naïve. I remember, we arrived in the city and ...' She furrowed her brow, as if trying to remember.

'You went into a chemist, to obtain pharmocopy for me,' I said.

'That's right.'

'You did not come out again.'

'What? Didn't I? I'm sorry. How rude of me! Ah well ... I remember now. I told the chemist what I wanted, for him to make up medication for a headless man, and he asked me some questions, and I told him the reason why. He was very shocked, I recall that. He was shocked that I had gone on such a journey, unescorted, with three headless. It was my first introduction to the prejudices of this city – the prejudice against the headless, I mean. He was *quite* shocked, I recall. He called the police, I think. After the fuss I came to find you, but you had all gone.' Her smile wavered. 'And, do you know, now that I look back – I haven't thought of this for a long time – but now that I think of it, that was *very* rude of me, wasn't it? Not saying goodbye. I apologise. But, then again, how could I find you afterwards, in so big city? Still, never mind. Never mind. You have fallen on your feet, as the phrase goes. What of the other two?'

'We were arrested,' I said dumbly, as if the need to explain it all to this woman – to this woman of all women – was somehow ridiculously improper.

Her smile was replaced by what I took to be her professional expression of concerned understanding. 'It is common amongst the newly headless,' she said.

'*Chevaler* Bonnard told us that you had been ...'

'I know *him* well!' she interrupted, in a pleased voice. 'The crusty old *chevaler*. I often rub up against him in my work. He has many dealings with the headless, of course, in his professional capacity.'

This was very nearly too much. I stalled over my words. It took great effort of will to say, 'He told us that you had been assaulted.'

She was puzzled. '*I* had been assaulted? Why would he say that? I haven't been assaulted. Or did he mean, perhaps, the car crash? I feel foolish even calling it a crash, it was nothing but a bump. I didn't really need to go to hospital; that was simply a precaution. I only wore the neck brace for a few days.' She laughed. 'I suppose stories can grow up about these things. Assaulted! The very idea! I shall have a word with the *chevaler*. Rumour is a strange thing, though, isn't it? But see, there again: that little accident was a full six months ago, and yet it feels to me like it happened yesterday. Whereas that walk, under the stars, all the way from Doué to Cainon, that feels to me like it happened a lifetime ago! But here comes my bus now – I must be off – how wonderful it was to bump into you again, James ...'

'Jon.'

'Of course, I'm sorry, Jon. Jon Cavala. I do remember! I'm so sorry that I have to go. I'm already late today. Which is to say, I'm early, but they've called a crack-of-the-day meeting so in *that* sense I'm late. It *was* so good to see you again.' And she hopped up onto the bus, and it pulled away, and I was left standing at the side of the road.

I stood for a moment without any thought at all in my mind. My feet moved almost of their own accord back to the door of the factory, prompted by some vestigial sense in my body that it would be a shame to let a whole month's wage go slide for the want of one more day's work.

'You're late,' said the supervisor, as my numb fingers pressed the data-screen to enter my name.

'I am sorry,' I said.

'I'll have to take a half-day from your monthly,' he said.

'Thank you,' I said. I said *thank you* because he was legally entitled, if he so wished, to dismiss me from employment there and then and pay me nothing. The words were automatic. I went through to the changing room and pulled on a plastic overall, and stepped on into the main chamber of the place.

I went through the motions of the job that day. What else could I do? I was aware of a thought in my head *I must think about this*, but I didn't know how to begin such thinking. I needed a wholly new paradigm. I needed to reorganise almost everything in my thoughts. This was too large a task. My mind was too exhausted to do this.

As the end of the working day approached I found that I needed to think what I was going to do – to think, in other words, in purely practical terms, even if I could not think through the fullest implications of it all. Was I to return to the house? Siuzan – or the woman I had been calling Siuzan, the woman who had deceived me – would be there, waiting, ready for us to walk away from the city and begin a new life. Could I do this? Was it a possibility? I had not loved her as a liar and an impostor. Could I begin a new life with her, now that I knew the truth?

I don't know what I thought. My thoughts were not coherent. I went through the motions of the job. Time did not pass in any noticeable manner. It seemed stuck.

It was late in the afternoon when two policemen came through to the work area. The supervisor, nervous at this intrusion of the proper authorities, hovered behind them. He was saying, 'How can I help? Please allow me to assist!'

All of us stopped working and turned to face the newcomers.

One of the policeman called out: 'Which one of you is Jon Cavala?'

'We have nobody here of that name,' declared the supervisor. 'Please. I know my workers. They are good workers, law-abiding though headless. There has been a misunderstanding.'

'If Jon Cavala does not come forward,' said the policeman, 'we are legally empowered to test the DNA of all workers in order to identify him. I should add that by not stepping forward when requested, Jon Cavala will add the charge of resisting lawful arrest to the other charges outstanding against him.'

I did nothing. I felt as if all motivation and passion had gone out of my body – almost as if an aperture had been opened in my heel and my total reservoir of willpower had literally flushed out through the gap. I simply stood there. I had become a great block of passivity on two legs.

The other policeman unholstered a DNA gun and stepped over to one of my colleagues. The dart made a *snk* as it popped through his overalls before snapping back into its home. The policeman spent a long time staring at the little screen on top of the device.'

'Well?' his colleague demanded.

'He is covered in animal fats,' said the second policeman. 'The animal DNA is confusing the device.'

Still I stood there, a perfect statue of passivity. As I look back on that moment I am surprised I did not at least *try* to get away: to run past the two men, to get outside, to avoid incarceration. I did not. It was not even that I saw the chillers hanging from their belts and decided against the attempt; although they did indeed have chillers on their belts, and *had* I made the attempt they would easily have floored me and taken me into custody. But the truth is I made no active decision at all. I simply stood there.

'I have a reading,' said the policeman, looking down at his device. 'This isn't him.'

'Hose the others off,' demanded the first policeman.

Again I stood perfectly still as the supervisor fetched a hose and sprayed the remaining workers, myself included. Once the animal soil was washed from our disposable overalls, processing the DNA was much more quickly achieved. The man to my left was processed. Then the dart snagged in my skin and was withdrawn.

'This is him,' said the policeman.

'Steelhand?' asked the supervisor, startled. 'But he can have committed no crime. He is a dependable worker ...'

'Come with me,' the first policeman said to me. His words acted as the command that provoked movement in me. I came, clankily, to life, like a rusty old automate or remote. I walked from the workfloor and out through the changing rooms, with one policeman ahead of me and one behind. I paused only to pull off my disposables and toss them in the chute. Otherwise I walked with a perfect and unflawed meekness out of the factory, and into the police car waiting outside.

Eight

What was going through my mind? Nothing at all. I was a clod of earth being moved by a spade. I was so forceless that they did not even bother handcuffing me.

They drove me to the police station, a journey that took perhaps a single minute. They drove into the area before the station reserved for police cars and pulled up. They got out and opened the door for me. I got out.

'You might as well take a look at the city,' one of the policemen advised. 'It'll be your last.'

I did not reply. But his words stirred a distant reaction inside me, something approaching regret. This was not a painful emotion, exactly. I think that, on that day, everything had been too thoroughly overthrown and cast down for pain. But, as I walked between these two men up the ramp, I did indeed take one last glance at the city. I stared at the four-towered marble box of the police station. One wall of this structure was gleaming pink with the light of the setting sun. It looked as if lit from within. Beyond it was the interrupted tessellation of rectangles and squares and diagonals of the Cainon itself.

A thought nagged me: I had not collected my month's wages. I supposed I would not need it now, but the thought upset me anyway. It was an incompleteness, a ragged edge that it would not have taken a moment to smooth.

Again there was that sensation of regret, very far away and deep inside. But what purpose would I have for the money now?

I stepped in through the main entrance. Here was the entrance hall, where I had waited, meekly enough, to be inducted into the military. The policeman behind the desk was a different individual to the one who had been on duty that day.

We walked through a heavy metal door and down a long corridor. At the far end of this corridor we turned left into a small interrogation room. There was no desk; but three chairs were set out facing one another at the vertices of a regular triangle. I was told to sit in one of the chairs. I did so. The policemen left.

I sat there for a long time. I am not certain for how long I sat there.

I contemplated the sensations of regret, such as they were, that needled in my heart. I considered this: that I had lived for the last few weeks in a state of happiness unprecedented in my life, and that over the last eight days that happiness had risen to an intensity I had never before known. This perfect globe had been struck away in a single day with a soundless, swift blow. Was that not reason for regret? But this, I thought, was not the core of it.

It was not the loss of my joy that gave me this twinge. It was the loss of my unhappiness. Or, to be more precise, it was the fact that so large a lump of anger and misery could have been transmuted into air, into, *Assaulted! The very idea! But here comes my bus*, so instantly, so effortlessly. It had been my whole life, a force more pervasive than gravity, for three years! And now I discovered I had been focused all that time on a nothingness, a deception or an illusion. That was the loss that desolated me. The severity of any suffering is made tolerable by the thought that it is at least significant, but that *significance* was precisely what had been taken from me. To live for years under the illusion of weight when in fact I had been the most weightless individual in the history of humankind! It amazed me that I had not floated away entirely. It is, I discovered, much harder to cope with the sudden loss of unhappiness than happiness. Very much harder.

The door trembled and flew open. Of course it was *Chevaler* Bonnard.

'*Sieur* Jon Cavala,' he said warmly. 'I hoped, and indeed expected, never to see you again. I had hoped you would go off and die in the wars, like a decent sort. But here we are again. Here we are again.'

He stepped in and sat down in one of the chairs. He was followed by one of the two arresting policemen, a thick-necked, tyre-muscled man in blue top and matching meadhres, who sat in the remaining chair. This second policeman unhooked his chiller from his belt and laid it across his lap, but the gesture was almost a disdainful one, as if to say, *See! Do you really think I would need this to restrain you? Can't you see how large and strong I am?*

Bonnard looked just as he had done before: his long face, his sharp facial bones, his retreated eyes, the cheerful ferocity of their expression.

'You look thinner,' he said to me. 'Altogether weaker. When last we met I remember being struck by how impressive was your musculature. That's all gone now, clearly. I suppose a diet of pap and menial work is not conducive with a well-developed musculature.'

The other policeman chuckled at this, as if to imply that *he* did not subsist upon a diet of pap.

'Very well, *Sieur* Cavala. You do not object to me addressing you as *Sieur* Cavala?'

I did not reply.

'Very well. The last time we met, I seem to recall, you had some fiddling moral objection to the honorific. But then again, the last time we met you were not hiding under a lie-name ... Steelhand, is it? Is that your current alias?'

He waited for a while, but I said nothing.

'You cut a pitiable figure,' he said eventually. 'I am sorry to say it. I have a great deal of experience of headless, and have become expert at recognising their body language. The last time you were here you were not so broken-down – you had spirit then. Do you remember attacking that other headless fellow? What was his name? The whole time in custody you were tense, full of your fury. Now look at you. Your arms hang limp!'

I did not reply.

'I see,' said Bonnard, with a little laugh, 'that you refuse to rise to my baiting. Good for you! And I am glad to see you patient. You'll need patience, where you are going. Charges? We must move on to the subject of charges. But you must not blame Siuzan Delage—'

I could not help stiffening slightly at this name.

'Aha!' said the second policeman, as if I had given myself away.

'Yes, you still have one button that may be pressed,' said Bonnard, smiling. 'That is good to see. It's good to see that the stuffing has not wholly been knocked from you. Well, I happened to have a meeting with Siuzan today. We often work together. She mentioned meeting you outside your workplace. She meant it kindly, of course. She was only gossiping, which is her manner. A pleasant woman, though not possessed of the most incisive of intellects.'

I should, perhaps, have stayed quiet. 'The All'God hates a lie, and a liar,' I said.

'A liar?' repeated Bonnard in mock surprise. 'A liar, such as the man who though named Jon Cavala would tell the world his name is Steelhand? A liar such as that?' The second policeman grunted at the justice of this observation.

I did not reply.

'But that is the least of it,' Bonnard said. 'False identity is a prison sentence of up to seven years, and we must observe the law in every particular. But after the seven years are up you will not be released, *Sieur*

Cavala; on the contrary, we will then pass you over to the army. Your file, it seems, lists you as never having been properly demobilised. Legally you are a deserter. Moreover, there are certain other charges, pertaining to breaking the duty of a bondsman upon another world. One of the terms of the Cessation Agreement has to do with either passing such criminals over to Ellaist authorities, unless we are prepared to punish them ourselves to the same standard as Ellaist law.' He shook his head. 'Death, I'm afraid. Unfortunate for you. But in the circumstances you should thank me that you will not face that fate for seven years. I am, I can tell you, a stickler for the letter of the law. You will be imprisoned for precisely that time. It will give you time to commune with your conscience. You could write your memoirs! You could meditate in writing upon on the fate that the All'God passes out to us!'

'You hate us,' I said.

'Indeed,' he agreed, matter-of-fact. 'Do you wonder at it? I see what your *type* has done, the crimes you commit that lead to your beheading. And I see what you continue doing even after decapitation. And you particularly, *Sieur* Cavala. I hate you in particular. Only last week I had dinner with my friend Georgis Benet. Bernardise was there.'

This was news from a very distant part of my consciousness. 'Bernadise,' I said.

'Years later and she is still marked by the shame of what you did to her.'

'I didn't rape her.'

Bonnard scowled at me. 'And you said yourself that the All'God hates a lie, and a liar! Oh, you mean you did not *force* yourself upon her. You mean you did not bruise or cut her, or bully her with your gym-built muscles. But you *pressured* her, *Sieur* Jon Cavala. Did you not? You applied *emotional force*. Do you deny it? You focused your expertise with language, the discourse of love and romance and all your mournful little poems, onto the malleable material of her soul. She *agreed* to have sexual relations with you? But how could she agree? She was a child; a twenty-year-old child. Afterwards she felt the shame and agony of what you had done to her. She still feels it. A girl of such purity, and her life now is bent out of shape. For that you deserved much worse than a mere beheading. But the law is the law.' He sat back, and the storm had passed away from his face. He beamed.

I said weakly: 'You told me Siuzan Delage had been raped. You insisted she was facing an inevitable decapitation.'

'Did I cause your sensitivities to suffer emotional pain?' he said absently. 'How can I express the height and depth and breadth of my sorrow for that falsehood? I assumed you would confess to save her, of course. I am a professional judger of character, and I judged that such would be your reaction to the situation in which I had placed you. With your confession it would have been easy to arrange an execution. I could have told the courts how necessary it was *not* to prolong Siuzan Delage's suffering by forcing her to testify and so forth. Your death, and justice! Justice for Bernadise. But you did not oblige. It still puzzles me. You refused to confess. Why was that? I wonder.'

I assumed the question was rhetorical, but he paused to give me space to answer. In a low voice I repeated: 'The All'God hates a lie, and a liar.'

'Oh I have no doubt the All'God hates all of us almost as much as He loves us all,' said Bonnard. 'That's of no consequence. The best I can say of you, *Sieur* Cavala, is that your moral cowardice surprised me. I suppose I had expected better of you. Which I suppose means that I thought there was *some* good in you. Still, I had ample reason to believe that a term in the army would be the death of you. You really should have died in the Sugar War. That was what *should* have happened. You were lucky.'

This word chimed with me, for some reason. I pondered. Then I recalled to myself that I had spent the previous night in an agony of uncertainty as to whether I had repressed the terrible memory of raping Siuzan Delage. My encounter with the real Siuzan had upended my certainties, certainly, but it had also – instantly, effortlessly, without intent – purged my soul of this worst of crimes. It had dissolved the sin wholly. Mark Pol, though annoying, was equally innocent of that crime. I was innocent myself. There was no crime for me to be guilty of.

This, I reflected, was something.

I felt another pang, but this time it was for the happiness I had known over the last few weeks and which now had passed away. It seemed to me, somehow, unfair that Providence had dangled the prospect of a new life and joy in front of me, only to withdraw it on the very day the happiness was calendared to begin. But *fairness* is a child's criterion for judging the cosmos.

I remembered that I had agreed to meet Siuzan, or the woman I had thought was Siuzan, outside the house after my work. We had been planning to walk away together. She was probably there now, waiting for me, wondering what had happened to me. She would wait until darkness. She would probably wait all night. In the morning she would be deeply saddened to think that I had abandoned her on the very threshold of starting a new life together. What would she think? She would be so disappointed in me! She would think I had run out on her, that I lacked even the courage to tell her directly that I could not go with her. She would think me a liar and a dissembler.

This was intolerable. It clicked something inside me. The woman I had thought was Siuzan Delage – what about her? Think of her. Had I, or had I not, fallen in love with her? Was she, or was she not, a good person, fair of soul? Had the happiness we experienced been *real* or *unreal*? Real. Yes, and good. Loved and loving. I had a responsibility for her happiness, too, even if she had lied to me. I could not leave her sitting on a doorstep all through the night without explanation of any kind. This, I think, was the first actual, active decision I came to since encountering the real Siuzan by the bus-stop.

'I must go,' I said. 'You must let me go. Not for my sake for the sake of another. A woman.'

'Indeed,' said Bonnard, managing to convey in that single word an eloquent combination of uninterest in my desires and certainty that I would never be released from prison.

'I must go,' I said again, more urgently.

The second policeman chuckled at this. 'Of course,' he said. 'I forget the precise legal phrasing – what is it? *Go from this place to another place there to be confined—*'

'—*There to be held. . .*' corrected Bonnard.

'Held,' mused the second policeman. 'It *is* a caring word.'

'Adequate care is one of our responsibilities,' agreed Bonnard.

But I had no time for this banter.

'I am sorry,' I said once more. 'I really must go.'

I stood up.

It was not desperation, exactly, that prompted me to this; neither a pressing desire to escape, nor even a strong belief that I deserved freedom. Rather it seemed to me simply that it was unacceptable that Siuzan, or the woman I still thought of as Siuzan, should be made to wait without any explanation of why I did not come. That could not be allowed. My certainty that this must not be allowed overwhelmed my rational or calculating mind, the part of the mind that thought of consequences. I could not help myself. I must impress this fact upon my captors. It may be that I believed I could convince them of this necessity by sheer force of will.

The second policeman stood up. His chiller was in his left hand.

'Sit down,' he said. He did not speak in an unkindly way.

I did not sit down.

'I do believe he feels *unable* to assist us with our enquiries,' Bonnard said, in a jovial voice with a chuckle running underneath it.

The second policeman flicked his chiller on. I saw the motion of his thumb.

I remember thinking: this is a situation that needs to be handled cautiously. There was going to be pain, I knew that; and there was a very real possibility of death. I was reconciled to the necessity of the pain. But the death was a different matter.

I straightened all the fingers of my left hand, and flopped the arm out, chopping the tips of the hand against the second policeman's Adam's apple. The organ seemed to pop inwards, inverting itself, under the pressure I applied. The man's eyes widened, his mouth snapped open. He made a curiously subdued noise, a sort of scraping or croaking sound. With a quick movement I put the four curled fingers of my right hand into his mouth, gripping him by the inside of his cheek, with my thumb on the outside. The fingernail of my ring-finger was slightly pointed, no more than a }, as it had been ever since my army days; I kept it this way, a habit of personal grooming. Between the point of this on the inside of the cheek and the pressure of my thumb on the outside I was able to pierce the skin of the cheek, and so get a grip on the slippery dermis, all in a single smooth moment. I pulled with all the force that was in my right arm and the man came tumbling forward. His skin tore through, separating the cheek into two flaps, but not before I had imparted a sufficient momentum for him to come tumbling down. I dodged to the right, and he fell forward. The charged chiller in his flailing left hand connected with his own right shoulder. He made a clumping sound as he hit the floor.

Of course there is no glory in causing another man pain. But, as I say, I was reconciled to the necessity of the pain. Possessing a head makes a man very vulnerable.

Bonnard was on his feet, his own chiller in front of him like a flick-knife. He waved it in the air between us as if to threaten me, but his eyes were fearful.

I wanted to knock upon the door in order attract the attention of the policeman out there in the corridor.

I stepped towards Bonnard with my left hand held outright, palm towards him. He jabbed the chiller at this target and discharged it directly against my skin. It was very painful. My arm seemed to burst at the seams of its nerves all the way up to its shoulders. This was a manageable pain. My fingers contracted about the end of the device, gripping it. With my other hand I took Bonnard's left ear in a grip that had been first demonstrated to me by a superior in camp one winter's morning. The difficulty in holding somebody by the ear is that it is a handle both small and flexible, and it too easily slips out of one's grasp. The way to counteract this is as follows: first take a hard grip of the ear, with the nails of the three main fingers lodged in the behind of the ear and the nail of the thumb jagged into the flesh in the main portion of the ear. Then – it is more easily done than described – force one finger into the ear canal. With a proper application of force this may rupture the eardrum, which is all to your advantage. The purpose of the exercise is not to damage the drum, but rather to give yourself a hold strong enough to permit – for instance – banging Bonnard's head repeatedly against the inside of the door as a form of knocker.

This, in a way, was the most delicate part of the entire business. It would have been easy, given the supply of anger inside me from which I was drawing, to have crushed Bonnard's skull with these blows. Perhaps he deserved death. I do not know, and it is not for me to judge, but it may be true. But I had made a vow, and I did not wish to violate it. Accordingly it was a ticklishly precise business hammering his head sufficiently to disable, without more seriously injuring, him. I knocked four times. There was a small window in the door, set a little too high for me to see properly through. The glass was thick and embedded within it there was a grid, like the graph paper schoolchildren have in their notebooks.

A face appeared at the glass, pressing close to see inside. I could see the face. Its expression changed from curiosity to one of alarm.

I pulled Bonnard's head away from the door. His ear had come partially off from his head, although there was still enough flesh to prevent it from detaching entirely. There was blood on my right hand. Bonnard's eyes were open, but the eyeballs had rolled up white.

I dropped him. He left his chiller embedded in my frozen, gripping hand and slumped to the floor. I reached round with my right hand and flicked the switch of this device to the off position. The pain stopped, although the hurting numbness remained. I had to pull the device firmly to extricate it from my fingers. My left arm dangled, uselessly.

I looked down at the two fallen men. The second policeman's body was twitching. It occurred me that he had fallen on his own chiller, and that the device was still on. This, clearly, might prove dangerous if prolonged. I pushed his body over with my right foot and he fell back, wholly unconscious. The hand with the chiller flopped free of his torso.

An alarm began to sound.

I faced the door.

There was a ratchety noise as a lock was unlocked, and the door burst open. A policeman burlied in. I put Bonnard's chiller in at his face, and he star-jumped backwards, his arms flying out so far that they banged against the door frame. I had to move quickly now. A single leap took me over his still falling body, treading up his chest as a ramp to hop into the air and directly into the man behind him. The chiller in my hand connected with this second fellow's neck, and he danced himself frantically down to the ground.

I stepped over him, turned right, and started back along the corridor. A camera panned to follow me. The alarm shrieked, its *chi-ii-chi-ii-chi-ii* cry enormously penetrating and loud. The door at the far end was open, and through it I could see people hurrying. A policeman in black plastic body armour put half of himself round the door. He aimed a rifle and fired. His weapon popped as it discharged. An object clanged, a tin can, off the wall near me, and clattered to the floor. Smoke as thick as dried ice began tumbling and gushing from one end of it. I saw the door at the far end of the corridor slam shut and then my vision was obscured by the gas. I flipped my neck valve shut, and took a breath from my army-fitted internal reservoir.

I was not certain how long it would take the police to ready their crash team, but I knew my supply of breathable air would outlast the supply of gas in the canister. Tucking Bonnard's chiller between the numb fingers of my left hand, I ducked down and picked the canister in my right. It was still spewing white steam, like a kettle that had broken its automatic off-switch. I could not be sure what the gas was, although it was making my skin sting.

I threw it into the cell which I had just vacated. Then I walked the length of the corridor through white opacity.

My left arm was still hanging limply. I tried flexing the fingers but nothing happened. I could shrug my left shoulder, but nothing more.

Nearer the end of the corridor I stopped and waited. I could see nothing in the white murk, but I could hear the sounds of confused motion, dulled by the door. There was shouting. A change in the timbre of the sounds indicated that the door had opened. There was another popping sound, and the clatter of another gas canister.

Moving quickly I located this by its hissing noise, picked it up and wedged it under my arm, with the smoke gushing out behind me.

I turned in the direction of the door again.

Coming forward very slowly, a black-armoured, black-snouted figure emerged from the smoke. He was holding a rifle before him, but I was able to step close enough to him such that he could not aim it at me.

What he should have done is brought the weapon up and struck me with the barrel as if with a baton, but this did not occur to him. I put the chiller in at the base of his spine and pressed the button, but the batteries of the device were now almost drained. He reacted, but did not fall. There was a flurried little dance as he tried to get away from me, but I slipped my good hand up to the back of his head and I pushed a finger underneath the strapping of his gas-mask. I didn't need to lever this entirely off before he had taken in a lungful of the smoke and collapsed, retching and coughing.

I walked forward until the door frame became visible. A second black-armoured and -snouted figure was in the frame, but there was enough space between his head and the side of the door for me to be able to throw the still spouting gas canister through the gap.

The policeman in the door swivelled his rifle towards me and began firing. He expected me to cower, or flee, or perhaps he expected me to fall backwards shot through with many bullets. I did what he did not expect: I reached out with my right hand and grasped the barrel of his rifle. Bullets clattered past me, missing my right flank by centimetres, but missing it for all that. After firing only half a dozen rounds the barrel was hot enough to scorch the skin, but this was a manageable pain. I pressed on the rifle-shaft as if I wished to angle it towards the floor. The policeman, his face unreadable behind its mask, fought my pressure, heaving to keep the gun level and trying to angle it further round to aim at me. A bullet shuddered the barrel and smacked into the floor at my feet. Another. I could feel the projectiles passing along the barrel as my palm burnt. Then I switched direction of my pressure, yanking it upwards, the same direction he was pulling it himself. Still firing bullets the rifle swung sharply. The barrel snapped into his chest. A round screeched off the visor of his mask leaving a scar of melted plastic and, in a panic, he dropped the gun.

I did not pick it up. I did not want a gun. It would have been very hard to preserve my vow holding a gun.

The man was already backing away. I leapt forward, rushed at him, pushing him before me and dominoing another of his colleagues imme-diately behind him. As they fell I jinked to the left and ducked forward as I ran. The hall behind was not large. Smoke from the grenade I had tossed had not filled it entirely, but it had done enough to disable most of the men there. One masked figure was hurrying forward to help his tumbled colleagues, and I ran straight past him. I leapt through the main entrance of the building.

I landed on my shoulders, as I had been trained to do, and rolled forward, flipping up onto my legs. It was night outside, and although the front of the station was well-lit it was only moments before I was swallowed by shadows.

Nine

The only real advantage I had possessed was surprise, which was itself a function of the ignorance of my captors as to the nature of my military training. The surprise was gone now. I ducked through a series of darkened alleys, and started my circumspect way through the city.

Bonnard had known where I worked, but I had never informed my workplace of my home address. Why would they be interested in such information? They only cared that I turned up to work on time.

Still, it would do to be cautious. Halfway to the house I came upon the fountain, the same at which Siuzan (the woman I had thought was Siuzan) and I had used to meet. It was deserted in the darkness, but I rolled in the water to wash off the stench of teargas, or whatever agent the police had used. The skin on my right palm was sore and burnt. I was starting to regain the use of my left hand.

I hurried on, keeping to dark or poorly lit ways as far as I could. Within twenty minutes I was back at the house.

The woman I had been calling Siuzan was there, sitting on the steps. She leapt up at my approach.

'Where have you been?' she asked. 'I've been here for an hour! More!'

'I met Siuzan Delage,' I said.

She did not say anything. After a while she sat down, and I sat down next to her. We were silent for a long time.

I listened to the sounds of the evening city, intermixed with which were several police sirens, dopplering towards and away from our location. I planned out my options should the police come to the building – which alleys were best to dash down, whether I could get upon the roofs of nearby buildings, which path had the best chance of escape. All this was part of my military training. But, in the event, we were undisturbed by the authorities.

'What is your name? I asked eventually.

'It is Siuzan,' she said.

'It is?'

'Yes. Siuzan. Though not Delage. But when you came up to me that day and addressed me as Siuzan, I responded genuinely.'

'But since then?'

'Since then,' she said, 'I have tried to be as truthful as possible. I'm sure that seems a poor sort of honour to you, but it's true.' She got up, agitated, and stepped away from the house. I watched her moving through the darkness, illuminated only by the light from one upper window. She roamed as far as the road, and then along, and then she returned to the front door and hesitated for a while. She sat down again. I didn't say anything.

Finally she spoke. 'To begin with I was surprised by how forcefully you seemed to recognise me. How certain you were that you knew me. I told myself: perhaps I *had* known you, in the days before the beheading. And at the beginning I was happy to have a friend, a roof under which to sleep, food, work, all these things. I listened to your story, of all the things you said about your time with the *other* Siuzan. Of course I understood that you had mistaken me. But then, as I grew to know you better, and as we talked, then ...' She tailed off.

'Then?' I prompted.

'Then, falling in love with you, it seemed to me that it had been more than chance that had provoked your misrecognition. What are the chances that you would confuse me with another woman also called Siuzan?'

'It's a common name.'

'It is,' she agreed. 'Well, well, of course I shan't hold you to an undertaking you made when you thought – thought I was another person.' She stopped. 'What will you do?'

'I must leave Cainon,' I said. 'Tonight, I think.'

She was silent at this.

'Do you love me?' I asked. 'Truly?'

'Enough to be ashamed of the misunderstanding that brought us together,' she said. 'But also enough not to – pester you with my presence. Yes, I love you. I thought fate had brought us together.' She was silent for a while, and then she asked: 'What happened when you met the – the other Siuzan?'

'She was not beheaded.'

Siuzan pondered this. 'I do not understand,' she said. 'You told me that she *had* been beheaded? You said you felt responsible, and that this Mark Pol was—'

'Indeed. I was deceived.'

'Well,' said Siuzan. 'Has a headed woman and a headless man ever made a couple? Has there ever been a marriage between two such?'

'It is not that,' I said, a little impatiently. 'I met her, and she was ... less than I remembered. There was much less *to* her than—' I stopped.

'Than?'

I had been going to say, *Much less to her than there is to you.* But I think she knew what I had been going to say. 'She was a very ordinary person,' I said instead. 'She chittered on about nonsense and gossip, and then she fled away on a bus.'

'Oh,' said Siuzan.

'What is your surname?'

'Visage. Even the surname mimics the sound of the other woman's, do you not think? Delage, Visage. Or, perhaps, it was only the urgency of my own desire that prompted my sense of the fatefulness of this coincidence. Perhaps there is no fate involved here at all.'

'I don't want,' I said cautiously, 'to adopt an interrogator's tone, for I don't have the right. But perhaps I may ask this: how much of what you said to me was true? Your changing attitudes to fate? Your life?'

'Oh, I tried to tell no active lie at all. When I had to lie I tried to lie by omission. But I know the All'God hates a lie, and a liar, and I'm certain He would not be impressed by the pedantic rationalisation of my sin. Everything I said *positively* was true. But some things I did not say, deliberately to allow you to continue in your false belief – that's where the lie was.'

'I do find the scripture alarming,' I said. 'About the lie, I mean. About the liar. Perhaps, as somebody once said, it means that the All'God must hate us all. For I spent three years worshipping an image in my memory, concocted largely from my own imagination, and telling myself that I loved it. But what I told myself was a lie. I do not love Siuzan Delage. I love you.'

'I didn't think that,' she began, and then stopped. She made another rush at a sentence: 'Perhaps the best thing would be—'

She stopped.

'We had better go,' I said. 'The longer I stay here, the greater the chance that events will conspire to prevent us both starting our lives anew. The longer I stay, the greater the chance something will come along to poison the happiness I have known with you, Siuzan, over these last weeks. The happiness...' She was trembling a little. So was I. '*That* hasn't been imaginary,' I said. 'It's the simple truth. Simple truth in a simple story. Sadness is the lie and happiness the truth. Let's both go to the Land of the Headless together and marry and do all we said we would do.'

'I've been waiting here an hour already,' she said. 'I'm ready to go.'

We rose together and walked, with our wandering steps and slow, away from that house. We walked out into the darkness and away from the city, and into the empty landscape.

Reader, we married. We live now in Montmorillon, and great things are in prospect, and not the least of those great things is a child, presently plumping Siuzan's belly. When we married, and since my name was poison, I took hers and became Jon Visage. We registered legal documents, at a cost of one totale and thirty divizos, with a local community legal centre, and this is the name in which all relevant documentation is filed. I had to supply DNA, of course, but I borrowed this from a friend who lives in the mountains, and who for his own reasons wishes to have nothing to do with the official world of Pluse. Some of the great things in prospect, of which I speak, have to do with this friend, and others like him. By the time this account is published I daresay they will have come to fruition.

In honour of my marriage and my new name I wrote a poem. This poem was my first composition for many years, and perhaps will be my last – for I am busy with other business now. But this poem has its place in this present account, for, of course, 'visage' means 'face'.

> *A windowglass:*
> *you on the far side,*
> *and my own face*
> *semi-reflected there*
> *where light and surface share.*
> *This is how we slide*
> *one into another:*
> *this superposition of faces.*
> *The connection of lovers*
> *is a union of graces*
> *as in prayer.*
> *The eye that sees itself*
> *and heart that frees itself.*
> *There*
> *is only one face in the glass.*

Siuzan, when I showed her this, thought it ironic that two headless people might memorialise their love through a metaphor of faces. But I've know some things more ironic in the world, and out of it, than that. It doesn't, to me, seem misapplied.

Acknowledgements

Thanks to Rachel, my sisters, my parents, and to Simon, my editor. Scott Eric Kaufman read the whole manuscript and made many helpful suggestions. *His* headless realm is at http://acephalous.typepad.com/.